GREAT
FROZEN CITY
CALLED GULAG

THE
WINTER
PALACE

EASTERN WORLD
OF PERPERTUAL
WINTER

THE
WINTER
KING

BABA'S
HOUSE

GINGERBREAD

BY THE SAME AUTHOR

Little Exiles

GINGERBREAD

ROBERT DINSDALE

THE BOROUGH PRESS

The Borough Press
An imprint of HarperCollins*Publishers*
77–85 Fulham Palace Road,
Hammersmith, London W6 8JB

www.harpercollins.co.uk

Published by The Borough Press 2014
1

A catalogue record for this book
is available from the British Library

ISBN 978 0 00 748888 9

This novel is entirely a work of fiction.
The names, characters and incidents portrayed in it are
the work of the author's imagination. Any resemblance to
actual persons, living or dead, events or localities is
entirely coincidental.

Set in Minion by Palimpsest Book Production Limited,
Falkirk, Stirlingshire

Printed and bound in Great Britain by
Clays Ltd, St Ives plc

MIX
Paper from
responsible sources
FSC **FSC C007454**

FSC™ is a non-profit international organisation established to promote
the responsible management of the world's forests. Products carrying the
FSC label are independently certified to assure consumers that they come
from forests that are managed to meet the social, economic and
ecological needs of present and future generations,
and other controlled sources.

Find out more about HarperCollins and the environment at
www.harpercollins.co.uk/green

For Kirstie

Who fears the wolf, should not go into the forest.

Belarusian folk saying

WINTER

When the car comes to a halt, the boy stirs from his slumber. The very first thing he sees is his mama's face, peering at him through the mirror. She has it angled, so that it doesn't show the sweeping headlights spreading their colour on the fogged glass, but shows her own features instead. Mama is tall and elegant, with hair at once yellow and grey, and blue eyes just the same as the boy's. In the thin mirror shard, she traces the dark line under one of those eyes with the tip of a broken fingernail, then spreads it as if she might be able to see more deeply within.

The boy shifts, only to let mama know he is awake. Outside, unseen cars hurtle past.

'Are we there, mama?'

His mother looks back. She has not been wearing a seatbelt – but, then, the hospital told her she wasn't to drive the car at all. This, she said as she buckled him in, would have to be their very own secret.

'Come on, little man. If I remember your Grandfather, he'll have milk on the stove.'

Mama is first out of the car. Inside, the boy sees her blurred silhouette circle around to help him out. It is not snowing tonight, though mama says it is snowing surely out in the wilds; in the city it is only slush, and that pale snow called sleet. It has fingers of ice and it claws at the boy.

Mama helps him down and crouches to straighten his scarf. Then it is up and over and into the tenement yard. On one side, the road rushes past, with rapids as fearful as any river, while on the other the yard is encased by three sheer walls of brick. Eyes gaze down from every wall, half of them scabbed over by black plastic sheeting, the others alight in a succession of drab oranges and reds.

The tenement is a kind of castle where Grandfather lives. Mama says the boy has been here before, but that was in a time he cannot remember, and might even have been before he was born. Together, they cross the yard, to follow an archway of brick and cement stairs to the levels above. The path goes all the way around the building, like a trail climbing a mountain, and at intervals the boy can peer down to see the car itself dwindling below.

At last, three storeys up, mama stops.

'Come here,' she says, and there is something in her voice which makes him cling to her without hesitation.

They are standing before a door of varnished brown, with a threadbare mat on which stand two gleaming ebony boots.

The boy is marvelling at these things that seem so old when his mama raps at the door. An interminable time later, the door draws back.

'*Vika*,' comes a low, weathered voice.

The boy's eyes drift up from the boots, up the length of mama's body, up the doorjamb broken by hinges. In the doorway, hunches his Grandfather. He seems a shrunken thing, though he is taller than mama, and taller still than the boy. On his head there is little hair, only a fringe of white hanging from behind, and his face is dominated by features that seem too large and out-of-place: a nose with a jagged crest; blue eyes shining, but eye sockets deep and dark. He is wearing a flannel nightgown, burgundy, tied up with a black leather belt, and though his eyes dwell first on mama, they drop second to the boy. He shuffles closer to mama's legs, and it is only then that he realizes that Grandfather's eyes have dropped further, to the boots on the mat.

'My jackboots,' he says. 'They're finished. Bring them, would you, boy?' Grandfather turns to shuffle inside. 'Oh, Vika . . .'

'We'll talk soon, papa.'

After mama has gone in, the boy picks up the jackboots and follows.

It is a small place, with a narrow hall and a kitchen at the end. Mama and Grandfather are already in that kitchen, with a pan rattling on the stove, but the boy creeps up quietly, stealing a look at the photographs adorning the walls. In them he sees people he does not know: a mama and a papa and a baby girl; banks of men in uniforms wearing jackboots just the same as those in his hands. He stops to scrutinize the grainy images, and sees long shadows cast at the end of the hall: the malformed shapes of his mama and Grandfather waltzing in the small kitchenette.

5

'No,' Grandfather says, the word stressed by the clatter of pans. 'I won't hear it, Vika. You were foolish coming here. It's giving in. It's *weakness*. I didn't bring you up just to let you give in.'

'It isn't *weakness*, papa. It's cancer.'

On the tolling of that word, the boy appears in the kitchen door. It is a small room, with a stove in its centre and a ragged countertop running around its wall. Pots are piled up haphazardly in a simple tin sink.

Across the stove, Grandfather's hand trembles as he lifts a pan. His eyes, desolate, fall on the boy. 'I made you a hot milk,' he breathes.

But mama puts an arm around him, and ushers him back into the hall. 'Come on. I'll show you your new room.'

There are two bedrooms around a turn in the hallway, and a third little corner with a gas fire and a rocking chair for sitting. Mama ushers him to its furthest end, past yet more photographs of times beyond the boy's memory.

The room at the end is empty but for a bed with two bunks and a chipped wooden horse standing on the window ledge. As they go through the door, his mama reaches for the light – but no bulb buzzes overhead. Still, she coaxes him in. Setting down the bag from her shoulder, she unrolls a simple set of bedclothes.

'What do you think?'

'It isn't the same as at home.'

'It's *my* home. This is where your mama used to sleep.'

Mama goes to lie on the bed. It is a ridiculous thing to think she might once have slept in it, because even the boy can see she is too big.

'Mama, look.'

6

Mama sits up, turns back to the pillow at which the boy is pointing. Where she lay her head, the pillow has kept a neat lock of her hair.

'Oh, mama,' whispers the boy.

In two simple strides she is across the room, snatching up the wooden horse from the ledge. She gestures the boy over and, torn between his mama and the hair she left behind, it takes a moment before he complies.

'This,' says mama, 'is my little Russian horse.'

The boy takes it. Once it was painted a brilliant white, with ebony points and a tail of real horsehair, plucked – or so the boy imagines – from the mane of some wild forest mare. Now its paint is dirty and in patches bare, its golden halter a murky brown. The chip above the left eye has given the trinket a look of immeasurable sadness, and the red around its open mouth looks bloody, as if the horse might have come alive in the dead of night and made a feast out of the woodlice who carve their empires in the fringes of the room.

'It was a present from my mama, and now it's yours.'

'Mine?'

'All yours.'

But the boy blurts out, 'I don't want it to be mine. It's yours, mama. You have to look after it.'

The boy grapples to push it back into her hands. Even so, mama's hands remain closed.

'You'll look after him, and your papa will look after you.'

The boy accepts the Russian horse, feeling its chips beneath his fingers. 'But who will look after you, mama?'

Mama crouches to plant a single dry kiss on his cheek. Once, her lips were full and wet. 'Get dressed for bed. I have to speak to your papa.'

After she is gone, the boy sits with the little Russian horse. By turning him in the light from the streetlamps below, he can cast different shadows on the wall: one minute, a friendly forest mare; the next, a monstrous warhorse rising from its forelegs with jaws flashing wild.

He does not get into his nightclothes and he does not climb under the blanket. To do either would mean he would not see mama again until morning, and he knows he must see as much of mama as he can. When he hears voices, he steals back to the bedroom door and out, back past the banks of photographs, back through memories and generations, to the cusp of the kitchen.

His mama's voice, with its familiar tone of trembling resolve: 'Promise me, papa.'

'I promise to care for the boy. Isn't that enough?'

'I want to be with my mother.'

'Vika . . .'

'After it's done, papa, you take me to that place and scatter what's left of me with her. You listen to me now . . .'

'You shouldn't speak of such things.'

'Well, what else am I to do, papa?'

His mother has barked the words. Shocked, the boy looks down. His shadow is betraying him, creeping into the kitchen even as he hides himself around the corner.

'I miss her, papa. On her grave, I haven't asked you for a single thing, not one, not since the boy was born . . .'

'Vika, please . . .'

'You do this thing for me, and we're done. I won't ask you for anything else.'

'It has to be there?'

When mama speaks next, the fight is gone from her words. They wither on her tongue. 'Yes, papa.'

8

'Vika,' Grandfather begins, 'I promise. I'll look after the boy. I'll take you to your mother. And, Vika, I'll look after you. I'll hold you when it happens.'

Then comes the most mournful sound in all of the tenement, the city, the world itself: in a little kitchenette, piled high with pans, his mama is sobbing. Her words fray apart, the sounds disintegrate, and into the void comes a wet and sticky cacophony, of syllables, letters and phlegm.

When he peeps around the corner, Grandfather is holding her in an ugly embrace, like a man in a patchwork suit at once too big and too small.

'And you don't let him see,' mama's words rise out of the wetness. 'When it happens, you make sure he doesn't see.'

S trange, to wake in a new home, with new sounds and new smells in the night. The tenement has a hundred different halls, and the footsteps that fall in them echo through all of the building – so that, when he closes his eyes, he can hear a constant scratch and tap, as of a kidnapper at his window.

Mama has her own room, across the hall in the place where Grandfather used to sleep. Grandfather has a place by the gas fire, in a rocking chair heaped high with blankets and the jackboots at his side. It is here that the boy finds him every morning, and here that they sit, each with a hot milk and oats. New houses have new rules, and the boy must not leave the alcove while Grandfather takes mama her medicines and helps with her morning ablutions. The boy is not allowed to see his mama in the mornings, but he is allowed to spend every second with her after his schooling is finished.

This morning, he is lying in the covers with the old bunk beams above, when the door opens with an unfamiliar creak. There is an unfamiliar tread, unfamiliar breath – and, though he wants it to be mama, it is Grandfather who tramps into the room.

'Come on, boy. Time for school.'

The boy scrabbles up. 'Is mama . . .'

'She's only resting.'

That is enough to quell the fluttering in the boy's gut, so he rolls out of the covers and follows Grandfather. The old man is retreating already down the hall, past the photographs of the long ago, when everything was black and white. The boy hesitates, eyes drawn inexorably to the doorway across the hall. Then Grandfather calls and he follows.

In the kitchen, he studies Grandfather as they eat. Once upon a time, Grandfather was only a story. The boy lived with his mama and only his mama in a house near the school, and in the days he learnt lessons and played with the boy named Yuri, and in the nights he came home and sat with mama with dinner on their laps. Now, Grandfather is real. He has a face like a mountain in the shape of his mother, and ears that hang low.

'What was mama like when she was little?'

Grandfather pitches forward, breaking into a smile that takes over all of his face. What big teeth he has, thinks the boy.

'She was,' he beams, 'a . . . nuisance!'

Then Grandfather's hands are all over him, in the pits of his arms and the dimples on his side, and he squirms and he shrills, until Grandfather has to tell him, 'You'll wake your mama. Go on, boy, up and get dressed.'

*

11

It used to be that mama walked him to the school gates, but the tenement is far from the school, almost on the edge of the city, where hills and the stark line of pines can be seen through the towers and factory yards, so today they must take a bus. The boy asks, 'Why can't we drive the car?' But Grandfather isn't allowed to drive, so instead they wait in the slush at the side of the road until a bus trundles into view.

As he puts his foot on the step to go in, he thinks of mama, alone in the tenement like a princess locked in her tower. He halts, so that the people clustered behind him bark and mutter oaths.

From the bus, Grandfather says, 'What is it, boy?'

'It's mama.'

'She'll be okay. She's resting.'

'I don't want her to be on her own. Not when . . .'

Grandfather's face softens, as if the muscles bunching him tight have all gone to sleep. 'That isn't for a long time yet.'

The boy nods, pretending that he believes – because even pretending and knowing you're pretending is better than not pretending at all.

He settles into a seat beside Grandfather and, as the bus gutters off, cranes back to see the tenement retreating through the condensation.

Sitting next to Grandfather is not the same thing as sitting next to a stranger, because in his head he knows that Grandfather was once mama's papa, and that, once upon a while, Grandfather took mama to school and maybe even sat on a bus just the same as this. Yet, knowing a man from photographs is not the same as sitting next to him and hearing his chest move up and down, or seeing the ridges on the backs of his hands. Every time Grandfather catches him watching, the old man grins.

Then the boy is shamefaced and must bury his head again. Once the shame has evaporated, the boy can look back; then Grandfather catches him again, grins again, and once even puts a hand on the boy's hair and rubs it in the way mama sometimes does.

'I bet you're wondering about your old papa, aren't you?'

The boy shakes his head fiercely. It is a terrible thing not to know which is wrong and which is right.

'I'm sure you've heard stories.'

That word tolls as strongly as any other, and he looks up. 'Stories?'

'Things your mama's told you, about her old papa.'

'Oh . . .'

'No?'

'I thought you meant other sorts of stories.'

They sit in silence, as the bus chokes through the lights of a mangled intersection.

'You like stories?'

The boy nods.

'Then maybe we'll have a story tonight. How does that sound?'

The boy nods his head, vigorously. It is a good thing to know which is wrong and which is right. 'Do you know lots of stories?'

Before Grandfather can elaborate, the bus stutters to a stop, the driver barks out a single word – *schoolhouse!* – and the boy must scramble to get off.

'Are you coming, papa?'

It seems that Grandfather will take him only to the edge of the bus, but there must be a pleading look in the boy's eyes, because then he comes down to the slushy roadside and, with one hand in the small of his back, accompanies the boy to the schoolhouse gates. There are other children here, and other mamas and papas, but none so old and out of place as Grandfather.

He looks for faces he knows, and finally finds one: the boy Yuri, who does not run with the hordes but paces the school fence every morning and afternoon, muttering to himself as he dreams. Yuri is good at drawing and good at stories, but he is not good at being a little boy like all of the rest. He is about to go to him when a figure, the vulpine woman who does typing in the headmistress's study, appears on the schoolhouse steps and begins clanging a bell.

'Will you come, papa, when school's done?'

Grandfather has a sad look in his eyes, which makes the boy remember his promise.

'Tonight and every night, boy.'

'And you'll look after mama?'

Grandfather nods.

Next come words the boy knows he should not have heard. 'And hold her, when it's time?'

Grandfather opens his leathery lips to speak, but the words are stillborn. 'Off with you, boy,' he finally says.

The boy turns and scurries into school.

In lessons, Mr Navitski asks him about his mama and he lies and says his mama's getting better, which will stop them asking and, in a strange way, make it so he doesn't have to lie again. Mr Navitski is a kind man. He has black hair in tight curls that recede from his forehead to leave a devil's peak, but grow wild along the back of his neck as if his whole pate is slowly stealing down to his shoulders. He wears a shirt and braces and tie, and big black boots for riding his motorcycle through town.

In the morning there is drawing, and he makes a drawing of Grandfather: big wrinkled mask and drooping ears, but eyes as big as silver coins and dimples at the points of the greatest smile. Yuri, who doesn't say a thing, works up a picture of a giant from a folk tale – and when Mr Navitski lines them up for the class to see, the boy is bewildered to find that Yuri's giant and his Grandfather have the same sackcloth face, the same butchered ears, the same bald pate and fringe of white hair. The only difference, he decides, is in the eyes, where simple flecks of a pencil betray great kindness in Grandfather and great malice in the giant.

In the afternoon it is history. This means real stories of things that really happened, and when Mr Navitski explains that, one day, everything that happens in the world will be a history, it thrills the boy – because this means he himself might one day be the hero of a story. He looks at Yuri sitting at the next desk along and wonders: could Yuri be the hero of a story too? He is, he decides, more like the hero's little brother, or the stable-hand who helps the hero onto his horse before he rides off into battle.

On the board, in crumbling white chalk, Mr Navitski writes down dates. 'Who can tell me,' he begins, 'what country they were born in?'

Hands fly up. The boy ventures his too late, and isn't asked, even though he's known the answer all along. This kingdom of theirs is called Belarus.

'And who can tell me,' Mr Navitski goes on, 'what country their mamas and papas were born in?'

More hands shoot up. Some cry out without being asked:

Belarus! Because the answer is obvious, and the prize will go to whoever gets there most swiftly.

But Mr Navitski shakes his head. 'Trick question!' he beams. 'This country wasn't always Belarus, was it?'

Yuri shakes his head so fiercely it draws Mr Navitski's eye. 'What country was it, Yuri?'

Yuri can only shake his head again, admitting that he doesn't know.

'Well, Yuri's half got it right. Because once, not so very long ago – though long ago might mean a different thing to you little things – Belarus wasn't truly a country at all. In just a few short years, it was part of many other countries and had different names: Poland, Germany, a great, sprawling land called the Soviet Union. And before that it was part of the Russias. Who knows what the Russias are?'

Though Yuri throws his hand up, this time Mr Navitski knows not to ask.

'It's an empire,' says the boy.

'Well, half-right again . . . Russia was a nation, with emperors called tsars, and it stretched all the way from the farthest east to the forests where we live today. What's special about those forests?'

Now there is silence, all across the class.

'Well, I'll tell you,' he says. 'Once, all of the world was covered in forests. But, slowly, over the years, those forests were driven back – by people just like us. They chopped them down to make timber, and burned them back to make farms. But this little corner of the world where we live is very special. Because half our country is covered in forests that have never been chopped or cut back. The oaks in those forests are hundreds of years old. They've grown wizened and wise. And those forests have seen it all: the Russias, and Poland, and Germany, emperors and kings and too many wars. Those trees would tell some stories, if only they could speak!

'And the truly amazing thing about Belarus is that, no matter how many times an empire came and made us their own, no matter how many soldiers and armies tramped through this little country and carved it up . . . not once, in the whole of history, have those forests ever been conquered. Those forests will always be, and have always been, ruled by no man or beast. And that makes them the wildest, most free place on Earth . . .'

The boy looks down. Yuri has been desperately drawing trees on his piece of paper. In between, he scrawls words: *wild . . . free . . . Belarus*. He presses down hard, promptly breaks the tip of his pencil, and looks up with aggrieved eyes – but the boy just keeps on staring at the page.

At the end of the day, Grandfather is waiting. As the boy hurries to meet him, something settles in his stomach: a promise has been fulfilled.

'Mama?' he asks, before he even says hello.

'She's . . .'

The boy pulls back from Grandfather's touch, shrinking at eyes that glimmer with such goodness.

'. . . waiting for you,' Grandfather goes on. 'She made you her *kapusta*.'

To get back to the tenement, they have to take another bus. This time, it feels better to sit next to Grandfather, which is foolish because the difference is only a few short hours. Now he can ask Grandfather questions, and Grandfather will answer: how long have you lived in the tenement? How old are you, papa, and what was it like so long ago? And, most important of all, what kind of story will it be tonight, papa, when we have our story?

The tenement is filled with the smells of spice and smoked *kielbasa*, that rubbery sausage on whose tips the boy remembers suckling, like a piglet, when he was very small.

He leaves Grandfather at the door, where the old man bends to remove his black jackboots, and gambols through the steam to collide with mama in the kitchen. He is too strong, and mama flails back, catching herself on the countertop.

'Easy, little man!'

She smothers him with kisses. When he pulls his arms from around her neck, he sees that she is wearing a kind of white handkerchief across her head. It gives her the air of a pirate, or a pilot downed in a desert.

'What is it?'

'I have a special job for you. But not until after dinner . . .'

'Papa's going to tell us a story.'

As he says it, Grandfather appears through the reefs of steam to join them in the kitchen.

'After we eat,' says mama. 'Now, go and clean up!'

Dinner is the soup of *kapusta* with slices of sausage, thin and flavoursome on top, thick like porridge at the bottom. It is for chewing and slurping, all from the same bowl. After dinner, the boy is to help mama with the washing up, but Grandfather wrestles her out of the way, so instead he helps his papa instead. As they work, Grandfather seems in a haze, quite as thick as the steam that still envelops them. It is, the boy decides, the rhythm of the work, working a kind of enchantment.

When they are finished, he finds mama in the corner room

18

with the gas fire burning. It is too warm in here, but he doesn't say a thing.

'Come here, little man.'

She is in the rocking chair where Grandfather sleeps, and on a pile of newspapers at her side is a pair of silver scissors, a comb, a glass of the burgundy juice that the hospital told her she has to drink.

'I'll need your help.'

She hands him the scissors, and unknots the handkerchief that has been hiding her head. The boy can see now, the patches where the locks have been left on the pillow. In places there is hardly any hair at all, in others a tract of downy fluff like a baby might have. From a certain angle, however, she is still the same mama, with her long blonde-grey locks framing her face.

She puts the scissors in his hands and lifts him onto her lap, which is a place he isn't supposed to sit anymore, not since the last operation. Showing him how to hold them steady, she runs her fingers in her hair and takes the first strands between finger and thumb.

'Just slide it on, and get as close as you can. See?'

The boy is tentative about making the first cut, but after that it gets easier. Blonde and grey rain down. Mama cuts his hair, and now the boy cuts hers too. As he takes the strands, Grandfather appears behind him, kneading his hands on a washing-up rag.

'Vika . . .'

'Shhhh, papa,' whispers mama. 'You'll break his thinking.'

There is another chair by the fire, a simple wooden thing. Grandfather settles in it, obscuring the pitiful blue flames.

'What about our story, papa?'

Grandfather says, 'A story, is it?'

Though he is concentrating on cutting the next lock, the boy sees his mama give Grandfather a questing look.

'What kind of a story would you like?' asks mama.

The boy pauses, too lost in thought to see the scratches he has lain into the papery skin of mama's scalp, too spoilt to see the way he has beaten back what is left of her hair like a forester managing a fire.

'One of the old stories, papa,' says mama. 'Like you used to tell me.'

This pleases the boy. The scissors dangle.

'Vika, I don't tell such stories.'

'Please, papa. For your little boy.'

There is a pained look in Grandfather's eyes, though what can be so painful about a simple story the boy cannot tell.

'There are other stories.'

'I used to like the woodland tales. Some of them, they're not so very gruesome, are they?'

Mama draws back from the boy, letting him stop his cutting.

'Your papa used to have so many stories. Of heroes getting their swords and their stirrups, back when all of the world was wild. He'd tell them to your mama when she was just a little girl. Until . . . you stopped telling those stories, didn't you?'

'Peasant stories,' whispers Grandfather.

The boy beams, 'I'd *like* a peasant story, papa.'

Grandfather looks like a man trapped. His wonderful blue eyes dart, but there is no escape from the boy's smile and mama's eyes.

'Go on, papa. It's only a tale.'

Seemingly in spite of himself, Grandfather nods.

When he speaks, his voice has an old, feathery texture that must work a magic on mama, because she softens under the boy, and when he looks she is beaming. The boy nestles down, half his work not yet done, and listens.

This isn't the tale, says Grandfather, *but an opening. The tale comes tomorrow, after the meal, when we are filled with soft bread.*

His eyes look past the boy, at mama. Silently, she implores him to go on.

And now, he whispers, *we start our tale. Long, long ago, when we did not exist, when perhaps our great-grandfathers were not in the world, in a land not so very far away, on the earth in front of the sky, on a plain place like on a wether, seven versts aside, there lived a peasant with his wife and they had twins alike as the snow – a son and a daughter.*

Now, it happened that the wife died of frost and the papa mourned sincere for a very long time. One year passed of crying, and two years, and three years more, and the papa decided: I must find a new mother for my boy and my girl. And so he married again, and had children by his second wife.

But a stepmother can think of old children like thistles in the wheat, and it happened that she became envious of the boy and the girl and used them harshly. They were beaten like donkeys and she gave them scarcely enough to eat. So it went until one day she wondered: what would life be like were I to be rid of them forever?

Grandfather pauses, with the simpering gas fire fluttering behind.

Do you know what it is to let a wicked thought enter that heart? he says, with sing-song voice and a single finger pointing

21

to the boy's breast. *That thought can take hold and poison even the very good things in you. So it was for the stepmother. So she brought the boy and the girl to her and one day said: here is a basket, you must fill it with fruits and take it to my Grandma in the woods. There, she lives in a hut on hen's feet.*

So, the boy and girl set out. They found nuts and berries along the way and, with their flaking leather knapsack filled with wild, wild fare, they entered the darkest wood.

There is a look shimmering in Grandfather's eyes that the boy can only describe as wonder. There are forests banking all edges of the city, rolling on into wilderness kingdoms of which the boy has only ever heard tell: the place called *Poland*, the northern realm of *Latvia* – and, in the east, the *Russias*, which once were the whole world.

On they went, the boy and the girl, and at once they found the hut with hen's feet. It was a most lamentable thing, and on its head was a rooster's ruff, with dark sad eyes. Izboushka! they cried. Izboushka! Turn your back to the forest and your front to us! The hen feet shuffled, the hut did as they commanded, and there in the little thatch door stood a witch woman, Baba Yaga, who was truly not a Grandma at all. The children were afraid, but they held to each other as children do, and said: our stepmother sends us to help you, Grandma, and we have brought fruit from our journey. And Baba Yaga, who was as old as the forest and older than that, said: well, I have had children before and I shall have children again, and if you work well I shall reward you, and if you do not I shall eat you up.

The boy watches as Grandfather says the final words. His throat constricts, and for an instant it seems that he has to choke them out.

22

That night, the boy and the girl were set to weaving in the dark of the hen feet hut. And as they wove, the boy cried: we shall be eaten. And as they wove, the girl said: we shall only be eaten if we do not work hard. If we work hard, we shall be rewarded. But a voice hallooed them in the dark, and the voice came from a knot in the wall, for in the wall were the skulls of creatures of the forest, and one of those skulls was the skull of a little boy.

Ho, said the skull, but you are mistaken. Your reward will be to be eaten, because for Baba Yaga to be eaten is a great reward. Heed me, for I was once a boy who got lost in the woods and toiled in Baba Yaga's hut.

But what can we do, asked the girl, but work hard and be rewarded?

You must run, said the skull, and take this ribbon. Be kind to the trees of the forest, for they will help if they can.

Well, the boy and the girl waited until dead of night, when Baba Yaga was abroad. And though the girl wanted to run, the boy was too afraid. So the girl said: I will run and find our papa and we will come back to help. And she ran.

But Baba Yaga knew a spiteful pine and the pine's branches whispered to its needles who whispered to a crow who brought Baba Yaga down. And Baba Yaga gave chase on her broom. At once, the girl remembered the skull's words. Be kind to the forest, and the forest will be kind to you. So she took the ribbon and tied it to a birch. And the birch was so filled with goodness that the trees of the forest, all but the spiteful pine, grew tangled and would not let Baba Yaga pass.

So the girl found her papa and told him what had come to pass, and the papa took his axe into the forest, but because the forest was kind it let him pass. And at last they came to Baba

Yaga's hut, but of the boy there was no sign. Now there was only another skull in the wall of the hen's feet hut, one to sit next to the other little boy. For the boy had been eaten up and now was part of Baba Yaga forever and more.

And from that day until this, two boys can be heard talking at night in the dead of the forest.

'Is it true?' marvels the boy.

Oh, says Grandfather. *I know it is true, for one was there who told me of it.*

The boy beams. It is the way a story is always signed off, a thing he has heard every time mama tells him a story. He looks around, to see if mama has loved the story as much as him, but he sees, instead, that her face is webbed in strange patterns, that her eyes are sore and red, that some monster has hacked away at her beautiful hair to leave her scarred, ugly, naked as Grandfather's pate.

'Come on, boy,' says Grandfather, lumbering to his feet. 'I'll make you a hot milk.'

Grandfather's hands find his shoulders, try to drag him from mama's knee. All around him, locks of blonde and grey shower down. His little hands reach out to catch them, but they slip away.

'It's okay,' says mama, 'I'll finish it. Don't cry, now.'

In the kitchen, the boy frets over a pan of milk that won't stop scalding. He can hear Grandfather and mama, and mama has lost all of her words. Then he hears the footsteps and closing of a door that tells him mama has gone to her bedroom.

Grandfather finds him wrestling with the pan, and gently sets it down. 'She wants to see you.'

A fist forces its way up the boy's throat. Though they have been with Grandfather only weeks, it is a law as old as time itself, one of the rules whipped up when the world was young, the forests were just tiny green shoots, and Baba Yaga only a babe: you must not go through mama's bedroom door, not after bedtime.

Grandfather ushers him down the hall and leaves him at the door.

At first, the boy does not want to go through. His hand dances on the handle and he is about to turn away, crawl into his bunk.

Then mama's voice itself summons him through. 'Don't be afraid. It was only a few little tears.'

It is a small room, with a bed with red patchwork and a cabinet with a lamp. On one wall there is a dresser, and around that more photographs of the kind he has seen in the hallway. In these photographs there are no soldiers, nor men in jackboots with rifles on their shoulders, but only the same woman, over and over again. It is, the boy knows, his own baba, who once was married to Grandfather.

Mama is on the bed but not in the covers. She has a shawl on her shoulders, the same one in which she used to wrap the boy when he was but small, and the knotted handkerchief is back on her head. Even so, it cannot disguise the fact that somebody has shorn off the last of her locks.

The boy hovers in the open door.

'Why were you crying, mama?'

Mama makes room for him on the bed. At first, he is uncertain; the room is a storm of different smells, alien even to the rest of the tenement. Only when he sees the pained expression on mama's face does he hurry over and scramble onto the covers. She folds an arm around him and he is surprised to find that she feels the same, even though she looks so different.

25

'It was only the story,' she says. 'Papa used to tell me all kinds of stories when I was a girl. Stories of the woodland and the wild, the kind of stories he'd heard from his papa, and his papa before him. Then, one day, when your mama wasn't so very much older than you, he stopped telling those stories. He wouldn't take us to the forest anymore. He wouldn't talk about the wolves and the stags, and I never knew why. I used to love hearing about my papa's time in the wilds, but from that day on he barely left the city. It was . . . nice to hear him that way again. That's all.'

The boy isn't certain he understands, but to say as much would be to betray mama, so he only nods. 'Papa has lots of stories of the forests, doesn't he?'

'They're all there, waiting, still inside him.'

'Do you think he'll tell me them, mama?'

'I hope so. But your papa, he's a . . . very old man, little thing. There are some stories he doesn't want to tell. Some he shouldn't . . .'

Mama means to go on, but there come footsteps from beyond the door. They hover, and they turn, and they click – as if Grandfather has put his old jackboots back on and is meandering up and down the hall. Mama waits for him to drift away once more.

'Listen,' she says, shuffling so that they can face each other on the bed, the boy nestled in the diamond of her legs. 'I need you to hear this.'

The boy stiffens. When somebody says *I need*, it means that the thing they will tell you is a terror, and must not really be heard at all.

'I won't be here for very much longer,' she says, with a finger brushing at his fringe so that he cannot hide. 'Your papa is a great man, a kind man, in his heart. But his heart can be buried. He lived in terrible times. You can see it in his eyes sometimes, those terrible things. It's why we haven't seen him so very much, not since your baba died. But I want you to know – you're of him, just as you're of me and I'm of you.'

Half of the boy wants to squirm, but the other half pins him down.

'He'll care for you and love you and, even when I'm not here, I'll be loving you too. I'll be in your head. I'll be in your dreams. You can talk to me, and even if I can't talk back, you'll know I'm listening. I'll watch over you.'

They sit in silence: only the thudding of two hearts, out of beat, in syncopated time.

'It's okay to be scared,' whispers mama.

'I'm not scared.'

'It's okay . . . to want it.'

The boy's eyes dart up.

'It won't be long,' she promises, with her lips so close to his face he can feel their warmth, smell the greasy medicine still in her mouth. 'It will be over soon. And then . . . then . . . I want you to make me a promise.'

The boy says, 'Anything, mama.'

'Promise me you'll look to your papa. No matter what happens, no matter what stories he tells, no matter what you see or hear or . . . No matter what you *think*, little one. Promise me you'll love him, and you'll care for him, forever and always.'

The boy doesn't need to think. He nods, and lifts his arms to cling from mama's neck, like a papoose made of skin and bone.

'Whatever happens, little thing. Whatever stories he tells.

Whatever you see in his eyes. Whatever happens in your life or his, he's yours and you're his.'

The boy nods again, head lifting only a whisper from mama's shoulders and held there by strands of tears thick as phlegm.

He is in school and making paper foxes with Yuri when Mr Navitski tells him, 'Today, Yuri's mother is going to take you back home.'

He has been to Yuri's house before, for a birthday party at which he was the only guest. Yuri has a stepfather who works on the railway that goes east, into all of the Russias, but more often than not he is away and it is only Yuri and his mother in the little flat above the workers' canteen. When he emerges from school at the end of day, white clouds are hunkering over the schoolhouse, and Yuri's mother is talking to Mr Navitski at the distant gates.

Across the yard, and Mr Navitski ushers him on his way. 'Take care,' he says. 'We'll see you . . . soon.'

'*Tomorrow*,' the boy says, with a hint of defiance.

Mr Navitski nods as if he does not really believe it, and then strides back to the schoolhouse.

Yuri's mother has eyes that nest in wrinkles and black hair scraped back in a bun. She has rings on each of her fingers and a coat with fur in its collar, but her boots are scratched and thin, at odds with the rest of her appearance, and it is these that the boy looks at as he approaches.

'Yuri,' she says, growing impatient at the boy still dragging himself across the schoolyard. 'Don't keep your friend waiting. We're taking the bus.'

The promise of the bus fires Yuri, and he is much more spirited as they puff their way to the stop. The boy follows. Yuri has a strange waddling gait, like a duck being plumped up for the oven. The boy thinks: he's like the boy in Grandfather's story, ready to be eaten up by Baba Yaga.

It is a bus he has not taken before, down past boarded-up shop-fronts. As they go, the clouds break, and fat flakes of white seal the bus in a sugary case. By the time they climb out, it lies thick on the roadsides. The city has changed shape, its corners grown less defined. Yuri's mother leads them on, past the railway canteen, and up a flight of frigid metal stairs. There, she takes a key from her purse and admits them to Yuri's world.

Yesterday's *kalduny* and *draniki*, heavy with fat, and a box of sugary juice for afters. While his mother is clearing up, Yuri takes him to his bedroom, which has bunks just like in Grandfather's tenement.

The boy sits on the carpet with his bowl between his legs. Yuri considers him silently, reaches out a hand with a wrist quite as big as its palm, and pats him quickly on the head. Then he turns to open a box. From it, he pulls two silver trains and a piece of toy track.

30

The carpet of Yuri's room is covered with a map, something Yuri has drawn himself, on the backs of envelopes and cereal packets. On the map are scrawled the most wonderful mountains and forests, rivers and roads. Yuri sets the trains down on a plain where a torn magazine front makes a ragged shore, and pushes one to the boy.

'Mother says you're not living at home.'

The boy rolls his train along the shore, bound for a head-on collision with Yuri. 'We have a new home.'

'A new home?'

'With my papa.'

Yuri swerves his train out of the way. 'What's your papa like?'

The boy remembers mama's words – your papa, he's a great man, but he lived in terrible times – and they must certainly be true. But there's another truth too: Grandfather has blue eyes just like mama, and a hundred different tales for the telling. He makes hot milk in a pan and, once, when the boy woke from a nightmare and cried, it was Grandfather who stirred and came into the bedroom and straightened his sheets and told him: hush now, it's only a dream. It didn't even matter that the dream was of mama, shrunk and desiccated in bed because they forgot that she was alive, because Grandfather's vivid blue eyes made it better.

'He's like my mama, but old,' the boy says.

'I have a papa too.'

Yuri digs again in the toy box and pulls up a photograph in a frame.

'He's the papa of my real father.'

The picture is much the same as the ones that line the tenement hall, but these men are wearing a uniform subtly different from Grandfather's own. In the image they stand in

31

a row against a brick wall, each with a rifle in the crook of their arm.

'He was in police, in the war.'

Yuri seems inordinately proud, and lands a plump finger on the man who is his Grandfather.

'What did your papa do, in the war?'

The war was a thing that happened in the long ago, in a time beyond all reckoning. In that age there were heroes and winters that lasted for seasons on end. There were kings with companies and they waged battles on ice-bound tundras, and took up brave quests. In truth, the boy does not know if Grandfather was in a war or not. It might be that those winter wars happened in his great-grandfather's time, or even an aeon before that. In the war, soldiers rode on woolly mammoths and unleashed great wildcats into battle, to cut down evil mercenaries with teeth like sabres.

'I don't know,' he says.

'My mama says I'm not to know, but I do. He was a police and he kept people safe.'

At that moment, the bedroom door flies open and Yuri's mother reappears. On a tray she has pastries, dusted with sugar, like the ones mama would take him to marvel at in the baker's window. She is about to set it down when she sees that Yuri is holding the photo.

'I told you! Put that dirty thing away or it goes in the rubbish!'

Yuri scurries to squirrel it back in the box, ducking his mother's hand.

Without another word, she tosses the tray on the bed and sweeps out of the room.

'It's because of my stepfather,' Yuri explains, deliberating over which of the identical pastries he should devour. 'My stepfather says the police were wicked in the war, but he doesn't really know. How can a police be wicked, when he's there to help?'

The boy shrugs.

'Maybe I can come to your house again. Then we can play without getting bashed.'

The boy nods, but it doesn't seem a thing that could happen, to have boys or girls to play in the tenement. The tenement is a place like that photograph now stashed away, where time is out of step and the real world awry.

They play on, and in stages the tray is cleaned of pastries, shreds, and crumbs. To lick the tray clean is a forbidden thing, but the crumbs taste better for being forbidden.

Soon, the snow is so thick against the windows that there is absolute dark. Through the walls, the boy can hear the tinny buzzing of a television set; Yuri's mama is, he says, watching her stories and mustn't be disturbed. There is the clinking of a bottle and, intermittently, she barks at the cavorting characters on screen, even though she cannot be heard. To Yuri, this appears to be the end of the world. He flushes crimson red, refuses to catch the boy's eye and mutters about a new game, anything to distract the boy from what is happening on the other side of the walls.

A clock above the door ticks – and the longer the games go on, the more persistent the ticking seems to be. Yuri chatters on, explaining new portions of his map and new games to be played, but all his words are drowned out by that simple, unchanging tick.

On the clock's face: seven o'clock, now eight, now nine.

Yuri has dragged a new piece of card to the foot of his bed, and is cultivating a dark pine forest in its corners, when the boy thinks he can detect another ticking in the air. This one comes with a different rhythm; it sounds more heavily, with a dull reverberation.

Time slows down. The hands of the clock drag, each tick tolling with a tortuous lag.

There come three short raps, of hands knocking at the front door.

Yuri spins around, as if caught in some mischief. 'But my stepfather isn't home until the weekend!'

It is panic that seizes Yuri, as he endeavours to tidy the room, but the boy sits still and listens to Yuri's mother crossing the flat to answer the door.

'Come in,' she says – and he hears, once again, the click of those jackboot heels.

After that, he knows what is coming. There is nowhere to run, and hiding would be useless. Yuri's mother appears again in the doorway. She does not speak, but a soft look in her eyes compels the boy to stand and follow her, back through the flat, into the living room where the door stands open, with winter flurrying up in its frame.

There stands Grandfather. His white hair is emboldened by ice, and his whiskers carry their weight as well. In that frozen mask his eyes are piercing bolts of cobalt. He wears gloves through which bitten fingers show.

The boy goes to him, stalls, goes to him again, crossing the flat's endless expanse in a stuttering dream. 'Is she in hospital again?' he says, with a tone that some might say is even hopeful.

Grandfather steps forward with clicking jackboots, crouches, and opens his greatcoat to put old and weathered arms around his grandson.

'No, boy,' he whispers with the sadness of mountains, of winters, of empty tenement flats. 'No, boy, she won't be going to hospital ever again.'

On the ledge by the window, its underbelly lit up by slivers of light shooting up through the floorboards: the little Russian horse that was a present from his mother.

It is cold in the tenement, and has been cold throughout the long, empty days. The boy counts them in his head: five, six, seven days since the jackboots clicked on the frigid metal stair, their steps tolling out the news. Now, with his eyes lingering on the little Russian horse, he waits for their clicking again. Today there has been nothing to do but wander up and down the hall, brooding on every photograph of the long ago, wondering at such things as soldiers and jackboots and guns.

When headlights roam the road outside, the Russian horse is trapped, monstrous, in the sweeping beams. The boy creeps up, as if he might peep over the ledge and look into the street below, but the creature leers at him and he is not brave enough to come near. He turns back, meaning to sit on his haunches in the corner of the room, but the horse's shadow dominates the far wall. The boy starts, turns back to the tiny wooden toy just as the headlights pass on. Now, it is just a flaking Russian horse again, with its painted eyes and preposterous eyelashes, its ears erect like a fox, a twisted little creature he must always look after, no matter how malevolent it has become in the week since mama disappeared.

It is only when the headlights are dead that the boy goes to the window. On tiptoes he can heave himself up and look out onto the tenement yard. Mama's car is parked at an awkward angle, one wheel up on the kerb. Ice still rimes the windscreen, so that the driver must have driven half-blind. Inside, a little heart of light glows.

When Grandfather appears, he is clutching a brown parcel to his breast. He takes off, but does not lock the car behind him. Soon, after he has crossed the tenement yard, he disappears from sight. The boy listens out for the click of his boots on the concrete. Then, he drops from the window ledge, upending the little Russian horse, and creeps to the bedroom door.

He will, he decides, make Grandfather a hot milk.

In the hallway, the photographs stare at him, and he in turn stares at mama's door. He has not been through since the night Grandfather brought him home from Yuri's, but he knows that Grandfather goes in there at night – not to sleep, but to make the sad baby bird sounds that the boy has started to hear after dark. Inside, a lamp burns; the boy can see the light in the sliver under the door. He drops to his hands and kneels and presses his nose to the crack, like the pet dog he has never been allowed. He thinks: I'll smell her still, in the air trapped like a tomb. But all he draws into his nostrils is dust and carpet strands.

He is in the kitchen, with the milk pan rattling on the stove, when he hears the familiar click of Grandfather's heels. A key scratches in the lock, and a flurry of cold air tells him that Grandfather has come in.

Quickly, he fills the mugs and ferries them to that place where the rocking chair sits before the dead gas fire. In the chair, mama's shawl is sleeping, curled up like a cat.

A voice flurries down the hall, 'You should be in bed.'

How Grandfather knows he is there, he cannot tell.

'I know.'

'Couldn't you sleep?'

Grandfather appears in the alcove, ruddy face still glistening from the cold. He looks different tonight. He has taken off his overcoat to reveal a slick black suit underneath. Grandfather has never looked as smart as he does in the suit, but it is a sad thing to see a man look so smart. His tie is done up tight and it bunches the loose skin of his neck, leaving a horrid red line like a scar. His hair has oil in it and is combed so you can see every strand. He has had a shave and all of his whiskers, once so prickly and wild, have gone.

'I see you made the milk.'

'It was to ward off winter.'

Grandfather's face cracks in a smile. 'Like in the story!'

It was one Grandfather told him on the night mama died, of the peasant boy Dimian and his forest home, and how he loved to take his fists to his neighbours and would do almost anything to tempt them to a fight.

38

Grandfather shuffles into the alcove, and, like a mouse afraid of being trampled, the boy scrambles out of the rocking chair to make space. Before Grandfather settles, though, there is the fire to be made. He keeps the brown paper package nestled in his arm and bends to turn a gauge. Then there is a match; a spark flies up, and the fire is lit.

'Come on, we can have a biscuit. I don't think she'd mind if you wanted a biscuit, would she?'

'Even late at night?'

'Well, it's a special kind of night.'

Grandfather retreats to the kitchen, returning with the package under one arm and a biscuit tin in the other. Inside are ten pieces of gingerbread with decorations carved into each: ears of wheat curling around a ragged map, and a star with five points hanging above.

The boy is reaching in with a grubby paw when Grandfather stops him.

'Maybe we should share one.'

Really, the boy would rather have one all for himself. These are special ones, made with honey, not like the ones with jam you can buy in the baker's. He feels distinctly more hungry just to see one.

'Can I have one for my own?'

'No,' says Grandfather. 'They have to last.'

It doesn't matter, in the end, because Grandfather has just a tiny corner, and the boy can suckle on his piece all night. It is rich and sticky in his mouth, coating his gums so that he will be able to taste it all the way to morning.

'Did mama make the biscuits?'

Grandfather nods. 'There's nine more.'

'Can I have another?'

'No.'

He doesn't ask why. Even so, he realizes he's being especially careful not to make crumbs.

After a great, honeyed silence: 'What was it like today, papa?'

Grandfather nestles, and might be readying himself for another fable.

This isn't the tale, he begins, *but an opening. The tale comes tomorrow, after the . . .*

'Papa, please.'

'It was quiet, boy. Snow on the cemetery. They brought your mama in a black car. I wanted to lift her down myself but she was too heavy. So the men from the parlour had to help me.'

'Did you . . . see her, papa?'

'Not today, boy.'

'It's her in the paper, isn't it?'

Both sets of eyes drop to the brown paper package in Grandfather's lap. Somehow, mama is inside. All of her that was, boiled down to nothingness and poured into a little tin cup. Inside that package are all the times she walked him to school, all the dinners she made, all the stories before bedtime. And the promise she made him make.

'Can I hold her?'

Grandfather offers her up. In his hands, she feels light as the air. She is the same as any package that might come through the door. He puts his ear to her and listens, but she no longer has a voice.

'When will we do it?'

Grandfather takes her back.

'Do it?'

'Take her to that place, in the forest.'

Grandfather's face is lined, and for a moment the boy thinks he doesn't understand.

He says, 'You know, the place where baba went.'

Grandfather shakes his head. 'Not there,' says the old man, lifting mama to marvel at her. 'We'll find a place here, in the city. A place near your old house. A special spot. Somewhere she loved to take you. And then, every time we want to talk to her, every time we want to hear her voice or see her eyes, we'll go there, you and me, and listen to the wind. What do you think, boy? Can you think of a place?'

Sitting at Grandfather's feet, with the prickling heat of the gas fire touching his back, the boy is somehow frozen. His fingers twitch, as if he might reach out for mama once again, but Grandfather's hands close protectively around her. He picks out Grandfather's eyes, but they are still so perfectly blue, that the boy thinks he must simply be mistaken.

'Papa,' he whispers. 'She wanted to be with baba . . .'

'She told you that, did she?'

The boy feels as if he is shrinking in size, barely big enough to perch on Grandfather's boots. 'No, papa, she told *you*.'

The silence of the deepest snowfall fills the alcove.

'When?' Grandfather begins, his voice a-tremble.

'It was when we came,' breathes the boy, as if fearful of his own words. 'You were in the kitchen and mama was crying and, papa, she made you promise.'

Grandfather hardens. 'Your mama would understand, boy, if you wanted her near, some place she could be with us. I don't want to take her to that place, boy. Do you?'

Though the boy is uncertain of the precise place mama meant, he has an image in his head. He was not there when the dust of his Grandma sifted through mama's fingers, but

41

she took him there in later years – and there he saw the fringe of the rolling forest, the tumbledown ruin which was a place of stories and histories as well. One hour out of the city, two hours or more, and the woods are wide and the woods are wild and the woods are the world forever and ever. It is, he knows, a place that baba loved through all of her life, a place mama would go to, over and again, to hear her dead mother whisper in the leaves.

'You *promised*, papa.'

Grandfather is silent. The boy wonders: does he know the meaning of a promise? Perhaps a promise is a thing only for little boys and girls, like schoolyards and alphabets and mittens.

'Sometimes, boy, you make a promise to stop someone's heart from bleeding.'

It isn't like that for the boy. He won't forget sitting at mama's side and putting his arms around her and making his oath: to look to his papa, to love his papa, to look after him for all of his days.

'Papa, she'll be upset.'

His fingers reach for the brown paper. At first, Grandfather lifts it away. Then, he relents. His fingers scrabble at it, find its corners, tear and touch the urn underneath. 'Papa, you wouldn't break a promise if mama knew.'

Grandfather's chest rises, fills with cold air. He breathes it out in great, slow plumes. In the make-believe grate, the gas fire flickers and retreats. 'You sound like your mother, boy. Papa, papa, *papa.*' Each word is like a flint being chipped from his lips: sharp, severe, showering sparks. He bends down, his face eclipsing the boy's, and there no longer seems any blue in his eyes. His lips are pursed and his brow is furrowed and the boy can see his fingers whitening around mama's little urn.

'Over and again, that's all she said. Take me to the forest, papa. Take me to the forest!' He rears back, and out of his hands the package tumbles. To the boy, it seems as if the world slows down. Mama's package turns, end over end, and rolls to a stop in the deep shag near the grate. 'Well, what if *I* don't want to go to the forest?' Grandfather snarls, whirling around without another look at the boy. 'This is my home. My life. What if I can't go back?'

Listening to the snarl still in his voice, the boy crawls across the floor and snatches up mama's urn. The lid is still in place and he thinks to lift it, peer at what still remains, but instead he turns to see Grandfather disappearing from the alcove. Heavy footsteps tramp back into the kitchen.

He clings to his mama. 'Why is papa so angry, mama?'

He hears the rattle of pans, the tramp of more footsteps, a single click as if Grandfather is donning his big black jackboots. Only when the tramping dies does he dare venture up, out of the alcove, and into the kitchen door. Inside, Grandfather has not donned his jackboots at all. He is hunched over a pan of milk and his heavy breathing fogs the tenement air.

'You're not angry, are you, papa?'

He is; the boy can see that he is. Even when it is not foaming on his lips, it is shimmering in his eyes. At first, he does not reply. He simply breathes in and, by breathing in, seems to force the anger back deep inside him. The darkness evaporates and his eyes sparkle blue all over again.

'I'm . . . sorry, boy. Your mama, is she okay?'

The boy offers up the urn. 'I don't think it hurt her, papa.'

It is a good thing when Grandfather takes the urn. The boy can feel his hands, cold and wet and scored with lines. They linger a little on the boy's hand, and it is like a little pat that

43

you might give a dog in the street. When Grandfather pulls his hands away, the boy's go with them, his fingers entwining with the gnarled old knuckles.

'Is it a tale before bedtime, boy?' the old man asks, almost contrite.

The boy nods. 'And mama can listen too.'

In the bedroom, Grandfather tells him of the little briar rose. It is a German story, and not of their people, but in it are forests the same as theirs, and peasants who might be like them, were it not for different tongues and different kings. In the story a mama and a papa want a baby of their own, but their lives are empty as the tenement today, until one day an enchantment gives them a daughter, the Little Briar Rose. There is a feast, but there is no place at the table for the thirteenth wise woman of the village, and in revenge she makes a prophecy that, on her fifteenth birthday, the Little Briar Rose will open her finger on a spindle and fall into an unending, poisoned sleep.

Grandfather's voice has the same sound, like feathers being ruffled, that is swiftly becoming familiar. The boy lets it wash over him. His thoughts, punctuated by mourning mamas and walls of thorn grown up to hem in the sleeping girl, wander.

'Why don't you want to go to the forest, papa?' he says, bolting up in bed so that his words pummel straight through the heart of Grandfather's fable.

This time, the old man is not so angry after all. 'That, my boy . . . that's another story. One,' he chokes, 'that your mama never knew.'

'We'll take her though, won't we?'

Grandfather whispers, 'I'm sorry, boy. I didn't mean to get cross. I . . . miss her, that's all. We'll take her tomorrow.'

The boy has closed his eyes to sleep, with Grandfather

retreating down the hall, when he realizes he is still wrapped up in mama's shawl. He has to be careful because one day the smell will wear out, so he takes it off and makes a nest in the corner. Then he plucks the Russian horse from the ledge and settles him down in the nest for sleep.

Outside, tiny crystals of snow are twirling on the wind. In the ragged orange of one of the streetlamps a man is hunched over Grandfather's car. With the door half open, the man rifles inside. But he finds nothing, and then he is gone, leaving the door ajar and the snow curling through.

The boy steals back to bed, whispers goodnight to the Russian horse, and closes his eyes. It blocks out the glow of the street-lamps, but it does not block out the strange, muted whimpers coming from along the hall.

In the morning they have to dress up warm, because it's winter and today is a day out. There are mittens and scarves that mama made, and big black boots two sizes too big. As Grandfather works them onto the boy's feet, he tries to find answers in the lines of the old man's face, but it is hard grappling for an answer when the question remains so out of grasp.

'Are you going to be okay, papa?'

The last boot goes on, and Grandfather looks up with furrowed eyes. His face is not scored with the same deep crevices as the night before, but this the boy does not brood on, because the night has a kind of magic and makes things all better by morning.

'Okay?'

'To go into the forest.'

In response, Grandfather lifts a hat from the edge of the rocking chair and lowers it over his head. It is a ring of brown and black that, so it is said, is made out of bear.

'We have to do it for mama, don't we?'

Grandfather nods, with steeliness in his eyes of blue.

The car, Grandfather finds, has been open all night. Snow ices the seats and the steering wheel is rimed in hoarfrost, so that when the boy crawls inside he is colder than he was outside. In his lap sits the little Russian horse – because mama must say goodbye to that poor wooden creature too – and underneath him, his eiderdown for a blanket. It is, Grandfather says, going to be bitter and cold before they are through.

'Do you know the way, papa?'

Grandfather says, 'I think I remember.'

'So you've been there before?'

'Oh, long, long ago, when we did not exist, when perhaps our great-grandfathers were not in the world . . .'

If it seems like a story is about to begin, it quickly turns to mist. Grandfather scrubs a hole in the windscreen and squints out. 'The winter might be against us, but you've the stomach for an adventure, don't you, boy?'

It thrills the boy when Grandfather says this, because the boy has never had an adventure, not a proper adventure of the kind he thinks Grandfather must once have had. Those photographs in the tenement spell out a kind of story, and perhaps he would find it as heroic as the fables Grandfather tells, if only he knew how to read it.

'What if we get hungry?'

Grandfather pats his pockets. 'I brought us *wings of the angel*.'

The city streets are banked in grey slush. This snow, Grandfather says, is not for settling. That Grandfather is not

47

always correct is quickly apparent, for once they have left the austere tenements behind, the drifts grow high at the banks and the blacktops are encased in ice as thick as a river.

It is frightening to leave the city. The city is school and the tenement and the miles and miles of empty factories where the boy is forbidden to play. In places, the boy knows, the forests have crept into the city itself, as if all of the streets and squares are held in a giant fist of pines, but outside there is nothing but the dark curtain of woodland and the barren heaths in between. The road weaves across them like an open white vein.

For miles the road is bordered by banks of firs but, deeper in, the trees are older still: sprawling oaks and beech, alders and ash. Once in a while an oak towers over the rest, and those oaks have stories and names all of their own. Somewhere, so deep that Grandfather says it might lie in some other country, stands the plague tree, whose branches cradled an ancient king while death ravaged his kingdom. There are oaks named after battles and tsars and emperors whose empires have long since ceased to exist, but these the boy knows he will never see, for the forest stretches until the very end of the earth and, if you follow its paths, you can never come back home. It would, he knows, be a very great adventure to see the edge of the forest; but mama is gone, and the boy has made a promise: he will not leave Grandfather to drink milk in the tenement alone.

They have gone many miles from the tenement when Grandfather pushes his old jackboot to the floor and turns the car onto a forest track. The branches above, laden with snow, have formed a cavernous roof, so that the trail here is almost naked, only lightly dusted with crystals of frost.

The boy chews his mittens off his hands and suckles on each finger for warmth.

48

'Are you so hungry?'

'No.'

'We should have brought soup.'

'I don't like soup.'

'You liked your mama's *kapusta*.'

'Which one is that?'

'Cabbage,' the old man beams.

There is a long silence.

'I didn't like it,' the boy finally whispers, his head bowed. 'I only told her I liked it.'

'Why?'

'She liked to make it for me, didn't she, papa?'

'I'll make you some.'

'Not like mama.'

'No,' Grandfather whispers, 'not like mama.'

When they are deep in the wood, Grandfather slows the car. The windows are frosting again on the inside and he rubs them with his sleeve to make sure he can see the trail. 'It must be somewhere near,' he says.

'Here?'

There is a trembling in Grandfather's voice; it might be fancy, but he thinks it is because of more than the cold. The boy watches him, but Grandfather is hunched over the wheel, squinting through the ever-decreasing hole in the windscreen, and betrays not a flicker. He guides the car to the very edge of the track, cutting the engine before they've stopped rolling.

'Come on, boy. We'll know it when we see it.'

It is easy, now, to see why Grandfather did not want to come to the forest. The trees have the visages of men. They leer, and grope, and they surround. Colonies of birds with watchful black eyes line the treetops.

When he climbs out of the car, the frost is the first thing to assault him; the trees simply stay where they are, *watching*, and for a moment that is the most terrible thing of all. Grandfather waits between the trees, and by the time the boy catches up his face has blanched as white as the ice-bound branches around.

'Are you okay, papa?'

'You don't have to keep asking, boy. We'll see it done and then be off home.'

They set off, Grandfather – in his eagerness to see it done – always two strides ahead. The trail leads them into darker reaches of the woodland, but everywhere shimmers with the same kind of spectral light, the sunlight trapped beneath the branches by a canopy of snow. This forest they walk in is a graveyard, and fitting perhaps for mama's end.

'The urn!' Grandfather mutters, opening his empty hands. 'Stay here.'

He sweeps around and, with shoulders hunched up, barrels back down the trail.

Now the boy is alone. He stands in the middle of the track and watches his breath rise. The tips of his ears and the end of his nose tingle. He has never heard silence quite like this. He thinks that, if he coughed, it would break some secret forest rule. It would be so loud the blackbirds would scatter from their roosts and the wild cats come hurtling from their hidings.

It smells of outside, of earth and bark and crystal-clear water.

He doesn't move until Grandfather returns, mama's package held between hands that have lost their gloves and look raw.

'Were you scared?'

He shakes his head.

'I was afraid, boy, the first time I found myself in the wilderness alone.'

The boy wants to ask more, because it sounds like there's a story in that, one quite unlike the fables Grandfather spins at night, but instead the old man tramps on and he is compelled to follow.

Before they have gone far, the trees thin, then peter out altogether. The forester's trail turns to follow the edge of the woodland, along a ridge that overlooks a clean, white pasture. In the roots of one of the tumbled yews, there is a big yellow depression and a trail of yellow droplets running away from it.

'Fresh!' exclaims Grandfather, and gives a shrill, throaty cheer when he spots the tracks. 'Roe deer. Do you see the two toes?'

He nods, even though he doesn't. How Grandfather knows such things if he never goes to the forests, the boy cannot tell. These are the things a woodcutter might know, or a hunter or a trapper, not the things of a man pottering in his towering tenement flat. He wants to ask, but when he looks up he sees that a glassy look, as frozen as the world, is in Grandfather's eyes. His face is haloed by the fog of his breath, and through those grey reefs he stares down the vale.

The boy's eyes follow.

At the bottom of the pasture, nestled against another rag of woodland, there hunches a house. It is a small thing – a girl might call it dainty – but it is old and sunken and the coal shed squatting out front is collapsed, crowned with more snow and specks of black peeking through. Most of the windows aren't glass at all, just wooden boards nailed together. There's a chimneystack, just reaching through the snow, with bits of broken brick lying around and a wood pigeon perching on top.

'This is it, isn't it, papa?'

Grandfather says, 'Did your mama ever bring you here?'

51

'I think . . . but not like this.'

'No?'

Sometimes, memories are like dreams. He remembers the house, but not the valley; the walls of stone, but not the ruin. In his head, it is summer. There is a cloth spread out in a wild garden ringed by forest, with the spectre of a house behind – but warm and welcoming, not frigid and alone like this thing feels. But then, he supposes, things must feel different after a death. The world is different to him, now that mama is gone, and so must be the house.

'Are we going down?'

Grandfather sinks to his haunches. He doesn't say a word, simply rocks on his jackboot heels, and when he draws himself back up he is changed: unwavering, resolute. He cups a hand around the back of the boy's neck. The boy tingles. His face bursts into a grin but, when he looks up, Grandfather is still staring at the ruin, as if he can see things in the tumbledown stone and colonnades of ice that the boy cannot.

Up close, the house is more afraid than it is frightening. Like the trees, it has the face of a man. Frost along its open roof is a fringe, and the boarded windows are eyes gouged out. The door, an anguished maw, has slipped from its hinges but is fixed into place by hard-packed ice. On seeing it, Grandfather's face is carved in the same sad lines as it was on the night he came to Yuri's – and the boy wonders if making him come here at all is breaking that promise he made to look after him, and love him, for all time and no matter what.

'Come on then, *Vika*,' Grandfather says, in a whisper meant only for the urn. 'We're home, if home this truly is.'

He heads for the door, but walks in an odd, circuitous way,

first parallel to the house, then turning sharply to approach the stone. The boy scurries to join him, plunging into snow as deep as his waist, but Grandfather turns and stops him with a word. 'Watch out. There was a garden wall.'

'Where?'

'Right where you're standing. It was to keep the pigs in.'

'Papa, how do you . . .'

Grandfather heaves his way to the house door. It isn't even locked, just warped and stuck in the frame. He sets the urn down, packing the snow tightly so it doesn't sink, and puts his shoulder to the wood. The door caves in and a tide of snow falls into the house.

Together they stand, watching the dust of ages settle in the dark passage.

'Don't you want to go in, papa?'

But Grandfather just looks at the black forest on the borders of the dell, the mountains in the canopy where snow and ice have crafted jagged peaks. 'Well, boy, I'd rather be in four walls than out there.'

Grandfather takes the first step, but the boy isn't so sure. Out here it smells clean and free, but there is something different coming from the house. It smells of dust and dark and being old.

It is only when Grandfather disappears that the boy dares to follow. First, he stands on the step and pokes his nose over the threshold. He can hear Grandfather shifting inside. There are pools of light up ahead, spilled no doubt through windows on the forested side of the house, and he sees Grandfather's shadow flit across them. For an instant it is pitch-black; then the light returns, as Grandfather moves on.

'Papa?' His voice echoes, lonely as he was all day yesterday. 'Papa?'

53

He creeps on. It is not, he decides, so very bad. The first step is the hardest. After that, all you've got to do is be brave. You've got to stop thinking about the smell, stop imagining all the ghosts that might live in a place like this. You've got to remember: you promised to look after your papa, and how can you look after him if he ventures on alone?

He reaches the doorway at the end of the hall and peeps through. Once upon a time, this was a living room. There is still an armchair in front of a big cold hearth, and a mirror on the wall covered in dust and what looks like wood-pigeon muck. On the farthest wall one of the windows is boarded up, and the other is encased in ice. Grandfather has already shuffled through another door. He can hear the old man kicking his boots in frustration.

It doesn't feel good, going into the room. There is little carpet left, only rags around the skirting board where mice haven't chewed it away. He can see the big wet prints left behind by Grandfather's boots. In the middle of the room the old man must have stomped in circles, circling the armchair and then striding away.

The room on the other side is a kitchen, and that's where Grandfather is crouched, rummaging through a cupboard. Mama sits on the countertop in her urn, and Grandfather keeps calling out to her, assuring her that he's not really left her alone. 'Vika,' he says. 'Vika, why do you drag me back here?'

The boy shuffles into the door between the living room and kitchen. It is lighter in here, because more light can pour through the backdoor. The glass is coated in ice, but it is less thick on this side of the house and, if you squint, you can even make out what used to be a garden, with a chicken coop and rabbit hutch and vegetable patch with a low stone wall.

Grandfather is down on his knees, buried in a cupboard under the sink. There are things scattered around his knees: old gloves, the handle of a trowel, a terracotta plot, a clod of earth.

'What are you looking for?'

Grandfather rears up with a sudden flourish: in his hands a single-headed, dark axe. His gnarled fingers are so tight around the handle that they look as knotted as the wood.

'Papa!'

The old man's eyes are raw, but he is smiling, his mouth full of gaps. 'We'll need kindling.'

'Kindling?'

'To kindle a fire.'

'How do you kindle a fire?'

'You do it,' says Grandfather, putting his shoulder to the backdoor, 'with kindling.'

Grandfather has to strain to force the door, but then it crunches and gives way. Outside, the snow is piled high, and Grandfather's hands are too big to reach through. Now it is the boy's turn to show Grandfather how. He reaches through the crack, shovelling enough snow away that they can both squeeze out, into a garden bound by winter. It is bigger than it seemed from inside, bordered on three sides by walls of forest.

'Do you remember it, boy?'

The memory is only faint, but the boy nods. 'Mama brought me, with a picnic.'

Grandfather whispers, 'She never told me.'

'Do you remember it, papa?'

'Oh, better than I ought. But I was a young man, then, and should have known better. Your mama was born in those four walls. Did you know that?'

The boy looks back. It is only a house, he tells himself, in the same way that those maps on Yuri's floor are real maps. It is like a story written down but screwed up and cast away when its teller can't find the words: out of shape, words and bricks heaped up without sense or form. It can hardly be a place where mama once lived.

'Here?'

'She was smaller than you when we left. I always hoped she wouldn't remember, but once something's in your head, you don't shed it so easily.'

'Why did you leave?'

'Because, boy, there are things in the forest, things not fit for a baby girl.'

From the tone of his voice, he does not mean to go on. He takes one big stride, then another, and in his wake the boy follows.

Although the snow is thick on top of what used to be a vegetable patch, under the trees it is only light dust. They tramp beneath the boughs and, only a few yards in, Grandfather stomps his jackboot down. The frost is like a layer of hard sugar, and it cracks under his heel.

He begins by stripping tiny twigs and dead bark from the trunk of a black alder. A little further in, an oak has long ago been uprooted and now lies dead on the forest floor, slowly rotting away. Mosses grow across its surface, like a bison's winter hide, but Grandfather scrapes a patch away and exposes the dead wood underneath. The axe sinks easily into the first layers, and chips of cold wet trunk shower down. The smell is cold and stagnant, and billows up in great clouds to make the boy sneeze.

'See,' says Grandfather. He has chipped deep into the trunk,

56

where the wood is dry and flaking. 'You can start a fire with this more easily than a match.'

The boy peers closely. 'But how do you know?'

'Don't you think your old papa might know how to start a fire?'

'I've seen you start a fire, papa. You turn the gas and strike a match.'

'Boy, that's barely a fire at all. Those are fires for poor old men in their tenements. I wasn't always so very old.'

The boy replies, 'But I'm not old, and I don't know about fires.'

'I wasn't the same kind of boy as you,' grins Grandfather. 'I was a little bit . . . wilder.'

Kindling, it turns out, is twigs and flakes of trunk and even bits of bird nest that the boy finds hidden away in a hole in the dead tree. With hands and pockets full, they go back into the house.

Grandfather says there hasn't been a fire here for years. He drops down at the hearth, props the axe against the stone, and piles the kindling in a dark mound.

The boy hugs the wall at the edge of the room. His eyes linger on the hunched figure of Grandfather, then flit to the threadbare chair, the crumbling stairs. Perhaps it should not take so very much imagination to see pictures on the walls, the windows opened up, a proper banister and bedroom above. Yet, when he tries to see mama here, the cobwebs in the corners fight back, and the idea of a baby crawling on these floors is preposterous. Only a baby animal could live here, some wild thing out of the forests.

Terrifying, to think of the long ago years before you were real; more terrifying even than to think of the things mama misses, now she is gone.

In the hearth, Grandfather has no matches. Yet, he has sculpted a model out of the twigs and pieces of nest that imitates fire exactly, licking up in the shapes of flame. His head is low, and his lips move in a whisper. Then, as if from nowhere, there is light. It spirits from Grandfather's lips and dances along the strands of nest. Tiny tendrils of red rush forth, spreading a fiery web.

'Papa!'

Grandfather turns, his face lit from behind by the stirring orange. 'It's been a long time, boy . . .'

Into the orange orb Grandfather piles the rest of his kindling. Soon, the glow is stronger. These, he explains, are embers. How they appeared, the boy does not know – for Grandfather is just an old man from a tenement, and surely he does not know sorceries and enchantments. The rest, the boy understands. To turn those embers into roaring fire you have to add scraps of cloth axed from the old armchair, and even a piece of floorboard. Then, when the fire darts and spits and dances in the grate, you can put a pot in and melt down snow.

If you melt snow, you get water. And if you boil up water, you can use it to soften the frozen ground so that the axe can dig down. In this way, Grandfather excavates a tiny crater in the roots of a black oak. Once he is done, he unwraps mama's urn. When the boy peeps in, he is expecting to see the bits of mama left behind, the bone of a finger with baba's ring still on it, a lock of hair or a piece of heart, but instead it is only grey dust. Gently, Grandfather upturns the urn and piles her in the hole.

'Go on then,' says Grandfather. 'Say goodbye.'

The boy looks at the pile of dust. Then he looks at Grandfather. 'Goodbye.'

'Not to me, you little . . .' Grandfather cuffs him, gently, around his shoulder. 'Did you think I was leaving you behind? Say goodbye to your mama.'

His eyes fall back on the dust. 'I won't see her again.'

'No,' whispers Grandfather, 'not like this.'

'But papa, we can come for . . .'

Grandfather cuts him off. 'Goodbye, Vika.'

Now a chill wind blows up through the alders and the peak of the little pile of dust is caught and spirited away. When Grandfather sees it he drops to his knees to cover mama's dust with dirt. Once that is packed down – the boy helps pat it flat – he smears the snow back over. The sky is heavy and, as soon as it starts falling again, there'll be no mark that mama was ever here.

'Is it a grave?'

'No, not a grave.'

'Then what?'

Grandfather's eyes are wet. 'It was summer when your Grandma . . . I didn't come here, boy, though she begged me to. It was your mama who scattered her in these trees. This forest, that's what your baba is now. And it's what your mama is too.'

He nods.

'It all goes back to the ground. Then it gets eaten up. And then there's trees and flowers.'

'And nettles and thistles?'

Grandfather nods. 'All the bad stuff too, but don't forget the good. There are wolves in this forest that ate rabbits in this forest that ate grasses that grew on your Grandma.'

The old man feels the boy's hands, tells him they are frozen, that they'll have to get warm before frostbite eats every finger.

This is a thing to set the little boy thrilling, because to lose a finger in the forest would be a very great adventure.

As they turn back to the house, the boy cannot help seeing the look in his Grandfather's eyes. It is not one he has seen before. He has seen him angry, and he has seen him sad, but fear has a way of making the eyes crease – and fear is what he sees now. His hand falls from Grandfather's own, and as the old man tramps inside, the boy looks back at the tree that will drink up mama, and the still dark beneath the branches.

If Grandfather is right, then the wilderness is baba – and soon the wilderness will be mama too. But, if it is really so, then there is nothing to fear in those long darknesses between the trees. It would be like in the story of Baba Yaga, and you would be kind to the branches and they would throw up walls of thorn to protect you from any bad thing in the world.

Then he remembers: there are other stories too, ones he does not know, ones it seems Grandfather will not tell. There are stories of this ruined house, and baba and mama. There are the stories scrawled along the tenement hall, of soldiers and kings and the wars of the long ago. And there is the tale mama never knew, of why, until this day, Grandfather has never returned to the forest and stopped telling his tales. Perhaps, in those fables, the forest is a wicked thing, and boys and girls would be better off staying in Baba Yaga's hen feet hut than running desperately for their papa through the chestnuts and pines.

Grandfather's shape hunches through the door and along the narrow kitchen. Beyond him, the fire burns strong. The old man steps into the light, rounds the corner – and then, for a moment, though the boy can still hear the familiar click of his jackboot heels, he is gone. As the footfalls fade, the boy finds himself torn

60

between mama's tree and the echo of Grandfather's jackboots. By the time he scrabbles back into the ruin, Grandfather is hunched over the fire, fingers splayed to drink in its warmth.

He joins him, feeling the lap of the flames. 'Mama must have liked it, papa, to want to come back here.'

'I suppose she liked it well enough.'

'So why didn't you live here? Why did you live in the tenement?'

'Stories, stories,' mutters Grandfather. 'Haven't you had enough excitement for one night?'

As the flames flurry up, Grandfather brings a piece of crumpled newspaper out of his greatcoat pocket. When he sets it down, the scrunched-up paper slackens and unfurls. There, in the light of the fire, the boy sees the nine remaining hunks of mama's gingerbread.

'Can I?'

'Of course.'

The boy reaches out and takes one of the hunks.

'I'll want a corner.'

'You can have a whole one, papa.'

Grandfather closes the newspaper bundle. 'No,' he says. 'They have to last.'

He turns the gingerbread over in his mouth, until it is wet and sticky and stuck in the crannies between his teeth.

After some time, the flames lose their strength. In the hearth's heart, the branches glow orange, but fire no longer licks up the chimneybreast, and the hiss and crackle has ebbed away. It does not matter, for the heat still radiates out. The boy curls in his eiderdown, and skims the surface of sleep, always the thought of mama hovering near, the reassuring presence of Grandfather, just beyond the line of his vision.

He must fall asleep, because the next thing he feels are bony fingers in his hair. He does not start. The heat has lulled him, and he opens his eyes to feel Grandfather near.

'Are you ready, boy?'

'Ready, papa?'

'To go back to the tenement.'

The boy hurtles up. 'Please, papa. We haven't . . .'

'I can't stay here, boy. Not in the forest.'

'But why not in the forest?'

'*Why* doesn't matter,' breathes Grandfather. 'Stop asking why. Why, why, *why*! I already kept my promise, boy. I did what I told her I'd do. Your mama loves this place. She's fine out . . .'

A shrill cry, one to pierce every room in the ruin: 'She isn't fine, papa! She's dead.'

If there was another anger bubbling out of Grandfather, the boy has shocked it back into place. Now he stands, merely numb.

'She'll be fine, boy. She doesn't feel the cold, not where she is. She isn't alone. She has . . .' He seems to hold himself, weighing up the words. '. . . all of the trees.'

'Papa, just a little more.'

Grandfather lifts his hands, as if in submission.

'Maybe you can tell us a story, papa? One for me *and* for mama.'

Grandfather says, 'Something to help the long night pass . . .'

'One more story, and then we can go.'

Grandfather breaks from whatever dream was holding him. 'I have a story,' he says, taking in the timbers and stones, the pools of orange and pools of black. 'But settle down, boy, for this tale is too long in the telling.'

The boy nods.

62

This isn't the tale, says Grandfather, *but an opening. The tale comes tomorrow, after the meal, when we are filled with soft bread.*

On hearing the familiar words, the tension rushes out of the boy. He wriggles back into the eiderdown, bathed by the dying fire. Up close, Grandfather wraps his arms around his legs.

And now, he whispers, *we start our tale. Long, long ago, when we did not exist, when perhaps our great-grandfathers were not in the world, in a land not so very far away, on the earth in front of the sky, on a plain place like on a wether, seven versts aside, came the war to end all wars.*

Now, war, as we know, is a most terrible thing. For a long time, war had been talked of between kings and in courts, but in the little town where our story begins, war was a faraway thing, fought by champions and knights, and not for the grocers and farmers and carpenters who lived in the town, kind and careful, without any thought for killing.

Yet, war . . . war changes everything. In the east, there was a great emperor, the Winter King, who lived in his Winter Palace and ruled his empire with an iron fist. And, in the west, there was a clever man, a calculating king who had fought in wars before, and been locked away, and risen to rule with a party of fierce companions, who all hated each other but hated others most of all. And, caught between these two evil kings, soon there was whispering in our little town that war . . . war itself would seek them out.

The boy is rapt. It is, he decides, unlike the stories of before, those of Baba Yaga, of Dimian the peasant, of the Little Briar Rose. There is wickedness in those stories, but there are certainly no wars.

But, before we find ourselves at war this night, Grandfather goes on, *this is not a story of the war, not of the evil Winter King, nor the calculating King in the West. This is the story of a little boy, much the same as you, and the stories he heard of the ghosts in the woods . . .*

That little boy was smaller than you when the kings made war. He was four or he was five, and he lived, like you, in a town on the edge of the forest. And do you know how big the forest was?

'The woods are wide and the woods are wild, and the woods are the world forever and ever,' whispers the boy, as if repeating an ancient rite.

For a little while, the wars of the Winter King were only stories to that little boy. For him the world was only his house and the streets and the finger of forest that cut into his town. It was many months before the war found him, but when it found him it changed his world.

For the King in the West had broken a promise, and turned against the Winter King, who he had sworn was his friend. Angry as the end of all things, the Winter King rushed to meet the King in the West in pitched battle, and in the morning, when the boy awoke, his streets were filled with tanks and soldiers and new sounds, and languages he could not understand. He watched from his window and saw soldiers a-marching, and he knew they were a different kind of man to his papa and brothers. These were men raised in a world where they had never before known the sun, or the summer. They were soldiers from winter itself.

And so it happened that the town changed. His papa became a clerk, working for those same soldiers who took his grain and commandeered his horse and took their pigs off for slaughter. He kept their stores and wrote in a ledger book every time they ate the sausages that should have been his. Some of the men in town hated his papa for serving the soldiers, and perhaps he even hated his papa little bit too.

'Were the soldiers very terrible, papa?'

Well, sometimes they were terrible, and sometimes they were kind. Mostly they were just soldiers, and took their delights as soldiers sometimes will. But that little boy's papa made friends with those soldiers and, in that way, stood guard over his little boy for two whole years.

Well, one day, things changed, as things often will. Because the King in the West was bitter that the Winter King had brought his soldiers to town, and so the armies of the King in the West marched and laid siege. And the King in the West had soldiers reared on hate, and the Winter King's soldiers were scared, and turned tail and ran. The new soldiers wore brown shirts and spoke a language more terrible yet, and they came in their thousands with murder on their minds.

'Murder, papa?'

Yes, says Grandfather, and for a moment his voice loses its sing-song lilt, and it might be that he is not even telling a story at all. *That little boy saw it for himself. For the King in the West had made a plan that certain mamas and papas and boys and girls must wear golden stars, and then the soldiers would know whom they should kill. Those mamas and papas and boys and girls were sent to live in a different part of the town. For a little while they were kept there. They had to make uniforms and cobble boots, and when they didn't work hard enough, a soldier would come and say: the King in the West has called your name! Now you won't know night from day! And that person would be taken away, and then that person might never be seen again.*

Well, some of the mamas and papas and boys and girls worked harder and harder, hoping the soldiers might let them survive.

65

But some of the mamas and papas thought: the soldiers are wicked, and their King is more wicked still. We must run away, or else be ruined and turned into dust. And one papa said: there are woods beyond town, and the woods are wide and the woods are wild and the woods are the world forever and ever. And there we shall be safe, because in the woods there is no King in the West, nor even a Winter King, and in the woods they will not find us.

'It's like the story of Baba Yaga, isn't it, papa?'

'How, boy?'

'If you're kind to the woods, the woods are kind to you.'

Grandfather nods.

Well, at night, our little boy would look out of his bedroom window. There, he could see the first line of the pines and know that things were moving out there, in a world he could never pass into. Because only little boys made to wear the yellow stars could go and live wild in the forest . . .

Well, that boy was watching one night, when out of the town there hurried a girl. She was older than the boy, but not yet as old as the boy's mama, and for many months she had been wearing a yellow star. Now, she went to the forest to live wild. But she had lost her way, and that night rapped one, two, three times at the boy's front door.

Please, please, let me in, she cried.

Do the soldiers chase you? came the reply.

No, for I go to make my home with the runaways in the wild, and live my life under aspen and birch.

Well, the boy's mama and papa let the girl with the yellow star in. The boy watched them in secret from the top of the stairs. And what he saw was not one girl but two, for the girl had a baby swollen in her belly and ready to come out. You must stay, said the boy's mama, and have your babe in these four walls. But no, said the girl, for the soldiers will find me and make my baby wear a star.

So she was fed and warmed and went on her way, deep into the pines.

Well, the runaways found her, cold and alone. They took her to their hideaways and fed her their kapusta, *and she slept a day and a night in a burrow. And, when she woke, the men were angry at her, for they had not known she was carrying a child. Now they saw her, with swollen belly ready to burst, and told her: you cannot stay. A crying baby in the forest is worse than a fire. A baby might tell the soldiers where we are camped and bring ruin to us all.*

And so, that girl made a terrible decision. Either she would roam the wilds alone, risking capture, or she would bear the baby and give it up, find a family who would raise it as their own and never breathe a word that it should wear a yellow star and be snatched by the King in the West.

When the baby was born, it was a beautiful girl, with black hair thicker than any baby the wild men had ever seen. She was, they said, a true baby of the forests, with fur to ward off the winter, and if she was theirs to name they would call her Vered, for she was certain to blossom a wild rose.

But the baby was not theirs to name, and nor would she be her mother's. Now the baby was taken to the edge of the forest, to that same house whose mama and papa had helped the girl on her way. And the mama in that house took hold of the baby and promised she would be safe forever and all time.

I know a place, said the mama, where she will be safe, and me and my boy will take her there and watch over her from afar, and know that the soldiers will never find her.

So the boy and his mama took a small road along the forest's edge, to where a little house nestled at the bottom of a dell. At the house lived a trapper and his wife. Once, they had had children of their own, but those children had perished young, and for many years now the rooms had not heard the sound of tiny feet, nor the cries of squabbling and bruised knees. The mama and her boy carried the baby to the step and laid her down, without a mother or a father or even a name to call her own. And they knocked on the door and hurried back, to watch with the trees.

The door opened. Two faces appeared. They looked down, and saw that they could be a mama and a papa again, and the baby started to cry. And the house was happy after that. The house had a little girl to run in its rooms and play in its halls. The mama had a daughter to dote on, the papa had a princess to give purpose to his days. And if, out trapping in the forest, he ever caught sight of ghosts flitting from tree to tree, if he ever heard the sharp cracks of gunfire as the runaways learnt to defend themselves against the soldiers sent in to ferret them out, well, he gave his silent promise that the girl would be loved and looked after and grow up in a world safe from soldiers and yellow stars.

And so ends the story of the babe in the woods.

'Is it true?' marvels the boy.

Oh, says Grandfather. *I know it is true, for one was there who told me of it.*

Outside, it is paling to light. Grandfather's story has lasted all through the darkest hours. The fire is low, and Grandfather stands, meaning to bring new kindling. For a moment, the boy watches him leave. His head is swirling with pictures of the Winter King, of brown-shirted soldiers, of wild men living out in the woods, things so magical that, even through their horror, he wishes they were true.

Grandfather's jackboots click as he disappears into the kitchen and, leaving the Russian horse behind, the boy scrambles to hurry after him. When he gets there, the door is propped open and Grandfather is treading softly across the night's freshest fall. He hesitates at mama's tree, and seems to gaze up at the branches, at the canopy bound in ice.

The boy creeps to his side. The old man is tired, of that there is no doubt, but there is another look in his eyes now, something more mysterious than simple fear of the forest. To the boy it looks something like . . . temptation.

'Are we going to go back to the tenement, papa?'

Grandfather crouches, tracing his naked fingers along the roots in which mama lies. 'Not yet, boy. I think . . .'

He pauses, because seemingly it does not sound right, even to him. The boy cocks his head. This is the same papa who wouldn't come to the forest, the same papa who would have broken his mama's dying promise and never set foot here again. Perhaps it is something to do with that fanciful folk tale. The boy looks back at the house, wondering.

'I think we'll stay,' he says, letting his arm fall about the boy's shoulder. 'Just for a little while. Just until . . .'

'Until what, papa?'

'Just until the stories are done.'

The boy watches as Grandfather's face shifts. His eyes seem suddenly far away. 'Papa,' he ventures, 'I thought you hated the forest. I thought you said you'd never come back. We can go now, papa. I don't mind.' He thinks to say it again, as if to make sure Grandfather understands. 'I don't mind at all.'

'Oh,' grins Grandfather. 'But neither do I. I think . . . the

69

trees might not be so wicked after all. Come on, boy,' he grins. 'If I remember at all, there used to be a stream . . .'

He lifts his jackboot, and in one simple step goes under the trees.

Watching Grandfather under the trees is like watching a wolf prowl the tenement. His hands light on trunks and his jackboots sink into the frosted forest mulch, and he stops between the oaks, as if to judge the way. They do not find the stream, but it doesn't matter; Grandfather says there will be other days, and in the dead of winter a stream sometimes does not want to be found. They stop, instead, at a stand of black pine and Grandfather shows the boy how to strip the branches of their needles. A scent like Christmas billows up to engulf the boy, and now he must fill his pockets with them, so that they scratch and prickle against his legs.

'What is it for, papa?'

'Aren't you thirsty, boy?'

The boy nods.

'I'm going to show you something. It saved my life, almost every single night.'

Once there are enough pine needles in his pockets, the boy follows Grandfather back into the house. He has unearthed a cast-iron pot and balances it in the new flames, adding the needles handful by handful as the snow melts to sludge and then begins to simmer.

'What do you think, boy?'

They drink it from unearthed clay cups. There is a pleasing smell to its steam and its sweet taste, of woods and wild grass, warms the boy through. When he looks up from his cup, Grandfather is holding his to his face, letting the steam bead in his whiskers, the thatches above his eyes.

'What's wrong, papa?'

'It's the smell. It . . . reminds me. There's nothing like a smell, boy, to put you in another place.'

The boy thinks he understands; it is not so very different when he drinks in the scent of mama's shawl. The thought of it, lying crumpled by the rocking chair in the tenement, makes him wonder. 'Are we going back to the tenement today, papa?'

'Not yet, little one.'

'I thought you didn't like it here.'

Grandfather breathes out, expelling pine-needle steam. 'You wouldn't want to leave her again, would you?'

This doesn't make sense, because it was Grandfather who said that mama was fine out there in the trees.

'Maybe we can take mama back with us.'

'No,' says Grandfather, and his tone means he will brook no more questions. 'We'll stay with her, for a while. She'd like that, boy. You'd like it. I'd . . . like it.'

Through the day the clouds are thick, so that night might

have already fallen for hours before the darkness truly sets in. With real night, however, comes real snow. Standing in the kitchen door to say goodnight to mama, the boy can barely see the end of the garden. It reveals itself only in fragments, catching his eye each time the driving snow twists and comes apart. At the end of that vortex, crusts grow over the roots where mama sleeps, but Grandfather says not to worry.

'I once slept in a hole six feet under the ice,' he begins. 'Three days and three nights, boy. Every time I closed my eyes, I thought I'd freeze. I didn't know, back then, that it was the ice protecting me. It was the ice keeping me warm.'

Grandfather turns to tramp back towards the hearth, but the boy is slow to follow.

'Papa,' he says, 'is it a story?'

At the fire, Grandfather bends to feed more wood to the flames.

'It is,' he says, 'but for another night . . .'

In the morning there is no talk of the tenement. Before the sun struggles into the sky Grandfather leads him off, deeper into the forest.

'I remembered the way,' he says. 'It came to me in the dead of night.'

'To the stream?'

'It runs underground but comes to the surface for just a little while . . .'

It turns out that Grandfather is looking for cattails. Cattails, he says, grow by streams and you can dig them up even in the dead of winter. If you cook them right they can taste just like a potato.

'But we have potatoes in the tenement, papa.'

They stand by a depression in the land through which Grandfather is certain the stream once ran.

'Do you want to go back to the tenement, boy? Is that it?'

'I don't want to leave her, papa, but . . .'

'What's in the tenement?' Grandfather sinks to his knees and runs his hands through tall bladed grass. He seems to be feeling their textures, teasing out the occasional one and following its stem all the way to its root. 'Your mama was the only thing in the tenement that mattered, and now she's here. In spring she'll be in every tree, just like baba.'

'Do you miss baba, papa?'

'Only every day. Might be I'd forgotten how much, until you made me come here.'

Now the boy understands: it is his fault. His papa pleaded with him not to make him come, but the boy pleaded back. There must be old smells and memories rushing on Grandfather every second. Maybe he remembers how baba smelt, how she spoke, the things that she said.

'Are the trees your friends, papa?'

'They saved my life, once upon a time.'

Grandfather plunges a hand through the crust. The earth seems to swallow him, up to his elbow. He fights back, gripping his arm with the other hand as if struggling with whatever cadaver lurks beneath the surface. Finally, he topples back, the cattail in his hand, trailing pulpy white flesh beaded in dirt.

'It's for dinner.'

'What about school, papa? I have to go to school.'

Grandfather's eyes roam the grasses, searching out another stalk.

'I never heard of a little boy wanting to go to school.'

74

'I haven't been since . . . before mama. They'll wonder where I am. What about . . . Yuri?'

'He's your little friend.'

The boy shrugs.

'You want to watch out for friends. When I was a boy, a friend was a dangerous thing.'

Grandfather's hand plunges back through the snow and comes out with another cattail root, wriggling like some poor fish just plucked from the water.

'Come on, boy. Aren't you hungry?'

Cattail mashed with acorn is not so very bad a dinner, if it's been two days since you had hot potatoes and hock of ham. By the time it is done the afternoon is paling and snow smothers the forest again.

Night means a different thing when there are no buzzing electric lights. Now Grandfather is ready for bed as soon as the darkness comes. He rests his feet, still in their jackboots, on a crate and sprawls back in the ragged armchair, tugging the bearskin hat to the brim of his eyes.

'Will we go back to the tenement tomorrow, papa?'

'We'll see.'

'We won't see, though, will we?'

Grandfather opens one eye. It rolls at the boy with a taunting sparkle. 'You need your rest.'

He really doesn't, but he gets under the eiderdown all the same. Soon he can hear the tell-tale wheeze that means Grandfather is asleep. He rolls over, the Russian horse lying rigid in his belly, and dares to close his eyes.

When he wakes, the flames are still dancing and an advancing tide of melt frost runs down the wall. Without clocks or the sounds of the tenement hall he has no way of knowing what time it is, nor how long he has been asleep. He squirms out of the eiderdown, leaving the Russian horse to bask in the hearth's demonic glow.

In the armchair, Grandfather does not move at all.

The boy steals over. There is a desperate silence in the room. It is the silence of snow, which devours all sound, save for the howling of storybook wolves or a foundling baby's cries on the doorstep. By the time he has reached Grandfather's side, that silence is overwhelming.

'Papa, are you awake?'

He dares himself to touch the thin, unmoving arms. Yet, when he does, it is a strange coldness that he feels. His eyes flit to the dead wood piled by the hearth; Grandfather's arm feels the same as those branches, brittle and somehow empty.

'Papa?'

When there is no answer, the boy relents, sits in a nest in the eiderdown and draws the Russian horse back into his lap. He studies his papa's face for a long time, as fingers of firelight lap at his hanging skin. He should be snoring. His head is thrown back in the way it always was in the tenement, but no sound comes up from his throat. His lips do not tremble, nor twitch; his chest, buried beneath greatcoat and dressing gown, does not move at all.

That must have been how mama looked: open-mouthed and bald, without any breath left in her breast. They wouldn't let him see her then, but the firelight plays a cruel trick and it is as if he is seeing her now.

He feels a fist of stone rising in his gorge, like a mother bird regurgitating food for her young. He fights it back down, but the stone must burst in his stomach, churning up whatever horrible slime lurks within. Back on his feet, and the room seems to be whirling.

'Papa!' he cries. And then, 'Papa!' again. But each time he has cried out, the silence is thicker; and, each time he has cried out, the idea that Grandfather is gone is clearer, more defined. Now he is like a storm-fallen tree, lying in the forest; he has the same shape as ever, the same ridges and fingers and branches and eyes, but what made him a living thing has disappeared.

The boy gulps for air. He doesn't know what to do with his hands. His feet want to run, but where he would run to, he has no idea. If only to stop that stone from rising back up his throat, unleashing his terror, he goes to the backdoor, thinking perhaps to ask mama for help. The world is silent. The snow no longer falls. But mama cannot help him now and never will again.

He goes back to Grandfather's side. 'I'm sorry, papa . . . I didn't mean to make you come. Papa, I have to get help.'

Doctors and ambulances have different kinds of sorceries. There is always a hope that their words can bring life back to Grandfather just like Grandfather's words bring life back to deadened fires. There is, he tells himself, always the car. If he finds the car, he can find his way to town. To squatting factories and endless streets, to a tenement with its window eyes gouged out. To help.

The boy steals down the passage. When he tugs the front door back, snow pours in, burying him knee-deep. With it comes winter, that relentless marauder. He gazes up the incline to the border of black forest, thinks he can make out the jaws of the trail he and Grandfather followed.

If he is going to do this he will need to be prepared. He retreats to the hearth and wraps himself in the eiderdown, one, two, three times. Now it is too stiff to walk, so he loosens the blanket and tests out his stride.

He is passing Grandfather when he sees the bearskin hat sitting proudly upon the old man's head. He does not need it now, so the boy lifts it down, awkward only when he has to wrestle it over Grandfather's ears. His eyes light momentarily on the old man's jackboots too, but they will not fit, and he does not relish the idea of seeing Grandfather's feet with their bulbous blue veins now devoid of all blood.

It is time to leave, so leaving is what he does.

Up the dell he goes, through luminescent snow. The woods in dead of night are no different from the woods at dusk, and for this the boy is thankful. The same light is captured in the snowbound canopy, the same ghosts move in the darkness, the same sounds startle and echo and live longer in the boy's imagination.

There are sounds in the forest, spidery things that scuttle on the very outskirts of his hearing, so that every time he whips his head round all he sees is frigid undergrowth. Every stem is crisped in white, every gnarled root iced with sugar like a wing of the angel. When he exhales, his breath mists, obscuring by degrees the deepening forest. It condenses in the rim of Grandfather's bearskin hat, so that before long he is wearing a crown of ice itself. Soon it encroaches onto the skin of his forehead. It pierces him and holds fast, binding head to hat.

In this way the boy huddles through the forest. His lashes are heavy, the ice creeping down his face to make a carefully crafted death-mask, but at last he sees the car between the trees. The whole body is draped in ice.

He tries the handle at the driver's side, but it is stuck. He heaves again, to no avail – and, this time, when he tries to let

78

go, he finds his naked fingers held fast. He tugs and tugs, but the winter has him in its grasp.

Panic takes him. He twists around, but he cannot twist far. Careful that the skin of his other hand should not touch the treacherous ice, he draws it back inside the eiderdown. A moment later he tries to prise his hand free. Cold is surging along his fingers and up his arm. He thinks: what will happen when it touches my heart? I'll be frozen forever, only to wake up in a hundred years, thawed out by some wanderer of the future.

He has a thought, and spits on his trapped hand. The saliva works a sorcery, thawing the thin ice and letting him work an inch of flesh free. He spits again, and then again – and, in that way, he is able to tear himself away.

At last, he remembers: when Grandfather lifted him out of the car, the door remained ajar behind him. He tramps to the ditch side and sees that door still open by inches. The winter has tried to seal the gap, closing the crevice with barnacles of ice just as skin grows back over a wound, but its work is not yet done. With effort the boy is able to force his way in.

The cold of inside does not have the same clarity as the cold of out. He heaves the door shut, to the satisfying sound of ice crunching against ice, and imagines he can hear the tiny clink of crystals interlocking.

The key is still in the ignition. All Grandfather has to do is turn that key and the car starts rolling. When the car is rolling, its undercarriage rattles and the floor gets hot – but when he puts his fingers around the key he finds it frozen in place, bound to the car by the same ice slowly smothering the forest.

Inside the car he cannot see out; through that icy cocoon all he can see are different shades of grey and black. Perhaps this is what Grandfather's ghost feels like, if it still lingers inside his corpse. He shrinks back into the eiderdown, holding himself. He thinks: if I sleep, morning will come, and with it the morning thaw.

It is not long after he closes his eyes that his teeth begin to chatter. He concentrates on holding them still, but to do so he must tense every muscle in his body and soon the effort is too great. It is only when he gives up trying that he begins to lose sensation: first his feet, then his legs, his hands and arms. At last, the only parts of him awake are his chattering teeth; then, even they pass out of all thought.

'Wake up.'

He turns, entangled in eiderdown, not knowing where, nor even what, he is.

'He's coming for you. You have to wake up.'

All he can feel is a circlet of pain running around the edge of his head. He is wearing an icicle crown and, rather than growing out, the icicles have turned on him, growing into flesh and bone. He shivers. It is not a shiver of cold, but a shiver of fever. It is the kind of shiver mama got every time they said they were making her better, and put the wires into her veins.

Mama's voice. He remembers it now. She says, 'Wake up, my littlest friend. He's coming to find you.'

'Who is, mama?'

'He's coming out of the wood . . .'

The boy's eyes snap open. No sooner is he awake than mama's voice is gone. He fights the eiderdown off to find himself trapped, somehow, on the inside of an ice cube. It takes a moment, but then: the car. I am in the car.

80

Outside, the snow dark is paling, but he cannot see the trees. All is occluded by ice.

Something moves.

As soon as he senses movement, other shapes fall into stark relief. Edges become distinct and distances become apparent – and, although the ice still magnifies and shrinks according to how deeply its scales have grown, he can make out individual trees.

He can make out, too, a figure coming lurching over a fallen bough.

In three great strides it is at the side of the car. Its hands seem to caress the windows and doors, but then it retreats. He thinks, for a moment, it is gone back to the forest, but then it appears on the ditch side of the car, brandishing a bough it has lifted from the winter wood.

The boy scrabbles against the furthest corner of car. His fingers find the handle, but it is held fast. He remembers the crunch of ice on ice, the sensation of the tiny crystals locking together, just as surely as this bearskin hat has become a part of his head. He tries again, unfeeling fingers fumbling – but still nothing.

'Are you in there?'

It can talk. The shadow man can talk. Its voice is distant, a ragged whisper as a thing might make if it did not need to take any breath.

The boy holds himself tight. It is only movement that he sees. Perhaps it is the same for this forest ghoul. If the boy does not move, he will remain invisible in his icy tomb.

'I can see you.'

He has to be lying. His body is held rigid, refusing to take breath. The ice from the bearskin hat is creeping down his face.

'I can see you, boy . . .'

At last, he exhales. Two great gulps, and a horrible pain explodes in his chest; he has swallowed air so frigid that veins of ice are spreading across his insides, groping from organ to organ like happened with mama.

The forest shade's hands grapple with the door. Now the ice relents. The shadow forces the bough into the tiny crack and, with a sound like shattering pipes, the door flies open.

The bright white of snow behind him is blinding. It takes long seconds for the boy's eyes to become accustomed to the glare. Slowly the silhouette gains features: a flat, crooked nose; eyes like sunken canker scars.

'Come on, boy, get yourself out of there. I'll have to start a fire.'

'Papa?'

'You shouldn't have run off like that. There's things in these forests.'

It feels as if his insides are coming apart, like a patchwork blanket with a loose thread that, once teased, begins unravelling and cannot be stopped. The sensation tingles up and down his arms, the wormy bits that make up his innards wriggling, uncontrolled. It is, he knows, a feeling of pure relief. He bobs in it, as if still cupped in the ice-cold waters of his dream.

'Is it really you, papa?'

'Who else would it be?'

The boy says, 'Well, there's things in these forests . . .'

'I just told you.'

'I thought you were a . . . thing.'

He allows himself to be manhandled out, to stand in the ditch alongside his papa. He knows it is morning only by the smell in the air, of the top dusting of frost constantly thawing and freezing over again.

'Why did you run?' Grandfather is inspecting the car, using the branch to fight the worst of the snow off the windscreen. If he is angry, the boy cannot tell. He moves awkwardly, constantly leaving one leg behind.

'I thought . . .'

'You thought what?'

'You wouldn't wake up.'

'I haven't slept so deep in . . . What is it, boy?'

'You didn't even snore. You always snore in the tenement.'

'You wanted to go back to school, didn't you?'

'Only if you want me to, papa.'

'Well, what do you want?'

He doesn't say: mama. Instead, he says, 'I only want to make you better.'

'Better?'

But even the boy does not know what he means.

'I'd be better if I had my hat, little one.'

The boy, alarmed at how he had forgotten, goes to whip the hat off his head.

'Careful!' Grandfather barks. 'It's frozen to your brow.'

'I think it's blistering.'

'You'll have to tease it off. You can do it later.'

'Maybe I *can* go to school, papa.'

'We'll have to bring this car back to life first.'

Grandfather sends the boy to unearth stones and, in a clearing in the woodland, they build a ring inside which they can harrow the earth. After that, it does not take him long to summon up a fire. The boy watches as the baby flames dance, maturing into darting oranges and reds.

While the fire beds down, roasting the rocks that keep it hemmed in, the boy and Grandfather tramp back to the ruin, dragging out the cast-iron pot from the hearth.

Grandfather asks, 'Are you sure you want to leave her?'

Shamefaced, the boy nods.

Once Grandfather is satisfied, they take the pot to their new cauldron in the forest. It nestles in the flames until it, too, is roasting, and then they pile handfuls of snow inside.

It takes hours of new snow-melt to excavate the car – but, at last, the thaw is complete. While the boy sets about dousing the fire in the wood, Grandfather bathes the frozen key in scalding water and turns it in the ignition. Like the Little Briar Rose being revived by a kiss, the car comes back to life.

It is another hour before they are stuttering back through the trees. The car is ailing as mama once was beneath them, but Grandfather doesn't hear, or, if he does, he doesn't care. They gutter around a turn in the trail and join the ribbon of black that snakes its way into town.

As the trees fade around them, the boy looks at Grandfather. Perhaps it is only the weariness in his eyes, but he thinks he sees heartache there, the same as the day mama disappeared.

'Papa, what is it?'

'It's nothing, boy. You were right. You . . . have to go to school.'

'It's what mama would want.'

'She always was wiser than her papa.'

'Then what is it, papa? What's wrong?'

Grandfather takes his eyes off the road; the car slews in ice and he wrests it back with birdlike arms.

'It's only . . . I don't want to go back to the tenement, boy. It's dead there. At least the forest's alive. It grows. It changes.'

'You never wanted to go to the forest, not until I made you.'

When Grandfather exhales, it might be a grin or it might be a grimace. 'Might be I should never have made that promise to your mama. But, you see, I've seen it now, those old woodlands. Older than me. It's only now it feels . . . right to be there.'

The boy thinks he understands. It is a kind of homesickness – because, no matter how long he lived in the tenement, it is the forest that Grandfather thinks of as home.

A strange thought erupts in him, one that must be given voice. 'That little boy in the story, papa . . . the one in the war with the Winter King . . .'

'Yes, boy?'

The boy loses his nerve. 'It *was* only a story, wasn't it?'

'Well,' says Grandfather, 'there's a little bit of truth in every fable.'

'Even Baba Yaga eating little boys and girls?'

Grandfather pales, as white as the snow, and in that instant he really is the forest shade the boy thought sent to catch him. 'Even that, boy,' he whispers, dead words to kill the conversation.

Plague oaks and black pines hurtle past.

What Grandfather does when the boy is at school is a riddle he cannot solve. The boy watches the car stutter back along the road, and wonders at the yawning emptiness ahead. Turning to the schoolhouse, he thinks: we should have stayed in the forest. At least, then, papa had cattails to cook and kindling to muster. At least the trees are alive, not like the tenement walls. It must get very weary to be so very old.

It is daybreak and there are children milling in the schoolyard. He stands on the edge of them, shivering – for he has left his eiderdown in the car, and his clothes still cling to him, soaked in forest frost.

Yuri is already here, prowling the corners of the schoolyard with his head in the clouds. The boy means to go and play with him, but before he gets there the schoolyard starts flocking, up the steps and into the schoolhouse. Yuri has already gone through the doors by the time the boy gets there. He pauses, because to go through them now would be a very strange thing. He can see children milling beyond and the caretaker, a young man they say is as simple as the most insensible child, is moving his broom as if to sweep them on their way.

He steps through the doors, to a wave of dry heat, quite unlike Grandfather's fires.

Almost instantly the caretaker's eyes fall on him. 'You can take off that hat.'

The boy goes to lift the bearskin from his head. Too late, he remembers the ice binding it to him. He pulls and the crystals tear at his skin.

'Jesus, boy, what happened to your head?'

He lifts his fingers to trace the raised skin where he wore the halo. Occasionally his fingers find tiny outcrops of ice still sprouting from the blisters, but they perish and melt at his touch.

'You little bastards don't look after yourselves. What kind of mother sends her boy to class looking like that?'

With the bearskin hat still in his hands, he hurries down the corridor. It is only a small schoolhouse, with not even a single stair. The tiniest children are in two rooms around a bend in the hall, but everyone else is gathered in the three rooms that flank the corridor. In the middle is the library with its open walls, where you can go and choose a storybook or have injections when the nurse comes to visit. At the very end of the corridor, boys and girls are scrambling for pegs to hang their coats, and then cantering for the best seats in the assembly hall.

The boy is halfway along the corridor when Mr Navitski's

eyes fall on him. At first his brow furrows, eyebrows creeping up to meet the point of his black fur, but then his eyes soften and he has a look less like bewilderment, and more like . . . The boy knows this look well. It is a look of: your mama's gone and you must be hungry.

As the rest of class scramble to sit cross-legged in the assembly hall, Mr Navitski picks a way through. 'We all wondered when you'd be back.'

'Am I late?'

'No, you're not late, but you are . . . Maybe you'd like to wash up before assembly?'

The boy peers through Mr Navitski's legs, to see the head-mistress already pontificating to the gathered school. 'Will I be in trouble for missing it?'

'No, you won't be in trouble. Better you . . . Look, I'll help.'

Mr Navitski doesn't seem to want to take him by the hand, but takes him by the hand nonetheless. There is a little bathroom just by the assembly hall, and together they go in. The water in the taps will take forever to warm up, so Mr Navitski fills a sink with cold and lathers up a cake of hard soap.

'How long have you been wearing this shirt?'

The boy shrugs, because something tells him he should not mention the forest.

'We'll find you a new one, from lost property.'

'Can I keep this one?'

'You mustn't wear it to class, but we'll keep it safe for you.'

Mr Navitski's hand strays from the boy's shirt to his hair, where he begins to tease out pieces of twig. When his hand brushes the blisters, the boy recoils. 'What happened here?'

'It was the ice.'

'Ice?'

'I was wearing my papa's hat, and it iced to me.'

'You're in his tenement now, aren't you? Doesn't he have the heating turned up?'

This the boy knows not to answer.

'When was the last time you had a proper meal?'

The boy remembers cattail mash, washed down with pine-needle tea. 'It was last night.'

'Really?'

'Really.'

'I have some leftovers my wife packed away for me. I'll have them warmed through.'

After he has rinsed his face and hands and even his arms up to the elbows, Mr Navitski finds a brush and tugs the tangles out of his hair. By the time they are finished the assembly is over, and it is time for class.

'You'll have some catching up to do.'

'I know.'

'Come on, then. We're learning about the war.'

'The wars of winter?'

Uncertainly, Mr Navitski says, 'Well, when the whole world was at war . . .'

'Was it when the Winter King fought the King in the West? And there were some men who had to wear stars, and went into the forests and lived there and ate cattail roots and pine-needle tea, all so the soldiers didn't catch them?'

A smile curls in the corner of Mr Navitski's lips. 'You mean the Bielskis, and people like them. They were Jewish partisans. They broke out of the ghettos and went into the wilderness, into the *pushcha* itself, and built a whole civilization there, and the Germans just couldn't find them. There were Russian partisans too. They went into the *pushcha* and found ways to fight back. Oh,' he beams – because some stories thrill grown men as much as little boys – 'men were crawling all through the *pushcha* during the wars.'

'When all the world was the Russias?'

'Well, one might say that . . .'

'And they might still be out there, even if they're gone, because the trees drink them up and everything that ever died turns into trees, doesn't it?'

This time, Mr Navitski hesitates before replying. He nods only vaguely, his brow creases again, and he shepherds the boy into class to join children who look at him differently, oddly – because, now that mama is gone, he is not really like them at all.

It turns out that the project is what our families did in the war. In turn, the boys and girls will tell about their own families, and what happened to them in that long-ago time. One girl tells how her Grandfather was a soldier and got put in a prison and had to spend the whole war there, learning ways to escape. Only, when he escaped, he found he was hundreds of miles from home and somehow had to get back. In those days there were no motor cars, and the trains were filled with wicked soldiers, so lots of people had to walk. Like those men in Grandfather's story, they had to live wild in hedgerows and forests, and some of them looked like cavemen and others more beastly still.

Yuri's project is a pile of crumpled notepaper and a map, like the one on his bedroom floor, which shows all the Russias and the countries along its side, places like *Latvia* and *Lithuania*, a big scribble called *Ukraine* and after that the tiny *Belarus*, coloured in with trees.

'Aren't you telling about your papa?'

'No,' scowls Yuri, scoring another tree into his map.

'Why no?'

'Because,' he says, poking a pencil in Mr Navitski's direction, 'he said not to do my papa, because, in the war, the police were no good. But how can a police be no good? Police are there to help.'

Yuri lifts his map and cups it around his mouth. 'I'm sorry about your mama.'

It is an incredible thing to hear. Such a little thing, but the boy's lips start to tremble, his hands hot and slippery as a fever.

'What's it like, living with your papa?'

Any words the boy might have would come out like sobs, so he swallows them.

'What did your papa do in the war?'

'Is it the wars of winter?' the boy finally says.

Yuri considers it. 'I think so. In the pictures, it's awfully cold.'

It is dark by end of day. Outside, mothers cluck around the gates and, as the boy ventures out, he feels Mr Navitski's eyes boring into his back. He stops to watch, because even Yuri, with a sleeve encrusted in spittle and bits of dinner, has a mama to run to. In the gloom at the end of the schoolyard, Yuri's mother scolds him, strikes him once around the ear and takes his hand to lead him away.

Grandfather is waiting on the other side of the road, prowling up and down by the car like a man in a cage. The boy takes flight, not stopping to look as he barrels over the road to find him.

'Papa!'

Grandfather looks up. 'I didn't know when this all ends,' he says, with what must be deep relief.

'Have you been waiting?'

'A little.'

'I'm sorry, papa. Are you cold?'

He beams, 'Well, they don't let you build cookfires in the middle of the street, do they? Jump in. It's getting dark.'

The boy's eyes drift to the skies. Clouds have gathered, but a half moon still shines. 'It's dark already, papa.'

'Not this,' Grandfather grins. 'I mean real dark. These people don't know real dark, do they? But we do. Your papa and you know about real dark. Woodland dark.'

The boy slides up front, and the car complains bitterly as Grandfather rolls it into the traffic.

'Where did you get that shirt?'

It is only now that he realizes he is still wearing the shirt Mr Navitski found for him.

'I'm sorry, papa.'

'Why sorry?'

Grandfather slows the car down to a halt, even though they are in the middle of a road, approaching an intersection where dark tenements huddle together.

'I don't know.'

'Don't ever say sorry, boy.'

After that they drive in silence. The boy wants to ask: what did you do today, papa? Were you lonely on your own? Did you talk to Madam Yakavenka or go to the shop and talk to the woman at the counter? Did you get a bread from the bakery or are you filled up with cattail? But he says nothing. He wipes at the condensation forming on the windows with his sleeve, and tries to make out by streetlights where he might be, how close to home.

It is only when he wipes the window clear for a fifth time

that he realizes they are leaving the town. The streetlights have grown infrequent, and in rags the trees grow more misshapen, not tamed by human hands like the ones that sprout from concrete along the city streets.

'Aren't we going back to the tenement, papa?'

'But what's at the tenement?'

'Well, nothing . . .'

'So why would we want to go back?'

This time, the way into the wild is familiar. They draw off from the main road, into the caverns of ice, and stutter on until they have reached the old resting spot.

'Are you warm enough in that shirt?'

The boy shakes his head.

'There's the eiderdown just there. But I found you a coat. There's a cellar, under your baba's house. There's a trapdoor outside, near the kitchen door.'

'I have a coat at the tenement, papa. It's the one mama got me.'

'This one's warmer.'

'But it isn't mine, is it?'

Grandfather stalks off, up and over the dead fire, loping like a hunchback into the trees.

'It's in the family,' he says.

Before they reach the ruin, the boy can see smoke curling out of the chimneystack. He can see the chimneystack too, no longer a crumbled mound of bricks but now excavated and piled high, churning clouds out into the night with the same relentlessness as the factories through which they have come. From the top of the hill, he can smell the woodsmoke.

Grandfather leads him down the dell and stops to lift a simple latch on the wooden door, no longer slumped and smashed into place, but hanging – if awkwardly – from hinges once again. When he opens the door, winter tries to rush in, but waves from the hearthfire try to rush out. A battle is fought in the open doorway, and through that prickly frontier the boy and Grandfather go.

'Papa,' the boy begins, begging a smile, 'what happened?'

Grandfather shrugs, as if to hide the smile that is flourishing in the corners of his lips. 'I found some . . . bits and pieces. This old house, it remembers me, boy.'

In the living room there are rugs. They do not extend quite to the edges as a carpet might, but they are deep and soft under his feet, and run all the way to the hearth, where a fire surges and rolls. Ranged around the hearth are two armchairs with a little table between. All of the brambles that once clawed in to take back the house have been hacked and bundled up, and now hang on strings above the hearth, drying out for future kindling.

In the hearth sits the cast-iron pot, and in the cast-iron pot spits and crackles a bird. Cattail roots bob, white strands trailing like Baba Yaga's hair, in the surface of the broiling snow-melt. Its smells lift, mingle with the woodsmoke, and reach out to tempt the boy.

He peers in the pot. 'What is it, papa?'

'It's like a chicken.'

'But what is it?'

'A grouse.'

The boy looks again, breathing in deep aromas of wild grass and wet bark. 'There are two birds here.'

'One's a starling.'

'A starling?'

'It's been such a long time since I ate a starling. Shall we say goodnight to your mama, boy?'

The boy follows Grandfather through the kitchen. Here, too, everything has changed. One of the smashed windows is covered with boards, and all of the pots are stacked in piles. A bowl by the tin sink is filled with cattail roots and acorns and other roots the boy does not know, all of them ugly as unborn children. In another bowl sits a handful of nuts, and in another still dry, sprawling mushrooms that look as if someone has rolled and stretched them out.

'Jew's ears,' says Grandfather, teasing one between thumb and forefinger.

'Jew's ears?'

'Just don't let your baba hear you call them that.'

Soaking up the heat of the hearthfire, the boy has forgotten how cold the winter night can get, and once outside he starts to shiver. Grandfather tells him to take a deep breath, they'll only be a minute, and pads to the bottom of the garden. As he follows him, he looks back at the house. Grandfather has excavated the snow from the walls, and in the crater he can see the cellar trapdoor, hard wood and iron clasp.

'See,' says Grandfather, staring at the roots of mama's tree. 'I told you he'd be back. He's done his schooling and now it's time for dinner. I'm making him a bird. He won't have tasted anything like it.'

While Grandfather is talking to whatever's left of mama, the boy imagines her working her way up the roots, into the trunk of the tree. In the spring, perhaps there will be leaves, and in the way the veins of those leaves spread out and bring colour to the leaf, there will be an image of mama. In autumn the leaves will fall down and rot, and the tree will drink them up again, and that is how mama can live forever and always.

Back inside, it is time for dinner to be served up. Grandfather even has dishes, and into each he spoons some bird and heap of roots. The boy sees, now, that there are pine needles in the broth, and chestnuts too, collected under trees planted by some ancient forester as a gift to the future. In the bottom of his bowl he finds a Jew's ear and turns it between his teeth. It is tough as the rubber bands Yuri chews on at school, but its juices run hot and thick down his chin.

'How do you like your real food?'

It is not like the dinners mama might make, but it is every bit as good.

'It's been an age since I ate like this, boy.'

'But when did you eat like this, papa?'

'Why, when I was young.'

'When were you young, papa?'

'In the long ago.'

There was not such joy in Grandfather's voice last night. There was not such sparkle in his eyes the night before. He wonders: what has changed? It must be the house that now looks so homely. It must be the woods out back and the snow that hugs them, the hearth with its proud cookfire, and the very trees themselves. Why would his papa refuse to come to the forests, when the forests make him so happy?

'What did you do during the wars, papa?'

Grandfather sets his wooden spoon down. The juices of grouse and starling, whose rangy skeletons now sit picked clean on his plate, glisten in his whiskers. 'Why would you ask such a thing?'

'It's . . . for school,' he says, though in truth it is for everything else as well. 'Was it like in the wars of winter? Mr Navitski says there really were people living wild in the woods . . . Maybe

96

there really was a baby. Maybe there really was a little boy who helped rescue it from the forest. And maybe . . .'

Grandfather's owlish eyes are on him.

'. . . maybe it was baba, papa? Maybe it was this very same house?'

'And what do you think?'

'You told me there was a bit of the true in every story.'

'Well,' says Grandfather, 'maybe you'd like another tale?'

The boy's eyes turn up. 'Yes, please, papa.'

There comes a sound from Grandfather's belly. It is a sound that says: settle down, boy, for we're safe and warm, while the world is white and wild, and this tale will be long in the telling.

This isn't the tale, says Grandfather, *but an opening.*

The boy's mouth follows the familiar words, surging ahead even before Grandfather has finished them.

The tale comes tomorrow, after the meal, when we are filled with soft bread. And now, he beams, *we start our tale.*

Long, long ago, when we did not exist, when perhaps our great-grandfathers were not in the world, in a land not so very far away, on the earth in front of the sky, on a plain place like on a wether, seven versts aside, there was endless, endless war.

The wars of winter had raged for a hundred long years, and time and again, our little town had fallen, first to the Winter King, then to the King in the West, then to the Winter King again. But the King in the West was strongest, and soon the little town became his dominion once and for all. The soldiers of the Winter King were frightened, but they could never give up. Do you know where they went?

The boy remembers Mr Navitski's words. 'They went into the forest, didn't they, papa?'

To the pushcha, *in the snow dark between the trees, for they were the soldiers of winter and knew how to live under aspen and birch.*

'And there were *partisans* . . .' He tries the word, and finds it almost fits. '. . . already, weren't there? Partisans with yellow stars? Because they knew about the forests too, didn't they?'

Grandfather nods.

But the woods are wide and the woods are wild, and the woods are the world forever and ever. And there was space in the trees yet, for the Partisans of the Yellow Star and the soldiers of winter. Sometimes they would find each other, and sometimes they would help each other – and if, when winter was fiercest, they met each other in the pines, they might share their potatoes, or share their milk. Or even their guns.

'Guns, papa?'

Oh, yes. Because the pushcha *was a place of great darkness. The King in the West wreaked terrible things and, sometimes, his men would lead their prisoners out, into places where only the oaks could witness, and line them up. Then they would cast terrible magic, and the prisoners would tumble between the roots and be buried forever.*

Now, trees are mighty, but a tree cannot move to help a creature in need. Some of the trees, they saw such things and screamed. Their roots spoke to their trunks, and their trunks whispered to branches and leaves, and all of the forests mourned for the men murdered in their midst. But other trees saw the work of the King in the West and were filled with joy. Because trees feed on dead things, and send their roots down to drink them up, and when the King in the West killed in the forests, some trees were tempted to feed on the murdered men. And those trees grew mighty and powerful, with branches made from dead men, and leaves that turned blood-red long before autumn's call. And to this day you

98

can see, out there in the forests, the trees that have drunk on the dead of the wars of winter – for those are the trees whose trunks have the faces of men. For that is their curse, to forever wear the features of the men they have eaten.

And that little baby, squalling on the step? Well, if she had stayed with her real family in the wild, she might have been drunken up by the trees as well. For her people were hunted down by the King in the West and, if ever they were caught, they were fed to the roots.

And so ends our story, of the good and bad trees.

After the tale, the boy finds that he is sleepy, lulled by the fire and the tale, but he does not want to close his eyes – not to images of trees devouring men – so, instead, he follows Grandfather back to the kitchen door, to wish goodnight to mama.

Moonlight scuds over the forest. He ventures out, tramping in the footsteps Grandfather's jackboots have left behind, but when he reaches the roots of mama's tree, it is not her that he sees in the branches. Instead, it is the mamas and papas marched out, lined up and shot down, so that all of the deeper trees could drink on their remains.

He has always known that the forests are home to wild things. Now, he knows that the forests are home to ghosts as well. He can almost hear them moaning, for the winter is whipping up a wind – and that wind is trapped, like a lingering spirit, beneath the canopies of ice. Deeper in, shadows stretch and dance in time with those mournful sounds.

The crunch of branches underfoot, the snap of a foot pressed down – but, when he looks up, it is only Grandfather that he sees.

'It must have been very frightening, to live so wild,' whispers the boy.

99

'Oh,' says Grandfather, 'it was frightening, but it wasn't because of the wild out there. It was the wild . . . in here.' He folds his wizened hands around the boy's and presses the bundle of fingers to the boy's breast, above his heart beating like an injured bird.

'Is it true?' asks the boy.

Oh, says Grandfather, with the deepest exhalation. *I know it is true, for one was there who told me of it.*

W inter hardens. When it is at its hardest the snow cannot fall. Grandfather says it is frozen in the sky, and to the boy this seems the most terrifying thing. When they cross the dell each morning, Grandfather cranes his neck so that his eyes are fixed on the low, jagged clouds, hanging above like a range of upturned mountains. In class, he listens to Mr Navitski's lessons and slowly composes his own report: what my papa did in the war. He makes notes about the little boy who helped the babe in the woods, and how that boy grew up in the shadow of the Winter King. Sometimes, Mr Navitski comes to read his notes and ask him questions. He gives the Winter King a real name – it is *Josef* – and says that the wars lasted only six years, not a hundred, and that if they had truly lasted a hundred years it would mean Grandfather was as old as the forest itself.

Going through the gates as each school day ends, he is beset by nerves, but Grandfather is always waiting near the car, fragile as a newborn bird in his greatcoat. Soon, he learns not to question why they do not go back to the tenement at the end of each day. It is because Grandfather is happier in the house in the wild, and for the boy that is enough, part of the promise he made. One week passes, then two, then a third. Then it is a month since he last heard mama's voice. It slips away from him, just as mama slipped out of her body, and Christmas is not yet rising when he realizes he no longer thinks of the tenement at all. The house in the forest called Grandfather back, but now it calls to him too.

This morning, Grandfather sleeps later than usual, but now the boy knows not to be afraid if the old man lingers longer in his dreams. Curled in the eiderdown, the boy waits, and waits, and waits some more. Dawn's fingers creep into the ruin, but Grandfather sleeps on. Only when the boy rocks and kneads at his arm do the old eyelids part, stirring life back to the blue irises underneath.

This morning: no words. Grandfather stokes up a fire and feeds the boy pine-needle broth, and then it is up and over the glade, into the trees to find the car. No words even as the boy climbs inside, no words as the engine fires up and the car belches back towards the road.

'Papa, are you all right?'

No words even now, and now they come to the edge of the forest.

The car is nosing out of the final stand of trees, to touch the black asphalt snaking towards town, but the engine slows and it simply hovers there, half in, half out of the forest. In the front seat, Grandfather cranes his neck forward, eyes glimmering as if to consider the sheltering sky. Then his eyes drop. His knuckles are white as they knead at the steering wheel and, every time he dares to look back up, they pinch and strain.

Then, at last, his head whips round. He fixes the boy with a look whose meaning the boy cannot fathom, and exhales deeply. 'Are you okay back there, boy?'

Words to make the boy's heart soar. 'I thought something was wrong.'

'No,' says his papa, and his foot finds the accelerator, guiding the car slowly out to the road. 'Nothing's wrong, boy.' He pauses, and in the rear-view mirror the boy can see him furrowing his eyes, thatched eyebrows to protect him from whatever he was peering at above. 'I just . . . can't wait for you to come home again. That's all.'

After that, no words anymore, not until the goodbyes at the school gates.

It is gloomy when he comes to school and darker yet when the last bell peals. It is even dark, though perhaps not impenetrably so, at the middle of the day when they are released into the yard to play or throw snow or to make teams and kick balls. Alone among them, Yuri walks the edges of the yard, because he is not welcome in games and, besides, would rather fill his head with stories and imaginings of what it is like at other boys' homes. Though he sits with him in class, the boy does not follow Yuri when it is time for lunch. Yuri has his own box from home, into which his mama has put a waxy apple and hunk of black bread, but the boy must sit with Mr Navitski at the teachers' table. Here, he eats half of whatever is on Mr Navitski's plate, but the *kapusta* does not taste like mama's, and the dark brown *macanka*, with hunks of sausage rolled in fat pancakes, does not have the same appeal as steaming hunks of starling and cattail strands frothing on top. Sometimes Navitski asks him why he is so dirty, why there is forest earth in his fingernails, why he does not change his shirt. These are questions the boy would rather not answer, but his silence seems to weigh heavily on the teacher. Some days, there are more clean shirts from lost property; once, a shirt from Navitski himself, cleaned and pressed and six sizes too big.

Today, it is the boy's turn to tell his tale. Yuri has gone only two days before, telling a story about his mama's own papa, who was kept in prison all through the wars of winter, and not the one he really wants to tell, of his father's father, a proud policeman. Now, the boy must stand at the front and everyone must listen. When Mr Navitski calls him, he is still scrabbling with his paper.

'Take your time,' says Mr Navitski.

At the top of the classroom, the boy surveys the class. More than anything, they look bored.

This isn't the tale, says the boy with his head buried in the page, *but an opening. The tale comes tomorrow, after the meal, when we are filled with soft bread.*

Among the children, Mr Navitski's face creases. The boy decides to carry on, like walking into a snowstorm.

And now, he says, *we start our tale.*

Long, long ago, when we did not exist, when perhaps our great-grandfathers were not in the world, all of the world was at war. The warriors of the Winter King fought the King in the West, and in the middle, there was my papa, and the babe in the woods. Now, in the long ago, men ran wild, but the forests were on their

104

side and saved them from soldiers, all but for the wicked trees, who feasted on the men marched out into the deepest wild . . .

There are titters in the classroom, and Mr Navitski holds up his hand. 'Class, we'll do some reading now.'

As the class rummage for their books, Mr Navitski glides to the front of the room and crouches at the boy's side. 'Don't worry,' he begins. 'We'll try again next time.'

'What happened?'

'We're doing history, you see. Not stories. Do you understand?'

The boy thinks: Grandfather's story *is* history. *His story.*

'Maybe you could ask your Grandfather to come and see me one night? Nothing urgent. But he might be interested, mightn't he, to come and see your school?'

The boy nods, but only because nodding will send him back to his seat. There, he finds Yuri, with an upside-down picture book in his hands.

'You're lucky,' Yuri whispers. 'They didn't make you do it *at all.*'

When the bell tolls for end of day and the children tumble out, the boy can hardly see the edge of the schoolyard. He can hear the distant calls of cars and lorries rumbling by, but that is the only sign they are there, for the fog has swallowed everything else.

Distinctly aware that Mr Navitski is watching him, he crosses the tundra of the schoolyard and stops at the gates. Moments later, Yuri wanders past and joins his mother on the roadside. She takes Yuri's chin in a brittle hand, rolling his head as if to inspect him for strange marks, and pushes him on his way.

From here, the boy can just about see to the other side of the road. The boarded-up shop-fronts are lined with cars, but no old man prowls between them, and he cannot see the car anywhere.

The simpleton caretaker trudges across the yard. Next will come the teachers, and something in that disturbs the boy; he does not want to see Mr Navitski's worried face peering down, offering him new shirts and hot dinners.

He goes between parked cars, but on each side the road fades into fog. In the streetlights it sparkles like glitter. He puts his hands into deep pockets and thinks of the hearthfire and bundles of kindling drying above.

'Still waiting, are we?'

He looks up, only to see Mr Navitski lurking in the mist.

'My papa's late.'

'So I see. Are you sure he's coming?'

'Of course he's coming!'

'Simmer down, boy. Perhaps you'd like to wait inside? It's warmer in the schoolhouse.'

Being in the schoolhouse after the bell is like venturing into one of the uninhabited flats in the tenement. Those halls are not supposed to echo with footfalls.

'Well, I can't just leave you here all night. What kind of a teacher would that make me?'

Mr Navitski is trying to laugh, but to the boy the joke doesn't seem so funny. 'Might you need a lift home, boy?'

'What if papa's . . .' He stops. It is not good to talk about Grandfather, just like it is not good to talk about mama too much. 'I'm supposed to walk today,' he ventures, uneasy in the lie. It is like climbing into somebody else's clothes for the first time, finding them ugly and ill-fitting.

'Oh? Then why are you waiting here?'

'I forgot.'

'Forgot, is it?'

More words will tie him in knots, so it is better to remain silent.

'So, do you want that lift or not?'

Because there is nothing else to do, the boy nods.

'Come on, then. If I'm late home, my wife starts . . . getting ideas.'

The way Mr Navitski stresses the last words makes a meaning the boy does not understand. He trudges after Mr Navitski, along the road to where a black motorcycle is sitting between the cars.

'I've never been on a motorcycle.'

'You just have to hold on. It's perfectly safe.'

It takes a few minutes for the motorcycle to warm up. When it is ready, Mr Navitski scoops him up so that he's sitting in the seat. Then, he swings onto the seat behind him, so that the boy is held tightly in the crook of his legs. 'This way, you won't fall off.'

'What will happen if I fall off?'

'You won't.'

'But what if I . . .'

The end of his question is lost, for the engine roars, Mr Navitski kicks down, and the motorcycle swings into the street.

Soon the city is rushing by. It is not like in Grandfather's car, slowing and stuttering in traffic, for Mr Navitski and his motorcycle swoop in and out of the cars, squeezing along narrow passes to reach the head of every intersection. They leave the main roads behind and ride along lanes between tenements, where the day's snowfall has not been cleared and grey sludge abounds. More than once, the motorcycle slews beneath them; Mr Navitski wrestles it back in line, and the boy

107

can hear him laughing as if, to him, it is all a great game. The tenement looms above, forlorn as a forgotten toy, and when the motorcycle comes to a stop he can hear the wheeze of wind in the gutters above.

'Should I come upstairs?'

'I'll be all right.'

'Oh, I'm sure you will . . .' Mr Navitski takes off his helmet. 'But I'd love a quick word with your Grandfather. He must be feeling awfully overwhelmed.'

'Over . . .'

Mr Navitski's face darkens, as if he has said something wrong and is anxious to unsay it. 'Well, I know he loves you very much, but . . .'

'I'll be all right,' says the boy, firmer now.

'As you wish. What if I wait here to see you safely inside?'

In spite of himself, the boy nods. He trudges along the tenement wall. Halfway along, he passes through the archway of brick and climbs the first flight of stairs. In the cold of the stairwell he is completely alone. Never have those steps seemed more alien. He tries to count the days since he was last here, but finds he cannot.

From the first landing he peers out, to see the diminutive figure of Mr Navitski and his motorcycle still waiting below.

He realizes: I don't have a key. I never had a key.

There is nowhere to go but up. He keeps his head down along the second landing, and finally reaches the third. Here he leaves the stairs behind, pushing along with his hood drawn high so that he does not have to see Mr Navitski's eyes tracking him from the verge. Past one door he goes. Past a second and a third. Now he is standing outside Grandfather's door, as old and unfamiliar as the ruin was on that very first day.

From the safety of his hood, he risks a look down. Mr Navitski is still watching. He whips his head back. The door handle is at the same level as his eyes, and seems to leer at him, screws for its eyeballs and a big hooked beak.

He closes his fist over the handle and pulls down.

It does not move. He pulls harder, thinks he can feel something give, but still it does not move. Once more, and there is a sound like grating stone. He turns his head, as if he can squint sidelong and see Mr Navitski, but before he has turned all the way the door swings open, dragging him with it. He pitches forward, over the step.

When his hand peels from the handle, he falls to his knees, scuffing them on the wire mat where Grandfather used to scrub his jackboots. He lies there for an instant, eyes unaccustomed to a darkness this soft around the edges. Then he stands. He shakes off his hood, looks back through the open door. Through that portal, the other side of the tenement yard is a cliff face, punctured with pits of orange. He creeps back to the threshold. Careful not to cross, he cranes to look down. Mr Navitski is still looking up.

Their eyes lock.

'See,' the boy whispers, adding just a little shrug. 'I got home, didn't I?'

Mr Navitski lifts a hand and presses two fingers to the side of his head. It is the kind of lazy salute Grandfather would have despised, because to salute is a very special thing and to do it so impudently is ignorant and ignoble. Even so, the boy finds himself doing the same.

Mr Navitski turns the salute into a flourishing wave and turns to swing back onto his motorcycle. Then he is gone, the motorcycle weaving wildly in the sludge, as disobedient as a toboggan.

After he has gone, the boy lingers on the threshold. Soon, he can hear the tramping of feet, footfalls echoing as they come up the concrete stair. Probably it is the neighbour, Madam Yakavenka, coming back from the bakery, but he must not be here to find out. Madam Yakavenka would say, 'Where's your papa?' And then Madam Yakavenka would know. She'd come with potato *babka* and *kalduny* stuffed with the pieces of gristle she calls sausage and want to take him into her flat and wrap him up and wash his hair.

The boy slams the door. 'Papa,' he whispers. 'Papa, I'm home.'

In the hallway it is not dark like the woodland dark. It is dark like being under covers in a well-lit room, or pulling your hood up to block out the sun. Light bleeds in, and it is the light of a city, the dirty groping glow of streetlights and cars.

'Papa, are you here? Teacher brought me . . .'

But there is no answer, and the boy knows there will not be one coming. He keeps on asking, just to fill the silence, but by the time he has reached the kitchen he is certain: the flat is empty as ever it was, not even the ghosts of the forest to fill it. Wherever Grandfather is, he did not come to the city today.

In the kitchen, he goes first to the cupboard. There is a can of Smolensk Stewed Beef and another of pickled cucumbers and a box of dry biscuits with only one rattling about inside. By the stove there is half a bag of sugar, but the milk in the fridge has long ago soured and not even the light in the fridge works when he opens the door.

To let more light in, he pulls back the ragged net curtain that mama always threatened to have washed. He pulls his coat tight around him and whispers the word again, though he knows it is useless. He is far too far away to hear. 'Papa . . .'

*

He is there a long time, long enough to hear Madam Yakavenka returning from work. The sound of her voice brings him back to wakefulness, and he decides to make a hot water with sugar, which is a kind of syrup you can drink if the winter gets too bitter. There is gas still in the stove, and this kind of fire is easy to conjure without needing any sorceries at all. He climbs onto a stool, twists a switch, and watches the blue fire flicker into life.

When the syrup is ready, he pours it into a mug. The drink works its magic, filling him with sweet, sticky strength, and soon he is brave enough to venture into the rest of the flat. Somehow it seems so vast, and he so small inside it. The flat is wide and the flat is wild and the flat is the world forever and ever. He leaves the kitchen and turns to the hall with his bedroom at its end, and there, in the alcove by the dead gas fire, he sees the rocking chair with a rag curled at its runner.

It is mama's shawl, and it cries out for him to take it.

He drops to his knees and snatches it up, presses it to his face and breathes in the scent. It is still there. It is like clouds and bluebells and the forest at summer. It is like the press of lips on his cheek and the red imprint they always left behind.

Now the tears come. They leak, hot and heavy, into the shawl. It is scrunched up, sodden in his hands and, too late he realizes what he has done. He is washing away mama's scent, the last thing of her that remains. He is corrupting it with the salt of his tears and the slime from the back of his throat.

Still clinging to the shawl, he comes down the hallway. The photographs leer at him from either side. He feels their eyes on him, but he does not want to look – for, suddenly, Grandfather is with him, staring at him, and his eyes are accusing.

He stops, to stare into a picture of Grandfather with a woman who must be baba. They are ringed by pines, and he wonders: is it the house in the forest where we live? Baba looks like mama used to do, and he tries to imagine her a squalling baby on the step. What is story and what is history? Grandfather's life, scrawled all around him.

He pictures what it must be like for Grandfather tonight. In his head a hearthfire dances, and a handful of frogs broil in snow-melt thick with Jew's ears and leaves. After dinner, though, there can be no tale to tell, for there is nobody there to hear the telling. Instead, Grandfather goes to the end of the garden and talks to mama. He stands in the curdling night until the ice solidifies around his jackboots to root him to the earth as completely as any old tree.

The boy sees Grandfather in the picture and fights back tears – it is not fair that there is nothing to ward off tears like a hot milk wards off winter – because another thought occurs: what if the car broke down, somewhere in the wild, and it took Grandfather long hours to get to school and collect him? Perhaps he is waiting there, even now, lurking at the gates of the empty schoolhouse, wondering what has happened.

He comes to mama's door. Inexplicably, the light still shines underneath. It makes his chest flurry because, for a second, he thinks that somebody might be through there. He presses his ear to the wood, as if listening for a heartbeat, but there is just the dull buzzing of the lamplight.

It is forbidden to go through the doors, but perhaps those rules don't mean a thing, now that mama is gone. His fingers find the handle, and the light rushes out to meet him. He stalls, lets it lap at his face, remembers the last time he went through this door and the promise he made. That promise is broken now. If mama knew he had left Grandfather out in the woods, she would never speak to him again.

He means to close the door, unable to face the ghost in the bedsheets, but smells rush out to seize him, and with them come memories. He snatches for them. The perfume she wore when she stepped out for the evening. The soap and soda she used to scrub the mattress every time she was sick. The *kapusta* she asked for in those last days, when she didn't want to eat and enjoyed, instead, the spice in the steam.

'Oh, mama,' he says, his voice so very small.

By the time he has the courage to venture in, he can see the dim outline of the dresser, the suitcase she brought from the old house and never really unpacked, in case it was needed in dead of night for a trip in an ambulance. He walks along the side of the bed, marvelling at how it has remained unmade, and trails his hand along creases in the sheets. He imagines their every ruffle like the contours of a map, the atlas of her body pressed into the bedspread.

It is only when he steps back that he sees the photographs on the walls. They lurk, just out of sight, more fragments of long-ago times. It occurs to him: before we lived here, this was where Grandfather slept. He didn't always sleep in the rocking chair. This is his bed, and these are his photographs . . . and this is his chest, sitting at the bottom of the bed.

It is something he has not seen before: a simple wooden box, with a brass lock and hinge. So worn and weathered are its corners that it looks like something that might have been unearthed in the ruin. He runs his hands over it, and when he lifts them up he can smell, not mama's perfume, not the detergent stench of her old sheets, but the musk of branches tied in bundles to dry over the hearthfire.

It opens at his first touch, with no need for a key. Inside lies darkness, old and stale – and, beneath that darkness, a leather pouch. He delves inside and lifts it up. It is, he sees, a knapsack, just the same as the one in the story of Baba Yaga.

He sets it on the bed and stretches it out. There are letters stitched into the strap, but they are letters the boy has never seen, strange things from another kingdom. He wrestles to unfasten the buckle, but the leather is tough, flaking as he works it out. At last, he slides his hand within – but there is nothing there. His hand comes out, trailing strands like spider's webs and, in the cracks between his fingers, he sees flecks of brown, like minuscule husks of seed – or pine needles left to dry by the fire.

He retreats to a chair by the dresser, with the knapsack in his lap. It is, he understands, a relic of Grandfather.

He stares at the bed, willing it to move. 'Mama, papa's in the woods.'

His voice is gone, swallowed by bedsheets as easily as snow. 'Mama, who'll look after him now?'

Then he remembers that mama's in the woods too, or at least what's left of her, and Grandfather talks to her in the roots at night. She can't possibly be in two places at once. Grandfather was right when he said there's nothing left in the tenement for either of them.

The boy is on his own, but that is not the thought that bores into him – for Grandfather is on his own as well, and there is a promise to keep.

Over his shoulder: the knapsack, empty but for the single tin of Smolensk Smoked Beef. He steals along the concrete row, the tenement above like a great sculpture of ice, something left

114

behind when the sun stopped shining. Alone, he hurries down the grey stair, mama's shawl wrapped around his shoulders.

He can find his way to the bus stop, but after that the city is as wild a thing as the *pushcha* itself. He tries to picture the route Mr Navitski brought him on his motorcycle, but the streets bleed into one another and it is difficult to tease one intersection from another. Even so, there is a place he remembers, one that has lodged in the back of his head: a place where buses come from all over the city, a warehouse near the railway bridges where Yuri lives above the canteen. Perhaps, if he can find his way there, there may yet be another way to Grandfather.

There are men gathered at the bus stop, faces masked by the fog of their breath. He stands with them, careful not to insinuate himself between them, lest they ask any questions. He looks up, as if he might be able to read the time in the stars, but all above is impenetrable cloud.

When the bus comes, the driver asks for a ticket and, when he doesn't have a ticket, asks for ten thousand rubles instead. When the boy pulls his empty hands from his pockets, the driver shrugs, wearing a wicked storybook smile. He is about to send the boy back to the side of the road when a man lumbers to the front of the bus, using his knuckles like an ape. With a mutter, he produces a note from his pocket, thrusts it at the driver, and turns to sit back down.

The driver curses, pushes a paper ticket into the boy's hand and barks for him to take a seat. With the scrap curled in his fist, he wobbles down the aisle. He thinks he should say a thank you to the man who helped, but he passes him by and nothing comes out.

Throughout the journey he keeps his eyes on the buildings that pass. At last he reaches an intersection he remembers. Here there hunches a canteen, where mama once took him for tea and a biscuit. Her hands wobbled as she tried to drink and she told him he didn't have to go to school until the afternoon, and in that moment it felt like the best day ever, even if that was the day she told him there was poison in her blood.

When the bus stops, he follows a woman wearing a headscarf to the kerb. He is sure the driver mutters dark things at him as he lowers himself from the step.

The roads are familiar and then the roads are strange, but then there is a spire to tell you where you are, or a tower to tell you when to turn round. In this way, he comes to the road of the school. He scours the parked cars for signs that Grandfather was here, but his attempts throw up no clues. Grandfather, it seems, did not make it out of the forests at all.

The schoolhouse is a sad thing, sitting in the dark and, when a cold wind gusts along the road, clawing at the building, it only reminds him of all that he is missing, out in the wild.

Retracing the steps to the bus he took with Yuri and his mama is easy enough. He lingers in the shelter of the overhang, as one bus passes and then another. None of these look like the kind of bus that might take a boy into the forest. At last, wary that darkness is already curdling around him, he gets aboard the next bus that comes along.

'Ticket?'

The boy pushes past, into the cramped interior, but the driver only barks again. 'Ticket, boy?'

He delves a hand into his pocket and comes up with the scrap of paper the first bus driver gave him – but when he presents it, the driver merely flings it back in his direction.

'Just what are you trying to pull?'

He stands there, dumb.

'Go on, get off, before I throw you off myself.'

Two more buses come before he has the courage to try again. This time, a glut of women, laden with shopping bags, rush to the door, and the boy finds himself swept up among them, lost in billowing dresses and coats open wide.

The condensation is thick in the windows and he cannot see the streets that pass. He thinks they might circle the cathedral, which is a place mama once took him, but then the streets are low and less crowded and the streetlights further apart. One after another the other passengers abandon the bus. He can see their blurred outlines waddling away, along dark avenues where the houses sullenly wait.

Soon there are only three other passengers on board, and one of those is asleep on the back seat. They gutter down a road where few cars pass and swing, at last, into a yard in front of a warehouse where great doors are open wide. The boy peeps up – and there, in the jaws of the warehouse, he sees rows and rows of buses, just like the one he is on.

'End of the line!'

Snow no longer swirls in the headlights, for they have come under the lip of the warehouse. Abruptly, the driver strangles the engine. 'Well, come on then, this is it . . .'

The boy noses to the front of the bus. He stands on the step, where the cold of night assails him. The other passengers must have been here before, for they tramp towards other buses. Some of them are lined up outside, capped in thin snow with their headlights blazing and their drivers smoking idly at their sides. The boy twirls around, wondering which way he ought to go.

'Where are you going, kid?'

He turns, to see the driver lumbering out of the bus.

'Well?'

He whispers, 'The *pushcha*.'

'You'll want the border bus, then. Are you going over?'

He must mean all the way over the forests, into that country on the other side. That country, too, used to be part of the Russias, and Grandfather says it really isn't so very different. It is the kingdom called *Poland*.

'Not over,' the boy says.

By now the driver has stopped listening. 'Well, it's over there. It says Bialystok on front.' He stomps off, passing a bench where some passenger has decided to slumber.

'Hey, kid . . .'

He turns.

'. . . should you be out alone like this?'

'I'm going . . . home,' the boy whispers, and knows that it is true.

'Well, lucky you.'

The bus marked Bialystok is waiting outside, with its windows speckled with snow. Even the tiniest flakes can cling there, because they freeze to the windows and make a pattern like a man going blind might see. There are dark hulks moving on the other side of the glass. One passenger has his face smeared up against the window.

One of the hulks comes down from the step. He is wearing the same shirt and trousers as the last driver, and he loiters for a moment, pitching the end of his cigarette into the dusting of snow. Then his eyes light on somebody further down the bank, and he strides off, bawling out a name.

The boy pitches forward. Now might be the only chance he has.

While the driver walks away, he scurries for the step. This

bus is higher from the ground than the last, and he has to use his hands to heave himself up. There are three steps, and then he is in the front of the bus, standing by the driver's vacant seat. The keys dangle in the ignition and a fierce heat radiates from the engine below.

He goes past the man plastered against the window, past a woman with a baby swaddled up in her lap, and finds a seat at the back of the bus. If he hunkers down here, he might not be seen. A boy can make himself so very small if he has to, and he sinks as low as he can. Moments later, an old man passes to take another seat, and does not even register the boy curled up there.

Soon, he hears a change in the engine's timbre, like a cat whose purr has taken on a new level of ecstasy. There comes a whine as the doors close, and the bus lurches forward.

When the orange orbs of streetlamps no longer glow, he knows they have left the city behind. He can smell it too, that change in the air that means they are beyond factories and roads and underworld trains. Now, only darkness rushes past on the other side of the glass. Tinny music echoes from the front of the bus. Bolder now, the boy leans over from his seat and peeps into the aisle to see the windscreen. Snow spirals hypnotically in the headlights, suspended in the air as if it is not even falling at all.

He has ploughed this road countless times with Grandfather, but it is difficult, now, to know exactly where he is. It is only when he sees a tiny black pine, growing so far out into the road that it seems an affront, that he knows he is near. Yet, the bus does not stop. It is crawling now, as the snow whips up around it, spreading the headlight beams in radiant array, and he sees it crawl past the turn-off that Grandfather always takes beneath the trees. He stands. He lurches forward. He stops. He cannot tell the driver, because then the driver would ask, and then the driver would know he sneaked aboard.

Every minute that passes now is a minute he is further from Grandfather. More than once, he creeps down the aisle as if he might demand the driver to stop, but every time he slopes back, like a beaten dog. One mile, two miles, three miles, four . . . Time has a way of slowing down, just like those snowflakes suspended in the windscreen. Snow distorts the world. It swallows sound and it swallows time itself.

He looks up. In the road ahead: a black ridge capped in pure white. The bus begins to slow, softly at first but then with increasing urgency. The back sways, as if refusing to obey what the front wheels tell it. In the seats opposite, two passengers wake from their slumber and exchange rapid words. Instinctively, the boy grips the seat in front.

The bus rolls to a stop, but this does not seem something that the driver can tolerate for long. He wrenches with the stick at the side of the wheel and presses his foot down; the engine roars but the bus will not move. He wrenches with the stick and tries again. This time, the bus stutters backwards before stopping dead. The driver stands, hits his fist against the dashboard, and the doors squeal as they come apart. Winter rushes in.

Through the windscreen the boy can see the driver inspecting the dark ridge that blocks the road. It is only when he has crept all the way to the front that he sees it for what it is: a tree that has fallen in a storm and been frozen there, bulging like scar tissue across the blacktop. He drops to his knees at the front of the bus and out of sight.

Now is his chance. He steals down the step. Outside, the

driver is kneeling in the snow, with his head tucked under the chassis of the bus itself.

Burying his hands in his pockets, he takes the last, fateful step.

The cold taunts him, working its way up his sleeves and around the rims of his ribs. Only his shoulders, still padded by mama's shawl, can fight it back – but even that will not be for long. He'll need a fire, a big one leaping like in Grandfather's hearth, and he'll need it fast.

He keeps flush to the side of the bus and darts away from the driver, turning out of sight while his head is still buried below. At the back of the bus a weak trail of exhaust floats up. The boy gags on it, but his body compels him to stay in its cloud, because at least the fumes are warm and dry. Fighting off the temptation, he crosses the road and flails up the bank. It is difficult, here, to judge how deeply the snow has grown, and he plunges up to his waist. The shock of the fall pummels all the wind from his lungs, but he pushes up with frigid hands and skids down the other side of the bank. Now he is in the forest. He is only a yard away from the open road, but already he feels warmer, as if the trees themselves are huddling up. There are creatures in this woodland that don't know how to build houses and hearthfires or to cook hot nettle tea in the flames. If they can survive it, so can the boy. All he has to do is be like the fox, the bison, the elk – the wolves up in their heartland, or the bear deep in his winter lair.

The conifers are few, and once he has left them behind there is not a leaf in sight, only the lattice of naked branches and the cavernous roof of snow above. He passes a low hornbeam, dwarfed by elms on either side, and watches a rabbit dart out of its hole underneath. The whiteness underfoot is not snow

121

but thick frost that crunches every time he takes a step. His shoes skid, and he holds out his arms to glide along, and for a while it is a game, like tobogganing without a toboggan, that only ends when his toes become snagged in a root and he smashes, face first, into frost and stone.

Dazed, he gets back up, scrambles to reclaim the knapsack from the roots onto which it has fallen. He walks on, mindful of the roots hiding just beneath the crisp white veneer. It is only when he sees the low hornbeam again that he realizes he has somehow been turned around. No doubt it happened when he took his tumble, and he rubs his hands together for warmth. Telling himself that it does not matter, he decides to plough back the way he has come. A few steps later, and a thought occurs to him: what if I wasn't walking straight lines through the wood? What if the trees turned me around and I came back at the hornbeam from somewhere else, and now I'm walking away from the track, away from the ruin . . . away from papa?

He turns in a circle, trying to judge which way to go, and as he turns a sickening thought spirals up from the pit of his stomach.

'I'm making it worse, papa.' The words burst out. He thinks he has shouted them, but they are mere whispers, slurped up by the trees.

He comes through a stand of oak, convinced he has been this way before, and a new smell hits him, a gust of wind like the steam that curls out of one of Grandfather's pots. He is almost upon it before he realizes what it is. What he thought was a log fallen in front of him is softer, splayed out in the snow light.

He staggers back. Dead eyes stare at him. Lying between the

trees is what is left of a deer. It seems a strange half-animal, its neck, its haunches all open or gone. Somehow its head seems untouched. It rests on a rucked-up root and fixes its gaze on him.

The boy scrambles back. Now the smell is thicker in the air. Now, noises crowd in on him from every angle: the snap of a branch, the rustle of feet pawing over roots, the shriek and whisper of wings in the branches above. The stench is on him like a coating. The cold sears it to his skin.

He crashes back, some treacherous oak tree rearing behind him. Winded, he sinks into the roots. He is still lying there, half-shrouded in darkness, when he sees something stirring on the other side of the ravaged deer. A new shape dissolves out of the darkness. Two silver orbs glow.

His lips make the word 'wolf' but dare not breathe it out.

He has seen them before, but only on the pages of his story-books – and this wolf is not like any of those. It is rangy and tall, missing one ear. It moves with a strange gait, never planting one of its paws, and its muzzle darts from one side to another, flashing warnings into the pockets of snow dark around.

Its eyes land on him. The boy wants to scramble up, hurtle into the forest, but his legs won't obey him. He closes his eyes, but nothing comes, only the whispering of night. When he dares to open them again, the wolf has its muzzle buried in what is left of the deer. There are soft sounds: of tearing, of shredding, of muscle shearing from bone. There comes a flash of silver as the wolf rears up.

It sees him. Here comes the silence. All shredding, all tearing comes to a stop. The wolf steadies itself, and out of its yawning guts there comes a low, cavernous rumble.

The boy opens his mouth to cry out, but the words do not come.

Something compels him to stand. No sooner has he got to his feet than the wolf is up, over the deer, its paws slathered in gore. It comes to a stop again, advances another stride, stops and lets its growl escape.

He thinks to say: please. And he thinks to say: no! But the wolf's silver eyes are on him, and there is only one thing he can do. His legs have come back to life. He heaves himself up, out of the roots, runs around the tree and scrambles off into the night.

He runs and runs, and when he can run no more, he plunges over a bank onto the frosted earth. Over his shoulder he cranes – but the tussocks of undergrowth at the head of the bank do not come apart. The wolf has not followed. He is alone again, surrounded by only the trees.

Time, like his body heat, leaches away.

He does not know, at first, when he stops feeling the tips of his toes. It creeps upon him gradually, and he only really understands it is so when the cold has crept up to his ankles. Now, he cannot feel any part of his feet at all. It is as if he is walking on stumps, a particularly unfortunate pirate.

'Papa, I need to get warm.'

He thinks: what would papa do? He thinks: papa had a story. He slept, for three days and three nights, in a hole in the ice. In the end, it was the ice that protected him. It is like in the story of Baba Yaga: if you are kind to the wilderness, the wilderness will be kind to you.

He reaches a small clearing where the canopy is broken to reveal the clouds above. Here the snow has tumbled down, gathering in great drifts against trunks and mounds of knotted root. He falls at one, reaching into the snow to carve it apart. By the time he has excavated a crater, his arms are numb up to the elbows. He pulls them inside his coat and rubs them together, finding a last cavity of warmth in the pits beneath his arms. Then he rolls into the hole he has burrowed. The ice bites when he curls up, but soon he does not feel it. He squirms one arm back into its sleeve and reaches for a fallen branch, hauling it across his hole like a blanket. With difficulty he reaches one more, and then one more again, and if it is not as comfortable as a real blanket might be, perhaps it will catch the snow in the night and fashion one for him.

In the hole, he reaches into the knapsack still hanging from his shoulder, and his numb fingers find the can of Smolensk Smoked Beef. He scrabbles to find the key, fold it back and release the meat – but his fingertips fail him, and the meat remains hidden.

He wriggles around in his coat, so that he can pull the hood up and cover most of his face. In here, his breath does not fog, and he can even feel its dewy warmth on his face.

It is not a fire, but he is a long way from fire tonight.

'Wake up.'

From far beneath the surface of sleep, he feels himself rising, desperate for air. In the dream he is trapped in the waters of a frozen lake. Fish locked in bubbles of ice float past, mouths open in circles of surprise, and all around is shimmering blue. He rises, rises further still, but the surface of the lake is thick ice. When his head hits it, it lifts, revealing a strata of air. He gulps at it greedily, but the ice forces him back down. In the water he turns, panicked.

'Wake up, my little one. You have to wake up.'

It is mama. Mama's voice. Though she is telling him to wake, waking is the last thing he wants to do – for, if he wakes, he will not hear her again. Now he knows this is a dream, he does not mind floating, breathless, in these crystal waters. The cold cradles him, but it does not matter. He fights the urge to rise, smash through the ice, and open his eyes. Better to stay down here with mama.

'Listen, little one. You have to wake up. If you don't wake up now, you'll never wake up. It will be too late. Do it for me. You wouldn't want to upset me, would you?'

There were times when he upset mama. He didn't mean to, but she snapped and cried and, once, she even struck out. It was his fault, and he doesn't want it to be his fault again.

'Wake up. Please wake up . . .'

There is a different timbre to mama's voice now. She is not telling him to wake; she is begging. 'Just open your eyes. This cold won't last forever. Just a little bit longer. You're not alone.'

A voice his, but yet not his, whispers, 'Mama?'

'Wake up, my littlest friend. Stay alive. He'll be here soon. He's already built you a fire. Cooked you a dinner.'

Silence, with only the muffled sound of the waters to hold him.

'You see, he's coming to find you.'

'Who is, mama?'

'He's coming out of the wood . . .'

The boy rises, his head forcing its way again into that stratum of air – and with one last heave, he smashes through the ice.

He opens his eyes.

It is still dead of night, though all around him the trees stand luminescent in the snow. The branches are still stretched above him, but they have frozen together, and ice has grown between them to make a trapdoor of frost. It is some minutes before he tries to stand. He reaches up to push open the trapdoor and, as the ice breaks and the branches fly back, he sees the shadow man above.

He opens his mouth to scream.

'Oh, boy. Oh, boy.'

Hands reach out to take him, and he is too weak to resist. For a moment he lies there, frozen into the earth, but then he is aloft, whirling through the air with different darknesses shifting on every side.

'Boy, can you hear me?'

The words come from so very far away. All the boy can really hear is the heavy drumming from deep in the breast against which he is held. When he does not reply, its beat seems to quicken.

'I didn't come for you, boy, but I've come for you now. Please, boy. Please don't . . .' Voice cracking, words fraying apart. '. . . hate me. Please don't hate a cowardly old man.'

Now they are moving. Trees sail by. The figure takes great loping strides, but then he breaks into a run. Now the trees hurtle past more quickly. After a short burst the figure slows, and the boy can hear a rattle deep in his breast. The heart beats an ugly, irregular percussion, and then the running starts again.

In this halting way, they come out of the wood. The snowy pasture is bathed in silver light, a gibbous moon showing between fragmenting clouds, and a wild wind whips in over the treetops.

He opens his lips, to find them parched dry. That cannot be right; he could not possibly be parched in a world with so much ice. 'Papa?'

The arms squeeze him tighter. The heart thunders its reply. 'We're nearly there, boy. I'll build up the fire.'

In the shelter of the ruin, the wind dies. Grandfather stops, holds the boy tight, and lifts one of his jackboots to force their way through the door. As they barrel inside, the smells of the hearthfire assault him. There has been a pot in the flames, and it is those rich scents that stir him. Suddenly awake, he squirms to be set down, but Grandfather's arms are locked tight.

The old man kneels in front of the fire, and lays him down in its glow. 'Boy, can you see me? Do you know where you are?'

Bitter cold is only a whisper away from raging heat. He feels as if he is inside the flames, tossed there like a piece of dead wood. The fire rampages over his naked skin, under his clothes, deep into his flesh.

'I can see you, papa. Are we home?'

The old man's face comes into focus. It is covered, now, with white down, wild whiskers curling down the line of his jaw. His brow, scored with such deep lines, is an atlas of unknown lands. Here are dark ravines, and here unscalable cliffs. His eyes, tiny craters on that atlas, brim with tears. He shivers, and the tears break free, to flow unchecked down his cheeks. Where they hang in his whiskers they glisten with firelight. 'Oh boy, I meant to come. I promise I meant to come.'

The boy manages to sit, though his body wants to curl up like a withering leaf.

Soon, Grandfather turns, dipping a chipped mug into the pot and bringing it up, filled with tea. 'Not too much, boy. Take it slow . . .'

'Papa!' the boy protests. 'Papa, it's burning me . . .'

Grandfather recoils, whipping the mug back. 'Your lips,' Grandfather begins. 'Boy, they're . . .'

The boy feels them with the tips of his fingers. They are swollen, hard in places and too soft in others.

'Papa, I promise I waited. I waited and . . .'

'I know, boy.'

'I went back to the tenement but you weren't at the tenement. And I went back to school and . . .'

Grandfather rocks back, lifting his knees in front so that he can put his arms around them and squeeze, like a spat-upon child. His chin is balanced precariously on the points of his knees.

'What happened, papa?'

'Boy, you're burning up . . .'

It cannot be. Only moments ago, he was freezing. Yet now he can feel the heat raging in him. His face glistens, his skin sears, and he shakes fiercely, sloshing pine tea onto the hearth. 'Papa, I don't feel . . .'

Grandfather springs to his feet, swooping the boy into his arms. Cradled again, the boy finds himself sailing through the room, past the tumbledown stairs and out through the back-door. Grandfather hovers on the step and holds him up, as if offering him to the night.

'Papa, I'm sick, aren't I?'

'You'll be well.'

'I want to be sick, papa, but I haven't had a thing to . . .'

'It will pass.'

'Was it the cold, papa?'

A voice, barely recognizable, whispers, 'Yes . . .'

'I got trapped in the cold, didn't I?'

A voice, even harder to recognize, utters, 'Yes . . .'

'What happened, papa?'

Grandfather's arms hold him tight, so that when he speaks the words vibrate from one body to the other.

'I came for you, the same as always. I went to the car.'

'It didn't start, did it, papa?'

'Oh, but it started. I turned her round and drove through the trees. But I reached the end of the trees, boy, and . . .'

His words trail off, and the boy feels the thunder of his heart dying.

'. . . I stopped.'

'You stopped, papa?'

This time he can only mouth the word 'Yes'.

'Was it because of mama?'

'I don't know.'

'Because you couldn't leave her?'

Again, 'I don't know.'

'Because she needs you, doesn't she, papa? And she needs me too.'

'It isn't just that, boy.'

Grandfather turns him, so that he is peering up into the old man's lined face.

'I couldn't leave the trees,' he whispers. 'They . . . wouldn't let me.'

The boy does not understand. He can see only one half of Grandfather's lips, so that it looks as if he is speaking from the side of his mouth, whispering dark incantations.

'I sat there for the longest time, boy. Don't think I didn't. I sat there until the darkness had spilled all over the world. Until it was deepening and hardening and freezing like the frost. I sat there when the snow began to fall. I waited until it had smothered me where I sat. But when I stepped out, into that snow, it held me there. I couldn't even walk out to the road.'

He lifts a hand to stroke the boy's head. 'Your fever's dying.'

The boy nods.

'I wanted to come for you,' he trembles. 'You do believe me, don't you, boy?'

'Of course I do, papa . . .'

'It just wouldn't let me.'

He turns to cradle the boy back into the ruin. In front of the hearth, he lies him down.

'I won't ever leave you again. I promise.'

'I was scared for you, papa. I thought . . .'

Tramping to his armchair, Grandfather looks over his shoulder. His eyes are full again, reflecting the leaping flames. 'I know,' he utters, and sinks into his seat.

Telling mama he loved her was as automatic as waking up in a morning and making toilet. But telling it to Grandfather is a different thing, because Grandfather is an old, old creature and might not understand.

The boy, accustomed to warmth once again, sees the knapsack lying in the hearth and crawls to pick it up. Inside, the can of Smolensk Smoked Beef is frozen as a ball of ice. He sets it aside, thinking it will make a broth for Grandfather, and goes to him.

'I brought it for you, papa.'

At first, Grandfather's eyes don't seem to see the knapsack in his hands. Then he reaches up, and old fingers take hold of old leather. 'Where did you find this?'

'It was in the tenement.'

The old man caresses it, wondering at its every wrinkle and flake. 'I haven't seen this thing in . . .' Grandfather's words peter away.

'You're okay, aren't you, papa?'

At last, holding the knapsack tight, he says, 'I promise.'

The boy throws his arms around his breast and buries his

131

head there, in the old man's shoulder. Both of them are crying now. The channels of their tears run together.

'I promise, too. We don't have to leave the woods, papa. If the trees won't let you, they won't let me either. I'll stay wherever you are. I'll look after you.'

'I'm the one who's meant to look after you.'

'We'll look after each other, papa. I promised mama.'

Tonight, he will sleep in Grandfather's lap. Tonight, he will curl up there like mama's shawl in the tenement chair, and listen to Grandfather's heart echo in his breast. He hauls himself up, feels the old man's arms close around him.

As their eyelids fall, a thought occurs to the boy. He voices it, though his tongue is thick between blistered lips. 'How did you know where to find me, papa?'

But Grandfather is already skimming the surface of sleep. 'It was the trees,' he breathes through lips that barely move. 'The trees showed me the way.'

H e does not miss school, for now there are different kinds of lessons.

In the weeks that follow – because, for once in his life, the boy must learn – Grandfather spills his sorceries. First, there are lessons in sculpting fires. Together they collect kindling and build the sculptures into which flames can be invoked. It is not like that night, lost in the wild, when he thought simple words could cast a spell; a spell is a more difficult thing, and to make the magic work you must take two pieces of wood, one with a dip in the middle, and drive a brittle branch into it, rolling it between your palms. In this way, a magic is born – and, out of that magic, the flames that can guard you in the long nights.

There are other lessons, too. In the forest, Grandfather sets traps. He leads the boy on his rounds, from cattail pond to open dell, and shows him the lengths of string, tied around trunks, from which frozen squirrels dangle, or the rabbit with its hind legs caught in a loop of wire. He shows him how to take the axe to the trunk of the black pine and how to roast that bark in a fire for biscuits, or grind it down for flour. He takes him to the fringes of waters where the frogs sleep, ready to be plucked out and put in the pot, and to the boy this seems the least cruel of all. Those frogs just go to sleep, waiting for spring, and never wake up.

He takes him between the trees, where the monstrous bison graze. Those beasts with legs like trunks and great humps above their heads, two devil horns. He whispers, 'I ate one, once. I scrapped with a vagrant wolf and won, and I feasted on him for six days and seven nights. It made me human again.'

'Is it true, papa?'

'Oh, I know it is true . . .'

The boy joins him for the final words. '. . . for one was there who told me of it.'

Soon, the boy knows how to spirit the flames and broil up a wild rabbit, and soon Grandfather trusts him to tend to the cauldron while he stalks the fringes of forest, rooting up nettles and pine needles to soak in the snow-melt. And, as he stirs those wild things round and round, he begins to think: the city, the tenement, the schoolhouse – all of those are the things out of stories. They are lost in the long ago, and the real world is here, in this little house.

Tonight, Grandfather returns from the forest with a brace of wood pigeons. 'Do you know what night it is?'

The boy stops, lost in steam from the pot. He wonders

what Grandfather might mean, but then a sudden thought occurs.

'Oh, papa!' He is filled with glee. 'New Year's night!'

Grandfather places the two birds on the hearth and, with a swing of his axe, takes off their heads. Their sad eyes spin as they roll away. Then it is up and over, and into the pot.

'Did you think I'd forget?'

It is the night the shaggy old man, Ded Moroz, will come from his wilderness home and bring him presents. Ded Moroz is like Grandfather, for he does not like to go into the cities. He goes but one day a year, to deliver his gifts, and they say it is like he brings the wilderness with him. To go at all, he must bring his grand-daughter, the Snow Maiden, and she must sprinkle pine needles wherever he treads.

'Will he know where to find us?'

'He'll know,' grins Grandfather.

Tonight, the pigeons taste better than ever – and, afterwards, because this is a special night, Grandfather produces a piece of mama's gingerbread to share. In this cold the gingerbreads have hardened, but Grandfather shows how to hold one on a fork over the fire, and in that way the middles turn soft and the outside singes black. It tastes as good as ever, and the boy thinks that the pigeon sitting in his stomach might even enjoy it too.

Now there are seven left and, just like before, Grandfather tells him, 'They have to last.'

They settle down in the deepening dark, as the fire turns the ruin to russets and red. In the hearth, the boy holds mama's Russian horse on his lap, and pets its flaking head, while Grandfather settles in the armchair with the shawl on his lap.

New Year's night is the night for a story, and from the way

he can see Grandfather nestling, he knows that one is coming to his lips.

This isn't the tale, says Grandfather, *but an opening. The tale comes tomorrow, after the meal, when we are filled with soft bread. And now*, he beams, *we start our tale.*

Long, long ago, when we did not exist, when perhaps our great-grandfathers were not in the world, in a land not so very far away, on the earth in front of the sky, on a plain place like on a wether, seven versts aside, a boy was in love.

'No!' cries the boy. 'Not in love! What about another story of the wars of winter?'

'And how do you know this story isn't of those very same wars?'

'Well, who was the boy?'

'Listen, and you might learn.'

Now, even though the King in the West was defeated and had smote himself in the barbarian palace where he lived, there was still much darkness in the world. It was called: the coldest war. The babe in the wood was grown up, and never did know her mother was a partisan who had lived under aspen and birch. But, for a certain young man, who had once been a boy, she was beautiful as the berries of the rowan, and this was her name.

That young man, who had once been a boy, had loved the girl since she was the babe in the woods, for he and his mama had been the ones to rescue her and leave her on the step. For many years he had loved her from afar, but now she was a woman grown, and it so happened that she was in love with him too. They courted in the forest and soon an agreement was reached that they should be married, and that a great celebration should be held. For love out of war is a beautiful thing.

The boy wants to grumble: there is too much talk of love in

this story. Yet something compels him to close his mouth and simply listen on.

Yet, as we know from the Little Briar Rose, the course of true love never does run smooth. For, even as preparations were begun to join the man and the woman, there arose a terrible darkness in the east. The Winter King, grown mad on power, had vanquished his enemies, but he had spent too long warring to know and love peace. And a King who knows nothing but war is more terrible than demons.

And so it was that the Winter King began his descent into madness, and sent out word that a great wall must be built to keep all enemies out. The wall was to be made of Iron, and would carve through all the kingdoms he had conquered in the wars of winter.

So men from all over the land were summoned to build this wall of Iron, and the young man who wanted nothing more than to marry his babe in the woods had to leave his home, perhaps forever, and join the new army of the Winter King.

This story, thinks the boy, does not make sense. It has no battles, nor heroes, nor ghosts. He thinks: it used to be that the Winter King was a good king, but now he is a terrible one. There ought to be good and bad, but not in the same person, never in the same person.

Well, the man went to build the Iron wall, and found himself a soldier of the Winter King, the very same as those soldiers who had, once upon a time, come to his town and changed his world. He toiled from north to south, and though he longed to get home to his babe in the woods, always the Winter King sent new orders. And soon he had not been home for many long months.

Well, the Iron wall was built, and all enemies of the Winter King were locked on the other side, and in that way a peace might have prospered. The soldier thought: now our work is done, we will go home, and I will marry my babe in the woods. But he had not counted on the madness of the Winter King.

For the Winter King had lived too long surrounded by enemies, and a man like that cannot begin to believe that the world is safe. Even his Iron wall was not enough to let him sleep at night. And, in the Winter Palace where he lived, his wise men began to whisper: our king is hungry for enemies to defeat, and if we cannot find enemies from beyond the kingdom's walls, we must find enemies within.

But where are our enemies? whispered one wise man.

It does not matter where or who, just so long as our king has enemies to defeat.

So they went out into the world. One, found a farmer. One, found a butcher. And to the farmer they said: you are sending poisoned bread to the Winter King! And to the butcher they said: you have a cleaver in your shop; do you mean to chop off the Winter King's head? And to both they said: you are enemies of the King. We banish you into the farthest east, to the world of Perpetual Winter. There you must live until the end of your days and toil in your King's service, in that great frozen city called Gulag.

Well, for a time, the Winter King was happy. He saw that his wise men had found the enemies in their midst, and rewarded them well. But, soon, the madness came again. And he said to the wise men: if this farmer was an enemy, if this butcher was an enemy, then our enemies are everywhere, in every house and street corner, in every town and farm. Go out into the lands and root out these men, and send them into the farthest east, to the world of Perpetual Winter, and there make them toil until the end of all time, in that great frozen city called Gulag.

So the wise men came together. And, seeing their King's thirst for enemies to vanquish, they said: we must go out and find more men to send to Perpetual Winter. We must find them in towns and farms, and offices and . . . even armies. For who else might turn against the Winter King, but a wicked soldier?

Well, far away from those wise men, the man who used to be a boy woke up one day and was given a letter, and in that letter it said: you may now go home, back to your babe in the woods, and prepare for a celebration and marry her under aspen and birch. And so that you might go to her, here is a ticket for an iron train, to take you all the way home.

It was news to fill the man's heart with joy, so in the morning he boarded that train. And the ticket gave him a carriage, all to himself, and when he went in, he thought: perhaps the Winter King is not so very mad after all, for what kind of madman would be so kind to a simple soldier, who only wants to marry in the forests by which he was born?

Well, the train rolled on, and home was near in sight. But when the soldier woke from a midnight slumber he heard a rat-a-tat at the carriage door. Let me sleep, he said, for I am a soldier going home, by permission of the Winter King. And a voice on the other side of the door said: no, you are mistaken, for we are wise men sent from the Winter King himself.

And the door flew open, and in its frame stood three wise men. The first stepped through and sat with the soldier, and the second stepped through and sat with the soldier, and the third stepped through and closed the door behind.

Did you receive a letter sending you home?

Yes, said the soldier.

And did the letter have a ticket to put you on this train, in this carriage, alone?

Yes, said the soldier, and now he was afraid, for the wise men knew things they should not.

Then you are not going home to marry your babe in the woods, and celebrate your wedding under aspen and birch. For we wise men sent that letter, and you are an enemy of the Winter King. You have a gun in your pack, and mayhap you mean to murder.

I am a soldier, and that is why I have a gun. I am a servant of the Winter King, and not his enemy, for I have spent many months building his Iron wall, when I would rather be marrying my babe in the woods.

Well, smiled the first wise man – for he had woven a trap of words, and caught out the soldier. If you would rather be in the woods than serving the Winter King, you are his enemy. So now you must be banished to the farthest east, to the world of Perpetual Winter, and there you must toil in your king's service, in that great frozen city called Gulag.

Grandfather exhales, soft and long. His eyes, sparkling with a vivacity at odds with his story, grow wide.

And that is how the babe in the wood's heart was first broken, he says. *So ends our tale.*

The boy crawls forward, the hearthfire at his back.

'It isn't a proper story, papa. A story has an ending. If it was a story, he'd get home. Or he'd get his stirrups and his sword and ride off and kill the Winter King. Well, wouldn't he?'

'Oh, but, boy, sometimes a story doesn't end the way we think.'

'Is it over?'

'Not yet,' says Grandfather. 'But that's for another night.'

Silence, thick as the snow.

'Haven't you forgotten?' grins Grandfather.

The boy shifts, uncomfortable. 'Is it true?' he whispers.

Oh, says Grandfather, *I know it is true, for one was there who told me of it.*

After the boy has stopped his questions, Grandfather produces another gingerbread and, tearing it in two, hands it to the boy. On the count of three, into their mouths the gingerbreads go.

Now there are six. In unison, staring at each other in the firelight, the boy and Grandfather say: no more now; they have to last.

His present, for New Year's morning, is a board for making fire, one for his very own. Ded Moroz has left it on the step. Scored with black lines, it has a perfect black crater and a brittle stick for twirling. He plays with it as the short days grow long, making countless cauldrons of fire in the garden ringed by forest.

Some weeks into the New Year, the snows come more softly – but his lessons are not yet done. At the edge of the forest, Grandfather teaches him tracking. Sometimes, a snare is enough to feed a boy and his papa for a day, but in deepest winter the creatures of the forest are few and far between, and bigger game must be stalked. Grandfather shows him the tracks of a deer, the scuff marks of forest pigs, the great swishing stride of the lumbering bison. You don't see them, says Grandfather. You see the things they leave behind, things like: indentations in the frost; spoor at the side of a trail; branches snapped beneath or sheared from a trunk.

The boy watches as Grandfather runs his fingers over ground he thinks untouched, and divines in the tiniest disturbance the direction of a boar, or the place where one of the behemoth bison stopped to snout in the forest mulch. Yet, it is not the bison's tracks towards which the boy's eyes are drawn. He stares, instead, at the crisp indentations of Grand-father's jackboots: sharp, pronounced heel, and thick pointed toe. 'Look, papa. You leave a trail as well!'

Grandfather draws back to his full height, and looks down. 'That's how they could follow me, boy.'

'Follow you, papa?'

Grandfather shakes his head, like a dog shedding snow. When he speaks again, he seems to have forgotten whatever it was he was dreaming of; probably it was just another fable.

'Do you think *you* could follow me, boy? If I went into the woods?'

The boy says, 'I don't know.' Really, inside, he is thrilling – because this sounds like a game. Even so, he isn't certain he wants to be alone in the forest again. The forest was not kind to him that night he came home, even though he tried his best to be kind to it.

'It's easy, boy. All you have to do is follow the click of these heels.'

Grandfather dances away, more light on his feet than the boy has ever known, and disappears behind the broad trunk of an oak. For an instant, the boy is alone. Then, Grandfather's grinning face reappears from behind the bark. 'Shall we?'

Eagerly, the boy nods.

To play this game, the boy must bury his head in his hands. Then he must count to ten, and after that to twenty – and, then, for good measure, all the way up to thirty too. When he opens his eyes, all around is winter light. He sees the oaks, but of Grandfather there is only one sign: the impressions of those jackboots on the forest floor.

He listens out. There is no click of jackboot heels. Wherever he is, Grandfather is hiding.

Sometimes, it is easy to see where the jackboots landed, for there is snow that has been disturbed. At other times it is more difficult, for there is only forest dirt, frozen hard by winter, and the impressions the heels leave are slight. Still, he keeps his head down and follows. Grandfather went up and over a fallen log; here, his heel scuffed up moss and rotten wood. Then he weaved down, along a stand of pine, into clearings where great oaks stand.

Here, the footsteps seem to stop. Such a thing does not make sense, for the canopy above is open and the snow has fallen more thickly – so Grandfather's bootprints ought to be plain to see. The boy wonders where he went wrong. Possibly, he has not been following Grandfather's trail at all. Possibly he has unwittingly wandered off after a forest boar, or some lynx with preposterous paws.

The heart of the clearing is dominated by an oak much taller than the rest. His eyes follow its enormous roots into a gross, misshapen trunk. Once upon a time, it must have been cleaved apart by lightning, for it grows in a great fork, and branches grope out from each.

In that fork, he sees furrows in the grain. They have bulged up, and in those bulges are terrified eyes, the gash of a mouth, the scarred mess left behind when an axe hacks off a nose.

A breath like winter catches in the boy's throat.

It is a murder tree, like the ones in Grandfather's stories. These very roots drank of dead men. He might be standing, even now, on the place where the King in the West led out mamas and papas and boys and girls and fed them to the . . .

A cold hand grabs him, closes over his mouth. He wants to scream out, but he has no breath left, his craw filled with old flesh like dirt and leather. His legs kick, but his arms are pinned to his side, and something lifts him aloft. It drags him back, holds him to it.

The murder tree recedes. The wan light of day passes from him as he is heaved under the branches. Only then does he feel himself clasped less tightly.

'Hush now,' whispers Grandfather. 'They'll hear.'

At once, Grandfather releases him. The boy staggers forward, but Grandfather snatches him by the wrist and holds him again.

He finds the old man's vivid blue eyes. There is such kindness in them that it quells the thunder in his chest.

'Papa, what . . .'

Grandfather lifts a finger, reminds him to be still. Then he turns that same finger and points it off, beyond the murder tree. 'Can't you hear them?'

The boy strains. He cannot.

'They're coming through the wood . . .'

Moments later, he knows what Grandfather is talking about. There are other voices, other footsteps. He tries to pick out words, but all he can hear is a low rumble: two voices, a woman and a man. Soon, he hears the crunch of their footsteps too. He listens keenly, for there is something not right about those sounds.

'There are three of them, aren't there, papa?'

'Hush, boy!'

The strangers hove into view, beating a path on the other side of the murder tree. He sees them fleetingly through the branches: a man the same age as Mr Navitski, with a scarlet coat flashing red in the trees. Beyond him there is a woman, with hair as blonde as mama's poking out from a navy woollen hat. To whom the third footsteps belong, the boy cannot see.

'Come on, boy. They're heading this way . . .'

Grandfather is about to lope off, when the boy tugs on his hand. 'I didn't hear you sneaking up. I thought you were a . . . soldier, or a ghost. Why didn't I hear your jackboots, papa?'

'Oh, your papa can walk silent as the snow, if he has to. It was one of the things the forests taught me, to keep me safe.'

Grandfather seems to be drifting into one of his bedtime stories again, but there isn't time to ask, for he whips the boy around and urges him into the trees.

'But . . . when, papa?'

The strangers must stop at the murder tree, for there is time to hunker down, with brambles as a shield, and hide as they walk past. Why they must hide, the boy is not quite certain, but he buries himself in Grandfather's greatcoat and tries to bear the brambles whipping at his cheeks. Grandfather's heart is a baby bird, squawking for its mother as a lynx climbs the tree.

The voices grow loud, and now the boy can hear them.

The papa says, 'It will be good for us, to be out of Brest.'

The mama says, 'This far out? Really?'

And a third voice, smaller than the others, says, 'I don't see why we shouldn't stay. I've promised to be good.'

The boy squirms against Grandfather, but Grandfather holds him fast. The footsteps grow so loud he can hear each from the other, and then they pass into view. From the brambles, the boy can see only their boots. But here comes the papa, with black mountain boots; and here comes the mama, with leather boots of green; and, trailing behind them, come the boots of a little girl: red and rubber, with flowers on top.

They tramp past, and the last thing the boy hears is the girl trilling a tune, her father barking at her. 'Some peace and quiet, girl! We're here for some peace and quiet . . .'

145

At last, Grandfather releases his hold and the boy can fight his way through the brambles to see the silhouettes of the family disappearing in the trees. He sees the back of the little girl's head – but after that, nothing.

'They're going to our house, aren't they, papa?'

'They're bound that way, boy.'

'But what should we do?'

'Do?'

'We should go and say hello . . . We can make them cattail root and acorn mash. You can catch them a rabbit.'

'Boy . . .'

There is a throaty growl in Grandfather's voice, but the boy is so keen to drag his papa along the trail that he barely notices it.

'Papa, come on!'

Grandfather is rooted to the earth, but then he relents. Quickly, they snake after the family's trail.

It is not so far to the house, after all. The woods are wide and the woods are wild and the woods are the world forever and ever, and it dawns on the boy that they are barely in its fringes, in a place the deeper forests would not even call the wild. With Grandfather slouching behind, they come to mama's tree.

The boy slows. 'Where do you think they are?'

Grandfather points, with a single long finger. 'You tell me, boy.'

Along the length of his arm, the boy sees the tracks in the garden snow. He picks out the prints of Grandfather's jackboots, and the smaller shoes that must be his own trotting alongside.

At first, he is not sure what Grandfather means – but then he realizes: there are too many prints in the garden, snaking

146

from the forest down to the door. There is another papa's boots, another mama's, another boot the size of his own foot, made for a little girl . . .

Grandfather barrels him into an outgrowth of briars. There they wait. Voices curdle up again, and out of the ruin appears the little girl.

She is older than the boy, though perhaps not by much. Her blonde hair stretches to the small of her back, and it hangs in a single plait. Her face, angelic as mama's in miniature, is dappled with freckles.

She noses forward, inquisitive as a dog, and seems to study the lattice of bootprints in the garden snow. She takes a step, to add to the patchwork, but then she is drawn to the remnants of one of the boy's practice fires.

After she has scrutinized it for some time, she looks up. Her eyes search out the darknesses on the edges of the garden, but what she is looking for the boy cannot say. It cannot be that she is looking for him, because nobody knows he is here, nobody in the whole wild world, save for the Grandfather who hunches at his side.

Why, then, does the girl draw herself up and stride across the garden? Why, then, does she trample his practice fires and come, at last, to the roots of mama's tree, to gaze up into the branches as if she has found the answer to some vexing mystery?

'Papa!' the girl cries out. 'Papa! Here! *Now!*' She swivels on her heels, stares at the empty portal of the ruin, and waits as another figure emerges – her father, swaddled up so tightly against the snow that he is more wool than flesh. 'Papa,' the girl declares. 'There's a face in this tree.'

Her father hangs his head, seemingly bracing himself for some inevitable storm. In the thicket, the boy's hand blindly gropes out to find Grandfather. He cranes to see what she is pointing out, this face that has appeared in mama's tree, but all he sees are ridges and knots in the bark. How can it be that this girl sees mama's face sprouting, soaked up by the roots, but the boy will never see her again?

The girl's father tramps halfway into the garden. 'Well,' he says. 'What do you think?'

'I think there's a face in this tree and you're not listening to me. *Again.* What do you think it is? Some kind of a witch?'

The boy bristles. Mama was many things, but she was never a witch; she would not come back that way. The tree could not warp her like that.

'I meant the house,' says the girl's father. 'What do you think of the house?'

'I think it stinks in there,' the girl declares.

'There must have been a woodsman.'

'A woodsman!? You mean people *live* in those woods?'

The father hangs his head. 'It was just somebody's camp. Come on, your mother wants to show you something.'

The girl turns from mama's tree and, with dramatic dejection, tramps back into the ruin.

In the briars, the boy clings to Grandfather's arm. 'What do they want, papa?'

A low voice, that he thinks is only half Grandfather, utters, 'I don't know.'

'What should we do?'

Grandfather whispers, 'You must go back to the forest.'

'On my own?'

'You've done it before, little one.'

'But what will you do?'

'I'll see them off, if I have to. But they mustn't see you, boy.'

'Why not?'

The boy's eyes meet Grandfather's own. The old man's shine with dew, so that he cannot see into their depths; then, the boy's do the same, so that two veils are drawn between them.

'Why not, papa?'

Grandfather says, 'You won't go far. Do you remember the frozen pond, where the cattails grow?'

'Will I wait there for you, papa?'

'I'll come.'

'You promise, don't you?'

Grandfather nods, 'With all my heart.'

With Grandfather's hand in the small of his back, the boy bustles back through the briars, beyond the line of the trees. He turns around once, only to see Grandfather urging him on.

It is not so very far to the cattail pond. Along the way, he sees a squirrel dangling from a noose, its eyeballs already gone where some famished bird has found an easy meal. He can see the track of a rabbit that has darted across the barren forest floor, and the gaping hole where a fox makes his earth. The wild points them out to him, like signposts telling him the way.

At last he reaches the slope where the cattail pond sits. He is sliding his way down, keen to drag up cattails and make Grandfather proud, when he loses his footing. When he stands, he sees mud clinging to his coat, thick and wet. It is such an unusual sight that, for the moment, he only stands there, staring. He dips a finger in and holds it up, and there is no doubt: the mud is not frozen; beneath a sprinkling of snow it squelches underfoot, oozing up around the sides of his shoes.

His eyes follow the slope. The pond is still covered in a sheet of ice, but at its banks he can see green waters lapping. He

149

crouches, his fingers find a stone, and he hurls it at the ice. With a satisfying crack, the stone disappears, leaving a perfect hole in the surface. More green water bubbles up, a portal to another world.

He is still standing there, long after, when he hears the click of jackboots and turns to see the dim shape of Grandfather coalescing from the gathering dusk.

'They're gone,' Grandfather whispers. 'You don't have to be afraid anymore.'

'I wasn't afraid, papa. I thought we could make . . .'

'You should have seen them, boy. Tramping around our home, wondering at the cookfire and the pot. Types like that have no business wandering the forest. What would they know about the wilds?'

When the boy does not reply, Grandfather comes carefully down the slope, listening to the mud squelching under his jackboot heels. 'What is it, boy?'

'Look, papa . . .'

Slowly, the boy steps aside. Where he was standing, fragile as the wind, a fist of green shoots rise between clods of frosted earth. Their green is more vibrant than the strongest pines, and at the top of each stalk dangles a single bell, as white as the ice that has entombed them since the months before mama died.

Grandfather crouches, opening its face so that the boy can see a smaller bell hanging inside, perfectly white and lined in another vivid green. 'Do you know what he is, boy?'

'Milk flower,' whispers the boy.

'Snowdrops.'

'But what does it mean, papa?'

'It means,' says Grandfather, gently letting the flower hang down, 'that things are changing.'

150

Together, they look into the woodland. Dusk is deepening, but already Grandfather seems to see new things, new depths in the forest.

'It means,' he goes on, 'no more cattail roots and acorn mash. My boy, the wild is going to be kind to us for a time.'

SUMMER

On the branches of mama's tree, peeking out from new tips of brown: the first leaves of spring, pale greens promising richness to come.

The boy comes from the kitchen to find Grandfather fingering the leaves with that strange, bewitched look in his eyes, the same one he has been wearing ever since summer dawned. He goes to him, and tries to take his hand, but the old man continues to finger the leaf, tracing its every vein as if lost in some reverie.

He is wearing a vest shorn from one of Mr Navitski's shirts and trousers with their ragged cuffs cut off to make shorts. He has no shoes any longer, for the shoes of winter are battered beyond repair. Over his shoulder hangs the leather knapsack with strange foreign letters, and into it have been piled bark-flour biscuits, seasoned with young hawthorn leaves from the edge of the dell.

'Boy, you take these.' Grandfather reaches into his greatcoat and produces the package of mama's gingerbreads, still wrapped up in paper. There are still six left, six reminders that she was once of the world.

When he presses them into the knapsack, the boy looks up in wonder. 'Really?'

'They're not for eating.'

'I know.'

'They're just for looking after.'

'They've gone hard, haven't they, papa?'

'Winter was good to them, but they'll be for fouling soon. Are you ready for your adventure?'

Proudly, the boy nods.

'Well, say goodbye to your Grandma's house. We have a long way to go.'

Grandfather is carrying a pack too, a bindle made from the vest he no longer needs. In the bindle is the pot from the stove and some other little implements scavenged from the ruin, but really all he needs is the axe. He has it pinned to his belt in a sling made from another rabbit skin, dried hard as rock over the fire. The boy spent nights kneading it until it was so supple that Grandfather could pin it and cut it and stitch it up again, a rabbit rib for a needle and sinew for his thread.

'Ready?'

The boy takes a long look at the ruin, sees the final whispers of smoke curling out of the chimneystack, and turns to follow Grandfather under the trees.

*

In summer, the trees are full of scent. Grandfather says you can find your way in a summer forest by keeping your eyes closed, because the smells rear up more potently, and you can tell if you are walking through stands of ash or alder or spruce. Though the boy tries it, to him the smells are a heady concoction, pulling him in a dozen directions all at once. He snags his foot and decides to keep his eyes open, better to soak up all of the forest.

In the days since spring shook off the shackles of snow, the boy has followed Grandfather yet further between the trees. At the pond the ice is gone, and the waters are slowly clearing as little black shapes stir into life and dart from one bank to another. The cattails grow more deeply, woody stalks with blades of green and darker bulbs unfolding on top. In the clearings where the snowdrops flourished and took their brief, grateful gasps of life, new colours are appearing; carpets spread from hidden crevices beneath dead trunks, tiny points of blue and yellow appear among the new leaves, and insects hum.

At the pond the boy collects water. He has a flask made from a crushed tin can, while at Grandfather's belt hangs a drinking pouch made from the hide of a hare. Still waters need to be boiled, says Grandfather, and the boy knows not to sip until the water has been sitting on the cookfire and the scum has been scraped away.

Today, they will go further than the pond. Further than ice and snow and the walls of winter. The boy does not know to which depths they head, but Grandfather can read the direction in the leaves. They reach a clearing with a fallen oak, and climb up and over. Grandfather goes first. On top, he is emperor of all the forest, and he reaches down to haul the boy up beside him.

It is easier to keep his balance, now that he no longer wears shoes. His feet squelch in the soft bark on top of the log. Teetering there, he looks down, into vaults of forest he has not yet seen. A ribbon of land is barer here, and at its apex he can see an oak, broader than all of the rest, its reach so vast that he begins to think of it as a kind of tenement, in which the boughs are hallways and the crooks between those boughs the rooms where a boy and his papa might live.

The woods are wide and the woods are wild and the woods are the world forever and ever. Together, they explore.

Grandfather seems to know these parts of the forest even more keenly than the trees around baba's house. As the boy follows him, he wonders if it can be so. He thinks: the ruin was once a house, where papa lived with baba and mama, but that was the long ago, and surely the forests have changed. He makes as if he recognizes alders, ash and spruce, greeting them as if they are old friends. He strides with a purpose the boy cannot understand. Perhaps he is following trails, but the boy knows about trails now and he does not see the mark of boar or bison at their feet.

In the afternoon they follow the shore of a woodland lake, where dragonflies hum and great birds dart. The day lasts long, and dusk comes late, as it has come later every day since he saw the snowdrops. Inch by inch, night is peeling back to reveal more of day.

As dusk falls, Grandfather leads the boy through the trees and revealed before him is a beautiful open sky in which reds and pinks swirl like the marbling of one of mama's cakes. Trees still line the horizon, but they are distant things, as unformed as the trees he remembers seeing on Yuri's maps

– and, between him and them, lie fields of undulating grasses, thick reeds and cattails, hummocks of land on which scrub clings. He smells stagnant waters, hears a distinct drone as a dragonfly drops into his vision, hovers there, and turns its odd pirouette to fly away.

'Here we are, boy.'

The boy stutters forward, still feeling the dark press of the forest behind. 'Where, papa?'

'I knew they were out here.'

'Is this where we've been coming?'

'I thought of these marshes in winter. I could see them when I slept. It was as if the trees were whispering to me, boy, putting them inside my head.'

The boy thinks: he's talking about dreams. But an old man should know what dreams are, for even little boys know that.

'Will we camp here tonight, papa?'

'Oh, tonight and more nights.'

Making camp means conjuring a fire. The boy uses his board; in moments the smoke comes. Soon, he has a cookfire raging, and has to hem it in with stones. Grandfather nestles the pot in the flames – and soon he is burying his face, rearing up with whiskers heavy with steam.

'How does it taste, papa?'

'Like I was a young man again . . .'

In the soup are the leaves of countless dandelions they picked in the long afternoon, and the stalks of a thistle on the cusp of bursting into flower. This thistle Grandfather calls the burdock.

'How do you like it?'

'It's like peppers.'

'It's good for the heart.'

'We haven't had a rabbit today, have we?'

'You're hungering for it, are you?'

'No!'

'Well, let's see what you've got.'

The boy upends his knapsack, making certain that mama's gingerbreads do not roll out. He sets down three bark-flour biscuits for Grandfather and three for himself, but he knows to pick the smallest three for himself because Grandfather's biggest and needs to keep his strength. Once he has spooned the dandelions and burdock onto the biscuits, he presents it to Grandfather.

'I'm looking after you, aren't I, papa?'

'There'll be berries soon, boy. Brambles and wild strawberry and bilberry in the clearings. Mountain ash too, and crab apple and wild cherry if we know where to look.'

These are magical things to the boy, because it has been a long time since he had stewed apples or brambles with a crumb on top, or the strawberries in jam that mama used to give him.

'And look at this . . .' Grandfather unfolds his hand. Sitting in his palm are three eggs, speckled and grey.

'Was there a nest?'

'It had eleven eggs, but I only took three.'

'Why only three?'

'There'll be other things wanting those eggs. Weasels and martens and stoats. All the other things of the forest. They're waking up, boy. They have babies to look after too.'

A terrible thought occurs to him. 'You don't think I'm a baby, do you?'

In the firelight, Grandfather seems to mull the question. 'Boy, listen to what the woods whisper. Do they think you're a baby?'

'They didn't let me freeze, did they, on the night I came back?'

160

'It's because they wanted you back. Just like they wanted me.'

The boy turns to the marshes. The wind in the reeds has a different sort of music to the wind in the branches. It is good, he decides, to see the sky after a long day beneath the leaves.

'How do the forests *want*, papa?'

'Well, you remember the story of Baba Yaga?'

The boy nods.

'And you remember the partisans in the woods?'

The boy nods again.

'The forests are alive, boy. They live and love and hate, just the same as you and me.' A thought seems to occur to Grandfather. He whispers into the fire, rousing the flames, and through that otherworld light beams at the boy. 'You want a tale, don't you, boy?'

The boy rises, just like those flames. 'Perhaps a summer's tale, papa?'

'Oh no. Tonight's not the night for that sort of tale. Our tales come from that land where it's always winter. If it's a summer's tale you want, boy, lie back . . . and listen to the forests. They'll tell you all the stories you need.'

Grandfather reclines, with a bed of reeds for a pillow.

'What about this?' the boy says, lifting the knapsack. 'Maybe this has a story, papa? Maybe you can tell me how you got it . . .'

He has been wondering on it since the night he brought it into the ruin. Every photograph must have a story, and every trinket too. He fingers the foreign lettering and wonders what journeys it must have been on.

Grandfather surveys him, with just one eye. 'No, boy,' he utters. 'That comes later, with winter's return.'

As if driven by the boy's question, Grandfather gives up his bed in the reeds and stands. Without further word, he turns, tramping through the long grass until he reaches the shallow rise where the trees begin.

'Papa, where are you . . .'

Grandfather waves back, forcing the boy down. 'Rest, boy. I'll be back soon. I have to . . .'

He does not finish the sentence, at least not before he levers himself over the ridge and back beneath the branches. The boy tells himself he will be back soon, that he is just going to make toilet, but as he arranges the reeds to make a pillow for himself, he feels the gnawing ache which means: you are lying, even to yourself. Grandfather has been roaming more and more, ever since the snows were banished and went east, into that land of Perpetual Winter, to terrorize that frozen city called Gulag. Some nights, the boy has woken in the ruin and not seen his papa until long after dawn. Tonight, it might be he is hunting, or foraging, but when the boy creeps after him, following the jackboot heels, he knows it is neither of those things. Grandfather is simply stalking amongst the trees, telling tales to them instead of the boy.

Back by the fire, he lays his head in the reeds. If Grandfather needs the trees, then Grandfather should have them. It is, he knows, exactly what he promised mama.

'Wake up.' The voice pulls at him, lifts him up, sets him on its knee and runs its fingers through his hair. He is at home – not the tenement, but that place he shared with only his mama, the place near school where he sat on the window ledge and watched the bigger boys traipsing to their classes, and wondered what it would be like when he too was old enough to march through the schoolhouse gates.

'Are you there, little one? Are you listening?'

He bounces on her knee. 'I'm listening, mama. I always listen. I'm a . . .'

'You're my best boy.'

'I love you, don't I, mama?'

'I know you do, little one. And I love you too. And . . . you love your papa, don't you?'

The boy knows what he must say, knows that he actually feels it too . . . but why, then, does he hesitate before saying it? 'Of course I do, mama.'

'Then listen to me and remember. He needs to know it, and he needs to know it now. Tell him.'

'Why, mama?'

'Promise me.'

The boy looks up. Mama's face is furry around its edges; he can see eyes, a nose, the line of her jaw out of the corner of his eyes, but every time he fixes on them they slip away, blurred and indistinct.

'I promise,' he whispers.

'And you must promise me one more thing.'

'What is it, mama?'

'Wake up, little one.'

'But I don't . . .'

'Wake up now. He's coming out of the woods.'

A great jolt, and he is awake. His head lolls back, and through the indistinct dark he sees a figure emerge from the forest. For a moment it hangs there, something the forest has remembered and conjured up, but then it lumbers forth. The ghost walks with a familiar lope. Its arms dangle, swinging back and forth. Its jackboots click.

Smoke still curls from the fire. He waves his hands to part it,

163

but the smoke must get in his eyes, for they start to water. By the time he has kneaded the stinging away, the ghost is upon him. It sinks down and, with arms like branches, bears him up, over the fire. The glow still left in the embers lights them from below and in those oranges and reds he sees his papa's face.

'Papa, you're back!'

'How long have I been gone?'

'I don't know, papa. I was sleeping.'

He looks for a sign of the sun's first light on the horizon across the marshlands, but dawn must still be very far away; the moon, a phantom, hangs over distant aspens.

'Were you hunting?'

Grandfather mutters a no, and takes a great stride, over the fire to where the first bulrushes grow. His legs force them apart, jackboots sinking into soft moss and earth.

In his arms, the boy sways. He feels as if he is caught in the branches of some toppling tree, a mad axe-man underneath. Grandfather takes another stride, and the boy feels the tops of the reeds tickling his skin.

'Where are we going, papa?'

'I think it's over there,' Grandfather whispers. 'On the other side.'

'All the way over?'

'All the way.'

'What is, papa?'

'The place I camped, when I first came home. An abandoned town, right there in the trees. Just like the camps I'd been in, but everyone gone. I thought: I could live in a camp like that, if everyone was gone. Just me and the trees. No other prisoners. No wardens. No wolves. Just aspen and birch. Not even a babe in the woods . . .'

164

There is a growl in Grandfather's voice, but the last words untie the knot forming in the boy's throat, because it means it is only a fable.

He clings to the old man's shoulders. 'Is it a story, papa?'

'No, boy,' utters Grandfather. 'It isn't a bastard bedtime story.'

He buries his head in Grandfather's shoulder, chokes the water coming back to his eyes. It cannot be smoke from the fire, because they have gone some distance now, and he can hear Grandfather's boots stirring up marsh water, the suck and pull as he lifts every step. He must be crying, then, but Grandfather must not know. Tears would upset him, and he has promised never to upset him.

Onwards, they walk.

At times the waters reach his papa's waist and seem to tug at his legs, but always the boy is held high, above the stagnation. At other times the waters reach only to his papa's ankles or knees, and the reeds grow so tall that neither man nor boy can see the moonlit horizon. An hour passes, and they reach a rise of land whose shores the waters do not touch. Here, there is no dead wood to conjure a fire, but Grandfather coaxes one out of scraps of nest and grass. Out of the nest come three brown speckled eggs, and Grandfather opens them in the flames. In one is a tiny bird, curled up and bald; its flesh glistens and turns gold, perfect for his papa to swallow whole.

Once sated, they move on, the boy flung high on Grandfather's shoulder, dangling there so that he can see the old shore receding. A tiny point of light marks the place where their campfire gutters out.

On this side of the island, the air is heavy with marshland smells. Grandfather seems to be nosing his way, more like an animal of the forest than a man from the city. But, the boy thinks, he has been more like that animal every day since mama died. The hunting and foraging. The roaming in the woodland. That day when the family wandered in the trees and, like a startled fox, the old man dared not go near. In his heart, he knows it is the way Grandfather looks after him – for how else to survive in the wilderness without feasting on the flesh of some other woodland creature? – but sometimes there is a clarity in the old man's eyes that betrays a darker ideal. What if, the boy wonders, Grandfather cannot leave the forest, not because the trees throw up walls of thorn to bar his passing, but because he *loves* it?

Soon, the ground does not pull so heavily at Grandfather's boots, and the reeds do not seem to grow nearly so tall. The boy feels the rush of air beneath him and, in great strides Grandfather – weightless after so long wading in the mire – bears him to the forest floor once again.

In the roots of a tall aspen his papa lays him down, but it is a long time before he wants to open his eyes. The ground is hard underneath him and, when he does peep back into the world, he understands that the earth itself is an unending lattice of roots, that the aspens around him are part of one singular tree whose roots have given birth to a forest of different trunks. All of the trees are the same, tall and straight, and there is moonlight enough tumbling through their branches to dapple the earth on which they stand.

Grandfather stalks off, jackboots clicking on the carpet of roots, returning with the axe in his hand and a bundle of kindling under one arm. Finding the place for a fire is difficult, for there is always a danger that the roots themselves will take flame, so he follows his papa deeper into the forest. The air in the aspens has a sweetness that offsets the stagnation of the marshes, and soon they find a brook whose waters run clear. When the boy drops his head to drink, he startles a hare in the undergrowth on the opposite bank. The hare takes flight, leaps once into the air, and then drops dead. Hardly able to understand, the boy looks over his shoulder to see Grandfather with a tiny stone in his hand, another just released to fell the running creature.

'I'll show you how later,' he says. 'Go and fetch him and we'll cook him up.'

The boy crosses the brook, feeling the cold water gurgling through his toes, and climbs up the other bank to push through budding bracken.

On the other side of the ferns he stops, looks back between the fronds. His papa is working in a circle, collecting fallen catkins for tinder. He has his head down, and moves so slowly, so deliberately, that he seems to fade into the trees. If the boy squints, his papa is gone, gone to the forest.

He shakes the sad feeling away, tramps on to lift the dead hare. Hare is tougher than rabbit, but this one was young; its flesh will be tender, its greases clear.

He is so focused on looking into the dead hare's eyes that he does not, at first, notice the barrows in the trees. Only when he drops the dead hare to his side to carry it back to Grandfather does he see them, a succession of strange mounds in the spaces between the trunks. The barrows are tall, their peaks almost as tall as the tip of his head and, upon their crests, strings of saplings rise. Other mounds are naked, save for the roots of the aspens around. Those roots have snaked their way up the sides of each mound, coiled together at their peaks, and in that way encased the earth below in a tangled vine shell.

'Papa!'

There comes a rustling, the click of jackboot heels on roots hard as city streets. The fronds scissor and come apart, and through them lopes Grandfather.

'Did you fetch him, boy?'

'But look, papa . . .'

Grandfather steps to the boy's side. For the first time, the boy sees flowers growing up the sides of the barrows, white and blue diamonds in the corners where roots are not strangling the surface.

'Are they graves, papa?'

Grandfather says nothing, steps closer instead.

'Why did you bring me here, papa? I don't like it here . . .'

He lets the dead hare drop and sits down with the bracken as his nest. As his papa picks a path between the first strange mounds, he finds himself reaching out again for the dead thing. He puts it in his lap and pets its ears so that they lie pinned back to its body. Every time his fingers run off, the ears spring back up, so he pets them harder, and harder, and harder.

'They're not graves, boy.'

The words startle him back to the present, and he lets the dead hare go limp in his lap. The old man is three banks into the barrows, standing halfway up a mound. The slopes of each are steep, but the roots snaking up their sides give plentiful footholes, and into these Grandfather's jackboots slip.

'What are they, papa?'

'It's houses, boy.'

'Houses?'

'This was where they lived.'

'Who?'

'Partisans.'

'Is it a story?'

'The woods have taken them back, boy, but they dug their houses in the forest floor, and lifted walls and built up roofs of timber and earth . . .'

'How do you know?'

At once, Grandfather rises, almost to the very top of the mound. His jackboots hover over the peak, but then softly come to rest, again, two steps down. 'Well, boy, I'll tell you how I know . . .'

This isn't the tale, says Grandfather, *but an opening. The tale comes tomorrow, after the meal, when we are filled with soft bread.*

The boy clings to the dead hare. On the mound, Grandfather's body moves, as if in a dance.

And now, he whispers, *we start our tale. Long, long ago, when we did not exist, when perhaps our great-grandfathers were not in the world, in a land not so very far away, on the earth in front of the sky, on a plain place like on a wether, seven versts aside, a poor man escaped from the land of Perpetual Winter, and left behind the cruelties of that frozen city called Gulag.*

Well, the man was far from home and he had many adventures, on his way back to his babe in the woods. And at last he came to those forests near his home. And he thought: these are the same forests that gave birth to my darling, for it is in these briars and hawthorn that she first came into the world. These forests looked after her people. Perhaps she is somewhere here, still, and, if she has not been enslaved by some great Russian bear, she may yet be my wife . . .

'Wait!' says the boy, his fingers still teasing the cadaverous hare.

'What is it, boy?'

'This isn't the tale.'

169

'Not the tale?'

'In our tale, the man only just went to Perpetual Winter.'

'So?'

'So you've missed out the adventures. What was it like in the frozen city of Gulag, papa? How did he escape? How did he get home?'

Grandfather's eyes darken. He stops his dance. The boy isn't certain but he thinks he hears, beneath the jackboot heels, another clicking, as of firewood drying and popping over the hearth.

'Those tales are not for the telling,' says the old man.

Before the boy can argue, his voice slips into that strange, feathery tone and he continues.

Well, the man came through the woods and, all at once, he came upon a marsh. And he said: there were not marshes in the forests I remember. Perhaps, if I cross this marsh, I will see trees I know and trees who know me. Then the trees will remember and help me on my way, for the trees have been kindest to me, in all my voyages through Perpetual Winter. It was the trees themselves who helped me escape that frozen city of Gulag. I would rather a tree for a friend than any person in the world, except of course my babe in the woods.

Well, the man crossed the marshes, but soon a terrible rainstorm came. And the man thought: would that I had stayed in the woods, for the woods would have sheltered me from this storm. And, with that thought in mind, he made for the nearest bank, which was two miles clear from the marshland in which he waded.

When he got there, he was cold and wet, but the cold and wet did not make fear in this man, for he had been through Perpetual Winter. He had learned the magicks to start fire from wet wood, and set about building a camp to warm him in the Long Night. And he was happy, again, to be under aspen and birch.

Well, when he lit the fire, he found he was in the woods and yet not in the woods, for in the woods a town had been built out of timber and earth. And it had houses and wells and larders and pens for keeping pigs. And, though almost all of the houses were empty, there he found an old man and his pig.

Ho, said the runaway.

Ho, said the old man, and Ho! said his pig. Name yourself, stranger.

I will not name myself, for too long I have had no name. I come from the east, from that land called Perpetual Winter, where stirs the great frozen city called Gulag. I am on my way home to my babe in the woods.

You have come to my town, and I am the only one left, for they say the wars are finished and men can go home.

But if the wars are finished and men can go home, why do you stay in the woods?

I stay because I have lived too long under aspen and birch. Since the wars began I have lived here, to hide from the King in the West, and though they say he is dead, the forests are my home and the trees my companions. And, when the time comes that I too shall die, I will take off my shirt and take off my shoes and walk into wilder forests yet. There the trees will drink of my dead body and my friend the oak shall wear my face for all time to come.

Well, the runaway thought about what the Old Man of the Forest said. And day turned into night many times before he had his answer. For he too had lived a long time in forests just like this, and like the Old Man of the Forest, he too thought the trees his friends.

I have thought, old man, about what you said, and I too would make my home forever under aspen and birch. But I left a woman

171

waiting, and if she still waits for me, in that little house on yonder side of these forests, I must go to her and make her my wife. I must forget about forests and stop living wild, for, once upon a time, I was a kind human being and I can be a human again.

Then go! said the Old Man of the Forest. Because, if you do not want the woodland, the woodland does not want you.

All at once, the Old Man of the Forest shed his skin. And his face peeled back and his hands grew claws, and his eyes grew dark, and as his skin flayed off there arose a great mane of fur. And he sank to his haunches and, now, he revealed himself a wolf. And it might have been that he was about to sink his teeth into the runaway, but instead he sunk his teeth into the pig and, with snout slathered in blood, turned tail and went to the wild.

I am no fell beast, thought the runaway, but I am still wild. If I stay in the forest much longer, I too will be the wolf. Needs must I leave.

So the runaway crossed the marshes and found trees he remembered. And the trees sang to him and their branches pointed the way. And that was how he became human again. That was how he found his babe in the woods.

The boy stands, palming the dead hare to the ground. As he advances, the barrows look different, almost inviting. Up ahead, his papa lifts a foot and inches closer to the top of the mound. Under his jackboots the roots complain, groaning like ancient floorboards.

'Is it true, papa?'

Oh, Grandfather says, lifting a foot and inching closer to the top of the mound. *I know it is true, for one was . . .*

Grandfather freezes. His body twists. There is a moment of pure stillness, in which he seems to be suspended there. Then a terrible sound reaches the boy: the groaning giving way to

172

splintering, the rasp as the earth comes apart, the painful grating of wood shearing from wood.

His papa looks at him, throws his arms forward – but he is too late. Beneath his feet the roots part, the earth vanishes like an enchantment dispelled, and his papa plunges into the heart of the barrow itself.

'**P**apa! Papa!'

The boy hurtles forward, weaving between the first mounds. His foot snags in a curl of root breaking the surface, but he does not go down. When he regains his balance, he is at the foot of the mound into which Grandfather plunged. He can see a thick length of root, dead wood pitted with holes, lying severed at his feet.

He slows, breath shallow and at odds with the pounding of his heart. 'Papa?'

Up close, the roof of the mound is level with the boy's head. To climb it will take some scaling, but the roots that encase it offer wizened holds for his hands and feet. When he puts his weight against it, it rocks forward; he knows, now, that the mound is hollow inside.

'Papa, can you hear me?'

Hand over hand, bare feet scrabbling for a hold.

'Papa, are you in there?'

His hand finds the edge of the gaping maw. He begins to haul himself up, but another length of root crumbles away and drops into the darkness of the void. It is a long second later that he hears it land. Next comes a moaning, softer still. The root has landed on Grandfather, forcing the air from his lungs. The realization comes with relief, for at least he is alive, but it comes with dread too.

When he feels the roots groan, he spreads himself out, edging up until he can peer into the jagged crevasse. Down there is only darkness so that, without daylight streaming through the aspen leaves, he can see nothing.

'Papa,' he ventures, 'are you down there?'

This time, there is an answer. It is not a word, only a sound.

'Papa, are you hurt?'

He puts his hand over the precipice. His fingers find nothing, and he claws to reach further. 'Papa, I can't reach you . . .'

His papa's sounds are louder now, the sounds he imagines a rabbit in one of their snares might make before contorting to take its teeth to its own leg.

'Papa, I'm coming down.'

He has not yet angled himself to go over the edge when Grandfather howls. From deep below, he hears the sound of a thrashing. Each thrash brings another howl, each howl another guttering gasp for air. He recoils, holds tight to the top of the mound. The howling ebbs away and, at last, he understands: his papa is telling him to hold back.

'What should I do, papa?'

A lower howl this time, something dirtier. Mangled impressions of words.

'Well, what should I?'

The boy slides away, stutters down the mound. Broken pieces of root lie at his feet and, as his eyes light on them, he has an idea.

He fumbles the dead roots together, ferreting at the base of every aspen for any other pieces of kindling he can find. Once he has enough, he finds a basin in the earth and sets about conjuring fire. As he whispers tinder to flame, kissing that flame to the kindling, he can hear Grandfather's low roar in the back of his mind.

Once the fire is stirred, he takes a length of dead root and plunges its head into the heart of the flames. It does not take long before the brand has taken light. Shielding it, he hurries back to the mound.

This time, he can feel earth breaking free underneath him, showering into the hollow. He has a premonition of being sucked under just the same as his papa, but he hauls himself to the peak and lowers the flaming brand. The heat rushes up the wood, scorching his arm and, though his instinct is to let go, he clings on, forcing himself to squint past the bright halo.

It looks like the ruin. The walls go deep into a crater in the earth, and there are beams, roughly hewn timbers keeping the walls in place. There are rafters too, little more than branches from the trees fixed into place with the earth heaped on top. Aspen roots have coiled among them, encasing the place in a fairytale shell: a castle of thorns.

He swings the brand. Along one of the walls a shelf is cut into the earth, and on its top more dead branches, bound into place by yet more creeping roots. Suddenly, he knows this for what it was: a home, just like his papa said. In the long ago, the partisans made homes in the earth and, when they left, the forest came and took them back.

'Papa?'

The light of the brand finds him: a dark shape lying in front of the shelf of earth. Perhaps he caught it on his fall, for around him lie scattered pieces of kindling thrown up from the earth. The boy pushes the brand further. At last, he finds his papa's head. He knows it only from its white whiskers, for the rest is pressed against one of the earthen walls. There is something wrong in the way he lies. His legs are tangled, the first bent and seemingly knotted in an inhuman way.

'Oh, papa.'

He lifts the brand. The precipice he is hanging over is held up by rafters that sheared beneath his papa's weight. There is, he decides, a way to shimmy down the rafters and slide down one of the old timbers.

He hesitates. Thinks of the murder grounds under the branches. Places people were shepherded to die. The things the forest drank to make its leaves, its roots. In that moment, he is not certain if he can go down to join them, in that place where dead men were made dinner.

The fire creeps up the brand and bites at his arm. Instinctively, he lets go. When the brand hits the bottom of the bunker, its light is dimmed but not snuffed out. Dry tinder at the bottom of the bunker suddenly takes light, and in seconds a cauldron of flames is stirring.

Light enough to guide him by. Light enough to convince him there are no ghosts in the earth; the ghosts stalk the forest above, but down there is only his papa.

He takes the knapsack from his shoulder and casts it down, to land beyond the fire. Now there is no way of turning back.

He takes hold of the branches that once made up the roof of the mound, testing them with his weight. Still bound in earth, he thinks that they will bear him, and slowly he goes into the hole. He scrambles for footing, but there is nothing beneath him. He dangles there, sensing the nothingness underneath.

Hand over hand, he finds his way along the rafter. There are hand-holds aplenty, for the roots make a tangle in which it is easy to tuck his fingers. Finding a way down one of the timbers is easier still, knots in the wood like the rungs of a ladder. Soon he finds himself on the shelf cut into the earth and, from here, it is a quick jump to the cavern floor. He stops, looks around. The fire throws spidery shadows, but at least he can make out the walls. There were steps, once, leading into a maw where now there is only fallen earth.

Grandfather is at his feet. In the air is a distinct smell that he takes for the cloying earth; it is some time before he realizes it is his papa himself who made that soil.

'Papa?'

The old man turns, his crusted mouth making a noise like some beaten dog.

'Papa, can you hear me?'

For the first time, the firelight bathes Grandfather's face: bulbous nose, smashed flat; flesh open above a purpled eye, half an eyebrow turned back like a white slug cleaved in two; down his cheek, a shining mask of red.

Grandfather opens his lips, and all the boy sees is a churning black mass. He makes a sound and, between those lips, his tongue bucks oddly, like a fish thrown onto land. Here is the reason his papa's words are all mangled: his tongue is torn in two.

'Papa, where does it hurt?'

More useless questions. The boy shifts so that he is not blocking the firelight. For the first time he sees a deep cleft in his papa's thigh, where the axe has bitten through its sling and carved his flesh. Though curiously dry, it gapes in horrible reds and blacks, made darker yet by the fire. The axe is at his side, its blade smeared. He picks it up, hurls it away. It bites into one of the timbers, and in reply the timber groans. The roots coiled above seem to shudder and, in terror, the boy scrambles up. His eyes are on the roof, the walls, waiting for them to tumble in.

When they do not, his eyes return to his papa. Now he sees why the legs are tangled. One of them is bent back, and from a point just below the knee protrude three jagged spikes.

'Papa, it's broken.'

It isn't the only thing. The boy hears the rattle every time he takes a breath. Probably ribs have been shattered. Probably he is broken inside.

He sits at his papa's side and he cries – softly, unheard, nobody to listen but the wild.

Night thickens. The fire dies. The boy recovers from his torpor to build it back up. Giving life to the flames gives new life to him as well, but he doubts it is doing anything for his papa. The old man stopped howling hours ago, and though he still breathes, he does so only in short, desperate gasps.

Once the fire is built back up, he sits at Grandfather's legs. The axe wound in his thigh is dark and dry, but the one below his knee has swollen to hide the jagged line of bone. A sour smell rises.

He opens his knapsack. Lying inside is the paper with mama's gingerbreads, now rock-hard and beyond eating, and beneath that her shawl. There is his board for making fire too. Dried Jew's ears and other tastier mushrooms. A little rabbit-skin pouch filled with moss for tinder.

Maybe the moss can pack the wound in his papa's thigh. He carries it over and holds it tentatively above the place where the axe bit into his flesh. Very slowly, he touches the wound. Through the moss it does not feel like very much, but then the warmth bleeds through. If he was Grandfather, he would buck and cry and complain, but Grandfather remains perfectly still. Perhaps his breath is more agitated than before, but the moss packs into the wound, its fibres clinging to raw flesh like cotton wool to a grazed knee.

Next, he unrolls mama's shawl. He presses it to his face but it hardly smells of her anymore. Mostly it smells of smoke and dry meat, but there is still something behind that, sweet like vanilla, that brings him instantly into mama's arms. He gets lost in the memory for a moment too long; then he brings it to Grandfather's side and kneels at his leg.

Gingerly, he rolls mama's shawl over the bulging mass. Stretched out like this, it is only a blanket. To bind the wound he must wrap it around, tie it off, somehow hold the leg together with woven wool embroidered with flowers – and, to do that, he must lift Grandfather's leg.

He puts his hands around Grandfather's shin, but the skin is slippery, and when he tries to lift it, it feels so light that he dares not. Instead, his hands creep up past the wound – which radiates heat – and to his thigh. He takes hold, and strains to lift. An inch is all he needs, enough to tuck the shawl underneath and drag it down around the knee.

Grandfather shifts. His sleeping arms snatch at something. His throat rolls back. A sound, like foxes at night.

180

When he is still again, the boy takes the ends of mama's shawl and draws them together. He rolls the shawl once more along the leg, wraps one corner into the other to form a loose knot. He draws it tight.

Grandfather opens his mouth, lets out a cry. One hand shoots up, the other shuddering savage at the shoulder; its fingers strain to claw for the boy. Even though they do not connect, somehow they have a hold of him. They gather him tight and cast him away.

'Papa, I'm sorry.'

For the first time since he fell, there seems to be intelligence in the old man's eyes. When they fix on the boy, they know that it is he, not some ghost of the forest dead, sitting there.

'I wrapped them up, papa. So they'll get better.'

The old man's eyes revolve to his legs. He lifts one arm, but it hangs limp. He lifts the other; this, at least, looks human. With his body rigid, he uses that arm to lever himself up. That he does it without crying out must mean something, thinks the boy – but perhaps it is only his forked lizard's tongue, keeping the words locked in his throat.

He opens his lips, only a fraction. Says something neither beast nor boy could ever understand. The language, thinks the boy, of trees.

'Water, papa? Do you want water?'

The boy turns to find his knapsack. Inside, the crushed tin can is still half filled. He takes it to his papa and puts the crumpled spout to his lips. Most of the water runs into his bloody whiskers, and what does find a way into his mouth makes him wince. Even so, Grandfather wants more. The boy drips it to him until it is almost gone.

'Papa, I think it's your foot too. I think it might be broken.'

The old man's head goes back, exposing a neck covered in thick white bristles. With an enormous effort, he hoists himself up on his one good arm. The boy follows the line of his eyes to the foot on the end of his broken leg. It must have been the one onto which he fell.

Grandfather cannot gesture with his hand, for it keeps him from falling back to the earth, so instead he tips his chin. He does it twice before the boy understands.

He goes to the broken foot. It, too, has started to swell; the flesh hardens and grows around the jackboot rim.

'I can't, papa.'

Grandfather's eyes tell him: you have to.

There are no laces or buckles on Grandfather's jackboots. The boy puts his hand around it and, as soon as he takes hold, Grandfather pulls back, smashing his head into the earthen wall behind. Some animal instinct has made him try and draw in his foot, but the mere attempt makes pain lacerate his body. The boy shudders backwards, sees a dark stain blossoming and spreading on mama's shawl.

Once Grandfather's breathing is under control, he paws at his eyes and gestures again at the boy.

The boy puts his hands around the jackboot. This time, his papa is ready. He winces, but he does not cry out. For a moment the boy simply holds on, but then the pulsing in Grandfather's body ebbs away. He does not turn around, for he knows that, if he were to look into his papa's eyes, his will would fail.

He tightens his grasp, and starts to pull.

Grandfather writhes, but he does not shriek. His eyes are shut tight, his one good hand closed in a fist. He seems to be biting down on what is left of his tongue.

The jackboot barely gives. It strains against flesh grown hard

182

as stone. With one hand he takes hold of its heel. The foot seems to resist, but then flesh reveals itself, marbled black as night.

The boy has dragged the boot half off his papa's foot when he looks up to see the old man basking there without any sound at all. He hurries to his breast, listens out for the rattle that will tell him he is still alive. Sure enough, here it comes: juddering, but somehow more peaceful than when Grandfather was awake.

If he is to take his chance, it has to be now. He returns to Grandfather's foot and pulls the jackboot off bodily. Its insides are slippery, and he throws it down, over the fire.

The foot he has revealed is hardly a foot at all. It is a ball of flesh, tapering to a point at which two talons protrude, the others engulfed. Somewhere in there are bones and tendons and veins, but of them the boy can see nothing.

'Oh, papa.'

He crawls to his papa's head and teases his fingers into hair like tough grass. Even this must hurt the old man, for the abrasions on his face seem to strain, the open flesh above his eye shimmering as it weeps.

He wants to hold him, but his hands won't let him; to hold him is to hurt him, and he is hurting enough already.

'I promised mama,' the boy whispers. 'I promised her, papa.'

All through the night: the old man's rattle.

T he boy stands between the aspens and feels the wind across his skin.

It has been six days since Grandfather fell. Six days and seven nights he has scrambled out of the old bunker in search of forage. In all of that time, not once has his papa eaten. He has stewed soups out of leaves, broiled the carcass of the baby hare, and dripped it to him from the crushed tin can. He has taken it back in sips, but the juices do not work sorceries on them like kindling to a fire. Grandfather's brow burns and his face looks gaunt, haggard as a winter wood.

At nights, the boy eats the mulch that is left. It fills him, and yet he feels empty.

Tonight, he creeps back through the mounds where partisans once made their homes. His pockets are stuffed with mushrooms, but he doesn't know which ones are full of flavour and which ones might poison him and send him to sleep for a hundred years. When he reaches the bunker, he sees only thin smoke rising up; he will have to bring a log to see them through the night. The axe is where he left it, its blade deep in the trunk of a tree. In the days past he has used it to carve a wider, lower entrance to the bunker, one he can drop through without risking himself on rafters and uneven ground. He ducks through and scrambles down.

His papa is propped up with his eyes half-closed. There are empty eggshells at his side, things the boy took from a nest hidden in the marsh grass. Raw eggs, it seems, are the one thing he can swallow and not scream.

The boy empties his pockets. Grandfather's eyes find the mushrooms and start rolling, as if to tell the boy which ones to set aside and which to toss on the fire.

'Papa, I want to go for help.'

Grandfather stops, only half the mushrooms counted.

'You helped me, papa. I want to help you too.'

The old man shakes his head, makes a dull sound, one simple syllable rolled on the back of his throat.

'I can . . .'

Now, the same dull sound again: a bark, a command.

The boy goes back to the fire. On a stone in its heart he has spread three chicks, snatched from their nest while their mother beat her wings in fury. They will all go to his papa, but he will not eat them; they will stay at his side and, in the night, the boy will creep over and suckle them instead.

His knapsack is fallen open and he sees, inside, the gingerbreads from the long ago.

'Papa, what if we . . .'

Grandfather's eyes flare. The left one has emerged from its swelling, the sore above scabbing over to make an eyebrow like crusted lava.

'There's honey, papa. It might be good for you. I can mash it with water.'

He shakes his head, only once.

The boy's head hangs. In the knapsack, the six gingerbreads stare back. They are shrunken now – hard – their decorations hardly recognizable as stars and ears of wheat. Yet, in their crimped edges, he can still see the depressions of mama's fingers, mama's thumb.

'Mama made me gingerbreads, didn't she, every time I was sick? And I always got better. Well, didn't I?'

Grandfather's mouth opens and out comes a sound like knotted words. The boy has heard him grunt and howl in the last days, but for the first time he thinks he hears real words smothered in the sounds.

His eyes lift, bright. 'Papa?'

Grandfather makes the sounds again. Three short, simple words – that is all they are, and yet he cannot truly hear them at all.

His head sinks again, the bunker filled with the guttering of Grandfather's breath. 'I'm hungry, papa.'

This time, when he looks up, the old man is nodding. He takes it as a sign and drags the knapsack into the middle of the bunker. From inside, he produces the package of mama's gingerbreads. He spreads them out, hard as rock.

The old man lets out a howl, forcing the first gingerbread from the boy's hand.

'Please, papa. We'll starve.'

The howl goes on. Desperate, the boy tries to block it out

186

– but it is reverberating in his head now and he cannot send it away.

Even so, his gut screams more loudly. He lifts the gingerbread again. With his eyes still on the fire, he puts one corner between his teeth. The crust is solid, but then he tears a chunk off. In his mouth it is dry, its surface rough. For a moment it is even painful. Slowly, it starts to soften. Tastes rush out, honey still the strongest of all.

When the corner is soft enough, he swallows it down. It feels tough, leaden as it makes its way down his throat – but that does not sate his appetite for more. He bites again, sucks again, chews and chomps down. He does it again and again until all of the gingerbread is gone, and the insides of his mouth are coated with sticky, sweet residue.

The aching is gone from his belly, but after a few moments he knows that his gut is not yet satisfied. The taste of honey, of ginger, of mama and the tenement and everything that went before, is burning in him, more vigorous than the fiercest of bonfires.

'Papa,' he says, pretending there is not a new haunted look in the fell creature's eyes. 'Just one more.'

His eyes fall on the next gingerbread in line, and he picks it up.

When he has finished all but one of the gingerbreads, the boy turns and doubles over. He can feel a great boulder rising in his gorge. He swallows, concentrates, swallows again. It takes an age for the sensation to ebb away, but at last he has it conquered; the gingerbreads remain in his belly, and ripples of warmth find their way to every corner of his being.

'Papa, have one. You have one too.'

The boy takes the last gingerbread, offers it up. But

187

Grandfather's clawed hand comes back, sends the biscuit flying. It rises up, arcs across the boy, and lands in the heart of the flames. There, it turns suddenly black. The boy watches the darkness spread.

It takes mere minutes for the gingerbread to die. He wonders how long it took for mama. He thinks: how long is it taking for papa, even now?

'Why, papa?'

Grandfather rolls his head.

We're all hungry, he seems to be saying. Then he lifts his good arm to flourish at the world above.

But the wilds are there. The wilds will provide.

And in the air: a smell like burnt honey.

Nights later, he is late in returning to the bunker. The sun has spilled glorious light over the aspens, but as he returns thin drizzle begins to fall, heralding the darkness. It has been falling for some time before it can filter through the trees, so that he only knows it is raining at all by a shift in how he senses the air. Still, the drizzle will bring new life to the budding nettles, the brooklime between here and the marsh's edge. In the morning the leaves will taste different, more tender somehow, and his papa will take them more easily.

At the bunker there is no smoke. He hurries through the last remaining mounds. The shadow men darting in the corner of his eyes have faces young and old, and they too are hurrying for the cover of their shelters under the advancing tide of rain. The boy hears the tramp of their feet descending into each mound. Fires doused and whispered words: the soldiers are coming, the soldiers are coming . . .

'Papa?'

Grandfather is there in the darkness. The boy descends, hand over hand, to find the fire low. He kicks through its ashes to reach his papa's side.

The old man has been sleeping. The boy nudges his good arm, to shake him gently awake.

'*Boy.*'

The boy stumbles back. This time, there is no doubt: it truly was a word.

'Papa, I brought mushrooms.' He empties his pockets, quite certain that these will not poison him. He found them growing on the earth beneath a fallen birch, could tell them by the depth of the cup and the scent when he dug a fingernail into the skin.

'*Boy.*' The word is thick, as if it is too big for his mouth.

'Oh, papa . . .' The boy wants to fling himself into Grandfather's lap, hear the word over and over. Yet, the leg still stinks, the wound and its ooze eating up mama's shawl, and though his foot is less swollen, each day that the swelling recedes it reveals the mangled mess beneath: the toes, a loose collection of fragments and flesh; the ankle gone, as if forced back inside the body.

'Boy, I . . .' Grandfather's tongue appears between his lips, dry and scaled.

'I got you some water, papa.' He scrambles to bring Grandfather the tin can, and holds it to the open abyss of his mouth. 'Papa, I have to go for help.'

The last water trails out from Grandfather's lips. 'No.'

There is no mistaking this word either.

'Papa, if I don't . . .'

'No!' The word is only an instant long, but by its end it is no longer a word at all. Grandfather brings his one good hand to his lips, draws it back covered in watery blood.

'Papa, your tongue.'

The boy brings him more water, but the old man knocks it aside.

'Please, papa. Please. I have to go.'

Grandfather tips back his head; his throat wrenches as he swallows something back. His eye locks with the boy's, and through great pain he utters, 'You . . . *promised.*'

Soon, Grandfather is gone to that restless world of sleep again. The boy builds up the fire, scuttles from one corner of the bunker to another. In the world above, he fancies he can hear the tramping of a hundred different jackboots as the soldiers come through the woods. He tells himself: they're only ghosts, they're only ghosts. Stories can't hurt you and neither can ghosts.

There's only one thing that can hurt you here, and he's lying next to you, an anguished giant under the ground.

He did promise. He sat there, in mama's lap, and he said: I'll look to my papa. But it's been nine days. Nine days and nine nights. He's fed him and brought him water, wrapped the wounds and built him fires to keep him warm. And still the smells rise. Still the rot festers. Perhaps, if he doesn't go now, there'll be no point going at all. Perhaps going is what he *has* to do, if he's going to keep that promise. Leaving now, finding help, that's what would make mama proud; not just lying here, in a hole in the dirt, petting his papa as he wastes away.

He goes up into the night. The axe is standing guard, with its blade biting an aspen root. He passes it, steals through the bracken, and in that way comes across the tiny brook and to the shores of the marsh itself. The drizzle has moved on but there is wind tonight – summer wind, with summer's smells.

Midges and mosquitoes descend, to make a banquet of his flesh.

He stands and gazes into the distance. There is moonlight enough from this hanging crescent to illuminate the tops of the canopy on the marsh's farthest side. His eyes scour the reeds and he finds the tiny island where he and Grandfather camped. What lies beneath, he cannot tell, but perhaps the marshes are drier than when they came across, so that he might find an easier channel.

He thinks to ask mama what he should do. The aspens would whisper to the marsh grass, who would whisper to the oaks on the other side, and they in turn would send the whispers down to mama's tree. Finally, she would hear and send her whispers back: come, little man; or, stay, little man, and care for your papa. Yet, he does not say a thing. He sits in the roots of the first tree and watches the moon.

Mama cannot help him now. Papa cannot help him. If he believed in stories, he would think: the trees can help me. But, if he believed in stories, he would have to believe in the Old Man of the Forest turning to a wolf – and perhaps, thinking of his papa, he would rather not believe in that.

Some time later, he thinks he hears a rustling in the bracken behind him – but, when he turns, he sees nothing, not even a ghost. He stands, because he thinks he has made up his mind to go to the marsh, but when he reaches the shore, the rustling comes again. He stops. His eyes are on the moon and the moon is telling him: turn around! But he will not turn around.

A cold hand closes around his ankle. He screams, kicks out. The scream scatters across the marsh, fading in that vast emptiness. The reeds rustle in reply.

The hand still holds him. He pitches forward, leg snapping

191

taut, and now he is on his hands and knees, with his face pressed into moist marsh moss. He reaches out, grapples onto the reeds, tries to haul himself up. Whatever holds him, holds him tight. He shakes his foot, manages to twist around. Now he is on his back, with his leg bent. He tries to scrabble backwards, but the thing, the creature, is holding him, and the weight is unbearable. He collapses, exhausted. His hands are sinking into the mire – and now, now the hand is crawling up his ankle, up his leg. He stares down the length of his body. Fat talons appear through the reeds. They grasp his knee. Next comes a hand, and with that hand a naked, purple arm.

'*Boy.*'

'Papa!'

The boy reaches out, touches Grandfather's arm. At once, his body relents. The hand does not grip him as fiercely, and the reeds whip him as he scrabbles to stand.

In the reeds, lies Grandfather. He sprawls, face-down, breathing heavily. His leg trails behind him, hanging out of the marsh like a dead body washed ashore. Standing tall, the boy can see the ugly smear where he has dragged himself through the bracken.

'Papa, how did you get out of the hole?'

'I . . . had to.'

'Papa, where were you going?'

'You . . . left.'

The boy sinks at his papa's side, pets his bloody head.

'I have to, papa. I have to get help.'

'No, boy. You promised. You *promised*.'

He barely recognizes the word, so gutturally does Grandfather speak. 'I'm not leaving you, papa. I'm going to come back.'

'They'll take you away.'

The boy is quelled. It is a fear he has not yet had, for his head is filled with stories and ghosts. It has been many months since he was last at school, but he can still remember the look on Mr Navitski's face when he dropped him at the tenement, when he thought to come in and talk to his papa.

He thinks to take Grandfather's leg and drag him back from the marsh, but it looks so ruined that it might shear off. Instead, he takes the hand of his papa's one good arm. He senses that the old man wants to resist, but the fight is gone from him. That hand has clawed his way up, out of the bunker, down through the aspens. Its muscles must be as shredded as the rest of him.

In a series of stuttering attempts, the boy hauls Grandfather around and lies him in the bracken beneath the aspen boughs. The midges and mosquitoes swallow them both in a cloud blacker than night. The boy tries to fight them away, but it is easier to fight a big, monstrous enemy, than a thousand insidious ones.

'Papa,' he says, sitting at the old man's side. 'I wasn't going to leave you. You know it, don't you?'

The old man gutters a reply.

'I'm scared, papa.'

Grandfather lifts his trembling good hand. With it, he finds the boy's. He tries to clasp him, but at first his fingers will not work. 'Don't be scared,' he says with forked tongue. 'The woods will look after us.'

'But how, papa?' the boy trembles. 'How?'

Grandfather's breathing goes up into the night, summoning further mosquitoes. 'I'll show you,' he utters – and those three words seem to demand more of him than all of his wounds, every inch of flayed skin. 'I'll . . . teach you everything, boy.

Everything I learned on that wild walk home. *Everything from Perpetual Winter and that frozen city called Gulag.* It kept me alive. It can keep you too.'

'Papa,' the boy whispers, feeling the chill in the summer's night. 'It is a story, isn't it?'

This isn't the tale, says Grandfather, *but an opening.*

Then, for the first time since he fell, he begins to cry.

'Bring me nettles, boy. Build me a fire. I'll be your eyes. You'll be my hands. In the morning, we'll make snares and pits and traps. I'll show you stalking. I'll show you kills.'

The boy stands. 'Yes, papa,' he says, and scurries into the trees.

In the weeks that follow: journeys at first light, to check new snares made from nettles and gather up the morning's forage; then long afternoons and evenings, sitting in a bivouac beneath the aspen boughs. No stories from his papa, nor even any stories from the boy for his papa to hear. Few looks, and fewer words. Grandfather teaches him, but he teaches in silence: snares and traps, and the stillness of stalking. It is long months since winter, yet he finds himself waiting for another kind of thaw.

Summer flourishes and summer grows old. With the rolling of the season, flesh comes back to his papa's bones, transforming the shape of his face by degrees more perceptible with each passing meal. His cheeks fill out, his eyes heal, but somehow he looks more drawn, his face longer, the corners of his lips turned neither up nor down. His chin loses its point, and his whiskers cling more closely to the flesh. No longer do they grow out; now they curl upon themselves instead, tight coils like fur. In the tracts where they do not grow, his skin is hard, as if permanently scabbed. The earth has left an impression on his cheek where he fell, a pattern of thin grazes that heal badly and somehow scar.

He holds one shoulder higher than the other, and when movement stirs again in the fingers of his broken arm, it is jagged, strings being played by a poor puppeteer.

One morning, the boy returns with forage to find the old man standing. His dead leg, bent and shorter than the other, still hangs useless, but he balances himself with hands on an aspen trunk. Today he just holds himself there, refusing to fall. The next day he takes steps, crude shuffling things that propel him forward at an interminable pace. The next day, he learns to prowl from one aspen to another. The boy watches as he picks his path back to the bunker, peers in at the ground that tried to feed him to the trees.

He looks to his papa, slowly healing into a new shape and wonders: mama, what have I done?

Because Grandfather does not mention his mama anymore. She is gone with the gingerbreads, gone from his thoughts and words. She is, or so the boy believes, gone from the forest itself.

Across the fire, the old man utters the same words, as if in a fevered dream.

This isn't the tale, but an opening.
This isn't the tale, but an opening.
This isn't the tale, but an
This isn't the tale

I'm the tale I'm the tale I'm the tale

In the aspens, the days turn to weeks, the weeks into months – and, in the branches above, the colours, just like his papa, start to change.

T his morning, when the boy wakes, he is distinctly aware
that it is darker than it was the morning before, or the
morning before that. By the remnants of the fire,
Grandfather still sleeps. A rattle comes up from his belly and
forces its way out through lips dry and scabbed.

He opens the embers, feeds them with pieces of bark and
steps out into the aspens. There is no doubt about it; there is
a bite in the air this morning, one he has not felt in many
months. He takes a deep breath and roars it silently out; a
gentle discolouring in the air tells him that his breath can make
fog once again.

It is time for the morning forage. There are still brambles
on the briars, and he hunts for ones the birds have not yet

found. Then it is time to check the snares. This morning there is only a lonely squirrel dangling from its noose, not nearly enough to sustain them through the day. The boy will have to go after rabbits, wood pigeons, whatever birds he can find. Eggs have long since disappeared, but perhaps there are frogs, huddling down in the reeds.

Dull light in the trees and no warmer, even after an hour running the range.

He is on his way back to the shelter when the wind starts to blow. It flurries up from nowhere, but he knows it will pass soon, just one of those idle gusts trapped in the trees. He retreats between the aspens and suckles on a hazelnut to keep off the morning's hunger.

As he suckles, he sees something he thinks he has forgotten: a single fracture of white sails down through the branches. It hovers before them, revolving as if to show off its crystal indentations, before it floats on, finally finding rest on the tip of a thistle. He goes to it, crouches, expects it to melt away – but it clings on; it remains.

At last, he picks his way back to the shelter, fingertips stained with the juice of the brambles he has devoured.

In the gloom Grandfather is awake and whispering woodland secrets to the fire.

'I'm sorry, papa,' he says, coming hand over hand into the shelter. 'There isn't much.'

Grandfather peers as the boy empties the knapsack and all of its treats. 'There's enough.'

'We'll be hungry, papa.'

Grandfather shrugs, 'I've been hungry before. So hungry, boy . . .'

'There's something else.'

Grandfather's eyes lift. 'What is it?'

'Come outside, papa. Please. Please try.'

The boy tries to take him by the hand. At first he will not be taken, but at last he relents; the boy folds his hand inside Grandfather's and, pretending that it is the old man leading him, teases him out of the bivouac and along the wild grass. They have gone only yards from the shelter when Grandfather stops. The boy feels his weight on him, realizes he is using him as a crutch.

'Does it still hurt?'

'It won't stop hurting now.'

'Look,' says the boy.

He looks into the aspens, but it is not the trunks that have drawn his eye, nor the empty darknesses between. It is leaves, the colour of rust. Even as they watch, they spiral to the earth. A carpet of russet and gold spreads between the roots.

'It's going to be cold soon, papa. Then there'll be frost. Then ice and snow.'

Grandfather nods.

'The trees survive the winter, don't they, papa?'

'Yes.'

'But we can't. We don't have bark.'

Grandfather gives him a look that means: well, that's not quite true.

'We don't have enough food. We don't have enough furs.'

Something in Grandfather seems to relent. He holds the boy's shoulder with a hand near as skeletal as the trees are soon to become, and levers himself to the ground. As the boy watches him go, he has a dreadful premonition: his papa, lying down there and letting the wild grass part around him, letting the

200

leaves float down to make him a golden shroud. The trees would drink him up and here, in this distant stand of aspens, a trunk would bulge with his papa's face.

'What about baba's house?'

'What about it?'

'There's always baba's house. Don't you remember the hearth-fire? We lived a winter there once, papa. It was in the long ago, but we can live there again. And have the fire and catch our rabbits, and find cattails by the cattail pond.'

'I can't walk, boy.'

'You can. You can, papa.'

'I'll need help.'

'What can I do?'

'The trees will help you, boy. Here, take my axe.'

Grandfather reaches to the sling, now back at his belt, and draws out the axe. When the boy takes it in his hands, it seems strangely light.

'What should I do, papa?'

'Go into the trees, boy. Cut me a stick.'

Now the boy understands – something to help him walk. He goes into the first of the aspens. Here are trees with trunks tall, without any protrusions, and he has to go deep into the reddening mist before he finds what he needs: a rowan, its trunk split, with fists of branches opening up from close to the ground.

The wood is still soft, and the axe blade bites easily. The bough that falls is as tall as he is, with a fork at the top where Grandfather might rest his shoulder. It is too supple, perhaps, but it will harden. The boy hurries back to where his papa lies. 'Will it work?'

Grandfather's tongue is heavy. 'Give it here, boy.'

Awkwardly, his crooked leg hanging behind him, Grandfather rises. First he slides the axe back into the sling at his side. Then, he tries the crutch. The bough fits neatly into his shoulder. He puts his weight on it; the wood warps, but does not crack. He takes a step, pushing the branch out first, grinding it into the earth, and then heaving himself forward.

It is no third leg, but perhaps it will do.

There is snow before morning ends. It does not settle. What flakes there are are few, and pirouette around the boy as he works the sorceries to conjure up a campfire and hems it in with rocks from the undergrowth. Over the flames stew nettles and wild ransoms. The boy watches as a tiny flake eddies above, dissolving in the curling steam to add its water to the broth.

Soon he will need more clothes. He brings a rabbit fur out of the knapsack. Grandfather has taught him how to use sinew to bind them together, but his patchwork will need to be tighter come the deepest snows.

In the afternoon they cross the marshes, the boy going first to pick a path that Grandfather might follow. More than once they have to double back as the ground gives way underfoot. By the time they have reached the other side, and lurch again under the opening treetops, the evening dark is already gathering. Dusk creeps upon them earlier and earlier, night conquering day as insidiously as mama's cancer.

Another night, another camp, another flurry of snow through the brittle leaves. This time it leaves a dust on the forest floor so that, come morning, the boy will see the switchback tracks where rabbits have been running, or the tell-tale signs of fox and wild lynx.

By return of dusk they have reached the emperor oak. Alone among the trees of the forest, its leaves still hold their emerald hue. Mottled yellow and reds creep along their veins, but the fringes of the leaves still live.

'Not far now, papa.'

Grandfather only tips his scarred chin in reply.

The blackness is almost absolute when they come past the cattail pond. The boy goes to fill his tin can, and finds the thinnest sheen of ice forming on the surface. It fragments under the tiniest pressure of his fingers, and the water he draws up is too cold to drink, even if it was clean.

'We'll build a hearthfire, won't we, papa? And boil the water and make a soup. And I'll get in my eiderdown, and you can have your chair, and . . .'

They go on, following the old trail, changed and overgrown since last winter. In places the briars are beating a retreat, leaving trails marked in the earth. The boy kicks their tendrils out of his path, listens to the satisfying crunch underneath his feet that tells him: here comes the first frost of winter.

He is some way ahead of his papa when he reaches the edge of the forest. That is why he does not cry out when he sees the light through the trees. Instead, he dawdles to a stop, disbelieving his own eyes. The undergrowth has risen thick along the edge of the garden, and he recoils as his hands, reaching out to find a way through, are raked by thorns.

He senses a shuffling behind him, Grandfather catching up at last.

'What is it, boy? Why have you stopped?'

'Look, papa.'

The boy finds a likely tree, and grapples with the bark to hoist himself up. As he scrambles into the lowest boughs, he sees where the light is coming from. There are squares of it, in the face of a proud stone house: two lights on top and two lights on bottom, and another tiny point of yellow glaring from the lock of the door.

He sees this house, with its windows and curtains and porch, but he does not see the ruin. He whispers, 'Something happened, papa . . .'

Below, Grandfather levers forward, using his staff to force a path through the wall of thorns. The undergrowth closes behind him like a set of jaws, and then he is gone.

He is out of sight for only a few shuffling moments. Then he reappears. From his vantage in the tree, the boy watches him venture into the space where the garden once lay. Light spills from the windows, and Grandfather steps into its flickering pool.

Nothing is the same.

He moves like a shadow, a thing with three legs, misshapen as he claws his way to the edge of the house. For a moment it looks as if he is going to take the handle and venture in, but instead he simply follows the wall, cups his hand to the window as if he can peer in past curtains drawn tight.

Now, the boy drops awkwardly from the branch. Quietly, he leaves the fringe of forest and goes into the garden. Grandfather is still there, camouflaged against the wall of the new house. 'Papa, it's all gone . . .'

At the bottom, the stones are pitted and weathered, wearing the scars of a hundred winters. The boy's eyes drift up, and here the stones are smooth, chiselled only weeks or months ago. There is mortar between the stones, just like in the city, and the windows are set in frames of hard wood. On the door: a big brass knocker, with the face of a fairybook wolf.

He hears voices coming from inside the walls. He feels the heat radiating from the windows.

'Somebody's been sleeping in our beds, haven't they, papa?'

Grandfather nods.

'And somebody's been sitting in your chair, in my eiderdown.' Grandfather nods.

'And somebody's been eating at our fire, haven't they?'

Leaning into his staff, Grandfather takes off past the boy, through the thorns and back into the fringe of the forest.

'Papa!' the boy cries. 'Where are you going? Papa!'

Too late, he understands what he has done. He hears a low growl, turns to the door to see the fairybook wolf glowering down. Now the growl erupts. The door quakes. On the other side, some fell beast hurls itself at the wood.

'Down, Mishka!'

This voice is the voice of a man. It quells the dog in an instant.

'What is it, girl?' the man goes on, voice muffled by the wood. 'Is something out there?'

Unseen, the dog whimpers.

'You'll have to get used to it, girl. This isn't Brest anymore.'

Frozen in the middle of a lawn freshly planted, the boy watches as the fairybook wolf jolts, its jaw moving up and down as somebody fiddles with the lock inside. There comes a click, and then a sliver of light appears along the edge of the door frame. He can hear the dog named Mishka scrabbling to get out.

He turns. He flees.

He plunges, without thinking, into thorn. He would flee further, into the welcoming arms of the woodland, but other arms gather him up. He finds himself buried against Grandfather's shoulder, struggling to fight past. The old man is down on one knee, his staff cast aside. He holds him fast.

The boy reaches up, whispers into his papa's ear, 'The dog can smell us, papa.'

'No,' Grandfather intones. 'She can only smell the forest.'

A bright pool of light has fallen out of the open door, and from it a man has emerged. Perhaps he is no taller than Grandfather, but he holds himself differently, his back upright, his head with no stoop. The boy has to look twice, his vision impaired by this unfamiliar light, to see that he is carrying a shotgun at his side.

'It's *him*, papa . . .'

'Who?'

'Don't you remember? We were in the woods, and we found the murder tree, and then they came past – a mama and a papa and a little girl . . .'

Grandfather's head turns, to consider the stalking figure. 'Is it him?'

'They've taken our house, papa!'

The dog, a wolfish creature yet certainly no wolf, stays at the man's side. Only at the man's command does it nose forward, running its snout close to the ground. It turns in frenzied circles, finally landing on a scent and following it to the undergrowth at the edge of the garden.

Grandfather's arms around him, the boy feels himself drawn back, past another tree.

'There's nothing out here, Mishka.'

The dog pants, dismissively.

'Go on, in!'

Reticent, the dog drops its tail and turns to follow its master back towards the light. As the door closes, Grandfather's arms soften about the boy. He reels out of them, down the bank, back to the thorns. It is a moment before he understands in the roots of which tree he is standing. He looks up. The branches are bare; only a single leaf remains. He reaches out, plucks it, holds it tight in his fist.

'Mama?' he whispers, begging for a voice he knows gone.

'Come on, boy,' Grandfather murmurs. 'We mustn't stay here.'

'But why mustn't we? Maybe they'll . . .' The words fail him. '. . . let us in. Maybe there's a room. Maybe they'll let us share.'

In reply: only the wind in the trees.

'It's our house, papa.'

But all that Grandfather says is, 'We can't build a fire this close to the garden.'

Then the old man turns. Three lurches and he is gone to the forest.

The boy remains, huddled in the roots of mama's tree. He watches as the lights die, one by one, in the house, until finally only one is left.

Something about that window, lit up in brilliant white light, captivates him. It is not like the drab oranges and reds that would stare out of the tenement walls like diseased, scabrous eyes. It is clean and bright. It is a portal into some other world, where the walls don't let in the wind, where there are beds and bedspreads and mamas and papas to put a little boy to bed, a world where the wolf is a loyal companion and not some rival to scrap with over a shred of red meat.

His eyes linger on the window for the longest time. Yet it is only as he stands to finally heed his papa's call that he knows why he has been staring. For there, in the window, its underbelly lit up by slivers of light coming up from beneath the ledge, stands the little Russian horse that was a present from his mother. Its chipped eye glaring. Its mouth, open and wild.

WINTER RETURNS

'What will we do, papa?'

The old man brings the axe from his sling, seems to study it in his hand. With a flick of the wrist, he sends it sailing over the cattails to bury its blade in the bark of the elm hanging there, its branches twisted as if to mock.

He opens his mouth and makes a gurgling sound, a rough approximation of words. Then, turning his shoulder, he reels down the incline to the waters. A thin pane of ice, already shattered in places, bobs in the surface. He stabs it with his staff, fracturing it further, and levers himself down to take in the water. He seems to have forgotten the lesson that he taught the boy in that long-ago winter: still waters must be boiled. Now he is like an animal, uncaring for the globules of black he takes into his lips.

211

The boy takes a tiny step after him, ventures the words so softly, 'Papa, what about the tenement?'

The old man looks up. Dusk has hardened to night and, without luminescent snow, the woodland dark is already impenetrable. His eyes sink, his brow creases, and the boy wonders: does he even remember the word?

'We could go back to the tenement. Papa, the car . . .'

The old man braces himself on his staff and rises. Coming back up the slope, his single jackboot slips. He sprawls forward, struggles to right himself. The boy reaches out, offers a hand, but the old man will not take it.

'Come on, papa. I'll take us there. I remember the way.'

To get there, they must go back in the direction of . . . He can no longer call it a ruin. He can no longer call it baba's house. How did he not know that, when that family came to the woods, they were coming to take his home?

He sets off in that direction, scenting chimney smoke ahead, but he knows after only a few steps that the old man is not following. Looking back, he sees him standing at the elm, with his hands wrapped around the handle of the axe.

'Papa, please?'

The axe sails out of the trunk, carrying the old man with it. In one oddly graceful motion, he swoops around and, still leaning into his staff, comes after the boy, his single jackboot heel clicking behind.

They emerge from woodland halfway up the dell, where the grasses sparkle with frost. The lights are still on in the house: not the light of hearthfires or a cookfire behind the kitchen grate, but buzzing electric lights like he last saw at the school-house. For a moment they stand on the fringes of the forest, hawthorn tendrils around their shins; then he thinks to venture out.

'No, boy!'

The boy's eyes plead with the old man, but the old man takes him by the scruff and ushers him back into the forest. 'They'll *see*.'

Even so, they skirt the very edge of the dell. As they go, the boy's eyes are drawn back to the glowing face of the cottage. He sees shadows move against curtains lit up like gold. He thinks he sees three: a mama, a papa and . . . the little girl? The same one from that day in the forest? She had hair as golden as mama's, and a scarlet coat with a hood that bobbed behind.

Soon they plunge back into the woodland. The shape of the forest has shifted through summer, so that now new branches claw out, and now new thickets of undergrowth have fought their way into being. The boy doubts he can remember the way after all, but it does not matter, for suddenly the old man is leading. He strides in front, his staff a third leg keeping him aloft.

They do not follow a trail. They weave between chestnuts and beech, and reel down a bank to where the car is sitting.

The old man lurches towards its bonnet, stepping aside to reveal it to the boy.

That thing sitting at the bottom of the bank used to be the car. It used to bounce him up and down as it bore him between the school and the ruin. Now it is a jagged, discoloured shell. Its yellow has gone, to be replaced by bubbling brown as he imagines a sea of lava. It is not only ice that rimes its windows and rims, but creeping greens too, moss of a hue that makes him think of disease. The wheels are bedded in thickets of their own, tough grass and thorns. A claw of briar grows from the darkness underneath and plasters itself across the back wind-screen like a splayed hand.

The boy sobs, 'But maybe she works, papa. Maybe she still works.'

The old man rounds the car. At first the boy thinks him inspecting it for wear, when really the damage is plain to see. Then he looks again: his papa has the same look as the storybook wolf on the new house's door. His fingers appear from his sleeve and stroke the sling at his side.

'No, papa!'

The boy starts forward, but already the old man has wrenched the axe from its sling. He lifts it high, brings it down in an arc almost magnificent, to strike the windscreen. Glass erupts. Snagged in the crumpling sheet, the blade keens. Weeping now, the boy presses his hands over his ears, watches through a blurred veil as his papa opens up the bonnet and plunges the axe inside.

He draws it back, trailing wires, black with ooze.

In an instant, all is calm. The old man cleans the blade on a tussock of wild grass. His mouth thick with tongue: 'She was dead already, boy.'

'I know,' the boy whimpers. 'But I want her back.'

'You ate all her gingerbreads.'

The boy draws away. He screams, 'I was talking about the car!'

Then, though he doesn't know it, he is on his feet and rampaging at his papa. With only a whisper of dark between them, he stops. He looks up through eyes thick with tears – but these are the tears of anger, of fury, and when he sees his papa it is like that time, last winter, when he was sealed up inside the car and saw a forest shade coming to stalk him.

'Why, papa? You ruined her, you ruined . . .'

'I didn't ruin her. It was cancer ruined her.'

The boy reaches up, thinking to drag the axe out of his papa's hand, but the old man turns back across the trail and into the trees.

'You're lying, papa.'

The old man stops dead. One turn over his shoulder, the ruinous half of his face. 'Lying, boy?'

'We *could* go back to the tenement. We *could* go back to baba's house. You just . . . don't want to.'

His papa glowers, the axe still in his hand. For a second, the boy hears the echo of some long-forgotten dream. *He's coming out of the woods.*

'Why can't we, papa?'

A whispered, mocking echo: 'Why can't we, papa?'

'Well, why can't we? They have a little girl, papa. They look after her. Maybe they can look after us.'

This time, the old man simply shakes his head. That there are no words, that there are no reasons . . . The silence explodes in the boy. 'You promised, papa. You promised you'd look after me!'

He takes off through the trees. He thinks he hears the whistle of air as his papa's gnarled arms reach out to gather him up, but in an instant he is through them, tumbling through familiar darknesses until he reaches the top of the glade.

Sky heavy with cloud, but no snow yet. He is about to skirt the glade but this time there is no old man to insist he must not be seen, so he strides on out. Each footstep is tantamount to treachery, but he loves them, each and every one.

By the time he reaches mama's tree, the lights are out in the windows of the house. He lingers in the forest and stares at the new façade. It is hardly believable that this rose out of the ruins of baba's house. Its walls are finely chiselled stone, its windows plates of glass inside which hang curtains and vases of flowers.

There is nothing to look at, nothing moving, and for a moment that itself is hypnotic: no branches stirring to tell him which way the breeze flies, no shadows darting as his eyes pick out quarry or tell him to run.

The coldness gathers. He thinks: winter's coming sooner than I thought.

He thinks: I could knock on the door and it would be rat-tat-tat, *Izboushka! Izboushka!* and the hut on hen's feet would turn and let him in.

But he does not cross the garden and he does not knock at the door. Soon, he hears the familiar click of a jackboot heel.

'Are you coming home, or not?'

The words have a smothering to them. They are like the snows that will come and banish the leaves. They cling to him and their flakes lock against each other to give him a new skin: a white crust, frozen, impenetrable, dulling everything that is good within.

He looks up. There stands his papa, a hunched shape in the snow dark.

Home, he said, and all the boy can picture are branches and demon trees with the faces of murdered men.

The boy nods, but by the time he has got to his feet to follow, his papa is already gone. He allows himself one last look at the dark façade of the house before he goes after him.

At that moment, up on the house's face, a square of light flares. He is so busy marvelling that their ruin now has an upstairs where there was once only empty air that he does not, at first, pick out the shadow on the other side. When he does, his eyes will not work; he cannot distinguish whether it is a mama or a papa, a boy or a girl. It is only when the curtains are drawn back, allowing that unreal light to spill out, that he sees.

The little girl.

She hangs over the ledge with the window thrown wide, as if breathing in the scent of the wind. Her hair, tied back, is even the same shape as his mama's, curled up and flicked out at her shoulders. The smaller features of her face are in darkness but, as she claws out for the window frame, he can see her in profile: as angelic as mama in miniature, her nightdress spotted with stars.

From deep inside, there comes a voice. 'Elenya, the window!'

'I'm closing it, mama . . .'

'You're letting the winter in!'

The boy watches until the window is closed, the curtains drawn, the electric light snuffed.

Elenya, he thinks, that one word filled with a thousand meanings. The little girl is named Elenya.

At the edge of the clearing: the camp. In the morning, the boy wakes before his papa. He uses sorceries to resurrect the fire and places chestnuts on a stone set in the flames.

At first light, the old man rises. 'You didn't have to wake early, boy.'

'I'm looking after you.'

The old man accepts the food. Its effect is almost visible on him, bringing colour back to skin webbed in blue, brightness back to his eyes.

'I don't need looking after.'

What his papa means is: I don't need looking after by *you*. But the boy doesn't want to hear it.

'We can't stay here, can we, papa? We need a home.'

The old man spits a charred shell of chestnut into the frost. He spreads his crooked arms. To the boy he is saying: look around you; there isn't a branch or root in this wild expanse that you don't call home.

'We had the bunker, didn't we? Maybe we could go back to the bunker.'

The old man snorts, 'Not across the marshes.'

'Is it too far?'

'Treacherous in winter, boy. The ice can tell lies about what's underneath.'

The boy busies himself stoking the fire. He finds stones to roast in the cauldron, things they can hold onto or put into the crooks of their arms to keep away the chills. So intent is he on his work that he does not realize his papa has unsheathed the axe, is lurching around the edge of the clearing with his eyes on the branches.

'What is it, papa?'

The old man brings back the axe, buries it in the crook of branch and trunk. The blade disappears. He wrenches it back out, swings again, and reels back onto his staff as the branch falls.

'For the fire?'

The old man gives a simple nod of his head. Then he utters five sharp, staccato words:

'There's going to be snow.'

It comes before the sun is at its height. Clouds gather to blot out the pale light, the whiteness deepens, and then the first flakes float through the branches.

By first fall of snow they have followed the trail past the cattail pond and into the shadow of the emperor oak. Great branches spread out above, still laden with leaves of russet and gold. For now, this will be shelter enough. What few flakes find their way between the branches are tiny, and eddy on the soft woodland breeze. When they touch the fire, they hiss and vanish, steam masquerading as smoke.

The old man leaves him to hunt. There was a time when the boy would beg to go too, but that was last winter; summer has come and gone since, and now he does not need to follow his papa into the trees. Instead he stays behind. The snows are already here and there is much work to be done. If they do not have the ruin, they must still have a home.

He starts by heaving the boughs his papa has severed towards the trunk of the emperor oak and piling them up. At his feet run rivers of roots, and between the roots are great crevices into which he can drive the end of each branch. He forces the first into one of the cavities and, when he steps back, it remains upright, like the post in a fence. He takes another and forces that into a crevice on the furthest side of the tree. Three more go between and, in that way, he has built a wall. Soon the ice will come to freeze them in place but, for now, they are sturdy enough.

He is about to set off, in search of pine branches to keep out the wind, when his papa reappears, dragging himself through the twilight under the trees. He comes empty-handed, his face turned down. He stops, looks at the boy's work. His eyes fall back to the fire. 'You let it burn down.'

'Papa, I'm making us a house . . .'

The old man levers himself over the flames and fans them back to life. 'If the fire dies, you . . .' Something chokes the words in his throat. 'Didn't I teach you anything,' the old man grunts, 'this summer?'

'Did you find anything, papa?'

The old man lifts his taloned hand, but he is holding no rabbit. 'I threw for one. I missed.'

'Is it your hand?'

'The cold got into it.'

'I can go, papa.'

The old man's eyes burn, just as fiercely as the new flames. 'There's nothing abroad. The snow drives them under.'

'We did it last winter.'

'Last winter we had snares.'

'I'll find more nettles. We'll make more snares. Or . . .'

The old man splays his fingers out over the fire and, in turn, moves each one back and forth. Only once he is satisfied does he speak again. 'Or what?'

He braces himself. He will try it. One last time. His papa's still in there, somewhere. 'What about baba's house?'

His papa's head hangs low, nostrils flared and breathing in smoke. 'What about it?'

'We can ask them, papa.'

'Listen to me, boy. It isn't your baba's house anymore. It isn't a place. The walls are treacherous. They grew up and changed and they don't want us anymore. What do you think's lying in those walls? The stones don't remember. Only the trees.'

The boy says, 'They're looking after the little girl, papa. They could look after us too.'

'I told you once before about friends. What did I tell you, boy?'

It was so long ago, but the boy remembers: 'Having friends is a dangerous thing.'

'Don't go down to baba's house, boy. It isn't for us anymore.'

*

It takes a season to raise a house from a ruin, but deep in the *pushcha* it can take mere days for a gingerbread house to be baked. The boy bakes it from branches and boughs, with roots for a carpet and pine needles to keep out the wind. He tends to it now, pressing the night's snowfall around its bottom, packing it hard so that he will have walls of ice. He takes snowballs squeezed between his hands and uses them to line the entrance, where two great severed boughs of pine scissor and come apart. He will make an archway of ice, and excavate a winding path across the clearing, something to guide his papa home.

Last night was four nights since the new snows fell, but the first night that the old man came inside. At first he slept out, curled crooked around the cookfire, but last night he could not settle; the snow filtered through the branches, dusting him, and the cold worked its way too easily into his bones. The boy was lying in the den when the pine fronds came apart – and in lurched his papa, dead leg dragged behind him, a vision of the woodland itself.

'You should have a fire in here, boy.'

'I made you a bed, papa.'

It was only a nest of more pine, but warmer than the hard forest earth. Without a word, his papa sunk into it. He had already closed his eyes, already begun to make his unearthly night-time noises, when his lips came apart and uttered those familiar words.

This isn't the tale, he breathed with eyes still closed, *but an opening.*

'Papa?'

The boy stole to his side, thought to lay his hands on skin as hard as bark, but hovered there instead.

222

The tale comes tomorrow, after the meal, when we are filled with soft bread.

'There won't be any bread, papa. There won't be a meal, not unless . . .'

The old man's eyes opened. He straightened himself, and now he was looking at the boy with a clarity he could not remember since before summer began: eyes bright enough not to reflect the branches that cupped them.

And now, he whispered, *we start our tale. Long, long ago, when we did not exist, when perhaps our great-grandfathers were not in the world, in a land not so very far away, on the earth in front of the sky, on a plain place like on a wether, seven versts aside, a man journeyed to the ends of the world on a train shut to the sky. He was a little pig sent to market and when the train stopped he was in the world of Perpetual Winter, at the gates of that great frozen city called Gulag.*

'Papa,' the boy whispered. 'Papa, are you okay?'

But his papa didn't answer, nor even seem to notice that anyone had spoken. And the boy thought: it's the story he didn't tell, the story he wouldn't tell . . .

With eyes open but blind, his papa continued.

Well, the great city of Gulag squatted on the Lena, whose ancient waters wended their way to lands where few men had ever trod. And the train released its prisoners onto tundra empty and white, and the train said: leave me now, go through the gates into Gulag, and know that your lives begin here, for all that happened before was a dream.

Well, some men gibbered and some men quailed, and they were the men who believed that this frozen city was the dream, and that they might wake up soon in the beds of their mamas and wives. But the great city gates of Gulag drew back, and through those teeth of ice they walked, and to the soldier it seemed as if he was being swallowed whole, by one of those great beasts who used to stalk the land in the days before men.

Gulag was wide and Gulag was wild and Gulag was the world forever and ever. On glassy streets of ice he walked, and in alleys and derelict squares he saw men turned to ice and rooted to the ground, like statues under enchantments and put to sleep for hundreds of years. Well, the new prisoners drifted into those alleys, and the soldier said to himself: what must I do, now that I am of Gulag, and where must I live?

He wandered aimless, following shadows in the streets, and those shadows had voices and some shadows had names. He went through empty buildings, empty halls, and climbed to the top of an empty tower, where yet more men were frozen and rooted to the earth. And he said: what magic happens in Gulag that men should freeze where they stand?

Soon the soldier heard the tolling of a distant bell. In the tower where he stood he went to the parapet, and from there could see the rolling roofs and minarets of Gulag, and it was strange to know that this was sky and this was street, for all about him was white.

Soon, he saw shadows in the street. And he took them for phantoms, because not since he came through Gulag's gates had he seen real men. But soon he heard footsteps in the tower, and upon turning saw a man appear to face him. Now there was silence as he had never known. The man's breath curled up, like a frightful dragon. He stepped forward, and it seemed he had murder on his mind.

Who are you? barked the soldier, who once was a little boy who believed in ghosts in the wood.

And the stranger held out his hand and said: do not be afraid, *for I am like you, lost in Perpetual Winter with hardly a friend. On his feet were gleaming black boots, which were called jackboots. And on his shoulder he wore a knapsack, with his name stitched onto it in the language of his home. It was a language the soldier did not know, for this man was of the Kingdom of the Finns, whose name is Finn Land, and had been captured there by yet more wise men of the Winter King.*

The boy listened to his papa's wheezing but for the first time tore his eyes from the old man's face. They fell, instead, on the knapsack in the corner. His hands reached out to trace the lettering on the frayed strap, dancing across the rim of his papa's last remaining jackboot.

What is Gulag? asked the soldier. And why do men freeze in the streets, to stand as statues?

Men are magicked if they do not serve, and stand cold sentry on the streets to serve as warning for others. For all men sent here by the Winter King must serve in the great underworld halls, where there is no night or day. We must serve so that Gulag grows, and they say if we serve we may go home.

Do you know anyone who ever went home?

I know nobody who ever went home.

Yet, I am a man, and I must go back, back to my babe in the woods.

The man, whose name was Aabel, looked forlorn and said: I have heard the fable before, for all men have their own babes in the woods, but a story is a hopeless thing, now you come to Gulag. Come instead to me and I will look after you, for I have saved food I have stolen and will share it with you that you might not starve.

But why would you help a stranger like me?

And Aabel said: if we starve, we will starve together, you and

I, for here in the heart of this frozen city called Gulag, a man knows good from evil, and I can see that there is goodness in your heart. From now on, we will call each other brothers and eat of each other's bread.

And the man, who once was a boy, wept for a crust, and in that way lived another day.

The old man opened his mouth to close the tale, but this time the words would not come. The bright blueness bled from his eyes; now they were grey and haunted again. He rolled over and did not look at the boy.

'Papa,' the boy said, crawling near, unable to look at the knapsack in the corner. 'Is it true?'

Dead words from a dead man, dead leg twitching as if in some fevered dream: *oh, I know it is true, for one was there one was there one was there.*

And all through the night, the boy saw the rooftops of that great fabled city throbbing in his dreams.

In the morning, the old man is gone for kindling and whatever kills his crippled hands can make. The boy takes a moment to stir up the fire, tossing on stones to keep the heat and yet more wood to feed it. Then he takes up his knapsack. He pauses to look at the distinct stitching on the strap and wonders: how can a thing from a story be here, in my hands? But he cannot dwell on it for long, for soon the day will be old, and instead he follows his papa's distinctive trail into the trees.

The gingerbread house is, perhaps, only an hour's walk from baba's house, but the boy does not head in that direction. He follows an escarpment down, to where he knows there are still a few hazels to be found and the berries of the rowan. He means to go after other treasures too: sweet chestnuts for roasting and the small brambles of the thorny briar.

It takes long hours to fill his knapsack. He has to resist the temptation to gorge on the woodland fodder he has foraged, and on an empty gut he makes the march back up the escarpment. He can find the trail to the gingerbread house by instinct now, and by the time he enters the clearing he already knows his papa is there. The smell of the camp smoke is strong; it seems he must have a rabbit, because in the smoke are the smells of grease and baking flesh.

The old man turns over his shoulder at the boy's approach. Splayed around him are the creature's entrails, its hide. He is crafting new moccasins for the boy to wear, something to spare his feet from the forest floor.

'What is it, papa?'

'Rabbit. What have you got?'

The boy has had his arm draped over the knapsack, as if to protect it from famished rooks and crows, but the old man's eyes have found it already.

'It's berries. Nuts.'

'No good. You need winter fat. To keep out the cold. We have to take a boar. A bison.'

'They're not for us, papa. I'm . . .'

The sad look in the old man's eyes makes him waver and he crosses the clearing to sit at his papa's side. Once there the smell of the rabbit is undeniably delicious. So that he might bring something to the feast, he sets out two handfuls each of sweet chestnuts and hazel. That, he says, is enough. The rest must be saved.

'Winter's not so deep that we need to starve on purpose.'

'No, papa, it isn't that. They're . . . for somebody else.'

The old man's hands sink into the fire to bring back the glistening flesh. The way he glowers is question enough to compel the boy to answer.

'It's for the little girl. To take a basket to baba's house.'

The rabbit breaks in his papa's hand, revealing flesh still pink and bones that ooze. He sets half down with his own hazels and sweet chestnuts and dangles the other half over the boy's hoard.

Then a word, soft as a snowflake: 'No.'

At first, the boy thinks he is going to go on – but it seems the old man has said it all. He lifts the carcass to his lips, slurping at the ooze that dribbles out.

'No, papa?'

'No.'

'Why no?'

'Look at you. Look what the wild gave you today. Why would you . . .'

'It's for the girl, papa. To have a taste of the forest.'

'A taste of the . . .'

'You gave me a taste of the forest. Why can't the girl . . .'

The old man sinks his teeth back into the creature. 'You don't know what the forest really tastes of, boy. I hope you never do.'

'Papa, please.'

'I thought you knew not to beg.'

'I'm not begging.'

'It sounds like begging.'

The boy feels as if he has his hands plunged into the cattail pond, but every newt he tries to snatch up just slips through his fingers.

It's now or not at all. The boy takes a breath. 'It's to make friends, papa. Like it used to be. I used to . . . have friends.'

The old man lays down the carcass and wipes his fingers dry on the rags clinging to his dead leg. Somewhere, among those rags, is what is left of mama's shawl. The boy's eyes try to find it, but it was gone long ago.

The old man grunts, perhaps in acquiescence.

'Then I can go?'

He grunts again, a sound neither no or yes.

Gingerly, the boy stands. Gingerly, he puts the knapsack on his shoulder. 'I'm coming back, papa. I just want . . . Do you want to come?'

The old man only shifts, as if nestling down into leaves and fallen pine needles. He does not look as the boy steals past him. He does not look as the boy disappears between the trees.

As he goes, the thoughts tear him like a lacerating wind. His papa went into the earth one thing and came out of it another, just like any old hibernating bear. It is as if the aspens sucked him under and tried to drink him up, their roots salivating for the taste of a man, just like in those stories of partisans and soldiers marching out to murder in the trees – but his papa escaped the roots too soon, so they could only drink half of him up. Now he is half man and half forest, lumbering through the branches gasping for words. And that story he started to tell . . .

The boy does not know he is so angry until he sees the lights in the face of his baba's old house. A little drift of snow has built up on the back step, so that he knows nobody has come through it today, and the kitchen windows are fogged. He steals along the edge of the garden and finds the gap in the thorn where he can peep around the side of the house. The pebble drive is a strange landscape of stone and pitted ice, but there is no truck sitting on it, and nor can he see one stuttering up the steep dell. Wherever the girl and her father have gone, they are not at baba's house today.

He retraces his steps and reaches the backdoor. The door knocker is frosted, the fairybook wolf glistening out of shape. He thinks he can hear the dog named Mishka snuffling on the other side, perhaps lonesome without the girl to keep her company, and he decides to sit on the step. A pet dog would be a fine thing to have in the wilderness. It could keep you warm at night even if there wasn't a fire.

After a little while, he hears the dog whimper and retreat from the door. Now it is time to do what he came here to do. He takes the knapsack from his shoulder, stands, and places it gently on the step. When he has it exactly how he wants it, he takes one last look and goes back across the garden.

The lowest branches of mama's tree are too thin to swing from, so instead he scrambles up a neighbouring tree, balances on one of the heavier boughs and, in that way, works his way into the crook of one of mama's taller branches. In spring this cranny would be cocooned from the world, with hardly enough air to breathe. Now he can see through the wraithlike branches and look down on the house.

He waits. After a little while, he sees starlings gathering like a funeral host. Soon, their caw goes up and he realizes why they are summoning each other. They begin to make raids on the knapsack, taking off with half-frozen rowan berries and brambles. To drive them off, the boy collects up stones, and rains them down from on high. The most determined birds still run the gauntlet, but he works out a way of keeping the worst at bay: a single stone thrown at the kitchen window will raise the ire of Mishka, whose unearthly din sends the starlings flocking back to the forest.

230

The light does not last long. Soon, dusk threatens. The boy's eyes wander the face of the house. If he screws his eyes just so, he can make out the Russian horse standing proudly in the girl's bedroom window. Wanting to see more, he finds a way further up the tree. Almost at the canopy, he is on a level with the window.

He is so focused on the Russian horse that he does not notice the deepening of night. Nor does he notice the distant hum of an engine. It is only when a door slams and he hears the now-familiar voice of the girl that he takes his eyes from the Russian horse.

'Daddy, I'm telling you, it was no such thing! I . . .'

Her father's gruff voice: 'I've heard enough of it, Elenya. It's a new school. You were going to behave.'

'I did behave! It was that dastardly . . .'

'Dastardly?'

'It's a word, daddy.'

'I know it's a . . .'

Now a third voice chimes in, a woman the boy takes for Elenya's mother. She has a voice not unlike his mama's used to be, soft but with an air of severity.

'That's enough, from the both of you. It's all I've heard ever since we left town.'

'I'm sorry, mama.'

'Don't you think you should say sorry to your father?'

'Perhaps.'

There is a grin in how she says it, something that must incite even more ire in her father – because the boy hears the stamping of heavy feet, the slamming of another door.

'Elenya, you'll be the death of him. He works and works and . . .'

'I know, mama. I'm ever so ungrateful.'

At last, the mother laughs. 'Elenya, I'll let you in through the kitchen. Take those dirty boots off before you . . .'

'Yes, mama!'

Before her mother has finished, the girl comes skipping around the side of the house. In the waning light, the boy can see why she was in such trouble: she is wearing a prim dress of embroidered flowers, but precisely half her body, from head to toe, is caked in thick mud, as if she has deliberately lain down in a puddle.

She skips ungainly across the garden and up to the backdoor. In the fogged glass of the kitchen window, the boy can see the face of Mishka, front paws scrabbling, excited beyond measure to receive the girl.

Elenya stops, her gaze drifting down to the step. She seems to consider the knapsack carefully before she ventures an approach. Crouching, she studies it from every angle. Then, she plants herself squarely alongside it. She is facing the forest now, and the boy can see the way her features contort, as if trying to puzzle out this conundrum. Her fingers hover over the frosted berries and nuts, and then dart down to snatch one up. She holds it up, looks as if she might toss it away. Then, quick as a snowstorm, she pops it inside her mouth.

'Elenya, I told you to . . .'

Her mother's voice rips through the walls, and the door flies open. In the light stands her mother, her father slouching somewhere behind.

'Elenya, you still have those filthy boots on! Do you want to stay out here all night?'

'Mama, be fair!' the girl protests. 'Look what I . . .'

'What have you got there, Elenya?' Her mother steps out, holding herself against the cold. 'Get off it, Elenya! It's filthy!'

The girl scrambles up from the step, leaving the knapsack where it sits. 'It's fruits, mama, and chestnuts too.'

'Your father's going to be . . .'

The girl lifts one mud-caked boot up and slams it down. 'Mama, it's not *mine*. I didn't do a thing. I was coming to take off my boots and do just as I was told, and then it was *there*.'

Calmer now, her mother lifts the knapsack. She must think it's a vile thing, because she holds the strap at a distance, between thumb and forefinger, as if to get it too close to her body might be to catch some woodland disease. 'Where did it come from, Elenya?'

The girl pouts. 'I *told* you. It was on the step.'

It does not matter that it's the truth, not when the truth isn't good enough.

'Inside, Elenya.'

The girl tramps towards the step, but her mother stands irresolute, blocking the way.

'*After* you've taken off those horrible boots.'

Once the girl is gone, the boy sits satisfied in mama's tree. He might have lost the knapsack, but the nuts and fruits, they're inside baba's house. It is, he decides, almost as if the woods themselves have gone through the doors. The idea makes him enormously proud.

It is almost time to go back and find his own papa, to unearth the old man from whatever leaves and snowflakes have fallen on him as he sleeps. He must go soon, but something makes the boy linger.

He senses movement in one of the bedroom windows and his eyes stray back to the little Russian horse, standing guard

233

upon the ledge. The girl appears, touches him gently on the head and rearranges him so that he is keeping watch on a different corner of the garden. Then she crouches down, her elbows poised beside the Russian horse. Together they seem to be surveying the treetops.

At once, Elenya reaches under the ledge and, with something held in her hands, scurries away from the window. For a while, only the Russian horse looks out. Then, the boy sees the door shudder and Elenya squirms out. Though dirt still smears her face, she is wearing a nightgown pure and white.

Mishka is desperate to follow, but Elenya battles him back. She lays whatever was in her hands upon the step, and then slopes back within. If she is as wily as the boy thinks, her mother and father need never know she was gone.

Moments later, she reappears with the Russian horse above. Mishka is beside her too, forepaws up on the ledge despite Elenya's protestations to sit – and together the three faces peer down.

The boy waits until his curiosity can wait no longer, and drops through the branches of the tree. As he steals across the garden to whatever treasure has been left on the step, he keeps his head low, resists the urge to look up.

In the dull light from the kitchen window, he can see a little bundle, wrapped up like a baby in its swaddling cloth. This, he remembers, was the way that the babe in the woods was found in his papa's fables.

The bundle is small and light, and he sees now that it is wrapped not in cloth but in thin paper, already matted with moisture. It is a moment before he recollects: this is tissue paper, the kind a little boy might once have used if he was making toilet.

Inside is a figure made out of . . . He sniffs it, and finds to his delight that it is made out of biscuit. There is a faint hint of honey, sugar, treacle. Ginger. He angles it to what light is left, and sees two raisins for eyes, and something like coloured frost to make pyjamas in blue and white lines.

He thinks to eat it there and then, cram it into his craw like his stomach is telling him, but when he looks at the little face, the make-believe bedclothes, the tissue paper blankets, he knows he is not holding tonight's dinner. He is, instead, holding a little friend. He will keep the biscuit baby for his very self, take it back to the gingerbread house and not even tell his papa.

He cradles it across the garden and back into the fringe of the forest. Once he is in the shadow of mama's branches, he looks up. Elenya still sits in the square of light, her face poised in the cups of her hands. He thinks he can see her eyebrows twitch, as if admonishing him for some imagined ill.

With one hand still holding the biscuit baby, the boy lifts a fist. At first, he is uncertain how to do it. His fingers remember before his mind. He shakes his wrist and his fingers open one at a time, to wriggle and dance, each out of step with the other.

In the square of light, the little girl suddenly perks up. She scrambles bodily onto the ledge, presses her face up against the glass. As she does so, her knee catches the little Russian horse, and he cartwheels out of sight. Mishka leaps up, but there is no more room at the window. The girl lifts her hand, shakes her wrist. The boy might not remember, but Elenya never forgot how. She waves.

In the forest below, the boy sees her waving. Suddenly, his hand remembers. He steps out of the shadows, waves again. In the window, Elenya freezes. She hesitates a moment, returns the wave; as if to mirror her, the boy does exactly the same.

In that way, minutes pass. Hours. Winter retreats to reveal summer, retreats to reveal winter again. His papa is well and mama alive; there are tenements, streets, schoolhouses, and all is as it was.

The boy turns and, with the girl still gaping in the window, disappears into the forest.

S ome nights his papa sleeps outside the gingerbread house, and some nights, if the boy is wily enough to leave the pine-needle doors apart, he can be tempted inside. Yet now there are more and more nights when the old man is abroad.

Where he goes, the boy does not know. He thinks he cannot roam far, because his dead leg drags behind him and more often he must throw himself into his staff to carry him through the woods. But there are nights when the boy tries to follow and, although his trail is a deep furrow on the woodland floor, from emperor oak to cattail pond the old man is nowhere to be seen.

At nights he stays awake and thinks about his papa's return. He is not alone, because in the corner of the gingerbread house sleeps the baby of biscuit. He talks to it as his mama once talked to him. He tells it the woodland stories, of baba's people and the wars of winter, and the baby in turn tells him stories of Elenya and Mishka, and the adventures of the Russian horse. Now that she has waved to him, he thinks of the girl more and more often. She is the one who sleeps in his bed and sits in his chair and eats all of his food. If she has his Russian horse, it means she has his eiderdown too.

A friend would be a very fine thing, when all you have had is your papa and the forest.

This morning, he would dearly love to have his eiderdown. Sometimes, when he wakes, his bones are stiff and it is not until he has conjured back the fire and filled himself with pine-needle tea that he can think about going out into the woodland, looking for forage. His new rabbit-hide moccasins keep his toes from freezing, but the cold can always claw in through the threadbare stitching of his rabbit-skin vest; nettle fibres are not good for everything.

The boy is awake before first light, but it is only as the sunlight is piercing the canopy that he crawls out of the gingerbread house to whisper the fire back to life. His papa must have been and gone already, because he has left two carcasses for the spit: a dead hare and a dead fox. The fox's pelt will be especially welcome, because the rabbit hides the boy is wearing are worn thin and fraying apart.

Once he has eaten his fill, he resolves to go after his papa. It is easy to see where the old man has gone. All he has to do is follow the trench carved by his trailing leg. This morning, he follows the track down past the emperor oak, as if his papa is following the old paths, all the way around the cattail pond and down to Elenya's house. In a depression between two dead elms he finds

238

the remnants of a fire where the old man has stirred a cauldron; that the ashes are warm tells him he has not long gone from this place. Yet, when he carries on, he finds another dead fire, and another one still – and, for the first time, he realizes that they are not bulwarked with stones in the way his papa always taught him. In fact, he can tell from the fall of branches in one that these were not fires built by his papa at all. They are ugly, ill-hewn things of the sort he himself might have built one whole winter ago, when he was stupid and young.

He is crouching, with his fingers deep in ash, when he sees the strange depressions at the fire's edge. At first he takes it for the print of some monstrous fox. If the ash has been shifted by the wind he might even take the print for one left by a woodland lynx. Only – he has seen the prints of lynxes before; he has seen the prints of foxes and wolves. This one is unlike any of those; it has great pads like he imagines a bear's, with three toes and talons that seem to be clipped in straight, ugly squares. When he looks closely, he can see the prints of four paws. And – lynxes would not come sniffing around a campfire. Foxes might look for something to scavenge, but wolves too would keep downwind.

He looks up: the flicker of shadows in the trees; the crunch of broken frost underfoot.

That is when he sees the girl coming through the wood.

She is still some distance away. He sees her only in the sudden shower of snow from a disturbed branch, the cry of a wood pigeon hurtling out of its roost. Yet he has no doubt it is her; the girl must be skipping, because there is strange music to the way her feet fall. At once, the boy understands the prints at the edges of the fire: the dog named Mishka is at the girl's side.

He is still squatting over the dead fire when he hears her

voice. She is, in a tone reminiscent of her mother's, admonishing the poor dog.

'You'll be for it when we get back! It'll be a bath in front of the fire for you . . . And you won't like it one bit. You'll whimper and wail and, if you start howling, father's going to come after you with his slipper!'

The boy counts: one, two, three . . . And here they come. He can see one arm swinging, the other wrapped around a big bundle of sticks. The girl appears to be wearing a coat three sizes too big, a thing that makes her seem like a sheep gone wild and unsheared for too many seasons. On her head sits a scarlet hood, lined in fur eerily akin to the bitch at her side. Her cheeks are pinched, her nose glistening where the cold has coaxed it to run.

They are about to come crashing into the clearing when the boy turns tail and flees. One bank of the clearing is still deep with dying bracken. Quickly, he loses himself in the ferns.

When he peers up, fingers forcing a gap between two fronds, he sees the girl march up to the dead fire. Oblivious to the boy's footprints, she dumps the wood she has collected straight on top of the ash. Seemingly aggrieved that it does not instantly burst into flame, she drops to her knees. As Mishka steals underneath to steal a stick, Elenya begins to toss them aside, revealing the obliterated embers underneath.

'Now I'll have to start again!' she declares, as if it is the poor mutt's fault that the night is black, the sun is wan, the snow is in the sky. 'Give that back, you brute!'

Mishka settles on the far side of the clearing, gnawing happily.

'I tell you, I'm going to make them give you a double bath, and dry biscuits for dinner!'

This the dog must understand. The stick rolls out of her teeth and she whimpers, sadly.

Elenya sets to work. The boy can see she has no idea what she is doing; this is a game, and the other dead fires he has seen in the wild are merely past attempts at playing the game right. She heaps up the sticks, but there is no air in the heap to feed fledgling flames, no careful grading of tinder and kindling to teach the fire how to burn bright. Besides, most of the branches she has piled up are thick with frost. They have green flesh instead of brown, life still in their severed veins. Plant those branches and they might sprout roots.

When she is satisfied, she steps back to marvel at her creation. In the bracken, the boy grins; that girl seems inordinately proud! She ferrets in her pocket to produce a book of matches, and now the boy grins more. Her papa ought to have taught her how to make a fire with a stick and a board. Instead, she is tearing off mittens, fumbling with fingers brittle and blue. More than once, the matchbook tumbles to the ground. More than once, she tears a match off and cannot keep a hold of it, so that it snuffs and dies in the frost at her feet. From behind, the inquisitive Mishka wanders over to look. Even she seems to understand: this girl is a fool.

At last, one of the matches lights and she tosses it onto the pyre. Yet before it has landed the match is dead. She tries again, miraculously finds light, and this time places it gently on top of the mound. Lonesomely, the match head burns away, the flame creeps down the matchstick – and goes no further. Now, all of the matches are spent. She turns to flounce away, sweeping up Mishka as she goes.

'It's because you're doing it wrong!' He had meant his voice to be small, but instead it shakes the snows from the trees. It

241

rises up and billows in the clearing, and pigeons scatter from their roosts and a single rook hurtles, screeching, into the sky.

The girl sweeps around. Mishka scrabbles to leap in front but, with hands clad in great mittens, Elenya bats her aside. If there is anything peculiar about her, it is that she does not seem afraid. She sets her rubber boots squarely, puts a hand on each hip, and fixes her stare on the bracken.

Between the fronds, the boy crawls forward, on hands and knees just like the dog. Only the fire is between them, not dead because it was never truly alive.

'What did you say?' the girl demands.

The boy tries to draw himself up, but finds that his body refuses to uncurl beyond a crouch. Probably it is that he can see what she is wearing, and knows he is naked by comparison.

Mishka drops her head, allows the rumble in the back of her throat to blossom into a growl. She is about to throw herself forward when Elenya grabs her by the scruff of her neck.

'Don't be so dramatic! It's that little boy . . . from the other night . . .'

She turns her gaze on him, as disparaging as any school-teacher. 'It is, isn't it? You're the little tramp who took my biscuit.'

These words are like one of his papa's snares; somehow, he's tied up in them. 'I still have him. You can have him back.'

'Have him back?' The girl is aghast.

'I was saving him.'

She eyes him suspiciously, and begins to prowl, cutting a circle with the boy and the dead fire in its centre. On the outside of the circle, Mishka waits with her head and tail both low. She too is like a snare, one wound up and ready to be tripped.

'I'm right, aren't I? You're the one who left the basket.'

242

The boy whispers, 'It was my papa's knapsack.'

'Filled with nuts and berries!'

He nods, glum though he can't say why.

'Well,' she says, stopping dead. 'Why?'

'Why . . .'

'Why did you leave a basket?'

'It was a present.'

At this, the girl seems satisfied. She begins to prowl again. She has cut two circles when, again, she pivots on her heel to face him. 'Where do you live?'

'What . . .'

'Live!' the girl declares. 'It's not as if there's any neighbours. I used to live in Brest. There we had neighbours. There we had a whole street and there was a party every New Year. I had a big bedroom.'

The boy does not like this question. It is like a circling hawk. It is like that day his papa fell through the ground and couldn't climb back out. He wants to say: you're living in my house. It belonged to my baba. It was where I went with my papa. And the Russian horse, that's my Russian horse. But he casts his eyes down, because he cannot say: there's a gingerbread house deep in the woods, way beyond the emperor oak. That's where I live.

'You don't say a lot, do you?'

The boy shakes his head.

'It doesn't matter. You don't need to say a lot. You'll have to do.'

'Do?'

'Well, I can't just play with this dumb old thing, can I?' Upon hearing the words, Mishka whimpers. 'I need *somebody*.'

The girl flounces to Mishka's side and throws herself at the ground. The dog rushes over and drops her head into the girl's lap.

The boy does not want to tell Elenya that she is sitting in snow, that soon the chill will work its way through even her thick coat, because then she might admonish him again. Instead, he creeps forward and hunkers over the dead fire. He can still smell the ash below the wet wood. 'You made it burn,' he says. 'Before.'

'Yes, but I had matches, and now it won't even burn at all. Some things are so inconsiderate . . .'

The boy begins to pick off the wet branches, one by one. Carefully, he stacks them at the edge of the fire, taking out three of the biggest to make a bulwark. Some of the frost has dripped into the ashes, and he begins to lift out grey clumps, so that all that is left is powdery and dry.

At the edge of the clearing, the girl sits upright. Mishka stirs, suddenly aware. She cocks her head, watches the boy.

'What are you doing with my fire?' Elenya demands.

'It's not your fire.'

'Not my fire? I gathered that wood myself!'

'Fires don't belong to anybody. That's what my papa says. Somewhere there's a great fire, like a forest that never stops burning, and all you can really do is ask it to come here for a while.'

The girl snorts, as if she has never heard a more ridiculous thing in her life. 'That's sorcery!'

The boy flushes scarlet red. 'It isn't sorcery at all.'

'Calling down fire like you're summoning a devil! That's witchcraft. Maybe that's what you are? A little witch boy, living in the woods . . .'

The boy's head bolts upright. He locks her with a stare. There comes a brittle snap: the bough in his hands, tearing in two. 'I don't live in the woods!'

The girl reels. It takes her a moment to regain her composure, but when she does, her face breaks into the most irrepressible grin. 'Who said anything about living in the woods?'

'I have a house!'

She beams, delighted at this sudden spectacle.

Silently, he scurries around the edge of the clearing, snapping off any dry wood he can reach. When he has a small bundle, he returns to the dead cauldron. The bigger pieces he uses to construct a pyramid on top of the kindling, something to funnel the flames. When he is done, he finds a curl of dried bark and a stick and rolls it firmly in his hands.

Soon there is smoke. It plumes up so that the boy has to whistle to keep it out of his eyes. On the edge of the clearing, Mishka lets out a single bark, enough to startle more birds from the treetops. Elenya's eyes are agog. She sheds her mittens and claps, loud and hard.

She does not notice when the sparks come. Stupid girl, but that is the most important part. Smoke opens the doorway to fire, but sparks are when he puts his foot through the door.

He brings his head low. He whispers. Up flurry the flames. They dance, as if he is himself breathing them out, and grow and ebb and grow again. When they are strong enough to live without his whisperings, he draws back. The kindling crackles, and the baby flames take hold of the pyramid of sticks.

'It *is* a sorcery!'

Now the boy hangs his head, not in shame, but embarrassment instead. 'It's only a fire.'

'It isn't only a fire! It's a *campfire*! What do you cook on it?' Elenya shuffles into the glow of the flames, with Mishka hanging reluctantly at her side. She opens her palms to warm them, takes down her scarlet hood. For the first time, the boy can see her thick blonde hair up close, the way the tops of her cheeks are coloured by clusters of freckles, the gap between her front teeth which she hides, calculatingly, every time she smiles. 'Well?'

'Well, anything,' the boy mutters, not wanting to say: cattail and crow; red fox and frozen frogs from the edge of the pond.

The fire spits up, and suddenly the pyramid collapses.

'It won't last long,' says the boy.

'Why won't it?'

'It needs more wood.'

'What's wrong with my wood?'

When the boy doesn't want to say, Elenya marches to the edge of the clearing, snatches up the frosted wood, and sends it crashing into the pyre. What flames are left hiss, as if recoiling in pain.

'It's because they're still living!' the boy protests, risking his hands to pluck back the branches. 'Dead wood's for burning, not green.'

'And how exactly would a dirty thing like you know?'

The words are terrible, but her tone tells him she is not really being terrible at all.

'It's because I . . . live here,' he ventures.

Elenya snorts. She doesn't understand. She must be thinking: well, I live here too, and *I* don't know.

'You look like you need a bath.'

It is astounding the way those few words wrench him from the forest and thrust him back into the tenement in the days when mama was still alive. In that instant, he might not be surrounded by bracken and wintering elm at all; he is squirming

246

in front of a bathtub, with a kettle of boiling water and a hard sponge caked in soap. Mama, her own hair long and wet, is helping him out of his school clothes and promising him hot milk and honey, if only he's good.

'I don't need a bath.'

'You do. Even Mishka has a bath. All your clothes are . . .'

The boy can feel his eyes burning. He turns from the girl, because to let her see would be a terrible thing. In two great strides, he is back at the bracken. He hesitates, hand reaching out to force a way within.

'Where do you think you're . . .'

'Home,' he interrupts.

'Well, where's home?'

He takes off again, parting the bracken to lose himself inside.

'Wait!' Elenya cries. 'What if I . . .'

'What?'

'What if I want to find you?'

'What for?'

'To play. Don't you know how *boring* it is in these woods? It isn't like Brest at *all.*'

The boy pauses again. 'I'll find you,' he whispers.

Then the bracken closes around him and, ignoring the girl's cries, he takes flight through the forest.

T hat night: snow beyond measure, and the caverns of the canopy are closed.

In the days that follow, his papa barely leaves the side of the fire, save to take the boy hunting in the wilds. He has fashioned from the guts of some strangled fox a sling with which he whirls stones through the air – and a stone slung by that sling is enough to end a rabbit, a fox, a wood pigeon in mid-flight. The boy watches him dance with it, and around him the dead things plunge.

With winter for a bedfellow, he finds himself thinking more and more of Elenya. He thinks: there had to be a reason she was wandering the wild, making those fires. He thinks: her face lit up, didn't it, when I showed her how to whisper those flames into life? What if I could make her face light up again?

248

What if we could play in the woodlands while my papa goes a-hunting? He wonders if she is out there, trying again, remembering the things she has learnt – but, when his papa roams alone and he goes down to the cattail pond, he sees only the husks of her old fires, kicked up by foxes or desperate birds.

Probably she has not ventured so far, now that the snow has come more fiercely. He remembers her harassed father and wonders if she might even be locked inside, forbidden from venturing out. Then he remembers: school. Little boys and girls go to school, and do lessons. It might be that she's there, slumped half-asleep in front of a blackboard.

He watches his papa lurch under the trees, carving a trail behind – and, though the old man mutters that he should follow, the boy simply watches him fade, just another skeletal oak with branches for arms. Then he sets off.

Down by the cattail pond, he pulls up roots and checks the nettle-string snare he set in yesterday's gloaming. Sure enough, a weasel has wandered unwittingly in. He collects it up and tosses it onto his shoulder. Then, with kindling collected and cattail roots in the crook of his arm, he makes for baba's house.

He picks a spot nestled in the first line of trees and spirits up a fire. When it is blazing, he suspends the cattail roots above and skewers the weasel whole. Once it has thawed, he will use a sharp stone to gut it and open the flesh to be toasted.

He does not have to wait long before, from the house, the dog named Mishka sets up a howl. In return the only voices are the cries of Elenya's mama, telling the dog to be still, and then Elenya herself. He thinks he sees her in the bedroom window, but when he looks back the only face studying him is the face of the little Russian horse. He wonders: can it see me too?

He is about to venture into the garden when the backdoor opens and Mishka hurtles out.

In seconds, she is up, through the trees and over the fire. He thinks she is come to savage him, but instead she bowls him over and proceeds to slather him with her tongue. A peculiar chill spreads across his features, fracturing every time his face creases: the touch of winter, working its magic on the dog's slobber.

'Mishka, down!'

The boy scrabbles from beneath the bitch, but she pursues him and bowls him over again in the roots of an oak.

'There you are!' Elenya exclaims. It takes a moment before the boy realizes she is talking to him, not the dog. 'I thought you'd never come. Don't you know how bored I've been?'

She stops, but still the boy cannot see her, the whole of his vision eclipsed by shaggy grey.

'Mishka, get off him! He isn't yours!'

Boots crunch, and Elenya bustles Mishka away. Now the boy can see again. Elenya looms above him. This time her hair hangs freely and she wears ear muffs of blue and brown. She stands with her legs splayed wide and her hands on her hips, and considers him with the steeliest of gazes.

'I thought . . .'

'You thought what?'

It is now or never: talk to the girl, or go back and live wild, with only his papa for company.

'I thought I could teach you more fires,' he ventures. 'I can teach you other woodland things too.'

'It isn't what friends *usually* do.'

The boy knows it. 'Does it mean we're friends?'

Elenya remains silent. Then, once she has considered it, she extends a hand, clasps his, and hauls him to his feet. Only when she has done so does she look at her hand and, seeing the blood and grease and forest dirt smeared there, wipes it fiercely on the nearest bark. 'I suppose it'll have to do,' she says, in a voice that means she is thrilled to be doing something, *anything*, that doesn't involve sitting in the house. 'But not so near my house! If papa gets back, he'll murder me. Didn't I tell you it was because of a fire we had to leave Brest?'

She turns to stride off, deeper into the forest, but the boy hangs behind, fixed by Mishka's eyes.

'A fire?'

'Oh, I wasn't anywhere *near*, but nobody would listen!'

The boy hurries to rescue his cattail roots and roasted weasel and plunges after Elenya. This girl cannot know about partisans, or soldiers, or the murder grounds between the trees, because she barely cares to stop and look at the branches. Fear doesn't touch her at all. Even when she reaches the murder tree, with its dead face glowering down, she doesn't flinch.

The boy flails after. 'Here,' he says, as the demon in the murder tree fixes him with its gaze. 'You can have this.'

She looks at the cattail root, but will not touch it. 'What is it?'

'It's for eating.'

'You're playing a trick.'

He brings up the toasted weasel, unrecognizable save for its blackened head. 'You could have this too.'

This time, the girl shrieks – not in shock, but in a shrill kind of glee. 'You've butchered that little thing!'

'It's cooked through.'

'It's hardly fit for Mishka!'

Mishka disagrees. As soon as Elenya says her name, she leaps up and takes the toasted carcass between snapping jaws. In seconds, she is hurtling into the undergrowth to devour it alone.

'Well, go on then. You can make a fire here.'

The boy's eyes drift up to the murder tree. 'I don't know . . .'

Elenya balks, 'You *dragged* me out here . . .'

'I didn't drag. I followed you. I . . .'

'Can you show me fires or not?' She stops, as if a thought has only just occurred. 'And where *do* you get those clothes?'

This is a burrow the boy would rather not follow – so, before she can ask him where he lives, where he comes from, why he's out here in the woods at all, he begins to craft a fire. First, he will show her how to pile the kindling up. Then, he will show her how to press and twirl the stick so that smoke flurries out. Last, he will show her how to make the special whisperings to invoke sparks.

The sparks are showering down when he hears a certain noise reverberating in the air trapped under the trees. It comes with a precise rhythm: a sharp click, followed by a soft pull. He stops, cocks his head. It is only as the sound comes into stronger definition that he realizes what he is hearing. He hears dark breaths, and darker words. He looks at Elenya. 'Maybe we can make a fire somewhere else.'

'I think you've got a perfectly good one here. Make it dance.'

The boy's eyes dart into the spaces between the trees. He sees a shadow lunge and haul itself forth, lunge and haul itself forth again. 'Come on,' he says. 'This way . . .'

He flattens his pyramid of sticks beneath his rabbit-hide moccasin and scrambles into the same thicket of brambles from which he once hid from the girl and her family. When it is plain that she will not follow, he darts out, grabs her by the arm and pulls.

'Just what do you think you're doing?' The girl must see the panic stained on his face. 'What is it?'

'He's coming out of the woods . . .'

In a daze, the girl allows herself to be drawn into the brambles. The thorns close around them, obscuring the clearing and the murder tree above. 'If it's hide-and-seek, only one of us should be hiding.'

The boy closes a hand over his mouth, as if to direct Elenya to do the same. Her face contorts into the deepest scowl, her eyes blazing with the fury of being told what to do, but she is silent all the same. Only after the moments linger too long does she dare a whisper. 'You know, you haven't even told me your name. If we're going to be friends, I'd expect you might tell me your name.'

Through thorns, the boy sees his papa emerge from the forest and drag himself through the roots of the murder tree. He has a dead pheasant dangling from his shoulder and the face of some other creature peeps from his greatcoat pocket. His breathing comes in fits, and between those fits his head is thrown back, peering into the snowscape above.

The boy strains to hear.

This isn't the tale, are the words hidden in those breaths. *This isn't the tale but this isn't the tale.*

'What *is* he?' grins Elenya, parting the brambles with a mittened hand.

The boy is on a precipice, about to say: he's my papa. Yet,

he will not say it; he does not know how this girl will react – and, above all else, he likes this girl.

In the clearing, the old man circles the murder tree. For a moment he disappears around the trunk, leaving only the face of the demon to watch them. Then he reappears – and with him come more words.

. . . when we did not exist . . . earth in front of the sky . . . seven versts aside . . .

'That old tramp's telling a fairy story!' breathes Elenya, her finger jabbing the boy in the ribs. 'I know those words!'

. . . we will escape, back through the jaws of the great frozen city called Gulag, and though we will find ourselves in Perpetual Winter, we are a brave company and will help each other through. There are eight of us friends, and the ninth is Aabel, and the tenth is Aabel's companion, and though we know him not, if Aabel says his heart is true, he will come with us and us be richer for his coming.

What will you do, said the leader of the band, to help us in our escape?

I will do whatever it takes, said the man who was once a boy, for I am sworn to get back to my babe in the woods, and would move mountains and wage unwinnable wars to get there.

How far is it until home?

It is all the way until summer, where the trees have leaves.

The old man drives his staff forward. Some flicker of movement must catch his attention, for suddenly his head cocks. The boy gets ready to bustle Elenya back through the thorns – but his papa directs his gaze to the snow dark beyond the murder tree. He hauls himself around – and there, gleaming in the perpetual twilight beneath the

254

branches, the boy sees two other eyes, and the silhouette of a frozen deer.

'Do you see it?' whispers Elenya.

The old man takes off. At the direction of his staff, the deer turns and bolts, showing only the white flash of its tail as it careens through the beeches. The old man's jackboot clicks as it rides the roots of the murder tree, and his dead leg bounces ungainly as he drags it through.

'Let's follow!' beams Elenya.

'Follow?'

'What, are you scared?'

'Not scared.'

'Then what?'

'I don't want to follow,' says the boy, grappling with her arm. 'We can . . . play here.'

'Play, with sticks and stones and dirty yellow snow? No, let's track him. He probably lives in a tree . . .'

'He doesn't live in a tree.'

'How would you know?' Her gaze is withering. 'You know, you still haven't told me where you live . . .'

The boy feels himself in a different kind of snare, scrabbling at the nettle strings to get away. There is only one way to chew through this particular snare, so he pushes through the brambles, skitters into the roots of the murder tree, and makes as if to go after his papa.

'Well, come on!'

'I'll lead. What would a little boy like you know about spy games?'

As soon as they have gone beyond the murder tree, it is obvious that she doesn't know a thing about tracking. The boy can see the furrow that his papa's dead leg has churned up, but

Elenya hardly seems to notice it at all. She heads in a different direction, allowing herself to be directed by fallen logs and branches. In this way, the forest would twist her up and take her far from home – but the boy is content to follow, let her think she is leading the way, when in truth his papa has roamed into deeper parts of the forest.

They have cut a circle, come almost to the cattail pond itself, when they climb over the stump of a rotten birch to see the same deep furrow in the ground. Though Elenya tumbles over, the boy stops. Something, it seems, has brought his papa back this way. The boy searches the ground for clues and sees, scored over by his papa's trail, the hoofprints of the fleeing deer. His papa is after it, and the poor beast hardly knows.

By fortune or not, Elenya follows the trail. This girl seems oblivious to the ghosts in the trees. She strides on, in ignorant bliss.

Then: his papa's voice, curdling up through the branches . . . *white and white and white, and only white forever more. That was the world of Perpetual Winter . . .*

Elenya stops. 'Did you hear that?'

The boy shakes his head.

'It's that old tramp, still telling his story. Who's he telling it to, do you think?'

'I think . . .' whispers the boy. 'I think he's telling it to the trees.'

Elenya snorts, 'Well, they're hardly bound to listen!'

The voice could be coming from any one of a hundred directions. It ripples along branches rimed in hoarfrost, along briars lying dead in the roots.

. . . for we are beyond cold and cannot understand that there

is still life in our veins. We have come five weeks since escaping that great frozen city called Gulag, but we can go no further. Our stomachs are empty as this vast white world, and our insides devour themselves to keep us alive.

And Aabel said: I have never been so hungry.

And the leader of the company said: I have never been so cold.

And the man who had once been a boy said: yet we cannot give up, for we must get back to summer, and my babe in the woods . . .

Elenya seems to be surveying the woodland. The voice flurries up around them, but at last she scents a direction. She takes a stride, banks left through the oaks. Here, a gentle escarpment drops away. She begins to descend – and, to the boy's terror, he sees his papa's trail doing the same, punctuated again by the prints of the deer.

In Perpetual Winter the nights last longer than the days, and so it was that the company of fugitives plunged through the blackness. And, ho, but the leader said: do you see that light in the distance?

It is nothing but a mirage, said another, for the snow is too thick to see even a campfire.

No, said the leader, it is a candle in a window, for we have stumbled upon the house of some forester or trapper.

Then we must not go near. The forests are filled with magickers and spies, and a trapper might lure us in with beds for the night, and then send word to Gulag that we are here. Then we would wake with the wise men, and be sent back to that frozen city.

We must take a chance in there, or starve to death out there. What say you?

And one after another, the companions said: yay.

And when it was Aabel's turn, he held to his knapsack and he said: yay.

And when it was the man who had once been a boy's turn, he too said: yay.

Then let us descend, and see what this trapper has in his larder.

Elenya reaches the bottom of the escarpment. Here, the trees grow more densely, but beyond there lies a clearing. The boy reaches her side, stops her before she goes through the trees.

'He's in there!' she whispers. 'Can you hear?'

The boy can: no clicking of heels, no driving of his staff, but he hears the soft whoosh of the axe, the keening of the blade, the wet sounds of flesh being torn apart.

'I think you should go home,' he whispers.

'Me?' demands Elenya. 'What about *us*?'

'Please . . .'

'Where do you live?'

The boy says, 'Not so very far away, on the earth in front of the sky, on a plain place like on a wether . . .'

'Oh, shut up with stories! I want to see what he's up to through there.'

Before the boy can stop her, she squirms through two elms and hunkers down in the roots on the other side. He can do nothing but join her.

In the roots they are barely concealed, with only more roots to hide them. It does not matter, for in the clearing his papa has disappeared inside his greatcoat and is facing into deeper reaches of woodland. His head is bowed low, the axe bites the earth at his side and spread out before him is the deer. Steam billows up from some unseen quarter of its belly and its cloud

258

churns around the old man's head. His hands must be buried deep in the carcass. The sling lies at his side and he wonders: could such a little stone really take down such a beast?

Well, the way was long and the way was frozen cold, but the promise of warmth and fodder kept the runaways from crumbling. And, when they reached the house, they saw that it was no mirage. It had four walls of timber and the light in the window was a lantern calling them on.

'What's he saying?' whispers Elenya.

But the boy only hears the sounds of the deer being butchered and does not reply.

Well, they knocked at the door but the door made no sound. And they knocked at the windows, but the house said: nobody's home. And the leader said: well, if nobody's home, it means we can go in, and we must take what we can, because without it we will starve.

Well, the door caved in, but the house was barren. All that was left was the little lamp on the ledge, and the leader said: they left it as a taunt. They have run away too, because in Perpetual Winter there is nothing to grow and nothing to hunt. We would have been better to stay in that great frozen city called Gulag.

Soon, despair took the runaways, for though there was warmth in the lantern, and though the walls kept out winter's bitter shriek, their stomachs were still shrunken and filled with hate. In the night, there were cramps. One man cried for his mother. And the man who had once been a boy sat long into the night, clinging to his friend Aabel, and shivered with the fever of starvation.

In the clearing, the old man rears up from the deer. His hand gropes out to take the axe. When he lifts it aloft, the boy sees that his fingers are covered in gore.

259

Elenya gasps, the sound stifled only by the boy's hand.

Well, deep in the night, the leader came to where Aabel and the man who had once been a boy sat and said: it comes to this. We are all of us friends, and all of us have suffered, but some must suffer more than most, if we are ever to make it back to Summer.

Of what do you speak? asked the man who had once been a boy.

One of our number is near to death. His name is Lom and he is a Cossack. Lom should die so that we may live.

Well, the man who had once been a boy and his companion Aabel did not comprehend.

We have come to this house, said the leader, in search of good meat.

Yet, there is none.

No, said the leader – and, here, the old man brings down the axe to sever a haunch of the deer – *for this house is full of meat. It is a larder rich with flesh. And we might dine on that flesh this very night. Do you see where Lom lies?*

And the man who had once been a boy peered across the dark cottage, and saw Lom breathing ragged in the range.

I will club him while he sleeps, and in that way spare him his torment, and in that way spare us ours . . .

Well, Aabel stood, and the man who had once been a boy stood.

You are a monster! said the man who had once been a boy. Man must not dine on the flesh of man!

And the leader flashed a smile: man needs meat!

The axe bites through the leg of the deer. Shreds of flesh shower up. Now his papa's words ebb away – and into the void come only his ragged breaths. He stands, hauling the haunch onto his shoulder, and turns.

In the roots, the boy turns to force Elenya down – but she is not there. He wheels back, sees her scrambling up the escarpment and away.

He is about to turn and follow her, when he hears his papa's voice, no longer the strange feathery one with which he tells his tales.

'Boy?'

'Papa,' the boy breathes, watching the final flash of Elenya's scarlet coat in the trees. His papa is looking at him with eyes of vivid blue; they sparkle with such life that, at once, the boy forgets the fable, forgets Perpetual Winter, forgets the flashing smile and *man needs meat*. In the clearing, his papa is draped in dinner enough to see them through the fiercest cold.

'I wondered where you were,' says the boy. 'I . . . came looking.'

'I found us the meat we need,' the old man replies, with genuine wonder in his tone. 'Will you help me carve her, boy? We shouldn't leave her to the wolves.'

The boy wants only to hurry after Elenya, but his papa's voice compels him to stay. He ventures across the clearing, looks down at what is left of the steaming deer. Entrails curl up in the nest of its open side. Its neck is thrown back, as if to invite the teeth of some woodland monster. For a reason he cannot fathom, he is surprised that there are not teeth marks there, scored into fur and flesh.

'Papa, why were you telling it a story?'

The old man lifts the axe, thinking to sever another haunch, but the heft is warm and slippery and he lets it drop through his fingers. 'Well,' says his papa, as if uncertain of the words. 'Some stories just . . . need to be told.'

He takes the axe and opens a great cleft in the other back leg, deep enough so that the boy can tear the rest free, to a grisly sight of gleaming white and red.

'I thought . . . you'd stopped telling those stories, papa.'

'I thought,' snipes the old man, 'that you were old enough not to believe in tales.'

He drags himself around, picking a path back to the gingerbread house.

Scrutinized by the deer's lifeless eyes, the boy follows. 'How does it end, papa? That tale?'

'It ends like all of them end.'

The boy is silent. Then, he remembers. 'Is it true?'

Oh, says his papa, *I know it is true, for . . .*

When he stops, the boy thinks he must have forgotten the words. 'One was there who told me of it?' he offers.

But the old man slopes on, into silence and snow.

At the gingerbread house, where the deer smokes on the cook-fire, the boy studies the old man in the firelight and tries to match him with the old man he first met in the tenement hall. What is happening behind those dark eyes that were once so blue? What wood still lives behind bark grown dead and rimed in ice? When hoarfrost hangs from a human skin, can that skin still hold a heart?

And yet, his thoughts keep drifting back to the little girl. 'What would you think, papa, if I went to play at baba's house?'

The old man eyes him, poking more deer into his jaws. 'It isn't baba's house anymore. They have the house, but we have the forest.'

Before sleep, there is more meat than the boy can remember, more meat than he can keep down. It is rich and red and tastes of the woodland, and his papa explains: you must eat it with the blood still pink, because then it will nourish you, for the goodness does not drip away like fat and sizzle in the cookfire. The boy takes as much of it as he can and crawls into the gingerbread house at once sated and sick.

Somewhere, out there, fox and lynx dine on what is left of the carcass, and a thousand other woodland beasts are summoned from far and wide.

Come morning, the fire dances high and his papa is gone. His trail, that one deep trench that follows wherever he goes, disappears in the direction of last night's pines.

The boy is warming himself on half-cooked broth when he sees three little mounds of snow on the far side of the fire. On the peak of each sits a bundle. He cannot see properly through rising smoke, so he sets the crushed tin can down and skirts the fire. And there, nestled in blankets of tissue now frozen solid with frost, sit three biscuit babies the same as the one in the gingerbread house.

He rushes forward, reins himself down, approaches cautiously. The biscuit babies have different decorations, different nightcaps and pyjamas. One is missing its raisin eye. Another has a mouth open in surprise, made from a sugared cherry. At first, the boy does not dare pick them up. He has himself set snares like this, only – instead of using gingerbread babies – for him it is bits of squirrel, or the heart of a stoat, anything to tempt a famished fox into the trap. He circles at a distance, feeling the sugar and encrusted honey calling out to him.

'Well, are you just going to *stare*?'

He reels around, searching every thicket of shrinking bracken. The morning light is wan, and the smoke in the camp obscures his vision – but there, standing between the three beds of snow, is Elenya. The dog Mishka hovers at her side, collar ruffed up against the cold.

'Well, aren't you going to say thank you?'

It takes the boy a moment to process what is going on. His shock turns to shame: that, somehow, Elenya has found the gingerbread house; that, somehow, she has crept upon him just as ably as he could creep upon her. This girl is not supposed to know about tracking. He scrabbles around, but there is no hiding the campfire, the house of branches and snow built up against the oak.

'Well, you could talk the other day! I don't see why you'd pretend not to talk *now*.'

The boy utters, 'I'm not pretending.'

'Then I think you should say thank you.'

'For what?'

'I brought you more, didn't I?'

'More?'

'More gingerbread babies. My mother bakes them, but I can't bear to eat them. They're too precious.'

Mishka shuffles forward, snout pushed out to smell the biscuits.

'Is this it, then? This is where you live?'

The boy fancies he can hear the snap of a branch underfoot, the soft thump of a deadweight foot.

'You can't be here!' he whispers, his voice somehow filling the forest.

'I knew you lived near, but I hardly thought it would be like this! What are you, some sort of wolf-boy?'

'A wolf-boy?'

'A boy raised by wolves. I heard they had one in Russia.'

'But this isn't Russia.'

'Russia isn't so bad. My daddy took me once, when he was thinking about moving. They have forests there like you wouldn't believe. My daddy's a woodsman.'

'A woodsman?'

'He does logging. Chopping down woods. I wish he'd hurry up and chop down this one. Then we wouldn't have to live here . . .'

She is at the door of the gingerbread house now, reaching out to part the pine branches and sneak a look within.

In three simple bounds, the boy barrels over the campsite, throws himself between Elenya and the branches. 'You've got to go!'

For a reason the boy cannot fathom, Elenya has a delighted grin upon her face. One of her pigtails drops out of her hood and she flicks it away. 'Go? But I've only just come!'

'My papa's going to . . .'

'Don't you want to play?'

'But if my papa . . .'

Elenya seizes her chance and shoots through the pine branches, into the gingerbread house. For a moment, the boy feels trapped, even though it is he who is without. Then, because there is nothing else to do, he follows her in. Mishka comes soon after, forcing her snout between the branches of the pine.

Inside, Elenya stands in the middle of the roots that make up the floor. In one corner lies the pile of soft branches that make up his bed – and, above that, a ledge for the biscuit baby.

Elenya beams. 'So, you couldn't bear to eat him either!' She lifts the baby down, cups it in her hands. 'What shall we do with him?'

'Please,' the boy whispers, 'you've got to . . .'

'I know! We'll make a guillotine and off with his head!'

The girl sweeps around, as if to leave the den. It is only as she hovers on the threshold that she stops and takes in where she is standing. 'Do you *really* live here?'

The boy seizes his chance. 'I don't live here. It's . . . a den. A secret place.'

'You do so live here. I can see your bed.'

'It's a hideaway.'

'It's *disgusting*.'

'I have a proper house. I do. And a mama and . . .'

Shaking her head, Elenya goes back through the pines. The boy, boxed in by Mishka, cannot follow. He tries to squirm past, but the dog's tail begins to beat, and she nudges him with her muzzle, expecting a game. By the time he has forced his way past, Elenya is already gone. He can hear her footfall, but in the whole world there is nothing else.

He emerges, squinting, into soft winter light. His head is low, but he sees her absurd pink boots standing at the edge of the fire. Something has made her stop dead, but all the boy can see is the wavering of the flames. Somehow they burn more vividly than only moments ago.

Between the girl's feet, something shines. It is the head of the axe, glimmering with snow-melt. The handle stands up proudly, as if tempting her to take it.

His eyes track up, to see her eyes wide open. He thinks she must be staring at the axe, the perfect guillotine for her ginger-bread man, but instead she is staring over the fire. He follows her gaze. Through the flames, he looks more haggard than he should – but there is his papa, hunkered down like a witch over her cauldron, half-propped up on his staff, hair stained in greys by the smoke curling out of the pot.

266

'Papa . . .'

On the other side of the fire, the old man looks up. There is a flicker of recognition, and then the bark of his face softens; his eyes light up. 'Who is she, boy?'

He hasn't even looked at her. He drags himself around the fire, until his face emerges from the parting smoke.

'It's the little girl, papa. From baba's house.'

Elenya turns, her pink boots ringing off the axe's blade. 'Baba's house?' she breathes.

'Elenya,' the boy ventures. 'This is my papa.'

'But that's just the wild man from the woods! The one who hunted that deer! You . . . made me follow him!'

The boy stammers, 'I didn't make you.'

'And he was telling that horrible story. Why didn't you tell?'

'It's . . . only my papa. He's . . . brought me camping.'

It is difficult for Elenya to tear her eyes from this wild man, but she tears them back to the gingerbread house. 'That was a rotten trick,' she says, and summons Mishka near.

The way his Grandfather holds himself, Elenya is almost as tall. The old man comes forward a few more paces; he seems so shrunken inside his greatcoat, like a tree stunted in a storm. 'You shouldn't be here, girl.'

Still, he does not look at her. He falls, instead, to the fire, sprinkling stripped bark into its heart, kicking up more stones to keep it hemmed in. Then his fingers are in the folds of his clothes. He produces dead things: a tiny songbird, a frozen shrew. He has handfuls of acorns, and the webbing of his fingers is stained with the juice of wild berries.

Elenya darts a look at the boy. 'Why shouldn't I?'

His papa utters, 'Tell her, boy.'

'Please, Elenya. You have to go.'

Before Elenya can reply, the old man's voice rises up. 'You shouldn't go wandering in wilds you don't know. They have a way about them, don't they, boy?'

Shamefaced, the boy nods.

'They'll turn you round and twist you up. Then you'll never find your way back home.' For the first time, the old man looks directly at her. 'Didn't your mama and papa ever tell you not to stray from the track?'

'I can find my way home perfectly well! Mishka will show me.'

A smile plays in the creases of the old man's face. 'That dog couldn't tell where it was without street signs to show it.'

'Well, I have a trail.'

'Breadcrumbs?'

'Yellow snow . . . Mishka's been marking her scent.'

The old man's head revolves, to stare through the canopy. 'Then you'd best run back to your mama. When this one breaks, it'll cloak us all. You wouldn't think you were so clever in the winter wilds at night, girl.'

For the first time, it seems as if Elenya has no response. Her gaze turns back to the boy. 'Well, maybe I *will* go home.'

'Elenya, I . . .'

Elenya sweeps across the campsite and snatches up the biscuit babies still perched on their mounds. She is almost at the line of the trees when Mishka springs up to follow, showering snow from her hind paws onto the cookfire. Behind it, the old man mutters some half-oath, and stoops to build it back up.

'Elenya,' the boy begins, 'I'll show the way.'

The boy is halfway across the clearing when Elenya looks back.

'I *know* the way. It isn't just wolf-boys who can live in the woods.'

268

'I told you! I *don't* live in the woods!'

'I found my way here, little wolf-boy.'

She steps into the snow dark under the branches; only a few steps and she is almost invisible.

'You'll get lost!'

The boy scurries to the tree line, but before he can go under the branches, his papa barks out. 'Let her go.'

'But, papa,' he says, swinging back round, eyes big and pleading beneath brows sparkling in frost. 'She'll get lost.'

'She should have thought of that, before she went wandering in the wild.'

'I want to go for her, papa.'

He did not mean it to sound so defiant. He did not mean it to propel his papa up and over the clearing. The boy freezes. He thinks his papa is going to barrel past him, or else snatch him up like he used to in the days of the tenement, but instead he heaves himself into position and drops down in front, sending the staff spinning as he falls. Now he must use the boy's shoulders to keep balance. His twig-like fingers are brittle and clasp the boy tight.

'She isn't for you to think about. She isn't for you to worry. Out here, you have to look after yourself.'

'And each other,' the boy whispers.

'*Each other.*'

He says, 'But papa, she came here to find me.'

'And how did she come?'

'Maybe she followed.'

'Might be you left her a trail?'

The boy thinks: all she'd have to do is find the furrow left by your dead leg. But he doesn't say it. He simply shakes his head.

He does not know why he cares. He knows he should not. He knows the world is his papa and only his papa. It has been that way ever since mama died. But seeing her try to build fires, holding her babies of biscuit, watching the dog Mishka trotting at her side: these are the things of which his last days have been built. He wants to go to baba's house and knock on the door and ask her if she might want to play. He wants to creep up to her bedroom window and hold his Russian horse. He wants to sit at a table with a knife and fork and have her mama bring him a dinner of *kapusta* or potato *babka*, or even the *kalduny*, no matter how gristly the insides.

He is used to silences, but this one feels as if it has gone on too long.

'Are you lonely, boy?'

The boy must shake his head, because he must not let his papa know: I want the girl, papa; I want a friend. I want Yuri and school and . . .

'Do you want to go back to the city?'

He whispers, 'It's not fair, papa.'

'Do you want to leave me here? On my own?'

'You have the trees,' he says, able to control the bleating in his voice but not the tears in his eyes. 'You always say you have the trees.'

'If you go to that girl, they'll come into the wilds and they'll find you there, in your house made of bark. A little boy, living in a house of bark, and they'll think I'm . . .'

A new fear ignites in the boy. The fire flurries up, and the boy himself flurries up with it. He wrenches himself from the old man's arms, whirls around in front of the gingerbread house. 'They won't think anything, papa! They'll know! I'm looking after you!

270

'How could you look after me, boy, if you let them take you away?'

The boy is silent. He sees it now. If men came to these wilds, they would take his papa for a monster. They wouldn't know about mama, or the roots, or how she lived a whole summer in the branches. They wouldn't know about the fall and the partisans and the ghosts in the trees. They wouldn't know how much his papa cared for him, teaching about sorceries and fires and of all the things you can catch and kill and eat. They'd want to scrub him, like Navitski used to scrub him, and dress him up and take him away. They'd want to take his papa too, no doubt. Only – his papa can't leave the forest. He tried once, and the wilds wouldn't let him. The boy would be in the city and his papa would be gone to the forest, with nobody to build his fires when he forgets.

'Elenya knows where we live now,' he whispers.

'Well?' the old man asks. 'What are we going to do about that?'

There is something glimmering in his papa's eyes, enough to unnerve the boy.

'She wouldn't *tell*, papa.'

'How do you know she wouldn't tell?'

'She's a good girl.'

The old man considers it, taking up his staff to stoke the fire.

'No,' he whispers. 'She'll tell.'

'Then what shall we do, papa?'

His papa is right. That girl was brazen enough to march into their camp; any girl like that will be brazen enough to tell tales. He shifts, awkwardly, from foot to foot.

His papa drops his staff, wraps his skeletal arms around

271

his knees. He sits there, bird-like, eyes lost to the fire. Then he looks up. His words, when they come, are a kind of keening. 'You'll stop her. Won't you, boy? You'll stop her, for your papa.'

The old man shows him how to carry fire. On nights like this, it keeps both winter and wild things at bay.

The cattail pond has a different look, lit in spidery shadows by the torch in his hand. The snows on its bank are like ridges of lava; the trees of charcoal, the icicles of tar. There are no tracks to show where Elenya and Mishka walked. He stops momentarily, struggling to get his bearings. He has seen the forests at night, but they do not only change with the seasons, they shift and change with the coming of every dusk.

He looks over his shoulder. The outline that looms in the snow dark is not just another tree bent out of shape: it is his papa, and here his papa will leave him. He lifts a single finger to his wound-like mouth, and flicks it out, as if to send the boy on his way. The boy tries to pick his path, but it is not

273

until he hears his papa's sibilant whisper that he is propelled on his way. 'I'll be here, boy.'

'Yes, papa.'

When he is certain of his bearings he comes past the cattail pond, down to the fringe of the forest and the roots of mama's tree. The house is dark, not a single window lit up. It is an easy thing to go into the garden. The only thing that is watching him is the fairybook wolf from the knocker on the door, and its fangs are even less fierce than Mishka's.

The lawn is hidden beneath snow packed hard, and in its centre there sits a figure of snow. There was no room to make a snowman when the boy lived in the tenement, but if there had been, this is not the kind he would make. Elenya must have gone out of her way to make him appear bent over, crooked. She has used a branch for a walking stick and piled boulder upon boulder to make a raggedy, segmented body like that of a millipede. His eyes are sunken cavities in which black coals sit. He wears no clothes, and his mouth is an open wound, a gash as might have been made with an axe.

He circles it, sweeping the torch up and down. When he has seen enough, he plants the torch in the snow and crosses the garden, eyes drifting up to the black hole of Elenya's window.

He reaches down to roll up a ball of snow, then brings his fist back and lets it fly. His first attempt falls short, looping up below Elenya's window, but with each attempt he gets nearer. At last, one lands squarely on the window pane. Perhaps it stirs her, but no lights flare. He has to try again, and again after that, until a cord is pulled and the eyes of the house open up. In stark silhouette, he can see the gaping face of the little Russian horse.

The curtains peel back and Elenya's wearied face appears in

a triangle of light. The boy feels a rush of relief that she made it out of the forest; then his nerves harden and he remembers why he is here.

'Where are you?'

The boy steps back, almost as far as the crooked snowman.

'I know it's you, little wolf-boy. Don't you think I'd *know* you'd come?'

The boy cannot follow this train of thought, but for some reason the girl seems terribly pleased with herself. He cups his hand to his mouth and shouts up, in a hoarse whisper. 'Elenya!'

'Are you down there or not?'

The boy reaches for the torch and heaves it back out of the ice. 'I'm here!'

'What have you got?'

'It's a fire stick. So I can see.'

Elenya drops out of the window frame. Now the only thing looking down is the little Russian horse. It has been an age since he petted the ill-hewn wooden mane, but its chipped eyes seem to be imploring him. Its open mouth might be speaking. At first he fancies it is asking him to come to its rescue; it has spent too long with an unruly little girl and wants the boy again, wants his mama. Yet, he is fooling himself. The Russian horse is telling him: everything's well. She's been looking after me. She's a good little girl, no matter what your papa might say.

Elenya reappears, brandishing something in her hands. When she fiddles with it, a beam of light erupts to roam the garden. 'See! I don't need a silly little fire stick, because I have a flash-light.'

'Turn it off,' whispers the boy. 'I can't see . . .'

The girl gives a dramatic groan and kills the flashlight. 'What are you doing here, anyway? Don't you know it's the dead of night?'

'I'm sorry about my papa.'

'Your papa! Why didn't you tell me he was your papa?'

'He isn't . . . bad.'

'Bad? I built a snowman of him and I mean to chop off his head . . .'

'And . . . I thought you might be lost.'

'Do I look lost? Here, in my pyjamas?'

The words stumble on his tongue: 'Do you want to . . . play?'

She leans, suspiciously, beyond the window ledge, shying at the flurrying wind. 'Now?'

The boy shrugs. 'I have a den you can come to.'

'I've seen your den.'

'It's another den, one my papa doesn't know about. It's by a cattail pond.'

'What's a cattail pond?'

'It's where the cattails grow.'

'You know, you're a stupid little boy. All I wanted was to be kind to you.'

'Please?' he breathes.

Elenya lets the silence linger, to be filled only by the sound of wind straining at icebound branches. Then she pulls the window shut and promptly disappears.

The boy does not have to stand alone for long. In three jerks, the backdoor pulls back and Elenya appears, poking her head into the night. She is in a nightgown, hair tied back but hanging loose at the front. On her feet she has big fur boots of scarlet red, each with the face of a fox: buttons for eyes and a smile stitched on.

'Just what do you think you're doing here?'

The boy scurries over. 'I'm sorry about my papa,' he repeats. 'I'm not like my papa. I promise.'

'Is that why you didn't tell me about him?'

'I thought he'd frighten you.'

'Frighten me? With his head in the side of a dead deer? Why would that sort of thing frighten me?'

'He isn't . . . well,' says the boy. It does not seem the right word, but it will have to do. 'We came camping in the woods and . . .'

'You can't just come to my house and think I'll come out and play!'

'Why not? That's what you did to me . . .'

'I thought you said that den wasn't really your house?'

The boy shrugs, caught in another snare.

'Just look at you! You'll have to come in quick. If my daddy wakes, he'll have my guts on a plate.'

'What?'

'It means he'll be cross. He's cross every time I open a window or leave a light on or set fire to a classroom. It doesn't matter if none of it's my fault . . . Well, don't just stand there! Little wolf-boys might like the cold, but I'm . . .'

'I don't want to come in,' says the boy. 'I want you to come out.'

'What's the matter? Don't you even dare come indoors?'

She stops, considers him methodically, as if trying to deduce the solution to a riddle. Softly she says, 'You don't really live in the woods, do you?'

'I'll come in,' he whispers, fearful of what his papa would say.

'Hurry up, then! I'm meant to be in bed without dinner.'

Inside, the warmth is astounding. It pummels him with

memory and fire. After only a few steps he feels a sickness rising in his gorge. He has to stop, clasp hold of the kitchen counter.

Around him, everything is different – and yet eerily the same. There is no longer an open range, but in its place a metallic oven with a polished top and circles for four pots to sit. The tin sink is set into cupboards of gleaming oak veneer and the upper walls are lined in cabinets with glass doors. Inside stand figurines of friendly woodcutters and benevolent wolves.

It was under that sink that his papa found the axe. But the sink isn't the same sink anymore – and, if he dared to look under it, he wouldn't find axes at all, only soap crystals for washing and rubber gloves.

He is in a daze, but a yelp from the girl brings him back to his senses.

'Look at you! You're skin and bone! Let's find you a treat.'

Before he knows it, Elenya has dragged a stool out from under a countertop and is scrambling onto it. She hangs there, poised like an acrobat, and opens one of the uppermost cabinets, there to reveal a clay jar full of biscuits. She teeters as she lifts it down. Then she delves a hand inside and comes back with a fist full of ginger and honeycomb breads, of shortcake and pastries. *Wings of the angel.*

'Here,' she says. 'Eat one.'

When the boy takes one of the treats out of her hand, he sees her skin as white as snow. Against it, his own skin is bark-brown, the colour of the wettest thaw.

'Well, don't be shy! We'll have to fatten you up, like a little piglet. That papa of yours isn't doing it. Somebody has to.'

'He goes hunting for us.'

'I don't need to hunt to find a biscuit.'

She struts on, through a doorway where there was once only

a crumbling arch of stone. More than any, it is this threshold over which the boy dare not stray. He hangs on the edge, suckling his biscuit – and feeling, for the first time in many long months, like somebody's son. He would stand this way on the cusp of mama's bedroom, knowing he was not meant to go through and see her coughing, wheezing, sweating into her sheets.

'Well,' Elenya says. 'You've come this far. What's frightening you now?'

'I'm not afraid.'

'I think you're afraid. How can you sleep in a wood with that old beast and be afraid of a few tables and chairs?'

Elenya treads back across the thick carpet to offer her hand. 'Come on, little wolf-boy,' she says, her tone softer, more motherly than he has heard before.

It has been so long since he held a hand that, at first, he does not know how he ought to take it, if the fingers should intertwine or if one palm should nestle crosswise to the other, like ragdolls stitched together. His dirty fingers are about to touch hers when, suddenly, Elenya recoils. Her eyes have dropped low, staring at his feet. 'Just look! You're leaving a trail!'

The boy follows her eyes. She is right; all across the kitchen floor are the prints of his feet, outlined in melted snow and forest dirt. He has even left an imprint on the very edge of the cream carpet, five half-moons of filth where his toes strayed over the line.

'I'll fetch slippers. Wait there!'

The girl darts away, her footfalls silent on the deep shag. While she is gone, the boy hovers in the doorway. The living room appears bigger than it was when he lived here. The windows on the farthest side are broader, with deep alcoves on either side of the chimneybreast where bookshelves climb to the ceiling. There is no longer an open fireplace, but a little wood-burning stove instead. A big mirror hangs above, reflecting back a coffee table with magazines, and a table with places set for breakfast.

Gone: his papa's armchair, with its threadbare hide and springs showing through. Gone: the nest by the fire where he used to sleep with the Russian horse looking down.

Elenya reappears from the staircase, and deposits at his feet a pair of big slippers. She is about to show him how to put them on when another face appears on the stair: the dog named Mishka. She stops halfway down, her muzzle pressed between the banister rails. A low growl erupts in the back of her throat but, curiously, her tail is beating hard.

'Mishka!' Elenya hisses. 'Back to bed!'

The dog does not obey. Now that she is acknowledged, she bounds to the bottom of the stairs.

'Yes, Mishka,' Elenya says, trying hard to ignore the dog as she forces slippers onto the boy's feet. 'This is the wolf-boy from the forest. Don't you remember? And he's filthier than you!'

Mishka whimpers, nosing under Elenya's arm to sniff the boy. One sniff is evidently not enough, for soon her nose is probing every corner of the boy's body: the cold cavities at the backs of his knees, his fingers with their nails yellow with dirt, the crevice of his backside itself.

Her tongue begins to work on the bare skin at his shin, revealing dirt in lighter layers, old scabs and scars from tumbles in the wild. So entranced is Elenya at watching the boy revealed, shade by shade, that she only realizes he is crying when the

280

first hot tears roll from his chin and cascade over her own face. By then they have picked up so much dirt that they paint a dark scar on her cheek.

'Mishka,' she whispers. 'You're hurting him.'

The boy's mouth works, but the sounds are indecipherable, a woodland language of whimpers and phlegm.

'Dry those eyes,' says the girl.

'It's all gone,' he finally breathes.

'Gone?'

'Everything but my little Russian horse.'

The girl rocks back and draws to her full height. 'What Russian horse?'

'It's mine, and it's in your window.'

'Yours?'

The boy nods, half-sadly, knowing she will not believe.

'Who are you really, little wolf-boy?'

The boy looks at her, her face distorted, but he cannot say, cannot let her know.

There is a great river of carpet separating them. Elenya reaches out, and this time she takes the boy's hand without recoiling. The boy hardly notices. He takes his first step into the room, and the slippers are soft on his feet and the carpet beneath them even softer. With Mishka still nosing at his every step, he allows Elenya to lead him across the bottom of the stairs.

The boy looks up. Spots of colour swim in his vision, a swirling vortex like looking straight into a snowstorm. The last time he ventured up those stairs, they stopped halfway.

'I don't want to go,' he says, straining on Elenya's hand.

'Don't you want to see that horse thing?'

'I want you to come . . .'

281

'No you don't. You don't *really* want to go back out there, do you?'

Instinct drives the boy to shake his head. The movement is so small, yet the guilt is so huge. He should be out there, even now, leading Elenya back to the cattail pond. There, his papa lurks between the trees.

'We'll have a game,' he says.

'What kind of a game?'

Before he can reply, Mishka lets out a single shrill bark. Elenya whirls around, as if to cuff her around the nose. 'Shut up, Mishka! You'll wake the whole house! Then we'll both be . . .'

Evidently, she has spoken too soon. From somewhere upstairs there comes the creak of a floorboard, the sound of a house much older than this. Elenya freezes, one palm up against the boy's breast as if readying to thrust him away. She keeps her stare on the stairs – but, when no more creaking comes, she relents.

'Come on. My room's at the top. We can get there without them waking.'

At the top of the stairs, the landing goes two ways. Elenya takes odd footsteps, long and zigzagging. At last, she takes one last stride and pushes open a bedroom door. The boy moves awkwardly behind her, careful to land only where she has been standing.

'Come on, wolf-boy. Quick! Before they hear!'

She disappears through the door. For a second, the boy pauses. Mishka sidles past, pushing the door with her nose and snaking after the girl. He is vividly aware of the walls, the slippers he is wearing, the sounds of an alien snoring from the other side of the hall. He is about to turn, take flight down the stairs, when the door reopens and Elenya's face peers out.

'What are you waiting for?'

She is holding in her hands the little Russian horse – and, after that, all thoughts of running away melt like the thaw.

Her bedroom is big, ten times the size of the gingerbread house, with a sweeping alcove for the windows and a radiator blasting out heat. The bed is big enough for three little girls, with an eiderdown covered in a pink, patterned sheet. At the foot of the bed sit a bank of teddies, as unlike bears as the fairybook door knocker, and a shelf full of books. An electric light buzzes, but it is a comforting buzz, one that tells you you are never alone.

The girl leaps onto the bed and sits, cross-legged, with the Russian horse in her lap. 'Well? Why are you just standing there?'

The boy knows he is being dumb, but he can't find any words.

'You can have him, if you want . . .' The boy lurches forward, dirty hands reaching out to grasp it. '. . . but first you have to tell me why.'

The boy couldn't snatch it, even if he wanted to; that dreaded Mishka is in the way, back to sniffing every corner of his body.

'It was my mama's.'

'Your mama's?'

The boy whispers, 'Then she died, and then it was mine.'

Elenya nods, unperturbed by this news. 'But it doesn't explain what it's doing in my house. My daddy gave me this Russian horse when we moved here. It was a present. He built this house himself.'

The boy shakes his head.

'What?'

'He didn't.'

Elenya straightens. 'Are you calling my daddy a liar?'

'No, I . . .'

'I wouldn't worry. He *is* a liar. He told me this house would be fun, but it isn't nearly as fun as our old house in Brest. There were shops and a café and you could go to the pictures at night. Daddy said the forest would be the best picture show of all – so I know better than anybody what kind of a liar he is.'

'This is *my* house,' the boy whispers.

'Your house!? I've *seen* your house, remember! It's a pile of sticks in the wood.'

The boy broils. He had a home, once. It doesn't matter if the stones are different stones; the earth is the same earth, the air the same air. The forest remembers.

'This is my baba's house, and you came and took it, and now you've got my little Russian horse!'

Elenya leaps up, scrambles off the bed. In an instant she is across the room, with her hand clasped around the boy's encrusted mouth. Mishka leaps up too, lets out another shrill yap. Still holding the boy, Elenya flails out with her foot. Mishka is repelled – but it is already too late; there comes a shifting from the other side of the wall.

'Now you've done it!' hisses Elenya. 'If that's my daddy, he'll have you locked up!'

She pushes him, bodily, to the other side of the room, where the radiator does battle with the draught coming in through the windows. Here, she forces him down. 'Take it,' she snaps, thrusting the Russian horse into his hands. 'But keep out of sight!'

The Russian horse: it's in his hands. So amazed is he, feeling the familiar chips, the cracks in its polished rump, that he does not even think about getting back up. He huddles down, hands

284

tracing every contour of the horse's wooden body. And in that second he is a real little boy again, somebody who sleeps in a bed and has breakfast in a bowl. Now he has it back, he'll never let go.

'Elenya!' comes a voice. 'What's going on in there?'

Not her father. Her mama instead.

Elenya scurries to the door. 'Nothing, mama. It's only Mishka.'

'Elenya, open this door.'

It is the kind of quiet command that means you mustn't disobey. Elenya opens the door a crack, enough to poke her head without. In a sudden flurry of excitement, Mishka forces her way between Elenya's legs to push out of the crack itself.

'How many times do we have to tell you? The dog sleeps downstairs . . .'

'I know, mama, but she was . . .'

'What are you doing in there, Elenya?'

'It's only a game.'

'It's two in the morning!'

'I know.'

'And you have school.'

'I know.'

'Your father's going to be furious.'

'Well, you don't have to tell him, do you?'

The boy keeps the Russian horse in his hand and creeps along the edge of the bed, certain that he is out of sight. At the end, he risks a peep around, but all he can see is Elenya's back to the crack in the door.

'Elenya, what have you done?'

'Nothing, I promise . . .'

'It *stinks* in there!'

The boy ducks back. There is room enough under the bed, and he angles himself to slide beneath. The corners of the pink eiderdown tickle him as he starts to crawl.

'It must be Mishka, mama. She's been stinking all day.'

'What have you fed her?'

'Maybe she had some scraps.'

'Scraps? What have we told you about . . .'

'Mama, please!'

The boy hears a soft thud; then footsteps. He peeks up, but there is only a hand's breadth between the hem of the eiderdown and the carpet, and he can see so little between. The footsteps, soft, come his way.

'Mother, *please*. I told you there's nothing!'

The boy tracks the footsteps around. Now they are at the window. He hears a whirr as the curtains draw back on their runners. He thinks he can feel the stir of the cold, the winter playing on the naked glass.

Elenya's mother turns on her heel. 'We'll talk about this in the morning.'

Then the boy tracks her footsteps back across the room, out into the hall.

The door closes. Elenya exhales, so loud that the boy believes it must be meant to summon her mother back. Yet nobody comes.

'Where are you?'

The boy reveals himself, Russian horse venturing first. As he uncurls, he sees Elenya beaming, a smile that stretches her face into something quite unreal.

'I thought we were done for!' she whispers. 'Good thinking!'

The boy wasn't thinking at all. It was instinct that drove him into his burrow.

'You don't know what they'd have done if they found you. That's why my daddy took this stupid job. They thought I'd behave if they brought me somewhere more . . . boring.'

Her mother can still be heard through the walls, clearing her throat as she settles back to sleep.

'How long have you been living . . . out there?' she says, turning to the glass. After hours of holding back, the skies have opened. Snowflakes, as big as the boy's fist, sail directly towards them, smearing themselves across the window pane. There they gather, or slip, or harden like barnacles.

'I don't know,' the boy replies. 'How long have you been living in my house?'

'You keep calling it *your* house. How is it your house? Isn't this my bedroom? Isn't this my bed?'

'It was after my mama died,' the boy begins. 'This used to be her house, when she was just a little girl, and I made my papa come to put her ashes in the tree, and he begged me not to, but I made him.'

'So?'

'So, once we were here, he just wouldn't take me back to the city. And you came and you made it yours and now . . . there's nowhere to go.' The boy turns. The slippers must have come off under the bed, for he realizes that he can feel the stroke of the carpet strands on the soles of his feet. 'I've got to go,' he says.

'Back out *there*?'

Elenya stares at the window pane, now almost totally obscured.

'Thank you for my little Russian horse.'

He opens the door. In the hallway, there is only darkness. By feel, he finds his way to the top of the stair. He can sense something moving down there: only Mishka, scolded and too afraid to venture back up. He takes the first step, but before he has taken the second, he feels Elenya's hand on his shoulder.

'Please,' she whispers, mindful of her mother. 'You'll freeze out there . . .'

'I won't. It isn't even winter yet. Not the real winter.'

He hurries down the stairs, back along the living room, and into the narrow spaces of the now chill kitchen. He can hear Elenya behind him, Mishka whimpering that something is amiss, but he will not look round.

'Stop!' she calls out, whisper as loud as a shout.

He turns. In her hands is the oversized coat with the scarlet hood that she wore every time he saw her wandering the forest.

'I thought you wanted me to come with you. I thought you wanted to play.'

He came here thinking the same thing. To take her down to the cattail pond, to that place between the trees where his papa has planted his roots, grown wizened and old. But now he has the Russian horse in his hands. She has cared for it, kept it company, put it with her gingerbread babies and petted it every night. He could not ask her to go to the forest, not with the horse's wooden heart thundering between his palms.

He shakes his head, stutters, 'I have to go to my papa.'

'Well, when will we . . .'

'Don't come into the forest, Elenya. Not without Mishka. Not without me.'

'Why not?'

'And don't tell. Please don't tell . . .'

Elenya's eyes drift upwards, to her sleeping mother and father. 'Take it,' she says, holding out the coat.

'What for?'

'To keep out the winter, on the way back to your house.'

Yes, the boy thinks, a coat like that really could ward off winter. Better than cattail root and acorn mash. Better than squirrel, hare and starling. Better even than a hot milk.

He steps into it, forcing the Russian horse down one sleeve and through the tight cuff at the other end. When he is done, he can feel the girl's hands, clasping tightly around each arm. The coat is too big by far. He could fit into it three times over, but its pockets are deep as his knapsack ever was, and already the warmth holds him. He shuffles along the kitchen, feeling like a giant.

He opens the door, to feel the full force of winter.

'When will I see you again?'

The boy looks back, the snow flurrying at his hind. 'Next time my papa's gone a-hunting. Next time he's on a roam.'

'I can come to your den . . .'

'No!' the boy cries out. Then he conquers himself; he calms. 'I'll come for you. I'll build a snowman in the garden. Then you'll know I'm waiting in the trees.'

He tramps past the crooked, segmented snowman. On the edge of the forest, he turns over his shoulder. The door is still open, but Elenya and Mishka are mere silhouettes, half-obscured by whirling snow. He lifts a hand to wave. The silhouettes do the same, retreating behind a closing door.

The boy goes under mama's branches. He clings to the Russian horse and finds, once again, the old path, the one that snakes down to the emperor oak and the gingerbread house which will always be his home. He is not yet at the cattail pond when he hears the familiar footfall. He stops and the noises stop; he starts and they start again. Yet there is no doubting what he has heard. That tread is so distinct that it can be nothing else: the snap where the point of a staff drives into the forest floor, the click of one jackboot heel, the slow ache, scoring a trench behind.

Eyes glimmer at him from the snow dark.

'Papa,' he says, heart hammering like a rabbit caught but not yet dead. 'You frightened me.'

The old man lurches to the path, stooping beneath a branch heavy with frost. 'You're on your own,' he rasps.

'I thought you were waiting at the cattail pond.'

'Don't you know how long you've been?'

The boy stammers, 'I'm sorry, papa. I tried to be faster.'

'Where is she?'

The boy is suddenly aware of his new scarlet coat. It smothers him like shame. He draws his hands into the sleeves, better to hide the little Russian horse, but his papa's eyes have found it already.

'She wouldn't come.'

He mutters, 'She wouldn't come.'

'I tried. She was going to come, and then her mama was awake and she wouldn't.'

These words seem to have a soothing effect on the old man. His eyes brighten, catching better the light captured in the ice all around. He drags himself to the boy, so close that the mists of their breath mingle in the air.

'She'll come, papa. I just need more time . . .'

'More time?'

'To make her want a game. To make her want to play.'

'She gave you a coat.'

The boy nods, head sinking low.

'Why?'

'To keep me warm.'

This time, it is the old man's turn to nod. 'She wanted to play when she came to our camp, didn't she, boy?'

He feels the words needling him, like clawing pine. 'I suppose, papa.'

'So why doesn't she want to play now?'

There are some moments when you have to lie, but in this moment the truth is enough. 'She's afraid, papa.'

'Afraid?'

'You frightened her. It's . . .' Now the lies resurface. Once, the idea of lying to his papa was a worse thing than mama's death. Yet, as the words take form in his throat, he does not care. So have the seasons changed.'. . . going to take her some time, before she'll come into the woods again. But she won't tell, papa. I promise she won't. Maybe I can . . . take her a present? I can make her a horse out of wood and leave it on the step.'

His papa seems to be considering the lie, turning it between his mandibles and testing it for points of weakness. He lifts his chin and turns to lurch onwards, towards the cattail pond. The fog of his breath whips behind him, coiled like a serpent around his neck.

The boy stands firm. His feet square. His own roots growing, down into frost and ice, down into earth where dead men lie and nourish the trees.

'What would you have said to her, papa, if she came into the forest?'

Ignorant of him, the old man lurches on. Behind him, the branches close.

'It's only talking, isn't it, papa? It's only to tell her not to say anything.'

The old man's voice whispers in the trees. 'The fire will be dead by now, boy.'

That is all that it takes for the roots he has planted to shrivel and die, the stems to shrink and retreat inside his body.

'Yes, papa,' he whispers, and lifts his feet to follow him on.

When his papa goes foraging, or tries to set snares, the boy takes himself down to Elenya's house. It is easy to tell where his papa goes roaming, because the forest itself gives him up; the trail cries out to even the most useless tracker, and he means to tell Elenya: when you see a trench in the forest, my papa is near. If you turn and the trench appears, my papa has been between the trees. If you wake and look down from the window and see a trench in the night's fresh snow, my papa has been in the garden, studying the house like a cast-out dog. These are the sounds that herald my papa's approach: a breath full of winter; the click of one heel; the long slow scrape of death dragged behind.

Some mornings, Elenya climbs into the black truck with her

father and disappears up the glade. On other mornings, she does not have to go anywhere at all, and for two days straight they can play together in the forest. In this way, the boy remembers days. He remembers weeks. And he remembers the feeling of a Friday afternoon, the interminable wait for the schoolhouse bell to ring and release him, Yuri, and all of the other children for two joyful, empty days at home.

They are called 'weekends', these two glorious days when he can be a little boy again, forget his papa lurching through the trees and play with Elenya down by the cattail pond. On most of their trips, Mishka comes too – but no hunting can be done with that loud, cumbersome beast snorting her way through the forest. Instead, the boy shows her how to build a den, one of stripped pine branches and dead wood, a gingerbread house in miniature. In here, they hide together from the curling snow. The boy shows her the things he collects: stones polished smooth, feathers of beautiful hue, a pigeon's skull perfectly preserved and plucked clean. She pretends to recoil, but takes each of the dead things and lines them up with the same delicacy as her gingerbread babies.

'You're a wild little wolf-boy,' she beams.

And then, because now it is a joke, 'I'm a wild little wolf-boy!' he returns. He barks, and Mishka barks too.

Those weekends flicker by, and soon the weeks between are a torment more tortuous than even the cold. He can stand snow and ice, he can stand an empty stomach, but the one thing he cannot bear is the aching loneliness of Monday mornings.

'I have an idea,' Elenya declares one day, as dusk's cold hand tempts her back towards home. 'You should come back to my house.'

'The house?'

'Your *baba's* house,' Elenya corrects. 'We'll tell my mama and papa you're a friend from school. If I bring a friend, they'll think I'm . . . fitting in.'

A thousand thoughts collide: can it work? Will it work?

'You'll have to get scrubbed first. I can hardly tell them I'm taming a wild little wolf-boy. I'll say Navitski made you sit with me in class and I decided . . .'

The boy's hand on her wrist and he whispers, 'Navitski?'

Elenya whips her wrist free; gentle as she is, hardly a second goes by when she doesn't tell him how much he needs scrubbing. 'That's my teacher. He's . . .'

'. . . my teacher too!'

'I didn't think little wolf-boys went to school?'

The boy would rather not talk about this. He would rather be showing her about how to eat a nettle, or where to find a dray. If you smash open a dray, you can find a squirrel. He might lead you to his hoard, and there you'll find enough winter treats to gnaw on all the day.

'I used to. I wasn't always so . . . wild.'

'Your papa was.'

'No,' says the boy. 'He wasn't.'

Elenya stops. 'What? Are you *crying*, little wolf-boy?'

He drags stiff rabbit pelt across his eyes. 'I'm not.'

'I didn't mean it . . .' She pauses. 'Do you know, I wish you'd just tell me your name.'

He wishes it too, but the word will not come up his throat. 'Can I really come?'

Elenya nods. 'Next weekend.'

It is an eternity away. Until then, five nights of forest and darkness. 'Maybe . . . tonight?'

295

'Don't push your luck, little wolf-boy. It'll take you all week to get scrubbed up.'

Sometimes his papa does not return to the gingerbread house at all. At first, the idea of a night alone with only the trees petrifies him, and he crawls inside the gingerbread house to bask in Elenya's scarlet coat and lie awake the long night through. He listens out for the tread of bison or deer, the foxes that come into camp when his papa does not curl by the fire, to ferret for whatever bones and scraps the boy himself has not devoured – but of all the sounds of the forest, the only one that stirs him is the click and soft thump as his papa returns to camp.

Tonight, he is dreaming of Elenya when he hears that trench being carved in the forest floor. The shadowy blackness that follows is his papa eclipsing the campfire. Soon, the fire has been fed; more crackling tells him the flames are flurrying up to repel the snow.

He peeps his head through the pine-needle doors.

'Come here, boy.'

His papa is not even facing him, so how he knows he has emerged the boy cannot tell. Even so, he steps out of the gingerbread house, to a welcome wave of heat. Forgetting for a moment, he scuttles to the fireside, sinks beside his papa, and opens his arms to receive the flames. Sometimes, a strong fire is more invigorating than a strong meal.

'Papa,' he begins, 'where have you been?'

'I went to the marshes.'

'All that way, papa?'

The old man snorts.

'Did you go . . . across?'

'The trees were calling me, boy.'

'From the other side?'

'From the other side.'

The boy remembers those trees, older and older again, the very same trees into which the Old Man of the Forest disappeared in the tale. He does not want to know how old the forests are beyond the aspens where the partisans lived. He does not want to voyage there, beneath branches where the ragged wolves roam, where there might yet be other papas who have turned wild and taken their little boys off to live among the trees.

This isn't the tale, says the old man, *but an opening. The tale comes tomorrow, after the meal, when we are filled with soft bread.*

'Oh papa, please, not a tale, not tonight . . .'

Well, the old man goes on, not registering the way the boy shrinks back, *Aabel and the man who had once been a boy had fled the cabin in the woods, for there men turned monster. And in his jackboots ran Aabel, and in his leather moccasins ran the man who had once been a boy. And it was not long before they heard cries in the night behind them. These were the cries of men, and such cries they had not heard since the day they escaped through the jaws of that great frozen city called Gulag.*

Well, Aabel stopped to help the man who had once been a boy along a ridge, where the black pine trees held them tight. And Aabel said: they are coming and they are hungry.

And the man who had once been a boy said: they have eaten Lom, and now they have a taste for the flesh of a man.

But they will not find us, for the trees are on our side.

Well, Aabel remembered a tale from his boyhood, and the tale was of Baba Yaga and her house with hen's feet. And in that tale, a little girl tied a ribbon around a tree, and that tree raised up

297

walls of thorn to keep the witch away. But Aabel said: we have no ribbons to tie around these trees, and without it we are gone.

No, said the man who had once been a boy, for I too remember a tale from when I was a boy. And in that tale, men lived wild in the woods, even though soldiers from the King in the West were sent to murder them. So we will be like those men, and trust in the trees.

Well, they ran, and were chased, and they ran and were chased, and they ran and were chased again. But the black pines crowded them, and would let no light shine through, and though the monstrous men from Gulag pounded after them, the forest floor covered their trails and hid them from view. And the black pines shifted and sent their pursuers along different paths, into parts of the woodland more dense.

Well, it happened that Aabel and the man who had once been a boy came to the edge of the woodland, and all about them were white heaths of snow. But not a flake fell from the sky. And Aabel said: they will follow us, where there are no trees to guard us.

And the man who had once been a boy said: but we cannot turn back.

And so they ran, and they were chased, and they ran and they were chased, and they ran and they were chased again. And soon, when they looked back, they could see the men who had once been their companions come from the forest.

They are stronger because they have eaten, said Aabel.

Eaten the flesh of man, said the man who had once been a boy.

The boy wants to hear no more. This is not like the story of Baba Yaga. She would feast on boys and girls too, but she lived in a house on hen's feet, and she rode on a broomstick, and she did not feel so very real . . .

'Papa,' he bursts in, 'is it true?'

But his papa's voice rumbles on, heedless of the question.

Well, Aabel was weak and the man who had once been a boy was weak, and as day turned to night, as Perpetual Winter closed his fist, they turned and saw the monsters almost upon them.

Where are the trees? cried Aabel.

The trees are too far! cried the man who had once been a boy.

And at once their companions were there. And there were five where there had once been eight, and the five had faces of scarlet and black and hands webbed in red. And Aabel said: I see you have not stopped at Lom.

No, said their leader, and we will not stop there! Do you not know that man eats man was the law of that great frozen city called Gulag? We are men and we obey the first law.

'Papa, is it true?'

At once, the man who had once been a boy begged the trees. And though the trees were far away, the trees answered his call. And into the night rose the howling of a hundred wolves. And a blizzard stirred up and out of the blizzard brawled those wolves. And the monsters saw the wolves and cried: what dark magic is this? And the man who had once been a boy cried: it is no magic, for the wolf calls out to its own, and he who is afraid of the wolf should not enter the forest . . .

Well, the wolves set upon the men, all but for Aabel and the man who had once been a boy. And Aabel and the man who had once been a boy ran into the blizzard, and the blizzard cupped them in its hand and kept them safe until the trees could succour them once more.

The old man's arms close tight over the boy. Each word is punctuated by a swift, sharp constriction.

So ends our tale of the men who ran away.

The boy is silent. He shakes.

'Are you bringing me that little girl, boy?'

'I'm trying to, papa.'

The boy squirms back, meaning to slope into the gingerbread house and wait until morning, the next morning, five mornings hence, but the old man's eyes are locked like a cage of roots and there is no gap to squirm through. He falls, instead, into the corrupted lap, listens to the hammering of an uneven heart.

Try, the old man breathes, *harder*.

On the day he judges to be Friday, he leaves his papa to his roaming and takes a long trail down to the cattail pond, eyes darting in search of his papa's trail along the way. There, he crawls into the den and lays down a hunk of ash hacked from the forest walls. In one hand he holds a stone with a point like the head of a spear, or an arrow without its shaft. He turns the wood against the stone's point and, in that way, carves down another layer, letting the shavings fall to the floor. Soon, a thin column emerges at each corner of the wood, legs with little bulbs at their bottom to make hoofs. Next, he gouges down so that a tail stands proudly from the rear. He stands it up, this thing without a face, and places next to it the little Russian horse. This new creature is like the Russian horse's bastard brother, uglier and unloved. Holding the stone closer to its nib, he scores a face, a mane, a pattern in its hide.

Hours, and more hours still, and scratch by scratch: a new little friend.

By the time he is done, the darkening has begun. This, he knows, is the start of the weekend. He knows it has a special power because sometimes he watches Elenya coming home, and on these nights there is a different spring in her step – because she, like him, sits out the inexorable weeks. In his head, she cannot wait to come back to see him in the forest.

300

Elenya's return is heralded by headlights over the rooftop. He waits in mama's tree until he can hear the engine of the truck; then the voices of Elenya and her father, bickering as they clamber out. This time, it seems, Elenya has *answered back*. Whatever this means, her father is sick of it. He doesn't want to know. School can wait, he says – but if she dares answer back to her mother tonight, Christmas will be cancelled.

Christmas. The word, so unreal, pummels into him like those other remembered words: Friday; weekend.

He does not have to wait for long. Mishka's barking tells him that Elenya has gone into the house – and, soon after, she appears fleetingly in the bedroom window, tearing off old clothes and wriggling into new ones. She presses her face to the glass, wiping away the fog with the end of her sleeve, looks down – and her face breaks into the wildest grin.

Elenya disappears and emerges, moments later, from the door at the back of the house. 'Where are you?'

'Elenya!'

At the edge of the garden, she finds him in the trees. 'I can't stay long,' she begins. 'They'll come looking . . .'

'I thought . . .'

'Not tonight, little wolf! *Tomorrow.*'

'Tomorrow,' whispers the boy. It seems another aeon away. He does not want to sleep in the gingerbread house. He does not want another story from his papa. He wants . . .

Elenya is staring at him with withering eyes. She mouths, 'I know who you are.'

The boy is about to offer her the new wooden horse when her words fell him.

'Who I am?'

'You're that lost little boy . . .'

'What do you . . .'

'There's a boy in class, some simple little thing. He doesn't have any friends, so he has to make them up. And there he was, just wandering on the edge of the schoolyard, playing with those imaginary things, so some of us went to see him and he said it wasn't imaginary at all, you used to be his friend and then you disappeared.'

'Yuri,' whispers the boy.

Elenya lifts a hand, presses it to his chest, propels him away. The boy, unsuspecting, stumbles back. Though he catches himself on the groping arm of mama's tree, the new toy horse slips from his grasp.

'It *is* true!'

The boy crawls back. One hand over another, and his fingers find the wooden horse.

'I made it for you,' he says, offering it up.

'I thought it was just another one of his games, but I asked Navitski and . . .'

She looms above him, with only the chipped wooden horse in between. He thinks he is going to push it into her hand, force her to see how much he wants to go through those doors, meet her mama and papa, perhaps even be a part of her Christmas – *Christmas*, such a terrible thing – but the word lodges in his head and slowly his arms fall. *Navitski.*

'Elenya,' he says. 'You didn't . . .'

'Didn't what?'

'. . . tell?'

'They were looking for you. Navitski said. There were police. There were posters. And . . .' She holds her breath before going

302

on; the boy holds his as well, for this must be the most terrible thing of all. 'I know your name. I'm your friend and you never told, but I know your name.'

Somehow he is back on his feet. He leaves the wooden horse where it has fallen, rolled over in the dirt. Even its eyes are accusing. He stumbles over roots, vaults a rotting log.

'Alek!' she calls. 'Alek, come back!'

But he will not, and he knows that, even if she were to follow, he could lose her in only a few simple strides. That, he admits through breathy tears, is because he is a wild thing, like the foxes, the ravens, the deer who lurk in these trees and barely ever get seen – and Elenya, she is of the world.

At the gingerbread house, the fire is dead – but he cannot see his papa's trench in the forest mulch, so there is time enough before he comes into camp, draped with the day's killings. He heaps up kindling, builds a pyramid and whispers to the embers to come back to life. Tonight, the resurrection will not take place as easily as on nights past.

Probably it is because his heart is hammering, his hands will not still, his breath will not stop coming in ragged fits. *Alek.* He has not heard it in so long, and now it is not right; using that name would be like putting on clothes, or sitting in a bathtub with soap suds dripping from his hair. It would be like potato chips and cushions and sherbet and birthdays. All of those things that used to exist.

Something compels him to dive into the gingerbread house, where Elenya's scarlet coat lies like a bedroll. He drags it to the pathetic fire his trembling hands have conjured and begins to feed it with a sleeve. The fabric is long in catching light, but when the flames take hold they do so with incandescent rage.

He watches as the threads turn to fiery snakes. They race up the sleeves, devouring, taking shoulders and hood.

If she were to tell, they would come looking. If they caught him, they would take him away. And then – then his papa would be alone, out here in the forests. He would live like the wild thing he is, and then he would die – be it this winter, next winter, or in a hundred winters' time – and then the trees would drink him up, turn him into branches more brittle than the man who stalks between them. And then, for all of time, the boy would know: my promise was broken. And if mama's still here, some-where in the trees, waiting for summer, she'll know.

The smoke of the scarlet wool billows up. It has a strong, acrid aroma, more bitter than burning wood. Enveloped by that smoke, he thinks: but if she told, they would be here *now*. If she *really* told, they'd have come and taken me away.

Perhaps . . . she meant what she said. She's his friend. His *friend*. Another thing from that long-ago time, but if *Alek* and Christmas and Fridays can come back, perhaps this can too.

Elenya's coat has gone and the fire is in deep retreat when he hears the familiar thump and pull. Birds roosting in the branches scatter, and then his Grandfather's shape resolves out of the darkness.

'You let her die.'

'The ice got in the wood, papa.'

'You should have smoked it dry.'

'I know . . .'

'Let me.'

The old man levers himself down. One incantation, and then another, and the flames rise. Once, his papa told him there was no sorcery in fire. Tonight, the boy might believe he has been lied to all along.

Across the fire: 'You've been to the girl.'

'I haven't.'

'I can smell it on you.'

His mind scrambles. He thinks: papa, she knows; he thinks: papa, they remember me. Yuri and Mr Navitski. All the rest.

He opens his lips. Words find a way. He says, 'I thought they might leave out scraps.'

'You don't take their scraps. We're wolves, not foxes.'

'Yes, papa.'

'So, did you ask her?'

'Ask her . . .'

'To come.'

The boy shakes his head. 'It's too soon, papa.'

The old man returns the words, through his broken crusted mouth: 'It's too soon, papa.'

'She's afraid of the forest.'

'Take her by the hand. Bring her to me. I'll make her afraid, so afraid she'll never breathe a thing.'

'She's a nice girl, papa. She . . .'

'Pretty girls tell tales.'

It boils out of him. 'They don't, papa! She won't! She's a sad little girl, papa. She doesn't say it, but she is. All she wants is a friend. I can tell.'

They drag the pot into the flames, and in goes the day's deaths, innards and all.

'Papa,' the boy ventures, 'did you know it's Christmas?'

'Christmas, is it?'

He trembles. 'What will we do for Christmas?'

But all through the long night, his papa won't breathe a word in reply.

He is awake before dawn, and his papa still sleeping. There have been foxes in the clearing, a vixen and a cub of late summer, and the pot has been upturned in the dead fire. Perhaps his papa did not wake, or perhaps he woke and simply watched. Whichever, the foxes were not afraid; to them, he is as much of the forest as the snow and ice.

He stokes the fire before he goes because, no matter what dark stories his papa now dreams, he is still his papa, and there is still his promise.

The faint light of dawn is threatening through the snow clouds when he reaches Elenya's house. Once there, he gazes up. It is not long before Elenya is gazing back down.

Moments later, she is at the backdoor, beckoning him across the garden.

'Elenya,' he begins. 'I'm sorry. I should have told you. Everything, Elenya.'

She does not seem interested in his apologies. She whispers, 'We have to get you scrubbed first.'

'Scrubbed?'

'They'll never think you're a boy from school, when you look like you've been eating dirt.'

'But – how?'

Elenya explains that they could scrub him in snow, which is a way of bathing she's seen on the television, but soap would do just as well. To get him soaped up, though, she must smuggle him into the house. Such a thing is possible, for it is a Saturday morning and this means her mama and papa lie in bed until late, and she is forbidden from hammering on their door, no matter what manner of strange sounds come from the other side.

Before they pass through the kitchen, Elenya reaches into the tin sink and produces a washcloth. Though she wrings it dry, it is still damp when she presses it to his face. She kneads, more fiercely than she might, and the boy reels back. Only Elenya's admonishing glare makes him behave. She scrubs again and brings back the washcloth, smeared in browns, yellows and blacks.

'See?' she says, presenting the dirt like evidence in a trial. 'You'd clean up to be a nice little thing, Alek, if you had a mother to look after you.'

The boy doesn't mean his lip to tremble; she is trying to be kind, but does not know what is kind and what is not.

'Oh,' she stalls as realization dawns. 'I didn't mean it, Alek. You must have had a nice mama.'

'I did.'

307

'She wouldn't want you living in the wilds with that old man, would she?'

'That's her papa.'

Elenya's face is flushed red, as if she does not know what route this conversation ought to take. Conversations, the boy decides, are like the trees of the forest: they can throw up walls of thorns and direct you along channels you would rather not climb.

At last, Elenya says, 'I'm running a bath. Then you'll be scrubbed up, and we'll say your papa dropped you off to play.'

'Will they be cross?'

'They'll be *delighted*. They think having a friend will keep me out of trouble.'

She leads him along the kitchen and to the foot of the stairs.

'Have you been in very much trouble, Elenya?'

She beams. 'That's *my* story, but you're not hearing that until I hear yours.'

Upstairs, steam rises from the tub. There is a shower. A toilet. He remembers: you sit on the rim and make a mess of the bowl, and after you don't need to ruck up dead leaves or forest mulch, just draw on a chain and let the water take it away.

She tells him to take off his clothes and get in the tub. He shakes his head. The bathroom walls are shiny and white, and beads of steam gather in the lines between the tiles. Soon, the steam obscures half of the room.

'Come on, Alek. It isn't that hard. You've had a bath before, haven't you?'

He shakes his head.

'Wasn't there even a bathtub here when this was your house?'

'You saw it,' he begins, peering into the mountains of foam. 'When you came with your mama and papa to look at it.'

'What?'

'It was last winter. I saw you, Elenya. You were in the woods with your mama and papa. Me and my papa were out a-hunting . . .'

'You little spy!' she shrills, with a mixture of horror and delight.

'There wasn't a bathtub at all.'

'Alek, there was hardly a house. When my papa said we had to live there, I didn't think there was a way *anybody* could live there.'

'We'd been there all winter. You found our camp. You . . .' He stops, wary of upsetting her. '. . . said it was disgusting.'

She steps back, studies him. 'You're not disgusting, Alek. It's that wild old man.'

She takes his hand, teasing him across the room. The water is soapy, hidden by a mountain range of bubbles, dreamy as snow clouds. 'Come on. It's good for you.'

Taking off his rabbit-skin pelts, the rags of his vest, is much harder he had thought. For too long they have been a part of him. When they are pooled around his feet, he feels like that same skinned rabbit, his pelt flayed off for all to see.

'Well, go on! Do I have to lift you in as well?'

He does not go until she manhandles him. Then, he lifts his foot. It hovers on the top of the bubbles and he bravely forces it down.

The water attacks him, more fierce than fire. He recoils from the heat, and the only thing to stop him from falling is Elenya at his back.

'Alek, you *have* to! Otherwise, you're as wild as your papa.'

Those words are a greater spur than any command. He puts his foot back, and this time pokes it slowly into the water. In an instant, the bubbles around his calf fade away, turning to brown scum on top of the water. His sole finds the bottom of the bath, and he levers his other leg in. Now he stands there, at the centre of a spreading dark tide. Elenya glares. It is a command to sit down.

Slowly, the boy lowers himself.

He is boiling. Burning. Only slowly does the sensation fade. He does not know what to do, so he simply sits there. A tiny rubber duck, as ridiculous as the fairybook door knocker, stares at him from the edge of the bath.

When she sees him returning the stare, Elenya lifts it down, sets it to bobbing on the dark tide. 'We'll have to do your face and arms as well.'

The boy barely hears her. Everything is so distant, seen through a veil of steam.

'I'll do it for you, then,' Elenya sighs.

It is as it was with mama. She lifts each arm to draw the sponge under it, tousles his hair, drips down soap suds that tear up his eyes. Then there is a measuring jug; she fills it with fresh water and pours it over him. All down his body run rivers of brown. At last, she pulls the plug and he watches as the silt of the forest washes away.

'Come on, quick! I don't know how I'll explain if they catch you in the bath . . .'

First, there is the matter of clothes. In her bedroom, she sits him at the foot of her bed, where a nest has been made of eiderdown and pillows. There, he faces the big bay window. From the glass, there peers the reflection of a boy he does not know, a boy with cheeks scrubbed pink; with wet hair hanging in tangles that nevertheless gleam from shampoo; with a towel

310

to hide his pure white skin, and a strange patchwork of rabbit skins hanging over his shoulder.

'What is it? Haven't you ever seen a reflection before?'

He is, he decides, as wild a thing as his papa. It doesn't matter that the dirt has sloughed off, that the thistles have been teased from his hair. The boy he is looking at now – that is not the same boy who lived in a tenement with a bedroom of his own. This is a boy who deserves only the forest, the endless trees, the marshes and the aspens beyond.

'I know,' says Elenya. 'First, we'll brush this hair.'

He feels Elenya's fingers in his hair, her comb, her brush. His hair, still somehow curled, grows longer and more defined: first past his neck, then his shoulders.

'Didn't your papa ever cut your hair?'

The boy shakes his head.

'It's nice hair, Alek. Long and thick, like a girl's.'

Elenya piles up the rabbit-skin pelts and ferrets in a trunk. Inside there are dresses and cardigans, things she decries too bad for the boy – but beneath is a blouse that might fit, and beneath that a pair of culottes that will pass for shorts. The boy barely moves as she dresses him, letting her lift and position his arms and legs as she might a doll.

These new clothes itch. He has to look at them in the reflection, and when he does, he does not see a smartly dressed boy, but a wolf in girl's clothing. She has tied back his hair with a band, and it stretches his face into something of a snarl. He turns, instinctively reaching out to wrap himself in the eiderdown from her bed.

'Oh, *eiderdowns*. I'd forgotten how much you like *eiderdowns*.'

The boy feels better, curled inside it, but she tugs it from him all the same.

311

'Time for you to eat something more than dirt, Alek. Come on, I'm making a breakfast fit for a king . . .'

The eggs are rich and yellow, and quite unlike the eggs of summer, which he roasted on stones or fed to his papa, soft and raw. It takes the boy a mouthful before he registers: these are chicken's eggs, bought from a market. Next to them are sticks of toasted bread, heavy with melted butter. Elenya calls them soldiers. Like so many others, the word thunders back into the boy. Soldiers, he remembers, are not just the wicked men from his papa's fables. They are pieces of bread too.

As they eat, the smells stir Mishka from her basket. Excited as she is to see Elenya, she is more excited to see the boy. Soon, she is in his face, covering him with her tongue, drawing in his strange scent of pungent forest and fragrant soap. Elenya tries to drive her off, but this morning Mishka will not be denied. Only the boy's hands, running through her shaggy scruff, will quell her. At last, she rolls in front of the wood-burner, exposing her tummy for hands to tickle. When they are not forthcoming, she rolls back and – as if to prove a point – whips a soldier from the boy's plate.

'Mishka!' Elenya cries, driving her off.

But the boy can only beam.

He devours the egg and soldiers so quickly that Elenya must offer him more. He says: another egg and toast, and I remember . . . bacon. Hot bacon, with streaks of fat, and cheese and biscuits and cake. Suddenly, all of those things are flurrying at him like a snowfall. Elenya rushes back into the kitchen, and while she is gone he sets to rolling with Mishka. By the time she has returned, Mishka has pinned him down, straddling him with all four paws and subjecting him to the worst assault with wet nose and tongue.

'What's going on down there?'

Not Elenya's voice. Her father. He tries to squirm from beneath the playful dog, but Mishka is too embroiled in the game to stop slobbering until Elenya's father barks again. By then, there is the clatter of footsteps. Wiping the slobber from his face, the boy sees two great tree trunks of legs descending the stairs.

'Papa,' says Elenya. 'This is . . . Alek. He's my friend. From school.'

She speaks each fragment as if she is daring her father to contradict her. Then there can be a fight, and then Elenya can win – for what other explanation is there, what better way to prove she has a friend and is fitting in at school than this boy now squirming on the living room carpet?

Elenya takes his hand, wrestles him upright. When he stands, he sees Elenya's father up close for the first time. Absurdly, he is wearing no shirt, only a pair of pyjama bottoms. His chest is covered in hair coiled up like fur. At the bottom of the stairs, he kneads his eyes.

'Elenya,' he says, more softly now, 'did your mother know you'd invited a friend?'

'I'm sure I told her, papa.'

'When did he . . .'

'Oh, his papa dropped him off. He was on his way over the border. He's coming back for him tonight. It's for *business*.'

Each fragment is another dare. Wearily, her father turns to tramp back up the stairs.

'Papa!' she calls. 'Aren't you going to say hello? His name's Alek.'

'I'll say hello when I'm dressed,' he mutters darkly.

One tramping foot, and then another; as he slips out of sight, Elenya spins on her heel wearing an absurd grin. 'He *likes* you!'

It doesn't seem that way to the boy. He finds that he has been shaking all along. The thought of another man, another papa, is as treacherous as being here, with four walls bearing down.

'Alek,' Elenya says, coming to his side. 'Calm down. It's only my papa.'

The boy takes deep breaths, but the only thing that properly calms him is to run his fingers in Mishka's long fur. 'What if they ask me? Where I'm from. Who I am.'

'You'll leave it to me,' says Elenya. 'And follow my lead . . .'

Dressed in corded jacket and jeans, Elenya's father is not nearly as terrifying as the boy first thought. Nor is her mama a terror, as she sweeps down the stairs and cries out a welcome, at the same time shooting Elenya a succession of serrated looks. There will, she declares, be a big breakfast and disappears into the kitchen, only to reappear an instant later.

'You made him breakfast?'

'Mama, he was hungry.'

'Did your father know you'd invited a friend?'

Elenya says, 'I'm sure I told him, mama.'

'And is he staying all day?'

'Yes, mama.'

Her father reappears from the front door, shaking snow from his collar. 'You forgot about our tree, of course.'

'Papa?'

'Our tree, Elenya. We were going to collect our tree.'

The boy's eyes beg explanation. Elenya mutters, 'For

Christmas. When we were in Brest we used to buy one, but now daddy says that buying a tree's for peasants. We've got trees all around, so we're going to chop one down.'

'Chop one down?'

He is aghast. It would, he decides, be like taking an axe to a person's legs.

Elenya's father, busy unbuckling his boots, must register the terror in the boy's tone, for he strides over, his meaty hands open wide. 'It's our first Christmas here, Alek. Why buy a tree somebody else has chopped down, when we have the forest?'

He thinks to say: but you can't go into the forest! Yet his throat is dry, his tongue sliced in two just the same as his papa's. He sidles closer to Elenya's side; here, Mishka forms a barrier of fur and flesh between him and her father. Even so, he wants to take her hand and hide behind her. It is, he remembers, exactly like that very first day at the schoolhouse, when mama had to leave him behind.

'The trees from Brest were better, daddy. Those trees, out there, they're . . .'

'Wild?'

'Horrible,' spits Elenya.

'Our Elenya's too much of a princess, Alek,' chimes in her mother, swooping back into the living room with a steaming mug for her father. 'We came here to get away from all that, Elenya.'

'We came here to get away from *everything*,' Elenya says – and, for the first time, the boy senses real bile in her voice.

When her father drinks, the sound is like his papa's jackboot sinking into marsh water and drawing back up.

'What about you, Alek?'

He trembles, wordless.

'What about him, papa?'

'Well, won't Alek have a Christmas tree this year?'

'Not from that old forest.'

Another slurp, with music like the marsh.

'The forest's the place for a Christmas tree. Ded Moroz himself lives in that forest. Did you know that, Alek?'

'Well,' interjects Elenya. 'I'm sure there are wild men living out there, but hardly Ded Moroz.'

Her father appears defeated. 'I suppose we haven't seen him yet,' he says as he stands. 'Maybe it's just a story. But you're not too old for stories yet, Elenya. Just remember that.'

Her father is crossing the room, bound for the kitchen and the better companionship of her mother, when the boy feels suddenly emboldened.

'I know lots of stories from the forest!'

The boy sees a thwarted look ghost across Elenya's face.

Before he has gone to the kitchen, her father turns around. 'So you do have a voice!'

Now he loses it again.

'What stories do you know, Alek?'

He whispers, 'Baba Yaga . . .'

'Well,' says Elenya's father. 'That was *a* forest. Who knows if it was this one? I haven't seen any witch-women out in the wood, or huts with hen's feet. Have you, Elenya?'

She shakes her head, only once, her jaw set rigid.

Now, the boy feels thwarted as well. His face burns, as if he has crept too close to his papa's fire.

'I know other stories,' he says. 'There were partisans in the forest and the soldiers went to catch them, and sometimes they took mamas and papas and boys and girls and fed them to the trees.'

316

Her father is silent. For a reason the boy cannot divine, he looks shocked, saddened even.

'It was the wars of winter,' ventures the boy.

'There were terrible wars, Alek, but that was long ago.' He crosses the room. In the window, where Mishka reclines like a wolfskin rug, there sits a case of books. When he crouches, he is tall as the boy but many times broader. He fingers the spines and plucks one out. Then he comes back to the boy, tries to press the book into his hands. Now that he is close again, the boy shrinks back. Instead, he must present it to Elenya.

'This old thing,' she mutters. 'This is for babies.'

'Folk tales aren't for babies, Elenya. They're for us all.'

He looks at the boy, half-hidden behind Elenya's back. 'It isn't history, Alek, but some of these stories are quite as bloody. Folk tales are just another way of telling history. They come from before the time when there was writing and books. Just families, in houses like this, staring into that outer dark and telling tales about what happened out there.'

'But there were still forests,' whispers the boy.

'And always will be,' he replies.

As her father tramps away, he lays his meaty hand on Elenya's head, half to stroke her, half to clout. 'You could learn something from him, Elenya. If you were so studious, we might have stayed in Brest.'

Outside, there is a strange quality in the winter light. The sun, seemingly lower than the canopy, gropes over the treetops. Where it pierces the branches, it cascades to the ground. As it advances, it illuminates first the gaping maw of a badger's sett; then the emperor oak with a ragged collection of sticks stacked up in its roots; then the open bones from a rabbit's breast, gnawed clean and cast down for the woodland scavengers to come.

This isn't the tale this isn't the tale I'm the tale I'm the tale . . .

Smeared against the ground, a wild man unfolds and finds himself alone.

In the bedroom, it is better. Here he does not have to tell lies or pretend. Elenya drops the book onto the bed and opens it up. Words and line drawings glimmer out. She traces them with her finger, but to the boy the symbols are inscrutable. He would rather read the etching in bark, the veins of a leaf; those things tell stories as well.

'Here's Baba Yaga,' says Elenya, her finger landing on the image of a wizened forest witch whose hair is curled around pine cones and acorn. 'And here's the bit where she eats the little boy.' She grins dementedly.

'Does it say about the wars of winter? What about the Winter King?'

'There are no wars of winter. There isn't a Winter King. Not in these stories.'

The boy crawls to the lip of the bed, balances his head on the covers, and scrutinizes the page. Elenya, busy turning the leaves, bats his head away as she might Mishka.

'They're in my papa's stories.'

'So?'

'So why aren't they in the book?'

'Maybe they're different stories.'

'The book has Baba Yaga.'

'*Every* book has Baba Yaga.' She hesitates. 'I don't like your papa's stories. What was he telling, when he was hunting the deer?'

'It was how the man escaped from Gulag to find his babe in the woods, and the other men started to starve and turned into monsters to eat each other.'

The way he remembers it sends a chill more precise than the winter into his veins.

'He told me another, afterwards. About how they ran away from the men and then the trees sent wolves to protect them.'

Elenya folds the book closed. 'I think your papa's gone wild in the head. Those aren't real stories at all. If they were, I'd have heard them. Didn't your mama ever tell you fairytales?'

'Not ones like my papa . . .'

'Then maybe they're not proper tales at all. A tale has to have a hero.'

'It has a hero. It's the man who once was a boy.'

'And it has to have a villain.'

He thinks: it could be the Winter King, but once the Winter King was good. He thinks: it could be the wise men, but the wise men only do what they think the Winter King needs. Maybe it's the great frozen city of Gulag, but a villain has to be a man, not a place.

'I'm bored of tales,' declares Elenya, slamming the book. 'Don't you ever get bored of tales, Alek?'

They used to thrill him. He remembers first coming to the tenement, gazing at his papa's face etched in lines and thinking: hiding inside are so many stories. Yet the ones he listens to now are like the insects that crawl into his clothes at night; they stay with him, cannot be rooted out.

'What about a . . . *game?*'

It seems that Elenya has been waiting for those very words. She leaps to attention, cartwheels to the furthest side of the window, and opens a big drawer. Inside, countless board games are piled. The boy can even remember how to play; there are pieces and dice and you take turns, and at the end there is a winner and a loser.

At last, she selects a box. The front depicts a forest more shadowy than the one revealing itself in the window light. A trail meanders between oaks and along it goes a girl, with a scarlet cloak and her hood fastened with a single silver clasp. From one hand there hangs a basket, piled with apples and pears.

'One of us is Red Riding Hood,' declares Elenya, revealing the disordered mess inside the box. 'The other is a wolf. We'll have to share the woodcutter out. It's meant for three players.'

The boy inches to the very edge of the bed, a precipice quite as frightening as any treetop.

'What do we do?'

'We roll a dice and Red Riding Hood tries to get to Grandma's house, and the wolf tries to eat her, and the woodcutter tries to kill the wolf.'

'How?'

'He chops off his head!' Elenya declares, mimicking the motion. 'He has an axe.'

'My papa has an axe.'

'I remember.'

The boy slides from the bed, to sit cross-legged at the edge of the board. It is an elaborate thing, though worn around the edges where it has been folded up inside the box. There are pop-up trees – he recognizes chestnut and alder – and fringes of black pine in every corner. A trail snakes all around the board, ending finally at a pop-up cottage in the centre.

'Who do you want to be?'

The boy is silent, still staring at the board.

'You be the wolf. I'll . . .'

'I don't want to be the wolf!'

'So you want to be the girl?'

The boy nods, sharply.

'Alek, you can't be the girl.'

'Then I won't be anything.'

Elenya gives a dramatic rolling of her eyes and hands him a tin figure. 'I suppose this makes *me* the wolf. But don't think I'm going easy on you. If I catch you, it'll be little boy or girl, or whatever you are, for dinner – and don't think I'll let some woodcutter stop me . . . Well, go on! You get a three-turn head-start.'

The game begins. After three rolls of the dice, Elenya takes her first turn. After three more, the woodcutter begins. After much wrangling, the boy is permitted to play the woodcutter too – because, really, the woodcutter and Red Riding Hood are on the same side. Soon, the boy is high on his knees, excited enough to shout out with every roll. Elenya quells him with her eyes, but it must be a good thing to see the boy beaming, for she returns every one.

'I'm going to catch you,' she says, reaching over the board to jab a finger in his armpit, taking delight as he wriggles back.

'You're not! I'm nearly at the . . .'

A voice cuts him off, reverberating around the house.

'Elenya! Are you getting ready?'

Her father's voice, big enough to shake the very walls. Elenya scrambles up. It is only as the boy tracks her to the door that he realizes the day has dawned. The sunlight, still weak, is spilling over the tops of the clouds, and what filters through has woken a ghostly world. With Elenya at the door, his eyes turn to the window, and the garden beneath. Mishka is out, running her snout over every new ridge of fallen snow. The boy sees the paw prints she has left behind.

They are not the only tracks in the virgin snow.

He flings a look over his shoulder, but Elenya is gone, out into the hall to bicker with her father. He turns back. Mishka has lit on it now, the very same tracks that cause his breast to tighten.

A single deep trench crosses the garden. It stops, circles the snowman, then crosses the expanse to reach the border of the house itself. There the snow is churned up in a deep crater. Somebody has lingered.

His heart hammers, but he finds he cannot look away. His eyes search for pockets in the darkness, the gaps between the trees where some creature of dead wood and thorn might be lurking. It is useless; every shadow has a face, every trunk the visage of a man.

'Alek . . .'

Elenya has come back into the room, only to find the boy huddled at the window.

'Look,' he whispers.

Elenya's eyes drift down, but they find only the dog. Following some strange canine instinct, Mishka looks up and returns the stare with a shrill bark.

'They're going to get the Christmas tree. They want us to . . .'

Before Elenya can reply, he hears the tread of heavy footsteps and knows that her father has come into the room. Even so, he does not turn around. His eyes continue to hunt out the darknesses, tracking the turning of the trench.

'Alek,' Elenya's father booms, 'how would you like a trip into the forest?'

'I've told you, papa!' Elenya shrieks. 'Alek's staying here with . . .'

The boy turns, ghostly pale.

'What is it, Alek?'

'Can't you see he's afraid?' Elenya retorts, planting herself between the boy and her father. Her eyes light on the book of folk tales and she whips it aloft. 'You're the one who gave him this thing! Now he thinks there's Baba Yaga and ogres and witches in the trees.'

'Alek, they're only stories.'

He thinks: but are they? There's a wild man down there. He isn't a story. He's my papa.

'Let us stay,' Elenya begins. 'We'll just play. There won't be any trouble.'

'You're not supposed to be on your own.'

'I'm on my own almost all of the time!'

At last, her father relents. 'I thought you might want to help us pick a tree . . .'

'Oh, *trees*,' Elenya mutters. 'I see a thousand trees every day.'

The boy listens to the heavy tread as her father goes back down the stairs. After he has gone, he turns back to the window. To his horror: a new trench, carved into the garden. This time, it barely reaches the snowman before it stops, circles around, and blazes a new trail back to the forest.

'Elenya, you have to stop them.'

'Oh, let them go! What do we need with . . .'

This time, at the window, Elenya sees the trench. 'Is it him?'

The boy nods, feeling as if it is he who has a knife at her throat. 'It's my papa.'

'He's come looking for you.'

The boy doesn't say: no, no Elenya, he's come looking for you . . .

From downstairs, he hears the opening of a door, can even feel the flurry of cold air that steals swiftly within, like fingers taking his scruff to drag him away. That cold hand is the hand of his papa. His papa is the woods and his papa is the wild, and his papa is the world forever and ever.

For a moment the figures below are obscured, too close to the house as they emerge. Then he sees Elenya's father, wrapped up in black with his hair flying free. Next, her mother, scarf wound tightly around her head. They stop on the threshold, and the boy realizes they must be locking the door. He looks again into the snow dark beneath the trees. He sees nothing. He sees nothing again. Then, a whisper of movement, as indistinct as a starling settling on a branch to disturb the snow. He stares, and it is only as Elenya's parents begin to cross the garden, with Mishka on their heels, that he knows he is right: it is his papa beneath the trees, watching as the family approach.

He opens his mouth. Wants to cry out. But his breath is frozen as his papa at night, and the words do not come.

Elenya's parents go under the trees, swallowed up by the snow dark.

'Alek, where is he? I can't . . .'

He says, 'Get down from the window.'

'He isn't there, Alek. I'd see him if he . . .'

He grabs her by the shoulders, wrenches her down. 'I said, get down!'

She reels back, rolling over the corner of the bed to lie, winded, on the floorboards at its side. When she looks up, her eyes are accusing, as if it is the boy who is the wilderness, and not his papa come to the house.

'This is my house!' she cries. 'You can't do that in my house!'

'No,' says the boy, vaulting over her to get to the door. 'It's my house, Elenya. It's where I lived. It's where my mama was born.'

She scrambles to catch him, before he ventures onto the landing. 'What if my father finds him, waiting out there?'

The boy says, 'What if my papa finds *him*?'

There is yet time to head him off, drive him away from the house. Before he goes, he snatches up his rabbit-skin pelt, hanging it over the strange clothes she has made him wear. Then he takes off, down the stairs, into the prickling heat of the living room. Through the kitchen and to the backdoor – but it holds fast, locked, and his hands cannot force it.

Not knowing what else to do, he thunders back. Elenya is standing on the cusp of the living room.

'I need the key. You have to let me out.'

'Alek . . .'

'If I go now, he'll never know I was here.'

'Why shouldn't he know? What's he going to do?'

'You don't understand. He thinks you'll . . .'

Her face makes him stop. Her eyes, directed at some place over his shoulder, sparkle with knowing. Slowly he turns. Along the barrel of the kitchen, past the counters and tin sink . . . a shape is pressed to the glass, and that shape is his papa.

He goes slowly, because his papa will only see him when a movement catches his eye. It is the same way that he hunts; his eyes grown weak, the dimming of the world. Through the glass, he can hear the wheezing of the old man, as strained as it was in those days in the bunker. A breath like winter itself rises up and pastes itself across the pane, obscuring him further. Now, he is only some ghost, his edges furred.

Then, his eyes are drawn to the door handle at the end of the kitchen. It trembles. It turns. The door holds fast, and then there is stillness.

'Get me the key, Elenya.'

'I don't have a key!'

'Then . . .'

A second more, and the handle turns again. The door resists, bucking in its frame. The handle stops, springs back into position. Then thunder, and the door quakes; thunder, and its hinges groan.

'Boy?'

He does not reply.

'Boy, are you there?'

He lifts his foot to go into the kitchen but realizes, too late, that it is a terrible mistake. Lifting his foot means he must put it back down and, as soon as he does, the handle twists again, up and down, up and down, each time more fiercely than the last.

'Boy, let me in . . .'

Silence.

'Open the door, boy! I'll blow it down if I . . .'

Elenya takes him by the arm, hauls him back to the living room.

'You could go by the front door . . .'

Here there is a key dangling from a nail. She leaps to snatch it down. Once, twice, three times – and it is in her hands. As she fumbles with the lock, the boy looks back down the barrel of the kitchen. In the frosted glass, his papa still moves. He thinks he sees an arm brought back, the flash of the axe's blade.

The front door swings open, and winter hauls him out. On the threshold, he takes Elenya by the wrist. 'Tell them . . . my papa came and picked me up.'

'Alek, why is he so angry?'

The boy says, 'I've got to go.'

He does not make his goodbyes. He steps into the snow and, dazzled momentarily by the winter light, hurries along the edge of the house.

When he steals around the corner, he sees his papa pressed against the backdoor, still bawling into the wood. Sometimes it is words – *boy!* – and sometimes it is just sound. He holds himself just far enough away that the old man could not claw out and grasp him.

'Papa, I'm here.'

The old man turns. He seems perplexed, as if he cannot understand how the boy has spirited himself through timber and stone.

'I thought they'd caught you,' sobs the old man.

It is not what he was expecting. He hovers, silently.

'Come on,' says his papa. 'We haven't firewood to last another night.'

His papa turns, to carve a new trail back into the forest. As the boy follows, he sees another shape in the frosted glass. Elenya, it seems, has crept along the kitchen to keep watch. As he reaches the edge of the tree line, he keeps looking back at her indistinguishable face.

Before they reach the branches of mama's tree, his papa looks down. 'You . . . what happened to you?'

'What, papa?'

'You *changed*.'

'It's only clothes. From Elenya.'

'It isn't clothes. It's . . .'

There is terror on the old man's face. Something, alive and stirring behind his eyes. 'She *changed* you,' he utters.

The boy finds himself hauled aloft. An instant later, he is cast down into the snow. Before he can stand again, his papa is bustling him forward. No longer does he have a hand on him, but the staff works just as well; he directs him forward, herding him like a dog might a goat. His feet, for too long warmed by radiators and floorboards, find scant purchase on the hard-packed snow, and he tumbles again.

In that way, with looks cast constantly over his shoulder, they go between the trees. Behind them, he sees Elenya's face framed in the kitchen glass. He looks again and she is gone. He looks again and she is back in her bedroom window. Her face is drawn. She can see everything, from on high: the boy, harried like prey; his papa, bearing down.

'Quick, boy,' the old man says softly. 'We haven't much time.'

'What, papa?' he says, panicked as a hare. 'What should I do? Please, papa . . .'

'Take them off.'

'Take what . . .'

'The clothes, boy! Quickly now!'

The rabbit-skin pelts come off in a second; then the blouse. Underneath the culottes he is wearing only the rags of his underwear, the same things he wore in the tenement in the long ago. Naked but for those rags, he trembles. He does not want to look, but his eyes are drawn upwards. Elenya can *see*. She has seen him naked, scrubbed every corner of his body, but now she sees him flayed.

'She put you in her bath.'

'It was to clean me, papa.'

'Look what she's done to you,' he breathes, bereft of all hope.

He looks about to collapse in an angular heap of legs and bones. If he did, he would look like any storm-fallen tree. The boy goes to him, thinking to feel the beating of his heart, but the old man recoils, as if he cannot bear to be touched.

'Get it off,' says the old man.

'What, papa?'

'The house, the girl, the *stink*. Get it off, boy! Please, please, get it off . . .'

He is already near naked. The only thing that coats him are the snowflakes that settle on his bare flesh.

'Papa, I . . .'

The old man drops, scooping up forest mulch in his taloned hands. He lurches at the boy, and though the boy wants to beat a retreat, the forest holds him fast. Then his papa's hands are on him, smearing the earth onto his skin.

He closes his eyes, head thrown back. When he opens them, Elenya's eyes are staring straight into his. She has pressed her face against the window glass like a spectre. Disbelieving. Despairing.

'She put you in a bath,' the old man snipes. 'But this is your bath. You're mine, not theirs. Didn't I look after you? Didn't I do what your mama asked?'

'Yes, papa. Yes, papa.'

'Then bathe in it,' he says: half beg, half command. 'If you like your baths so much, you should have one.'

It is a second before realization dawns. He thinks his papa is going to come for him, crown him with more earth, scrape the lichen from the trees and knead it into him. Yet his papa simply watches.

'You're a big boy, aren't you? You want to be a big boy.'

'Papa . . .'

'Well, you can bathe yourself.'

The boy sinks to the ground, with his clothes strewn around.

Tentatively, he scrapes up the muck of rotten forest leaves, the disintegrated mulch of pine. He presses a fistful to his chest. 'It was only a bath, papa,' he sobs, forcing fox dirt back into his hair.

'So is this,' rasps the old man.

He is scouring his breast with another fistful when a sound in the forest stops him. He wrenches his head around, but all he can see is an amorphous mess of black, brown and the dirty white between the trees. Dropping the mulch in his fingers, he rubs away the tears. Now, though, his eyes sting and stream. As he lumbers to his feet, it is all he can do to keep himself from crying out.

'Who said you could stand?'

'Papa, I didn't mean to upset you. I . . .'

There it is, again – not just a sound in the trees, but a voice. *Voices*. Elenya's mama, her papa, coming back to the house.

The boy whirls around. Another shape in the darkness: Mishka. She resolves from the gloom, tongue lolling. In seconds she is on the boy, covering him with her tongue. Seconds later, she is gone again, lying winded and spread-eagled in the roots of an ash, as his papa looms above him, fist drawn back.

'Papa, she's only . . .'

Mishka turns her head towards the boy and the old man hanging above. The boy thinks she might be about to bare her teeth, leap for his papa's neck, but instead her eyes betray something like fear, something like total and utter obedience, and she turns to disappear.

'On your feet,' the old man whispers.

Like Mishka, the boy obeys.

'Which way are they coming?'

The boy does not know.

'Which way!?'

'They went that way, papa,' he says, lifting a hand.

The old man herds him on, directing him with the staff. At a halting pace, they move between oaks, pines, oak again. Sounds whirl and attack in strange, insidious ways: one minute, voices on their left; the next, on their right, ahead, behind.

'Not this way, papa!' the boy shrieks. He lifts a hand, points at impressions in the forest earth. There he sees the snaking paw prints of Mishka the dog. He crouches, snuffles after them. Soon he can see bootprints.

'They came this way, papa.'

In the same instant, the voices reach a clarity like never before. No longer are they just strings of sound. There are words, questions, sentences.

'Papa, quick! They're coming this way!'

The old man is slow, his eyes on the footprints.

'They're coming *back*!'

The boy lopes between the alders. Only yards from the trail, they stop, look back. As the old man catches up with him, the boy can see the trench he has carved, cutting straight across the tracks Elenya's mother and father left behind.

It is a moment before they appear. They are lumbering because they are dragging a tree behind them, a baby pine barely nine feet tall. Its springy branches drag in the dirt. The dog Mishka appears at their side. For some reason, the dog is subdued. It goes to Elenya's mother, pushes her with its muzzle, tail beating only softly as she begs to be fussed over.

Then they lumber on, tree trailing behind.

His papa beside him, rattle in his breast. 'You did good, boy.'

The boy squirms from his touch.

'The tree,' the old man whispers. 'Where are they taking her?'

'It's Christmas, papa. Don't you remember? Ded Moroz. It's a tree for the house.'

He looks up, only to find his papa's mouth contorted in the most unimaginable smile. Across that face are written both the good man he was, tending to his dying daughter in a tenement flat, and the beast, the creature, the forest he is now.

It is no wonder he is wearing such an expression, thinks the boy. A tree of this great wilderness sitting inside Elenya's house is as inscrutable a thing as his papa going back to the city, as impossible a thing as the boy seeing those streets ever again.

He wants to drag himself back to Elenya's house, but when morning comes the fire is dead and he knows not where his papa has gone. It should be perfect, he should feel safe creeping back to the garden to wait for her in the trees, but the look in her eyes still haunts him; he cannot risk her seeing that again.

Once the fire has been invoked, he scours the snares and roasts what miserable dead things he can find. Some distance into the forest, he finds his papa's trail. Uncertain whether it is a trench he carved last night, or a trench from some past night, he follows. Soon he knows exactly where it is going, for these are channels he has followed once before; his papa is bound for the edge of the marshes, there to gaze into the aspens beyond, that reach of the wilderness into which the Old Man of the Forest disappeared.

He watches his papa's trail wend its way through the trees, and thinks: there was no Old Man of the Forest in Elenya's book. Where do papa's fables come from, if they're not make-believe?

He does not venture further, but retraces his own footsteps back to the gingerbread house. It would be safe to visit Elenya now, but perhaps she ought not to see him after all.

He comes into the camp to see the pine-needle doors pushed apart and, lying in the snow on the edge of the fire, one of her gingerbread babies, peering up lost and forlorn.

He hurtles forward, vaulting the remnants of the fire. He is about to go through the pine-needle doors when something catches his eye, moving in the darkness. He stops, listens out for the familiar click and pull of his papa's gait. Then, at last, he sees the two eyes watching him. At first, he takes them for Mishka – but it is only a fox, come to scavenge in their camp.

Before he dares go through the doors, he plucks up the gingerbread baby from its snowy bed, half-frozen and half-stale.

He claws through the doors. There, Elenya sits. She stands to receive him, breathing out the deepest sigh of relief, but he will not step into her arms. Instead, he casts down the gingerbread baby. It catches on the branches, and off comes its head.

'What was it? A sign?'

'To tell you I was coming . . .'

'To tell *him* as well!' the boy cries. 'I told you not to come into the forest!'

'I had to find you, Alek.'

'Stop calling me that.'

'Stop calling you your *name*?'

'I don't like it.'

'Alek, I had to come . . .'

'You didn't have to do anything. You're the one who can stay. You're the one who has a bed and a mama and a papa. You're the one who goes to school and . . .'

Elenya ventures a hand, and rests it on his shoulder. 'Alek, it's all right.'

'No it isn't,' he whispers. 'It hasn't been, not since my mama.'

'Where is he, Alek?'

'There's a place he's been going,' says the boy. 'It's the place where he fell. He keeps roaming back there, like he wants to cross over again. I don't know how long he's been . . . The fire was dead when I woke. It means he went in the night.'

'Good,' spits Elenya. 'After what he did.'

He whispers, 'I'm . . . sorry, Elenya.'

'Sorry? What should you be sorry for?'

'You didn't have to see.'

'See what that monster did to you? Alek, he's meant to be your papa.'

'He *is* my papa.'

'My papa never bathed me in dirt, Alek. He yells but he never lifts his hand. Is he always like that?'

The boy turns over his shoulder, shifting the pines to keep out a finger of wind.

'He wasn't. He was my papa and he lived in a tenement, and when we went to live with him he was kind. He made hot milk. He told tales, but not bad tales, only tales like Baba Yaga and Dimian the peasant. And he didn't want to come to the forest, but I made him come to the forest, and now . . . I think it's because of the trees. They did terrible things, the trees. They got into him. Drank up whatever was good and left the rest behind. Now he can't leave.'

'He can't leave, but you can.'

335

The boy shakes his head. 'I made a promise, to my mama. To look after him. Only, now he's wild. And I don't know what to do.'

Elenya leans forward, folding a hand over his. 'What do you *want* to do?'

'I want it back the way it used to be. I want to live in the tenement, with my papa the way he was. And . . . I want my mama.'

Elenya says, 'It can't be that way.'

'I know it.'

'Then what do you want now?'

'I . . . don't know.'

'I know one thing,' says Elenya.

'What?'

'I know it's Christmas soon.'

The boy nods.

'And I know Ded Moroz won't be bringing you any presents, so . . . maybe I'll have to.'

She shifts, to reveal that corner of the gingerbread house she has been hiding. There, he sees a package of shining red paper. Awkwardly, she passes it to him.

'For me?'

'For you, Alek.'

He presses his ear to the paper. He runs a finger along the lines where the present has been taped up, prods it, pokes it, lifts it up and shakes. At last, he leaps on the package, as fiercely as a lynx upon its kill. He tears back the paper, and as he does the present itself seems to grow larger, opening like one of the blossoms of springtime. The red paper has been holding it in, but in the middle lies an eiderdown.

He sits back, unable to touch it. It must have been packed

tight, for it relaxes, stretches out. It is warm, as thick as any eiderdown he has ever touched. He breathes in, and though it is not his mama's scent it is something similar: vanilla, and dust, the scents of a house where a family might live.

'Thank you, Elenya,' he whispers.

'Alek, there's something else.'

At first, he is too buried in the new eiderdown to listen. Only when she repeats it does he look up.

'What?'

'It's those stories he tells.'

'You said they weren't real stories.'

'Alek, I asked my papa. I know what Gulag is.'

The boy says, 'The great frozen city . . .'

'It was prison, Alek. Big prison camps, from Russia.'

'No,' says the boy, shaking his head. 'It's Perpetual Winter. That's what my papa says.'

'It's real, Alek.'

'Baba Yaga isn't real.'

'But partisans and soldiers in the *pushcha*? What about babes in the wood?'

The boy tries to hold the words back, yet they spill out nevertheless: 'I think it was my baba.'

'And if that was your baba . . .'

The boy does not want to reply. The stories fracture and begin to unfurl in his head. The wars of winter, real; the Old Man of the Forest, some creature out of legend. The partisans and wicked soldiers, real; the Winter King's wise men, plucked straight from the heart of a fable. He cannot tease one from the other.

Even Mr Navitski said the Winter King was real. He had a real name, and that name was *Josef*.

Elenya ducks her way to the edge of the gingerbread house, prepares to go through the pines.

'Alek, I want you to come back with me. We'll make it right. I don't know how, but we'll . . .'

Click, and soft thump. Click, and soft thump.

The boy claws out, taking her wrist that he might make her stay. 'Elenya, wait.'

She lifts her wrist, if only to show that she could leave if she wanted. 'Why, is he going to bathe me in dirt too?'

In that moment, the boy believes she will defy him, stride out into the camp and spit bile at his papa. Then his papa would take her up and bear her into the trees, and if she came back she would be a wild thing like him or she would not come back at all. He opens his eyes, begs her to remain. Perhaps it is only the thought of seeing him upset that stays her. She softens. She sidles back around the boy, to slump into the eiderdown nest and lift up the little Russian horse.

'It isn't right, Alek. *He* isn't right. He isn't your papa, not anymore.'

The boy turns into the pine-needle doors. When they part, he can see the back of his papa, bent over the fire. Around his feet are strewn the dead things of the forest: a brace of birds and more; furred creatures he has not seen before, dragged feet first from their winter burrows.

'Papa,' he says, venturing near. 'There you are . . .'

'Where else, boy?'

'Have you been to the marshes?'

'How did you know?'

As the old man's head turns, the fire spits and crackles.

'Were you thinking of going across, papa?'

'It's wilder there. Deeper. Those trees don't know men, not anymore.'

'Not since . . .' The boy hesitates before going on, because perhaps the question is better not asked. '. . . the wars of winter?'

'Yes, boy, they knew men then.'

The boy thinks to stop there, but his eyes dart at the ginger-bread house and he fancies he can see a dull shape moving on the ice-bound walls: the shape of Elenya, shifting on the other side. No, he thinks. I have to – *want to* – know.

'Why are you looking at me like that, boy?'

He stutters, trying to find the right words. 'I was . . . thinking of your fable, papa. About the man who escaped from winter.'

The old man takes the axe and carves up the cadaver at his feet. This he dangles down, a bloody worm for the boy to suckle up.

'Did he make it home, that man?'

'You already know he made it home. He found the Old Man of the Forest.'

'And the Winter King didn't catch him again?'

'Oh, the Winter King died, boy. He choked to death in his Winter Palace, and all his wise men were around, but they were too afraid to save him.'

'So that man,' the boy whispers. 'He had a happy ever after?'

The old man makes a broken sound.

'And he found his babe in the wood. Well, didn't he?'

At last, his papa says, 'Yes, boy. He found her.'

'And had a little baby of their own, in the house near the forests . . .'

The old man turns his back on the boy.

'Well?'

The old man breathes, 'Well?'

339

'And that baby, that was mama. Wasn't it, papa? Well, wasn't it?'

This isn't the tale, utters the old man, *but an opening.*

'Oh, papa . . .'

The old man's eyes are gone again, as empty of life as the trees around them. The boy wants to reach out, towards the gingerbread house, but he fancies he can hear Elenya inside, breath held in her throat, and to move towards her would betray her.

The tale, the old man rasps, *comes tomorrow, after the . . . man needs MEAT!*

Man needs meat, said Aabel.

And: man needs meat, said the man who had once been a boy.

And: man needs meat, mocked the trees and the mountains and the snow in the sky.

But Aabel and the man who had once been a boy had walked seven days and seven nights, through pine forests dark and over open heaths of white. And sometimes they heard the wolf pack in full cry, and sometimes they heard the runaways howling their names, and sometimes they could not tell who were the runaways and who were the wolves, for Aabel said: they are all of them monsters now, and all of them will feast on our flesh if they find us. So they must not find us.

Well, that night Aabel and the man who had once been a boy made camp in a forest gully, and in that forest gully the man who had once been a boy conjured up fire. And Aabel said: I have never known a man to conjure such fires. And the man who had once been a boy said: I know how to whisper to fires, for there were once ghosts in the forests where I grew up, and I would follow them and learn of their magicks.

We have a fire, said Aabel, but what will we eat?

340

We will not eat, said the man who had once been a boy, but keep on until our hearts give out.

In front of the fire, the boy thinks he sees the corners of his papa's lips twitch, as if daring a smile. Perhaps it is just an illusion cast by the spitting fire, for the rest of his face is implacable as those faces in the murderous trees.

Well, sleep did not come to the man who had once been a boy, and he was sore aggrieved, for without sleep he could not dream of his babe in the woods. And when morning came, he watched Aabel pull back on his jackboots and put his knapsack over his shoulder and say: the company is near, and they are running with wolves. We must make haste.

Well, the way was steep and the way was narrow, and the way was dark beneath the pines. And Aabel said: we must chew on this bark, so that we will not starve. But chewing on bark just taunted their stomachs, and soon the hunger gnawed more and more and . . . man needs meat.

Man needs meat.

Man needs meat.

The old man moans it, again and again.

Well, night returned – and of the runaways there was no sign. The man who had once been a boy took them to a camp beneath a stone ridge, a place the wind could not claw, and fell to making fire. But hunger is a terrible thing, for it starts in the stomach but ends in the fingers, and now his fingers would not obey. He tempted up smoke but he could tempt no fire, for no longer was there any fire inside him.

And he and Aabel lay together and Aabel said: we have run and we can run no more. And the man who had once been a boy said: I am glad to die beyond the walls of that great frozen city called Gulag, for though I die I am a free man.

341

Then came endless sleep.

The boy rears up. 'But papa!' he cries. 'They didn't die! They didn't die, did they?' He pitches across the fire, heedless of the raging heat. 'He made it back, papa.' He crawls into the old man's arms, all fear evaporated. 'He made it back for his babe in the woods, and he had a little girl and she had a little boy, and that little boy's me, and I'm still here . . . I promised, papa! I promised to look after you . . .'

The old man's branches fold around him, locking like warped wood.

Well, now dreams came. And in the dreams he saw his babe in the woods, and she was but a babe on the doorstep where he left her. And in the dreams he saw her grow up and grow beautiful as the forest. And in the dreams he saw her take his hand, and he saw her kiss his lips, and he saw . . . Boy, he saw that she was good and just, and he saw that she was beautiful and fair. And he saw that nothing else mattered, not wars of winter, not the Winter King, not the Iron wall or the King in the West, not Perpetual Winter and that great frozen city called Gulag.

And he opened his eyes. And there, at his side, Aabel still slept, his heart beating ragged in his breast, for the hunger and the cold had not claimed him yet. And the man who had once been a boy said: I will go home to my babe in the woods. I will go home to my babe in the woods, no matter what it takes.

And he stroked Aabel's hair from his brow, and brought back Aabel's head to show a throat red raw and mottled in beard.

And into that throat he sank his teeth.

'No, papa. Please, papa . . .'

Well, Aabel woke, and Aabel thrashed, and Aabel choked up blood and screamed: why!? But the man who had once been a boy bit harder, and the man who had once been a boy tasted iron and salt. And the man who had once been a boy drank back, and chewed and spat and chewed and spat. For now there was fire in him again, and now his fingers would work. Now, he summoned up fire, and now he baked flesh. All to get home to his babe in the woods . . .

And now, now, now, now, he feasted on the flesh of a Finnish man.

At once, his papa's arms release him. They pitch him, propel him back over the fire. The boy lands awkwardly, one leg still trailing in the flames. He whips it back, thankful for the bitterness of the snow in which he lies.

And now I was strong, moans his papa. *Now I was warm. And I took his axe and I carved his flesh. And I took his knapsack, and filled it with flesh. And I took his jackboots and I walked in his step. And I ran and I ran and I ran . . .*

Is it true? He barks the question at himself, as if there are two men inside him, one desperate to get out.

Oh, I know it is true, for I was there!

Scrabbling back, the boy looks at his papa. The old man's whiskered face is etched with the same patterns of ice as the boy; through the telling of his tale, his tears have been falling.

Without another word, he picks himself up, pushes through the pine branches and into the gingerbread house.

In the eiderdown nest, Elenya is waiting.

'I've got to go,' she says, a trembling in her tone.

'You can't,' the boy replies. 'He'll know you're here . . .'

'I heard him, Alek. I heard him . . .'

'It was only his tale.'

'It wasn't a tale, and you know it!'

At the last, her voice climbs into a shriek. Outside, the boy hears his papa shifting. He thinks: he's coming into the gingerbread house; he's coming now. But then he hears the familiar sound of new boughs being piled into the fire, the click of the jackboot heel as his papa shifts around.

'That was him, Alek. He did that. He . . .'

'He didn't,' says the boy, though he can see pictures of his papa, his face buried in the man named Aabel's throat, seared onto the backs of his eyes. 'It was a story, like Baba Yaga.'

'Baba Yaga ate little boys,' says Elenya. 'Little girls too . . .'

But the boy shakes his head. 'He's my papa,' he whispers. 'He wouldn't . . .'

'I've got to go,' Elenya sobs.

The boy throws himself between her and the gingerbread doors. 'Just a little longer,' he begs. 'Until he's . . .'

'Get out of my way, Alek!'

The boy tries to grapple her back, but his moccasin is caught in tangled root, he cannot catch his balance, and he plunges down. In seconds, Elenya clambers over him, clawing at the pine-needle doors. He reaches out, fingers flail for her ankle, but she kicks back – and then she is gone.

When the boy follows, he thinks he will see his papa, bearing down. He thinks he will see him with his bough-like arms closed around her, but instead there is only the fire. Elenya is on the other side of it, making for the forest.

He sees the trail his papa has left behind, snaking off under other branches.

'Elenya!' He vaults the fire to reach her. 'I'll take you home.'

In the snow dark she clings to his arm.

'Come with me,' she finally says. 'My mama will look after you. You shouldn't be out here. You should be inside, with a bed and a blanket and . . .'

She stops, as if something so simple has just occurred to her.

'It isn't a game anymore. He's a monster, and it isn't a game. Someone has to know.' She teases her arm out of his grasp, takes three steps into birches heavy with ice.

'I . . . can't,' says the boy.

'Why can't you?'

With a breath like winter, 'Because I made a promise, Elenya. I promised mama I wouldn't leave him, no matter what.'

'Did she know what he was?'

The boy listens to the soft tread of her footfalls, as her scarlet coat fades to grey. 'She knew he's my papa,' he whispers, and watches her go.

After she has faded, he tramps back across the clearing. There is a smell in the air. It is a smell of closeness, of clarity, of lucid dreams. He wishes it wasn't so, but he could not go with her. He can never go. Girls like Elenya can get on and grow up, but boys of the forest can do none of those things. They stay little boys, all because of a promise they made, and promises can't be broken. Monster or not, the wild man will always be his papa.

He has turned to go into the gingerbread house when he sees the new trail on the edge of the clearing. Tracking it round, he sees his papa reappear with yet more pine branches.

'Papa?'

The old man drops, his body curled around the fire like a cauldron's edge. Moments later, the boy knows he is asleep. In his dreams, he thunders through these forests on legs that still work, a young man desperate to get home.

He is about to pile up the pine branches, when a sudden thought strikes. Throwing the pines onto the fire, he takes the eiderdown and lays it over the old man. He tucks him in so that only the tip of his head is open to the night. In this way, he looks like any old man from the city.

The boy stands. It is not enough.

'Papa,' he says. 'Is it true?'

In response, the old man snorts.

'Papa,' he says. 'She thinks it's true, that you're like Baba Yaga, that you eat little boys and girls. She's going to tell. And . . .'

He crouches low, thinking his whispers might infiltrate the old man's dreams. But what thoughts fester in his sleeping head, when such stories bubble on his waking lips?

'. . . she thinks you're a monster, papa. But it's only a story. Please, papa, let it be a story. This isn't the tale, papa, but an opening. The tale comes tomorrow, after the meal, when . . .' His voice cracks, but he will not cry. '. . . we're filled with soft bread.'

He sits by his papa's side, until the snow has cloaked them both, as crisp and white as the eiderdown keeping his papa warm. It strikes him: that eiderdown is the only thing making him human. Without it, he might be just another beast of the forest. Was it like that, once upon a time? Did his papa escape Perpetual Winter and feast on a man, just to get back to baba? Is he like the Old Man of the Forest, a wolf in the skin of a man? What if, one day, he sheds that skin altogether, sinks his teeth into the flesh of the boy, and cavorts off, into deeper woodlands, to live and die wild?

If Elenya tells, it will be like his papa once said. They'll come into the forest. The promise will be broken. Wherever mama is, she'll know that he failed.

He doesn't want to fail.

He steals out of the clearing, refuses to look back. Back through the alders, back past the frozen cattail pond, and up to the house which he longs to be his. The lights are out now, the family asleep, and he does not need to hide as he crosses the garden.

One fist of snow at the window, and another and another. When the light flares, he gets ready.

'You came!' Elenya gasps, hanging out into the tendrils of white. 'They wouldn't believe me, Alek. Said I was telling tales. But they should know – tales can be true, just like with your papa. Wait there. I'll wake them . . .'

'No!'

Elenya's face hardens.

'You can't tell, Elenya. You mustn't.'

'Can't tell, Alek? Can't!?' Her face purples, in spite of the incessant snow.

'If you do, they'll catch him.'

'They'll catch you too. Give you a good scrubbing! Put you in proper clothes and proper food and a proper house. They'll find you a new mama! Isn't that what you want? A new *mama*?'

She means it to hurt him, like loosing a stone from a sling-shot in the forest. The stone finds him, stuns him, knocks him down. But there is breath within him yet.

'Please, Elenya . . .'

'I'm telling Navitski in the morning. Then you'll see. Then you'll know it isn't a story.'

The light in the window dies.

Navitski, he thinks. She's going to tell Navitski.

He prowls the edges of the garden, churning up a trail just like the ones his papa leaves behind. More than once, he digs down into snow packed hard, brings his hand back with a stone in his fist. He means to loose it at the window, compel Elenya to face him again, but the thought of stirring her mama and papa puts more fear into him than his papa's fable, and he casts each stone back into the forest. He goes to the door, takes the

347

fairybook wolf in his hands, but cannot rain it down. Snow, and snow, and more snow to come.

How to stop her, before she tells?

He thinks: I'll pounce on her in the morning, before she goes to school. But then her mama and papa would see, and know it wasn't just tall tales. He thinks: I'll tell my papa, and we'll go deeper into the wilds, cross the marshes to the aspens, go deeper where only the Old Man of the Forest might dwell. But then he'd never see her again. Never sneak into the house and play games. Never hear of the world beyond the forests.

There is, it dawns on him with a dreadful clarity, only one way he can catch her.

He creeps around the building. At the front of the house sits the black truck. On the back, the flat-bed is covered with a thick tarpaulin. He finds a way to scramble up, the tarpaulin springy beneath his feet. For a while, he simply stands there, wondering: can I? Can I do this at all? Then he finds a corner where the tarpaulin is fastened down and, using frozen fingers, peels it back. All it needs is a corner. Then he can crawl underneath, into a cavity dry as bone.

He closes his eyes. Compels the night to come asunder.

When he wakes, he does not know where he is. It is voices that remind him. He can hear Elenya and her father, close, closer still.

Doors slam. An engine gutters to life. The metal beneath him, warming slightly, begins to tremble. The chattering of his teeth.

The truck is away. He feels it slough, struggle to grip the snow, before bucking hard and taking off. It has been so long that panic seizes him – but this morning panic will not be his master. He holds onto the ridges in the flat-bed floor and, using them like the rungs of a ladder, hauls himself along. The corner of tarpaulin through which he crawled down is still loose. He pushes at it, disrupting the snow on top, and peers through. White rushes past, and then all is darkness; they have reached the top of the glade, gone under the trees.

The truck settles, at last, onto a path its tyres have pounded many times before. He watches the glade recede, sees the path behind snaking away.

He does not peer out again until the truck banks right, the sound of its tyres suddenly smooth. The wind rushing past has a different clarity now, and no longer does the flat-bed rattle with the same regularity. Behind, the black ribbon of the road, banked in white, twists away. He cranes his head forward. Past the cab, he sees distant orbs of yellow and white.

The town is getting closer with every passing second. He is going back home.

I n the woods, a wild man wakes.

He stirs slowly, to find himself iced into the earth. The fire at his side has long since died, its embers nothing but crystalline frost. His hands curled in strange attitudes, gnarled as the branches that cover him, he tears himself from the ground, leaving behind clumps of whiskers white as ice. What is left covers his face in an impenetrable crust, a pitted landscape of crevices and craters, strange monoliths of twisted hair in burnt sugar shells.

He rolls over. He sees the opening of the gingerbread house on the other side of the fire, the eiderdown and the Russian horse. But that is all he sees.

He stands, mutters indecipherable sounds. Whether words or not, only the trees are there to say. He pitches forward, onto the dead wood that is his staff, and in that way crosses the camp.

Over briar and bramble. Through hawthorn and rowan. Land so deathly that the only sound is that of his breathing, deep and querulous in his breast.

The click of his one jackboot heel, soft thump of his dead foot trailing behind.

Down by the cattail pond and along a trail he used to know, and there is the house that once was his. He stands in the shelter of skeleton trees, remembers dimly the roots at his feet.

Empty ache in his stomach. Axe at his side. He lifts it from the sling, runs a finger along its dull blade.

Coming out of the trees is like stepping into blinding light, even though the vaults above churn with clouds, pregnant with the promise of the blizzard to come. He heaves himself across the garden. At the windows: nothing. At the door: a sound, somebody humming, the snuffling of a dog.

He puts his shoulder to the wood. It gives. Dead wood good for nothing but kindling. No roots to bind it. No resin in its veins. Warmth rushes out, the staff falls from his hand, and now he is in a kitchen, and now he is hauling his way along its narrow hall, one hand on either surface. Fire blasts from an iron rail. His hand against it, too numb to feel the burn until it is deep in his flesh.

From around the corner, a grey hulk hurtles. The din of a wolf, but this an impostor. It comes at him, howling, but he quells it with a look and it shrinks back. On he lurches, into the path of the bitch. She scrabbles in retreat, tail between legs. Then she is gone.

The old man stands in a doorway. The hearthfire dead, but

heat from somewhere. A stair where there was a ruin. Footsteps on it, coming down.

A woman steps into view. She stops, breath in her throat.

From the old man, guttural sounds. Behind him, only the bitch understands. Her tail reappears, her hackles rise high, lip curled back in the hint of a growl.

The woman mouths, 'Who do you think you . . .'

'Where is he?' This time, the words decipherable. Each of them short barks, spoken from the gut and not the tongue.

'What?'

'The boy.'

The old man steps forward. The bitch does the same. In the same instant that she leaps for him, his fist finds the axe at his side. Wrenching it from the sling, he drives the handle into the bitch's neck. What growl was in the creature becomes a muted whimper. She spirals back, crashes into the stones of the hearth. There she lies, gasping for air, the fur of her collar dark and matted black.

The old man brings his fist back to his side, the axe handle glistening in red. As the woman's eyes tear from the fallen bitch, he steps towards her. Her eyes wide, but not looking at him; looking straight through him instead, along the funnel of the kitchen, at the winter woods roaring behind. The noisome, taunting trees.

'Where,' he utters, 'is my boy?'

Outside, the morning dark has barely disappeared. It is a strange thing to see the hulks of factories and tenements rushing past, stranger still to breathe in the acrid smell of exhaust, see traffic lights changing from amber to red. These things are from the long ago, yet only hours from where he has lived his life.

Soon he knows where he is. At a particular intersection he lifts his head, recognizes the boarded-up shop-fronts and canteen. Now he is content to sit upright, keeping his head bowed only so that Elenya's papa might not see him in his mirror. He knows the corners, the parked cars, the building yard still derelict and the playing field beyond.

They come to the schoolhouse while the last vestiges of morning dark still linger. There is no place to park, so Elenya's papa pulls the truck into the side of the road; through the glass, the boy can hear him urging his daughter to jump out.

Now is his chance too. He scrambles up and, in a second, is over the rim of the truck, scuttling between two parked cars to reach the kerb. There he hunkers down, watching as Elenya puts her arms around her papa's shoulders, plants a kiss on his cheek, and lowers herself from the truck. As the truck forces its way back into the traffic, the boy tracks Elenya with his eyes. She weaves her way to the kerb, coming past a motorcycle squeezed between two cars.

The boy remembers: I was on that motorcycle once. I sat squeezed tight between Mr Navitski's legs and he took me to the tenement.

He takes his chance, pounces onto the kerb. He thinks to hurtle straight for her, tear at her arm and roar: you can't tell! But before he is halfway there, some girl he has never seen has linked her arms with Elenya's and together they head for the gates.

He opens his mouth to cry her name – but there is only silence. Instead, he creeps along the railing, reaches a spot between the gates from which he can peer into the schoolyard. Snowmen and barricades, and gangs in scarves and mittens, bound up against the cold. His gaze loses its focus – he tries to picture them in the trees, with papas just like his – and when his focus returns, he sees Yuri, kicking his heels on the schoolyard's furthest edge, alone among everyone: his head full of stories, thoughts full of maps.

'Yuri,' he whispers.

At once, he is back in Yuri's bedroom, looking at the photograph of Yuri's Grandfather. Yuri said he was a policeman during the war, but now the boy knows better: he was a soldier of the Winter King, or a soldier of the King in the West. They are real, and the things his papa did to get home, they were real too. Perpetual Winter and Gulag, they're places in the real world. His own baba: the babe in the woods.

Man needs meat and his own Grandfather, Baba Yaga come to life.

Into the morning air comes the pealing of a bell. He cringes from it, but he might as well be cringing from the sky. When he looks up, the children have turned. As one, they bound for the doors of the schoolhouse.

The boy's eyes pick out Elenya in the crowd. She is flocked by other girls. She looks over her shoulder; the boy thinks she might even be smiling. Smiling. Could a girl wearing that smile be about to break open his world?

She cannot tell. She cannot tell.

He takes the deepest breath, and approaches the gates.

At the schoolhouse door, he can see through the glass. First, a teacher he does not recognize, shepherding some tiny children along their way. Then the headmistress, appearing from her study door with spectacles halfway down her nose. Along the corridor, he sees the caretaker, propped on his broom in such a way that an image forks, like lightning, across the backs of the boy's eyes: his papa, leaning into his staff, lurching along a tunnel of snowbound trees with the branches groaning on every side.

He banishes the image and goes through the doors.

It is warm in here, so warm he might as well be sitting in the hearth while his papa whispers up a fire all around him. He comes, tentatively, around the corner, evading the sweeping gaze of the headmistress in her study door. The caretaker seems to be sleeping standing up, so heavy are his eyes, and the boy navigates his way around him. The schoolhouse walls are close, closer than they have any right to be, and he hears the scratch and tap of countless shoes scuffing the polished floor.

He passes the library corner with its rows of neat books. Yuri is ferreting on one of the shelves, but when he hears the boy approaching he stuffs whatever he has been reading back and, not bothering to look up, scuttles to catch the rest of the class. At the end of the corridor, they are milling at the entrance to the assembly hall. In gangs of twos and threes, they wander in to sit cross-legged on the floor. The boy approaches dreamily, the schoolhouse so unreal he might as well be lost in one of Elenya's tall tales. And there she is, surrounded by friends; one of them reaches up and whispers into her ear.

Halfway along the corridor, he stops. He sees Mr Navitski emerge from the classroom and, using his hands like shovels, steer the remaining children into the hall. It is the strangest thing, but he does not look as tall as the boy remembers, nor as lean. His hair is still black and tightly coiled, and he walks after the children with an air almost meek.

The doors to the assembly hall close, and the boy is left alone, the sounds of his breathing echoing all along the empty corridor.

After a while, he creeps further, past the library and toilet door. He stops at the classroom and peers inside. There is nobody here, and it gives him the courage to wander through. On the board are written the morning sums, and the date in luminescent green chalk. Some of the children have been here already; there are coats on pegs, a ruler and a pencil with a broken end.

The tables are exactly as he remembers. He winds his way

between them to take his seat at the back, the desks more ordered than the trees of the forest, so that he stubs his toe and collides with a corner, unused to walking in straight lines.

There is a coat here already, and a wet pool on the floor where snow-melt has trickled down the sleeves. Above the desk, on a board of stained cork, are pinned pictures and maps, the projects of boys and girls from the seasons he has missed. There, in the middle, he sees a picture he recognizes: the very picture he made of his papa, in that time so long ago. On the paper the eyes are vivid and blue; his lips suggest a smile and his big ears hang down with the air of a mournful dog. His eyes stray across and find Yuri's old picture tacked up alongside. A crude fairybook ogre stares out, with hollow holes where its eyes ought to be. The boy cannot look at it for long, because to look at it is like admitting a truth he would rather remained buried out there in the forest.

He hears footsteps. He stops, cocks his head as he might at the sound of a rabbit trying to sneak past out of his line of sight. By degrees, he turns so that he can see the classroom door out of the corner of his eye. Somebody hangs there, eyes boring into his back.

'It's . . . you.' In the doorway stands Mr Navitski. His sleeves are rolled up, his tie hanging loose, and his face is etched in lines. Even as the boy watches, those creases deepen.

He lifts a hand, both palms open and empty. Then he just stands there. To the boy he seems to be making himself as big as he can, like a man trying in vain to frighten a bear.

The boy's eyes dart, left and right.

'It's okay,' Mr Navitski begins. 'I'm not going to come near you. I'm just coming into the room.' He comes closer, though they are still several desks apart. 'I'm going to stand here,' he goes on. 'I'm not going to move.'

The way he is speaking does not make sense. The things he says are calm, banal, but there is something stony in his tone, something that tells the boy he is struggling not to do something else. He is like a tight blossom, ready to explode and shower down its seeds.

'Alek,' Mr Navitski ventures, 'are you all right?'

The boy takes a step back, feels the cold glass of a window at his back. Mr Navitski must think he means to open it and scramble away, for suddenly he takes another step, and then another.

'Alek, I'm not going to hurt you. I want you to know . . .'

The boy nods, whispers – but not a word.

'Alek, are you well?'

Again, the boy nods.

'Alek, where have you come from?'

Then it is relief that floods the boy's body – for, in those words, a secret is being revealed: Elenya has not spoken to him yet; Elenya has not *told*.

There are other sounds now. The assembly hall doors being pushed open. The babble of children bubbling out. The boy sees their fuzzy-edged shapes gather in the corridor beyond Mr Navitski. There is pushing and shoving, and now they are streaming in.

'I've been at . . . home.'

The children flock at Mr Navitski's back, but he pushes them back with a half-turn over his shoulder. In that same second, they fall silent.

'Where is home, Alek?'

'I live at the tenement.'

'I've been to the tenement, Alek. It's been boarded up for more than a year.'

Now the boy knows: this is a trap, quite as subtle as the trap that sucked his papa down into the earth and spewed him up different, changed, touched by the forest.

So he says nothing. Shakes his head.

'Mr Navitski?' comes a tiny voice. 'What's that dirty little thing doing in the class?'

Mr Navitski turns, as if to shield the boy from the herd of children behind. 'Back into the corridor,' he says.

'But Mr Navitski . . .'

'Now!' Mr Navitski barks. 'It's library time. Everybody into the library.'

A voice pipes up, 'You said the corridor.'

'Well, now I'm saying the library. Everybody. Now.'

As one, the children move sluggishly back through the door. Among them, there stands Elenya. She resists the pull of the tide, even though her friends are crying after her. Her eyes lock with the boy's. She has no words, but the boy knows what her eyes are asking. He nods, tells her he is all right; he has come to make things better. Yet, as she turns to follow the rest, something lurches inside him. He wants her, needs her, to stay.

'Elenya!'

In the doorway she stops. 'Mr Navitski, there's something I've got to . . .'

'No!' yells the boy. He doesn't know how to say it without telling Navitski too. 'No,' he repeats, his words fading to a whisper. 'I'm here. I'm here now.'

Mr Navtiski's eyes are cold. They fall on her. 'I said the library, Elenya.'

'But look at him, he's just a sorry little boy . . .'

Something softens in Mr Navitski's eyes. 'I'm not angry with Alek, Elenya. We need to help him. So, if you could give us just a few moments . . .' Mr Navitski pauses. 'You too, Yuri.'

The boy looks around. Somehow, unnoticed, Yuri has crept into the classroom and taken his seat beside the boy. He has a pencil in one chubby fist, a notebook open, and he is patiently copying down the sums from the board.

'Elenya,' Mr Navitski concedes. 'Stay here with Yuri.'

He looks at the boy, his back still pressed hard against the window. 'Alek, I'm sorry, but I'm going to come over to you now. Do you understand?'

Of course he understands. Mr Navitski seems to think that a few months living wild has robbed him of all words, all thought. He is about to cry out, tell him it isn't so, when he remembers his papa, keening in that hole in the ground. The forests drained the words out of him. The forests drained his thinking too. He feels the dirt and foliage still tangled in his hair and wonders if it's been doing the same to him all along.

He nods, but even so he doesn't take a step until he feels Mr Navitski's hand gently touching his shoulder.

An hour later, he sits beyond the forbidden staffroom doors, where none but the naughtiest or sickest child has ever come. Stripped to the waist, he stands on the tiles of a little kitchenette with a bowl of soapy water at his feet and another steaming on the counter. Mr Navitski lifts one of his arms and rubs at his ribs. Water as dirty as any stagnant pond dribbles down Mr Navitski's arms, soiling his own shirt and polluting the bowl so that, every few minutes, it has to be changed.

From the corner of the kitchenette, the headmistress watches keenly. Her hands are wrapped around a mug of some hot drink.

The boy has one too, coffee spooned full of sugar, but its taste is far too strange and he leaves it unsipped on the counter.

'Nikolai, I'm sorry. I wouldn't believe it if I didn't see it myself.'

Mr Navitski does not look up at the headmistress's words. He simply carries on sponging the boy's mottled skin.

'How long has it been, now?'

'Longer than a year since you were last in a lesson, isn't it, Alek?'

The boy nods, but cautiously so, careful not to betray any secret.

'And there he was, just sitting in class?'

'I wasn't sitting!'

Mr Navitski stops.

'I hadn't sat down yet. I didn't know if it was still my seat.'

Mr Navitski's face erupts in the most wonderful smile the boy thinks he has ever seen.

'It's still your seat, Alek.'

As Mr Navitski continues to scrub him, finally returning to the dreaded task of untangling his hair, the headmistress comes and goes. Each time she returns, she leads Mr Navitski out of the kitchenette to share whispers on the other side of the staff-room. Once, another teacher wanders in, peeks her head around the door, and then retreats, shaking her head in a strange mingling of sadness and wonder.

Mr Navitski puts down the soapy rag and drapes a towel around the boy's shoulders. 'There you are. Good as new.'

'Isn't it time for lessons?'

'Soon, Alek.'

Mr Navitski stands. 'Alek, I'm going to leave you here now. I'll be back very soon. Do you understand?'

There it is again: now, it isn't enough to say a thing; you have to ask if it's understood as well.

Mr Navitski pushes him gently into the staffroom proper, where big armchairs are lined around the walls, and a table in the middle is piled up with magazines. There is a fresh towel on a chair. There are shoes too, battered brown slipper things that get handed out if a boy's been kicking and has to have his own boots taken away. Mr Navitski helps him to climb into them.

'You can read any of the books while I'm gone. But why don't you just have a rest?'

There is a big blanket, and the boy sinks into it. Though it hugs him close, it has a scratching texture, not like the needles of a pine or an eiderdown thick with dirt.

Mr Navitski returns to the kitchenette, gathers up the pile of clothes he used to wear and winces as he ties them in a bag. Then he strides across the staffroom, flicking a smile over his shoulder as he reaches the door. 'Be good,' he grins.

He disappears. The boy's keen ears pick out the scrape of a key in the lock. He hurries over, tries the handle. It is locked fast and, when he presses his eye to the keyhole, all he sees is Mr Navitski striding away.

For a fleeting moment, panic holds him. There is still a chance Elenya could tell it all. He hurtles to the window, if only to catch a glimpse of the outside, but condensation fogs the glass and all he sees are sweeping blacks and greys, the schoolyard and the street beyond. Traffic hums. He searches for a way to force the window open, but no sooner has he found the latch than the panic leaves him. He can feel the heat throbbing out of an old oil radiator, still smell the dregs of the coffee. He sinks down into the big woollen blanket.

'Just like mama's shawl,' he mumbles. He wonders what happened to it. Maybe his papa still has it tied around his leg, the skin healing over it to fuse one to the other. He remembers what Mr Navitski said: the tenement is still there, boarded up. Waiting, he thinks. The tenement is waiting for me. There'll still be mama's picture in the frame. There'll still be mama's hair on the pillow.

Some of his warmth has bled into the blanket now. It hugs him tight. These new clothes feel as peculiar as a new skin might, but the longer he wears them, the softer they feel. They are, he decides, just like the wilderness itself. You get used to anything in the end.

He puts his head down, only for a second, and closes his eyes.

'Wake up.'

Some derelict city street, shop-fronts boarded up and walls caved in. Between every stone sprouts a sapling. In places, roots cascade out of a crack, or burst up like a rupturing volcano. Ivies cling to the brickwork, the blacktops.

In this wild city he stands alone. He has been running. He clings to a trunk, but the trunk is too slight to hide him and, instead, he has to spread his arms and legs into a mockery of branches, a foolish trick that will not last long. Out of the corner of his eye, he sees shadows darting.

'Wake up! Please, boy, wake up and . . .'

The voice halloos him from far above. He gazes up, along the edges of towers rimed in dark moss, but sees only a pale grey sky.

'Here!'

This time the voice drags his eyes to the face of a ruptured building, four storeys up. It seems that trees have been growing inside, for where the brickwork has collapsed there is the face of a thicket. Inside are open floorboards, around which roots cling like coiled rope. Trees have grown high into the ceiling and through into the rooms above, and others have exploded, opening clear gashes in the tower's face.

In that gash, half-shrouded in falling leaves, stands his mama. 'Little one!'

He is about to break cover and run to her when her hands flail at him, driving him back.

'Mama?'

'Stay where you are,' she says, her voice a whisper even though it reaches him across the divide. 'Keep your head down.'

'Mama, I want to . . .'

'No, little one!'

'I want to come to you, mama.'

He takes flight. It doesn't matter what she says, doesn't matter what she wants. It's been too long. He breaks free from the tree that hides him and, as he pounds across the reclaimed street, he sees the shadow dart after him. With one final effort, he flings himself at the face of the building, scrambles through a door and hurls it shut behind him. Slumped against it, he feels somebody crashing into the wood. It shudders, bucks against him, but somehow he holds it fast.

When he is certain the figure has gone, he stands and looks around. The innards of this building are as corrupted as the street. From the floorboards a carpet of briars has risen. Along the briars grow roses. Fronds of bracken grow from the rails of a ruined staircase. Nettles and thistles abound.

The boy picks his way through the brambles, parting the curtain of ferns to climb the stair. The steps, here, are not as crumbled as he imagines, and soon he is bold enough to take three at a time. He emerges into another storey, where the floor has been eaten away and a lattice of roots grows between the floorboards. He goes up, and up, and up again.

At last, he reaches the storey with the ruptured face, so far up that he can see across the city: down into streets reclaimed by wild; the schoolyard, a pasture of cattails and reeds. In the heart of the misshapen grove, there stands mama. It must be cold, for she is holding herself. Gusts of wind set ripples flowing across the nightdress she wears.

He crosses briar and rose to find her.

She gathers him up. Her face touches his. Her lips on his cheek.

'What is it, mama? What's wrong?'

'You shouldn't have come. You should have stayed where you were. You should have woken up already.'

'Mama, this looks like the tenement.'

'I know, little one.'

'How did the woods get in the tenement?'

Mama's voice, immeasurably sad: 'Little one, you brought them with you . . .'

Down in the street below, there is a strange keening.

'Papa hasn't been looking after me at all, has he, mama?'

Mama has a look about her, at once sad and admonishing. She whispers, 'And you haven't been looking after him.'

The boy draws back, but not far enough to tumble out of mama's arms. 'Mama?'

'I'm sorry, but you haven't. You made a promise. That you were to love him and care for him, for all of his days . . .'

'He turned wild, and I didn't know how . . .'

'He needed you, like you needed him.'

'It was the trees, mama. First, they wouldn't let him leave the woods. Then they drank him all up.'

'Come with me, little one.'

She bears him, still in her arms, to the precipice, where wind plays on the ruined walls. With her face pressed against his, they lean into the rushing air. It is a long way down. Even the tops of the trees are far, far away. The boy feels them, lurching in and out of focus.

Between those trees there moves a thing of shadow.

'Look at him.'

'What is he, mama?'

'It's your papa.'

'And, mama, what's he doing . . .'

'He wants to come into the building. I've been keeping him out, but I can't do it anymore. You see, he doesn't need the trees, not now. He brings the forest with him.'

She stops, swallows a sob. 'Little one, you have to wake up. Wake up and run. Out of the school, as far as you can . . .'

'Why, mama?'

'Well, because he's . . .'

The boy feels himself torn from mama's arms. He whirls through the air, crashes back down. His eyes snap open and he finds himself staring into the face of Mr Navitski. The headmistress hovers behind.

He scrambles up, realizes he is entangled in the blanket. He wants to fight it off, squirm out of it like smothering arms, but Mr Navitski is holding him. His face is creased in deep consternation.

'It's okay,' he says. 'You were sleeping. Alek, you were babbling . . .'

The boy calms.

'Alek, can you hear me?'

The boy nods.

'I'm thirsty.'

Mr Navitski nods at the headmistress, who disappears inside the kitchenette. Moments later, she reappears with a beaker full of water.

Mr Navitski presses it to the boy's lips. 'Is that better?'

It dribbles down his chin, but it soothes his throat all the same.

'Alek, you were dreaming. Thrashing around. Do you remember?'

He could not forget. He takes another pull at the water, softly nods.

'Well, Alek,' Mr Navitski begins. 'What did it mean?'

'What did what mean?'

'You were saying it, over and over. Shouting it, Alek.'

The water has cut a cold channel all the way down his throat; now it chills all of his insides.

'What did I say, Mr Navitski?'

Mr Navitski stands. 'It was the strangest thing. You were . . . rolling, and your fingers were grasping, your legs were kicking . . . And you kept saying it, over and over.' Mr Navitski's eyes drift to the watching headmistress, and then back to find the boy. 'He's coming out of the woods, Alek. You kept saying: he's coming out of the woods.'

The woods. The trail. A car long ago abandoned, marked by an axe.

He drags himself beneath the oaks, scoring a trench into the frozen earth.

Then: a ribbon of black road, curling into the winter dark.

A lone motorcar gutters past, its driver bawling incomprehensible words out of the window, fist pumping to threaten the old man.

The wild man bawls something back. Famished rooks in the trees, and the glaring eyes of some road-killed lynx.

One foot, and one foot trailing useless behind. He puts forward his staff and starts to walk.

When the bell rings for midday, the boy is still in the staffroom. In the schoolyard the snow falls with dogged persistence, too blinding for boys and girls to be dispatched outside for games. Instead, they must lounge in classrooms, in assembly halls, in libraries and whatever other nooks and crannies they can find. In the staffroom, the teachers complain as bitterly as the children.

When the room has almost emptied, Mr Navitski crouches by his side. 'Alek, there's somebody who'll come and see you this afternoon.'

'Who?'

'It's a man from . . . the police. Missing people.'

'But I'm not missing,' the boy whispers. 'I'm right here.'

'I'm sorry, Alek. It was me who reported you missing. After you stopped coming to school, I . . .'

'I didn't mean to.'

'I didn't know what else to do, Alek. They'll only want to ask you some questions. They'll want to know what happened to you and your papa. Is he still alive, Alek?'

When the boy will not reply, Mr Navitski goes on. 'I've asked if you can stay with me for the night.'

The boy twists away, feeling suddenly treacherous in his new clothes. He did not mean to come to the city forever. He meant only to come, stop Elenya, and scuttle back into thorn. In the wilderness, there is a fire that will need building. There is an old man who lies down in the snow, who needs the pine branches and eiderdown piling on top so that the forests do not take him during the night.

Mr Navitski tries to take his hand, but to the boy it seems some kind of betrayal, so he curls his fist and climbs to his feet without needing to be told.

In the classroom, the children are rebellious, waiting for Mr Navitski to return. When he appears, they quit their games of upturned chairs and balled-up paper. Mr Navitski guides the boy to his seat at the back, where Yuri considers him with bewildered eyes. When the boy finally sits, Yuri delicately picks up a pencil from the corner of the table and slides it over. The boy takes it in a fist, uncertain how to handle it.

Yuri directs him with a nod, his face opening in a beatific smile. 'Are you coming to play after school?' he asks, as if a whole year hasn't vanished between them.

At the front of the class, Mr Navitski begins. This afternoon: not stories, nor sums, but a problem instead. He draws on the blackboard, explaining about mountaineers trapped on a mountain and the time it takes to reach them, but the boy feels lost, in a haze. His eyes pick out the faces of the other children. At last, they settle on Elenya, on the far side of the classroom. Intermittently, she rocks back on the legs of her chair, balances there and beams. A fountain pen dangles out of the corner of her mouth. More than once, it drops and skitters across the ground, only to be recovered by some other boy whose eyes dote on her.

'Elenya!' Mr Navitski calls out. 'What do you think?'

The chair almost slips from underneath her. 'About what, sir?'

'Were you listening at all, Elenya?'

'Sir, I was . . .'

Mr Navitski's sigh is a perfect imitation of her father. 'Pay attention next time . . .'

As Mr Navitski moves on to the next problem, summoning answers from all the other children, Elenya returns to her rocking. This time she takes the game too far; the back legs slide out, and she crashes down in a cacophony of arms and legs. Around her, the other children shriek. Down on the ground, Elenya too is beaming. It is her trick, it seems, to be the centre of attention.

Defiantly, the boy springs up. In a second, he has weaved between the desks. At the front, Mr Navitski calls for silence – but the sudden flight of the new boy seems to have stirred the class to acts of greater hilarity. Navitski begins to stride over, but already the boy is helping Elenya to her feet.

'Did it hurt you?'

'I practise doing it all the time.'

The boy cups a hand, presses it to Elenya's ear. 'Did you tell, Elenya?'

371

'Alek . . .'

'Did you? Did you tell?'

She wants to use his shoulder to lever herself up, but the boy will not let her, not until she has replied.

'I didn't tell, Alek. But you have to. They have to know what he . . .'

With Navitski halfway across the room, Elenya finally uses the boy's shoulder to hoist herself up. The boy ducks to lift up the chair, and when he rises again, Elenya is facing the window. He nudges her, trying to put the chair back at the desk, but she does not move.

'Alek, back to your seat, please.'

The boy turns to go, but Elenya is holding him by the cuff of his over-long sleeve. He strains, but she pulls him back.

The window is broad as the wall, but the outside is obscured by a veil of grey. Elenya has used her other hand to rub a porthole in the condensation, and through it she peers across the playground. The porthole is slowly closing as the greyness steals back, but she shuffles sideways so that the boy, too, can look out. To do so, he must stand on his tiptoes.

'Do you see?' whispers Elenya. For the first time, there is uncertainty in her voice. Those three simple words tremble.

Outside, the playground is a perfect blanket of snow. Snow drives over the building, but does not plaster itself across the window, collecting instead in drifts on the farthest bounds of the yard.

He might be forgiven for thinking the world a virgin white, but across the playground snakes a single deep trail. It comes out of the whiteness, with a churned-up bank at either side, weaving in a great arc around the schoolhouse itself.

'It isn't, is it?' Elenya breathes.

The boy lifts a sleeve, rubs fiercely at the glass to scour it of more condensation. The trench swings close to the building, only yards away from the window to which his face is pressed, before swinging away again, around the corner of the assembly hall and out of sight. He is hurrying along the wall, dragging his sleeve to expose more through the glass, when he feels the hand clamp upon his shoulder. Thinking it his papa, he lets out a gasp, whirls around; Mr Navitski's face looks down.

'Why don't we sit down and get on with our lesson? I promise it won't be long. Then we'll have this mess all sorted out.'

How to say: there is no mess? How to say: I have to leave? How to say: these are the sounds that herald my papa's approach – a breath full of winter, the click of one heel, the long slow scrape of death dragged behind . . .

A hand in the small of his back, he finds himself steered back across the room. All eyes are on him now, but only Elenya understands. When he drops back into his seat, Yuri offers up another pencil, this one chewed so diligently that it looks like a twig.

The boy wheels around. Behind him, there is another window. This one gazes out at the back of the school, the playing field where, in summer, boys can go for races – but the glass is so thick with fog that he cannot see even an inch beyond. There might be a face lurking there, pressed to the glass, and still he would not see.

His eyes hunt out Elenya's own. They plead with her. They beg. Even though Navitski is watching, she reaches over her shoulder to clear the glass and look through. When she turns back to the boy, it is with an almost imperceptible shake of the head.

At the front of the classroom, Mr Navitski throws out

questions. One after another, answers rain down. They come with metronomic rhythm, but that is not the only rhythm the boy can hear.

From the glass behind his head: the click of one jackboot heel.

T he boy throws his hand up. It is only as it dangles there that he wonders: why? It is instinct that has driven him to do it, but it seems to work.

Mr Navitski looks up from his desk. 'What is it, Alek?'

'I need to go.'

'Go?'

He nods. 'I can take you in one minute, Alek.'

As he drops his hand, he realizes: he thinks I mean the toilet. But I don't use toilets. I use holes in the earth and snow for paper.

'No,' he whispers. 'I have to *go* . . .'

He is about to continue, but a knock at the door silences him. In his seat, the boy's skin blanches white as winter. Elenya kicks her chair back, as if ready to run.

The door opens. There, in the crack, hangs the bulbous face of the caretaker.

'What is it?' Mr Navitski asks, his voice almost a snap.

'Phone,' grunts the caretaker. 'In the staffroom.'

'The *telephone*?'

'For one of your lot. Some girl called Elenya.'

'Elenya's in *class*,' Mr Navitski says, stressing the last word as if it is something the caretaker might not understand.

'Suit yourself. Says it's urgent, though. It's her mother.'

Elenya rises, to a clatter of chairs. 'Can I, Mr Navitski?'

Besieged on both sides, Navitski gives a wearied nod. A wave of his hand sends Elenya halfway across the class. As she reaches the door, she looks back, with eyes meant only for the boy.

No words are exchanged. Elenya disappears, and now – in a room full of people – the boy is truly alone.

He stands, heedless of Yuri's sudden cry, and scrubs at the window pane. Outside, the playing field is barren. Yet the trench has been carved only a yard from the window, punctuated by strange circles of scuffed-up snow where his papa has paused, twisted as if to change direction, and then lurched on. In the trench, he sees shreds of pine branch, a blade of thick cattail grass. His papa leaves a trail like the forest itself.

'Alek, what are you doing?'

'I have to go,' he says, turning from the window.

'I said I'd take you in a minute . . .'

The boy bares his teeth, scrambles bodily over table and chair. 'I said now!' he cries. 'I have to go now!'

Across the classroom: gasps, titters.

In a breath, Mr Navitski is through the tables. His big hand closes over the boy's wrist. 'Okay, Alek,' he says, soft and yet firm. 'We'll go now.'

At the door, the boy thrashes, pulls back. 'Not to the toilet! Not there! I have to go back, I have to go back to the wild!'

With Navitski's hand still wrapped around him, they come through the door. On his left, the doors to the assembly hall are sealed. Directly in front, the toilet door flutters, ajar. Somebody must have left a window open inside, for the cold is suddenly unutterable. A breath of winter has stolen through. It rushes up the passageway, clawing at the books in the library cranny. A scrap of screwed-up paper, caught by that wind, flutters like snow.

Navitski tugs him in the direction of the toilet, but he throws his roots down, into the cold linoleum floor, and resists. For he knows, now, that the cold does not come from those bath-room stalls. He turns to look up the corridor. The wind rampages down it, howling to escape through windows, walls, the rafters in the roof.

The smell is like the forest at dawn. It comes, borne on that wind.

The sounds, sharp and soft: click, and thump; click, and thump. Click. Click. Click. Click.

A darkness rounds the corner, bringing those sounds, those smells, into clearer definition. It is tall as a man, and it walks on three legs.

Mr Navitski's fingers tighten around the boy.

With each step the darkness unfolds. This darkness has arms. This darkness is crowned in white, its strands stained at their tips, matted and bound.

'Alek, get back in the classroom.'

The boy can hear another sound now: the sound of malformed words and a tongue cleaved in two.

'Who is it, Alek?'

He finds his strength, rips his hand from Navitski's grasp. 'It's my papa,' he sobs, seeing the jagged slashes of dark through the crook of Navitski's arm. 'Oh please, but it's my papa . . .'

All that is behind him is the classroom, the assembly hall, the toilet itself. Dead ends, each and every one. Mr Navitski thrusts him back into the classroom. Crashing past the door, he tumbles in front of the desks. Somebody cheers. Somebody cries out. Somebody, more prescient than the rest, stands and skitters back.

Mr Navitski stands in the open doorway. 'Stay there, Alek.'

Too late, the boy stands. Mr Navitski slams the door shut, trapping himself in the corridor. And, all the while, the click and soft thump, click and soft thump.

'Can I help?' Mr Navitski begins. Then, bolder: 'I said, can I help?'

The boy goes to the door, grapples on the handle. He pulls, forces the door open a crack – but Mr Navitski's hand is closed around the handle on the other side, and he heaves it shut.

'You don't understand!' the boy wails. 'Open up! Oh please, but open up!'

The door gives again. This time, only the thinnest of slivers. Enough to see Mr Navitski, standing firm. Enough to see a slashing of black as a single jackboot appears.

'Papa, please! Don't, papa, don't . . .'

He sees a wizened hand disappear in a greatcoat. He sees it come out, with a slice of silver in its grasp. Then, all is black. Mr Navitski's hand slackens on the door.

Through wood and wall, the boy hears a crash. Mr Navitski cries out, the words stunted in his throat.

'*Where?*'

That voice, the voice of his papa, so indistinct it might be any bestial roar.

'He isn't here,' utters Mr Navitski.

Breathing, long and laboured.

The boy's hands, still curled around the handle. He looks over his shoulder. Some of the children are standing. Beyond them all, Yuri sits low in his chair, head balanced as if decapitated on the edge of his desk.

'I haven't seen him,' Navitski goes on, his breath returning.

'*Here?*' a wild man rasps.

'No . . .'

Beneath the boy's fingers, the handle rattles.

'It's just a classroom. Just children. Don't you . . .'

The door strains. Instinctively, the boy presses himself against it. He slumps to the floor, tries to brace himself against the wood – but he can find scant purchase, keeps slipping forward.

'*Boy?*'

The boy whispers, 'Yes . . .'

'*Boy?*'

The boy whispers, 'No, papa . . .'

The door flies open, propelling him across the classroom floor. As he picks himself up, the screaming begins. Tables, chairs, clatter, as the children fly back, forming huddles on the furthest edges of the room. Only Yuri remains at his desk, holding himself, head buried.

In the doorway hangs a branch of gnarled, weather-beaten wood. Beside it, the black jackboot webbed in lines of white. Above them both, a creature in whom he cannot believe. Only half of it is his papa. The rest is ash and oak, earth bound together by roots. Only one eye turns behind hair like hanging ice, a sunken ball of black.

Out comes the staff. It grinds to the ground. Next comes the jackbooted foot. A screeching click as it lands, dragging the body behind. Last through the door comes his trailing leg. A flash of marbled green flesh, under the ice.

'Papa, what are you doing here?'

Against the ground, the boy crawls backwards. Very quickly, he can go no further. His head crashes into the leg of Mr Navitski's desk, sending papers tumbling.

In the classroom, the screaming has stopped. All is silent as a winter wood. One girl makes as if to dart for the doorway, but the wild man still hangs there, with only a sliver of light behind. The girl stops, careens against a table.

The old man halts. His head revolves, breath erupting in plumes of phlegm and fog.

'The windows! Open the windows!' Mr Navitski's voice, on the other side of the wild man. It brings the children back to life. Tiny fingers grapple at a window latch.

'It won't open!'

The boy sees Mr Navitski's shape rising behind his papa. 'Smash it!' Navitski yells.

Somebody lifts a chair. They swing it hard at the window glass, but the chair simply bounces away. Somebody else lifts a foot, a broom handle, a broken table leg.

'Alek!' Mr Navitski calls – but, before he can call any further, the screaming returns.

It takes a moment for the boy to understand why. Then he sees it: the axe, hanging in his papa's hands. The wild man drags himself forward, axe reflecting the buzzing electric light. For the first time, he reveals the door behind him.

Mr Navitski strides through – but when he, too, sees the axe, he stalls. 'There's no need. There isn't any . . .'

His papa is on top of him now. He stares up. 'Papa, please . . .'

'*Papa,*' the wild man groans, '*please.*'

'I only came to school. It was to help. It was to stop Elenya telling . . .'

The wild man casts his staff aside. An ugly assortment of limbs bend down, a hunched back out of shape. Old hands, one maligned beyond measure, find the boy. He wants to resist, but the hands grasp him. Knuckles and fingers and bulbous bones where there should only be flesh. The knots in a dead branch meant only for the fire. He feels the old man's breath, rank as the dinners they have been eating, and then he is aloft, borne into the air to the tune of his papa's laboured breaths.

The arms close underneath him. One hand still clings to the axe, the flat of its blade in the small of his back.

The wild man turns, dead foot sending the staff halfway across the room. How his papa can walk without it, the boy does not know. One foot shuffles, and when his weight is on the other his body must quake to find balance.

In the doorway stands Mr Navitski. 'Put him down.'

The wild man takes another step. Mr Navitski does not move.

'Please,' whispers the boy.

'Alek?'

Navitski does not know it, but it is to him that the boy is pleading.

He tries again. 'Please, Mr Navitski . . .'

There is movement behind, a change in the air. A roar, strangely diminutive, and the air sliced apart. Something catches the wild man, and he staggers out, away from the blackboard, into the desks.

In the corner of his eye, the boy sees his papa's staff come down in an enormous arc. On the other end of it, his tiny hands clasping its bulb, stands Yuri. The bedraggled boy has his feet planted squarely. His cheeks are ruddy with effort. He gulps for air, straining to lift the staff again. 'Put him down!' Yuri squeals.

The boy feels his papa sinking beneath him. He hears the clatter of feet as Mr Navitski comes forward, but all the world has slowed, his teacher is wading through snow as high as his waist, and will not reach him in time. The wild man's arms come apart, and through them the boy crashes back to the ground.

By the time he has caught his breath, all he can see is the scissoring of the old man's greatcoat. Without the boy in his arms, he catches himself on a desk, knuckles his way backward – and, with taloned hand, plucks the staff out of the air.

Yuri clings to the other end. His fat fingers strain white.

At last, Yuri can hold on no longer. The wild man rips back the staff, whips it up. The bulbous end catches Yuri beneath the chin, driving him back into the desk where he should have stayed hidden. His head snaps back, exposing the pale pink of his throat. He crumples, catching the corner of the desk as he falls. There he lies, with a thin rivulet of red cutting a course from the top of his brow.

The boy feels hands around him: real hands of flesh, blood, bone. Mr Navitski has hold of him. He takes him by the chin, forces him to see. 'Run,' he says.

'What?'

'Run, Alek!'

Hands rush him to the door. He hangs there, staring back at his papa, at Yuri bloody beneath. Mr Navitski propels him on. He flails into the winter cold of the corridor. Along its length, other teachers, other children hang out of their class-room doors.

'Stay inside!' Mr Navitski thunders, waving a fist to drive them back. 'Run, Alek! Do what I say and run! I'll hold him here . . .'

The boy takes a step, takes another, and soon his little legs are pounding. He falls, scrambles back to his feet. Up the corridor, past the library cranny. With every breath, he palms off the walls, drives himself on.

He is almost at the end of the corridor. So consumed is he that he does not notice the figure rounding the corner ahead. Too late, he barrels straight into it and crashes to the ground. He is lying there, thinking his papa must have woven some sorcery to leap in front, when he hears a familiar voice.

'Alek, just what are you doing?'

Elenya holds out her hand, helps him to his feet. He says not a word, but he doesn't have to. 'It's him, isn't it?'

The boy nods.

'It was my mother, on the phone. Your papa went to the house. He thought we'd caught you. Alek, he . . .'

Elenya's face darkens. Her eyes are fixed on something beyond the boy. He does not have to turn, wills himself not to, but something in him will not obey. From the classroom at the end of the corridor comes a strangled cry – and then, darkness visible, darkness rising, his papa appears from the door.

'He axed my mother, Alek. She called as soon as she woke . . .'

The boy takes Elenya's hand, drags her up the hall.

'Alek, he killed Mishka.'

'What?'

'Dropped her dead . . .'

They hurry on. At the corridor's head, the path diverges, right towards the classrooms where little ones gather, left towards the front of the schoolhouse, the offices and staffroom beyond.

'Where's Navitski?'

The boy heaves her left. 'I think my papa . . .'

At the front of the schoolhouse, the hall is empty. The light has a strange quality, for the glass in the doors is plastered with snow and none of the daylight can fight its way through. The boy hauls Elenya towards it.

Click, and soft thump. Click, and soft thump.

He lunges for the door handle. It turns, but will not give. While he fights with it, Elenya staggers back. The corridor is still, but sound echoes up it, like the scuttling of rats.

'This way,' she says. 'We can call the police.'

'We can't,' the boy sobs, knowing it impossible. 'He's my papa. He's mine . . .'

No sooner has he said the word, the door flies open. Snow and wild wind rampages in. It takes the boy in its fist, pummels him back.

'Come on!' the boy cries.

He is about to plunge into the snowstorm, when a figure rushes the steps outside to battle back the door. For an instant, he believes it his papa, somehow given new form. Then he sees it for the caretaker.

'What are you two bastards doing out of class?' He reaches out to haul the door shut.

'No!' the boy exclaims, but his hands are not fast enough, his arms too weak.

The door is closed, but the wind does not die. The boy wheels around, looks at Elenya. The clicks ring more loudly. The thumps toll.

His papa appears, hauling himself to the front of the school-house.

Now, it is Elenya dragging the boy. Together, they tumble through the staffroom door. Smells of coffee and dirty dishwater. Elenya slams the door behind. She yells for him to follow her lead. The first sofa is heavy and fixed to the ground. The next creaks as they heave it out of place. The carpet rucks up, resists as they push it. Outside the door: click, thump, click, thump. At last, with a great shudder of complaint, the sofa conquers the carpet and they slam it against the door; in the same instant, the door opens. They battle it back.

As the boy strains to keep the sofa in place, Elenya leaps across the room. On a table beneath the window ledge, there sits a telephone. She picks up the receiver, but she has not yet pressed it to her ear before the boy bounds across, snatches it from her hands.

'What are you doing!?'

A handle turns. The door bucks.

'You can't!' the boy thunders, wrenching the wire from the wall.

'Why can't I?'

'Because he's my papa!'

On the other side of the room, the sofa slides forward, snagging again where the carpet has torn. Behind, the door hangs ajar. It can go no further. In the gap between door and wall, the face of his papa appears like some apparition. A hand reaches through. An arm. At its end, the staff can reach over the sofa, slicing the air in the centre of the room.

'*Boy.*'

That one word is like a blizzard.

385

The boy's eyes beseech the girl. 'Because he's my papa,' he repeats.

For a moment, she might be about to relent. Instead, she charges back, throws herself at the sofa, forces it back into the door. The door slams, trapping the old man. His face bulges, grotesque. It smears him against the wall, with one hand groping out. The shock causes his fingers to cramp, and the staff slips from his grasp, rolling past the girl and into the room.

'Help me!' Elenya barks.

The staff lands at the boy's feet. Uncertain whether he should take it, he looks up. Held between door and wall, his papa thrashes.

'*Boy.*'

'Stop it!' he yells. He throws himself at the sofa, but stops before joining Elenya. His hands close on her wrist.

'What are you doing?'

'He's my papa,' he cries. 'You're hurting my papa!'

A look like bewildered fury colours Elenya's face. For a second, she stops – but a second is enough to free the wild man in the door. He drops back. First, he is gone; then, from beyond, silver crashes down. Something bites into the door, showering splinters of wood. Its teeth rear back and it drops again. This time, a jagged shard tears itself away. The third time, it sinks deep into the door. Now the boy knows: it is his papa's axe, felling the door as fiercely as it would take the branches of a tree.

In the corners of his vision, shapes move through the snow smeared on the window glass. Children fleeing the building? The caretaker, summoned to whatever commotion rises within? Whichever it is, he does not know. The axe takes its final bite, obliterating the top of the door, and into the serrated portal comes his papa's face.

'*Boy.*'

Elenya's scream rents the air. Above her, the wild man stares at the boy.

He searches, desperately, for sadness in the eyes. He searches for pain, for terror, for signs he thinks himself betrayed. Anything that would show him that his papa still lived, somewhere in that walking wild.

'Papa,' he whispers, 'I'm sorry, papa . . .'

The wild man reaches out. At last, the boy understands. He reaches down, takes up the staff, offers it up. His papa's hand clasps around it. He thinks: I'm helping him; I'm looking after him, mama. But, too late, he sees that something does live in the creature's eyes: it shines venomously; it hates; it *laughs*.

His papa heaves on the staff, drawing him near. Too slow to let go, the boy finds himself dragged across the room. By the time he rips his hands back, he has landed, with Elenya, on the sofa. The wild man throws the staff behind him, grapples out to take him in his hands.

'*Boy!*'

He rolls left, plunging from the sofa. His papa's hands cannot reach him now. Instead, they drop down, finding Elenya's hair, her shoulders, her throat. His crooked hand strokes her lips, silencing the scream that threatens to erupt. Forcing the scream back inside her, he lifts her up.

Elenya cannot hold on fast enough to keep him from dragging her through. From the floor, the boy watches her go. Her knee digs into the back of the sofa, but his papa is stronger. By degrees, she is disappearing.

He leaps up, wraps himself around her legs. For a second,

he can hold her still. Then, one foot tears free of his grasp. Now, he dangles from the other leg. He slides forward. Behind the sofa, what is left of the door slams shut. He could not follow her now, even if he wanted. He feels his strength fading away. First her ankle, then her toes, and now the last part of her slides through the devastated wood.

He presses his face to the rent in the door. Along the passageway, Elenya hangs over his papa's sunken shoulder. Click, and soft thump; click, and soft thump. The wild man lopes away.

It takes him too long to haul the sofa back, force his way through a gap in the door. By the time he has pounded to the end of the passage, the only sign of his papa is the schoolhouse door, flying wide. The storm claws within, and he forces himself to the precipice. On the schoolhouse steps, the caretaker lies in a heap, scarlet in the snow where he has been thrust against the stone.

He gazes out: pirouetting snow and endless white, gust doing battle with gust so that, everywhere, miniature storms wage war. He cannot see the drifts at the far side of the playground, for between them the flakes are more impenetrable than the forest.

All he can see is a single trench, disappearing into the storm.

A long the roads, between cars. The boy tries to keep pace with his papa's trench, but every time he thinks he sees a figure lurching in the mists, it resolves into the face of a pillar box, the jut of a tumbledown wall. Soon he stops bawling out. The figures he passes turn at him oddly; one barks out, demanding to know if he is okay. The boy only carries on, over intersections where the traffic is packed, nose to tail. Soon the cars are fewer and far between; the buildings give way to sprawling yards and hunkered tenements, with their eyes gouged out. A factory pumps out noxious smoke; a bus sits broken at the edge of the road. All around, curling snow – and quickly the imprint of his papa is gone.

In the distance, distorted sirens and flashing blue lights.

At last, there are dark smudges in the whiteness. The skeletal trees appear. As soon as he is able, he leaves the road behind, tracks it instead from the shelter of the forest. Through the trees he can make faster time, for he is a wild thing not meant for the blacktops and asphalt. And there, guttering from oak to blasted ash, is the trail of his papa.

He tracks it for miles, until night has come upon him. He thinks his papa must have conjured a fire, but nowhere can he see empty cauldrons or bulwarks of stone. Foxes do not have fires, nor bison nor boar. When a man has turned wild enough, he does not need fires either.

In places, the trail evaporates, but every time he finds it again. If it is not in the scoring of a jackboot or the trail of dead leg, it is in the snapped twigs on the trees, the three lines scored into bark where Elenya has clawed out, dangling from his shoulder. He is buoyed to see it, for it means his papa has not turned Baba Yaga and devoured her yet; he bears her into the woodland, but she is still alive.

'Papa!' he yells, but the only answer comes from the trees.

Go back, they whisper. *Go back.*

He had forgotten: the trees are on my papa's side. If his stories are real, it was trees that kept him from the men who escaped from the great frozen city of Gulag; they threw up walls of thorn to protect him. Yet – why would they protect his papa? Why not Elenya? Why not . . .

He tears through the trees and finds himself at the head of the dell, his papa's trail disappearing in a swirling vortex of white.

At the bottom of the glade, he can see the outline of the house, so spattered with white that it seems to meld into the sky, appearing like a ruin once again. Down there, a blue light dances, off and on, off and on, like one of the Christmas

390

lights wrapped around Elenya's tree. He looks for tyre tracks on the glade, but the snow has cloaked them so that he cannot tell how many men are already there.

He is about to duck back into the forest when a vile rumbling comes through the snowfall. The boy cocks his head. He would know that sound anywhere.

From behind, a ball of blackness erupts through the veil: the same black truck that unknowingly ferried the boy back to school. Down the glade it plummets, sloughing around in front of Elenya's house. The boy watches as, with the door still hanging open, Elenya's father leaps out and pounds towards the front door.

At the bottom of the dell, light spills out of the house. He sees other cars here – one, two, three and more. A motorcycle, its every contour familiar. Shielded by the snow, he steals close, skirting the house as if to sneak into the garden behind. In the garden, the drifts have grown high. He can hear screaming within, thunderous cries.

More light spills from the kitchen door. Some fool, heedless of winter's malice, has left it ajar. Footsteps churn up the snow on the step, fading under the constant fall as they wend their way into the woodland.

He steals to the step. Along the barrel of the kitchen, two policemen stand with Elenya's mother. His eyes track down. There, between the policemen, lies Mishka. She does not move. Her jaws are open. A dead tongue lolls.

'Oh, papa,' he whispers.

In reply, the taunting trees: *oh, papa.*

He turns, hurtles under mama's branches. Up and over: the wild ways, the old lanes; frozen cattail pond and emperor oak. By the time he approaches the gingerbread house, he can see his papa's trench winding through the trees. Yet – there is no smoke in the air, no scent of the fire.

He comes, tentatively, into the clearing. Everywhere, there are tracks: fox and wild cat; his own moccasins; Elenya's boots, preserved from the night before – but, above them all, the deep tread of other men.

His eyes are drawn to the gingerbread house. Its walls tremble. At first, he thinks it his papa, using it as a hiding. Moments later, a silhouette appears in the doorway of the gingerbread house. It steps into the light. This is not his papa. This is a man younger than Navitski, with a coat of navy wool and a furred cap. A policeman, like the ones at baba's house looking for Elenya.

'Just some tramp,' the policeman mutters darkly, oblivious to the boy.

Behind him, a second policeman emerges. In his fist hangs the little Russian horse. One gulp of fresh air, and he turns to retch into the roots. The horse rolls away.

'He has *children's* toys,' he says, wiping the slime with his sleeve.

'You think he brought it for the girl?'

'Who knows, with these bastards? Come on, let's report it back . . .'

The man freezes. Eyes that were once unseeing have landed on the boy. '*Biladz,*' the man utters. 'Is that her?'

The boy thinks to run, lose himself in the trees. He could do it if he wanted. He'd vault the fire and snake between them, lose himself under aspen and birch. They'd try and track him but end up tracking a deer, a fox, each other. These men don't know about running wild.

Yet, he stays still. 'Where is she?' he utters.

'Where . . .'

'Elenya!' the boy barks. 'Did you find her?'

The policemen share a bitter look. 'What are you doing here, boy?'

'You don't have her, do you?'

The first policeman ventures a step forward. 'What are you,' he says, 'her brother?'

'No,' says the boy, the single word melting. 'I'm her . . . friend.'

At the house that once was a ruin, more policemen gather. As they shepherd him back under mama's branches, he fancies there must be six, seven, eight cars lined up on the dell. Flashlights roam the undergrowth, while radios crackle with static.

Among them, he sees Mr Navitski. He is different now, wearing a woollen coat the same as the rest. One of the policemen is helping fit a radio to its belt when he sees the boy being ushered across the snow dark.

'Alek!' he cries, bustling the policeman aside. 'Wait. Hold him there.'

The two policemen hardly listen, pushing him instead along the thin funnel of the kitchen. They bring him to the living room. A blanket has been laid over what remains of Mishka, but from it her snout still pokes, as inquisitive as it was in life.

By the wood-burner, Elenya's mother sits with a police-woman. Half of her face is purpled, and to it she holds a cloth soaked in water. She is murmuring to the policewoman and the policewoman translates those murmurs to a book in her hands.

'This one mean anything to you?'

Elenya's father turns. His eyes light on the boy. He is about to speak, when Mr Navitski forces his way between.

'Alek, we can handle this.'

Elenya's father says, 'Alek, what are you doing here?'

Between wintry breaths: 'I've come to find her.'

'Find her?'

'I can find her, I promise.'

He does not believe. The boy can tell; the look on his face screams it out, more clearly than black skies scream out thunder.

'It was my papa,' whispers the boy. 'I'm sorry, but it was my papa. He came to the school and . . .'

'Your papa?'

'He brought the woods with him.'

Silenced, Elenya's father looks at Navitski. 'Did you bring him here?' he says, accusing.

Mr Navitski says, 'He wants to help.'

But Elenya's father rages, 'How can he possibly help?'

'It was my papa,' the boy repeats, as if reading a rite. 'My papa. My papa.'

Elenya's father strides forward, sinks to one knee. This close, he is enormous, a bear of a man. 'Alek, listen to me. What do you know about the man who took Elenya?'

The boy is lost, with only one thing he can possibly say: the truth.

'She was going to *tell*. She said she had to. That we couldn't carry on. I went to town to stop her, but my papa came too. I thought he'd come for me, but he took her.'

Her father's face is set, like one of the faces grown out of the murder trees. He lifts his head to stare at Navitski. 'What is he talking about?'

'They live out there,' breathes Navitski.

'Out there?'

'In the *pushcha*.'

394

The boy sees the truth resolving on her father's face. He stands, rocks back.

'It isn't his fault,' the boy whispers. 'It's because of the trees. He wasn't always so wild. He was good. I promise, he was good.'

'Alek,' Mr Navitski interjects. 'This is important. Can you hear me?'

The boy nods.

'Your papa, Alek. Do you know where he went?'

The boy looks from each face to the other: her mother, face shining and swollen; her father, with murderous eyes.

'No,' says the boy.

All three of them exhale. Fists clenched and gorges full.

'No,' says the boy, 'but I know how to find him.'

Snow, and more snow, and more snow to come.

There are more than he expected: Navitski, Elenya's father, and more police than he can count, fanning out through the woods. They have forced him into a woollen coat just like theirs, too thick and cumbersome, but he would not let them restrain him in such stupid things as mittens and scarves. By the time they come back to the gingerbread house, most of the policemen are gone – but he can still see the beams of their torches roaming under the trees, distant flashes of spectral light.

The gingerbread house looks tormented, empty and alone. Its roof has slipped, and the emperor oak that claws up makes it look like some meagre pile of kindling cast into the roots.

'It's where we lived,' says the boy.

'Here?'

Elenya's father strides forward. The shotgun over his shoulder dangles like a taunt. He crouches, plucks something from the ground. Too late, the boy realizes what it is: he is holding the little Russian horse.

'This is hers,' he breathes. Eyes like fire turn on the boy. '*Hers.*'

'No,' says the boy, with the firmness of the forest. 'It was mine. It was my mama's. It was all I had, and she had it in her window. She gave it back.'

'Did she give you *this* too?' He lifts the eiderdown from beneath the crust of snow, trampled with dirt.

'It was . . .' His stomach tightens. '. . . to keep me warm. I put it on my papa, but it couldn't keep the forest out.'

They gather, as if at some museum of the arcane, marvelling at such simple things as a fire, a ribcage picked bare, a house made from sticks.

At last Navitski says, 'Which way did he go?'

The boy searches for his papa's trail. It criss-crosses this expanse in deeper degrees. In some places, it has been camouflaged by falling snow; in others, it is still as severe as it was the day it was carved.

It takes some moments before he realizes: they're looking straight at it, but they can't *see*. All they see is the snow dark. They don't see the marks where the axe has bitten the trees. They don't see the crunch underfoot, or the snaking roots. They don't know what to look for at all.

His eyes light on a trail deeper than the rest. He leads them under the branches, away from biting snow. He sees the disruption in the frost where his papa approached the clearing. His gait seems stranger than usual, heavier and more crooked; it must be Elenya, still hanging over his back. He crouches, crawls along. Soon the trench is plain to see.

The boy surges ahead, finally kicking off the slippers they

forced on him in the schoolhouse. With naked feet, he is freer; he bounces from roots, over storm-fallen boughs. With Navitski's breathing fading behind him, he scrambles up an escarpment where the trees grow more sparsely and there are yet gaps in the canopy for snow to stream through. In the time they have been in the forest, the fist of night has closed completely. It is the time for cookfires and shelter – but only for men like Navitski, like Elenya's father gasping his way up the hill behind. The boy needs nothing, not while there is still warmth in his veins. If that makes him a wild thing, if it makes him a little wolf-boy, he does not care. He flies.

In the gaps between the trees, his papa's trail is harder. Here, he stopped. Here, he set down Elenya. Here, he lifted her again. The boy glides past and, slowly, begins to recognize the faces in the branches, the particular stoops of trunks. He kicks through a shallow bank of white, dead bracken beneath his toes and stutters to a halt.

He has come this way before.

He knows, now, where his papa is heading. First, there will be the marshes, treacherous beneath skeleton layers of ice; then, the aspens; then, strange mounds, relics from the long ago, with their underworlds beneath. Beyond that: the wide, wild woods, forever and ever, that place in which history and story are the very same thing, that other wild into which the Old Man of the Forest turned wolf and disappeared.

Navitski and Elenya's father appear on his shoulder. Behind them, two policemen labour their way up the hill.

'Is he near?' gasps Navitski.

The boy stares into the snow dark, to find his papa's trench disappearing again under the trees. Where the snow can light on it, its edges erode. By morning, it will be gone. He takes a step after it, lets them follow. Under the trees, the trail is more defined. It climbs over a ridge, forging a path where the wraithlike woods give way to pines.

For a moment, the boy sets off towards those pines. Their scent is strong. Then he crouches, as if fingering a trail – and, when he gets back to his feet, he shuffles so that the pines are in the corner of his vision. Now he stares into leafless trees, sculpted in white.

'He went this way,' he says, indicating a way down, into the skeletal valleys below.

Elenya's father takes a great stride. 'Here?'

'He isn't far,' lies the boy. 'He's getting tired.'

Mr Navitski's hand, trembling, finds his shoulder. 'Are you certain, Alek?'

'Please,' the boy breathes. 'Please, Mr Navitski.'

The boy thinks to follow them down, but they gather around him and their eyes implore him – and, once again, it is he who must lead.

The valley is sheer. He has to stop, so that the men following can stutter down its slopes. He takes Mr Navitski by the hand, shows him how to shimmy sideways down the escarpment, using the roots of clinging trees to steady his falls. Then, when he is certain he has led them so far that they could not find their way back, he hurtles forward.

At first, Navitski does not realize what he is doing. It is Elenya's father who barks out: 'Slow!' Then: 'Stop!' By then, it is too late. The boy is wilder than they, and they could not follow his footprints any more than they could follow his papa's trail. Alone, he takes flight.

The trees throw up walls of thorns to protect him. He whispers his thanks.

Only when he is certain he has forged too far ahead does he turn back, cutting an arc through a stand of wintering ash to find another way back up the hill. He knows when he is level with them for he can hear their voices, echoing in the trees. He thought he could take them to his papa, thought it was for Elenya – but he was wrong. He made a promise, and it's a promise he's going to keep.

At the top of the valley, he goes back to the pines. His papa's trail has dimmed under the relentless snowfall, but under the branches it still shimmers. He hurries on.

The path meanders with the lie of the land. He follows it along a ridge, with a sheer face of earth on one side and a rolling precipice on the other. The pines grow on the ledges here, and he guides his way through them just as surely as his papa.

Soon the land levels out. The ridges soften, one bank rolls into the next, and he emerges from the thick pines to see the mixed woodland beneath him, a seascape of ice with occasional flourishes of fir cresting the surface. Here, his papa's trail is more visible still. It wends its way down, and the boy follows.

Under an ice-bound canopy again, he begins to notice dead bark stripped back, axe marks where branches have been hewn away, a hole cleaved in the ground where his papa must have thrown the axe to take down some wretched woodland creature. Each is a sign he is close, each a sign his papa is growing tired.

Wind stirs beneath the branches. Cringing from it, he pushes on. Now, the trees come apart. Now, he sees a rippling curtain of white. He lifts his foot, but there is nothing beneath it, for the land drops away in a steep bank. No longer any trees to protect him, he gazes out across the marsh.

By a line of encrusted reeds, whipped into a frenzy by the

wind winter breathes across them: oranges, reds, reefs of grey. How this fire burns in the blizzard, he cannot know. It is, he understands, a magic learned in Perpetual Winter, some gift from the wilderness that kept his papa alive after he fled that great frozen city called Gulag and made his wild walk home.

Down there, his papa is only a shape in the storm. He is hunched over the flames, feeding them with handfuls of bark plucked from his pockets. From where he stands, the boy can see only the long sweep of the greatcoat down his back. Beyond the fire, Elenya is huddled in reeds, curled up like a closing fist. Her blouse sleeves torn, she wraps her arms around her knees.

The boy steals forward. He thinks: they will not hear me in this raging wind. Yet, no sooner has he scrambled down the bank, he knows he is wrong. His papa would hear the faintest sound in a night filled with maelstroms.

Slowly, the wild man turns.

'Oh, papa,' he whispers. 'What have you done?'

His papa snorts out dark plumes of breath.

'Is she okay, papa? Is she okay?'

He stutters to the edge of the marsh to reach her, but his papa shifts, like a vagrant wolf protecting its kill.

'Elenya?'

In the reeds, the girl unfolds. Her eyes are raw, but intelligence still sparkles in them. The same cannot be said for his papa. His eyes, black orbs, roll in their orbits.

'Did he hurt you?'

Elenya shakes her head. 'Is *my* papa coming?'

The wild man casts a final handful into the fire. Smoke explodes, flecked with shining sparks.

'He is, papa. He's coming, and he's not the only one.'

The wild man gives him a questioning look.

'There's police in the house. Police in the woods. The teacher's with them. Papa, *why*?'

This time, the wild man tries to find words. They seem to ride up his cleaved tongue, themselves being cleaved in two.

'Drink, papa. Drink, papa.' The boy cups snow in his hands and lifts them to the wild man's lips. He buries his lips, his whiskers, in the palms.

'Is it better?'

The wild man nods.

'Papa, they're coming to get you.'

The old man brings his staff down in an arc over the fire, better to indicate Elenya.

'He said you'd come,' a small voice pipes up. 'All through the forest, he kept saying it. *Boy. Boy. Boy.*'

'For *me*?' the boy breathes.

'I think he thought, if you wouldn't come with him, he'd make you follow.'

'Papa, I didn't leave because I wanted to. I left because . . . I didn't want her to tell. I wanted to stay, and be with you. Because I promised, papa. But now . . .'

'*Boy* . . .' The word breaks apart. The old man stutters, as if to take hold of it, but instead he chokes up whatever pieces of bark he has been chewing through the long day. The boy cups his hands to melt more for him to drink, but in a single motion the wild man sweeps him aside. He drops the staff, cups his own hands, fills his cheeks with the raw, frozen snow.

As he bends over the fire, the boy rushes to Elenya's side. 'She's freezing, papa.'

He rips off the police coat, wraps her in it. Above him, the wild man shakes.

'Papa, what if she . . .'

He takes Elenya's hand, as if to tease her from the reeds. Only now does he see the blue black bracelets around her wrists. He sees the same discolouration on her shoulder, where her blouse has been torn apart.

'He hurt you, didn't he?'

Elenya whispers, 'He wouldn't put me down.'

'What did he do?'

'Alek, I'm cold.'

He pushes her to the very edge of the fire. 'Papa,' he ventures, 'I have to take her back.'

The old man stands.

'They're coming for you, papa.'

The wild man opens his encrusted mouth, as if to let loose a roar, but into the silence comes a different sound: the air above being torn apart in relentless rhythm; a sound like his papa's staff constantly whirling in the air, the suck and pull of air in its wake.

The sound intensifies. The snow begins to dance in different directions, a new blizzard forced on them from above.

Light bursts over them like the dawn. It illuminates the canopy of the forest in brilliant whiteness, intensifying as it approaches. The wild man cringes, spreading himself over the fire. The boy finds his arms draped around Elenya, as if he might shield her from it.

As quickly as it comes, the light goes. The boy can see it sweeping over the forest. The sound diminishes. Now, it is only a distant storm.

'Are they close?' asks Elenya.

The boy squints upwards, tracking the retreating light.

'I left Navitski in the forest, with your papa. I sent them the wrong way . . .'

'What if there's more?'

The sound is returning now, the light bearing back. He stares at his papa, tries to find some shred of man left in those eyes of blue. The cold sinks its teeth into him, like Aabel being devoured, and he thinks he finds a way.

'It was like this before, wasn't it, papa?'

'*Boy.*'

'They hunted partisans here, didn't they? Police like Yuri's Grandfather and wicked soldiers from the King in the West. They sent airplanes, and the partisans crossed the marshes and made their home under aspen and birch . . .'

'*Boy!*'

'And . . .'

The boy swallows. He fancies he can hear the tramping boots of those wicked soldiers coming through the trees.

'. . . it was the same for you, wasn't it, papa? When you escaped that frozen city called Gulag and had to cross Perpetual Winter. The soldiers of the Winter King chased you, and when they stopped chasing you, it was the other runaways chasing you. But you got away, didn't you, papa?'

This time, no anger, only sadness: '*Boy . . .*'

'You were wild then, papa. And you're wild now. It isn't your fault. I promise, papa. You're not Baba Yaga. It wasn't really you . . . It was the trees. They got into you then, and they've got into you now. But . . .' The boy wipes at his eyes, for his tears are freezing as they trickle down his face, and he feels as if he is wearing a mask made out of ice. '. . . you can't come back, papa. You can't let them catch you. You have to run. They have to hunt. But, papa, you've got the wild on your side. You're a wolf. They're just dogs.'

The wild man holds his breath. No clouds of grey envelop

his head. No click, nor soft thump. He stands still, stares at the boy.

'Run, papa! Please, papa! Please, run!'

He pounds across the flames, kicking up burning logs as he comes. On the other side, he throws his arms around his papa's broken form. At first, the wild man stands, resolute as any of the trees through which his hunters are coming. Then, he stops. The boy can feel him tremble. He buries his head in the stinking greatcoat and feels fingers in his hair, cold taloned branches but fingers nonetheless. They stroke him.

'*Boy.*'

The boy draws back, his papa's fingers trailing after.

The wild man makes a movement, as if he might whip the boy onto his shoulder.

The boy shakes his head. 'Run, papa! Run. I'll be . . .'

The wild man turns, drives out with his staff. He hauls himself one stride into the reeds. He stops. Looks back. Blackness in his eyes, but not only blackness. The shreds of something else, too, some memory entangled in bramble and briar.

'Go!' the boy thunders.

The wild man takes another step, falters again.

'He wants you to follow,' Elenya whispers from the other side of the fire.

'Go!' the boy sobs. He takes up a fist of ice and snow, lets it loose to catch his papa's jaw. 'Get out of here!' he cries. 'Please!' he begs. 'They'll follow if I come! They won't give up!' He takes another ball, and another. The first hits his papa's breast, the second the top of his head. To that wild man they are like snowflakes. They barely seem to touch him at all. The boy reaches back, finds a branch that has rolled from the fire. Taking

404

it by its flameless end, he hurls it into the marshland. The flame drives his papa back, one step, two steps, and more. Again he stops, staring blankly at the smouldering bough.

The boy reaches for another. He is about to loose it when he hears sounds in the trees: voices bellowing his name, bellowing Elenya's. It is Navitski's voice, but he is not alone. There are countless other footsteps as well.

He takes the second flaming branch and charges after his papa, deep into the slicing reeds. He cuts the air with it, trailing fire in the blackness. His papa stumbles back.

'Go!' he cries. At last, no wavering, no begging in his voice. 'Don't you know what you've done? You kept me here, papa! You kept me in the woods. And you . . .' He falters. Has to choke the words out. He does not mean them, does not believe, but he thinks of the things Navitski will say, he thinks of the teachers in the school and Madam Yakavenka in the tenement, and he lets their crowing come to his throat. He will spill out every vile thing if only it will drive his papa away, make his papa think that he hates him, when every fibre in his being, every muscle and sinew, compels him to follow. This, he knows, is the only way of staying true to his promise.

'You kept me here and wouldn't let me go, and you fed me dead things and you made me freeze! You went into that school, papa, and you dragged her away. You hit Yuri. Do you really think I'd come with you? You can't really . . .'

The wild man moves, as if he might lunge forward, but the boy wheels the flaming branch.

'I want to go back, papa. Back to the city. To the tenement. And . . . they're kind to me, papa. They're good. I don't want you, papa. I don't . . .'

The wild man lunges again. This time, it is not to lash out

405

or snatch up the boy. His arms open, as if he might wrap them around the boy. He tries, but they are too broken now, their joints too jagged to ever complete the circle again. The boy lifts his fists, still clasping the smoking branch. He forces it between them. The wild man's arms dangle. He pummels him in the breast.

'Go,' he whispers. 'I don't want you, papa. I want . . .'

'*Boy.*'

The wild man lifts a hand. One taloned fingertip traces the line of his jaw.

But the boy will not look in his eyes. Even if there was memory in them again, to look into his eyes would be to betray the lie. Instead, he buries his face, fixes only on the tangled reeds. He feels his papa step back. There is no click and soft thump, not as he steps into the marshes, not as the veil is drawn.

When he looks again, there are only the reeds.

He is huddling with Elenya when her father storms out of the forest, flanked by more policemen than he can count. Navitski is among them, but though he tries to reach the boy, burly arms muscle him away. A meaty fist forces the boy to stand. He says: he wasn't here; my papa's already gone. When they ask him where, he tells them: he has turned into the Old Man of the Forest, but in the end he wasn't Baba Yaga after all. They get even less sense out of the girl, but perhaps that can be forgiven; she is tinged in blue and slurs her words, and a police medic proclaims that it is only the fire keeping her from a long and dreamless sleep.

Soon, there is a cordon. Soon, flasks of hot, sweet tea. Then, the police medic sets down his pack and rolls it back to reveal a simple metal tin. He lifts off the lid. Inside, in perfect rows, sit biscuits engraved with a familiar design: ears of wheat curling around a ragged map, and a star with five points hanging above.

The boy cannot hold back his tears.

'Don't cry, little one. They'll warm your insides, give you strength.'

Tentatively, the boy reaches in and takes a biscuit in his grubby hand. He does not eat it. Not at first. He lifts it to his nose and breathes in the scents of honey and ginger. He strokes the ear of wheat and ragged map, touches each point of the simple star.

When he takes a bite, it rushes to every corner of his body. He suckles until his mouth is coated with flavour, takes one more bite for good measure, but he will not eat it all – and he knows, in that moment, that he will not taste this taste ever again.

The police are fanning out now. There are blankets and a sledge, the better to take Elenya back home, but the rest are looking for footprints in the earth. They will not find them. Not one of them knows what they ought to be looking for: a simple trench, wending its way into the reeds, as the man who used to be his papa makes his way across marsh and aspens to the lost world beyond.

NEXT WINTER

On the ledge by the window, its underbelly lit up by blue and white fairy lights: the little Russian horse that was a present from his mother.

He has been up for an hour, but he has not yet ventured out; it is New Year's morning, and if you venture out too soon, Ded Moroz will not come up from the forest and leave presents in the hearth.

He is sitting with the Russian horse when the tiniest of taps sounds at the door. In the light between door and wall appears Mr Navitski's face. Now, the boy must call him Nikolai. His eyes are heavy but his face is bright, and he is still wearing checked pyjamas of the sort the boy has hanging on the back of the door, ready for the moment when he wants to wear pyjamas again. Mr Navitski tells him it will happen one day, but it hasn't happened yet.

'Are you ready, Alek?'

The boy nods.

'Better get some clothes on, then.'

The boy has a drawer full of clothes. He tugs it open at the foot of his bed. The bed itself is untouched, for he sleeps instead in a nest of eiderdown and branches on the floor. Mr Navitski takes away the branches every weekend, but it is easy to find more; there is a tree in the garden denuded of bark, and more along the way to school, whose lowest branches have been mysteriously hewn away over the long months of summer.

In the drawer he finds a shirt, some trousers. Socks and underpants. Beneath them all: a patchwork vest of rabbit-skin pelts. If Nikolai knows he has it, he doesn't say, so it must mean he doesn't mind. Even so, today is not a day for dressing like that. Sometimes he puts it on after dark, but only after Nikolai and his wife Nastya are themselves tucked in. Then he can curl in it and remember the smells of the wilderness. Dressed like that, he can better remember his papa.

Once he is dressed in shirt and short trousers, he leaves the bedroom and follows the hallway.

'Well?' grins Nastya, appearing at the bottom of the stairs with tinsel in her hair. 'Don't you want to see?'

The boy nods, but remains at the top.

'I'll bring you a hot milk, should I?'

The boy shakes his head.

'Okay, Alek. We'll be down here waiting – but we're not opening any presents until you come!'

After that, it doesn't seem fair that he should sit on the top step all alone. He isn't even certain why he wants to. He comes down the stairs slowly. In the living room, Nikolai is sitting cross-legged in front of the tree, with his daughter Ana squirming in

412

his lap. She is eighteen months old, chubby, with hair the same tight dark curls as her father. Behind them, the hearth is dead.

'Come on, Alek, you're letting the team down. We're freezing down here!'

It feels good to be asked, so he bounds down the last of the stairs and scurries across the room. In the hearth, he drops to his hands and knees. There are matches and fire lighters piled up, but Navitski knows he doesn't need them. When he is finished, the fire is a burning crimson ball.

On seeing the burgeoning flames, Ana claps as she always does. She reaches out a fat fist and snatches to take hold of the boy. At last, he gives her his finger.

In front of the tree, there are presents. Ded Moroz has been. Ded Moroz did not really live out in the forest, because if he did, the wild would take him, turn him into a feral creature, and he'd have no thirst to hand out presents any longer. But it is a story the boy would like to believe, so he crawls over and opens the first one.

Later, with his new winter coat and hunchback knight, he sits in the back of the car, with Ana strapped down in her special seat beside him. Through the city they go, to that railway yard with metal stairs and the hovel above. Yuri is already there, sitting on the step. Without wailing out a goodbye, he tumbles down the steps to join them, awkwardly clambering into the car.

'Isn't your mama coming?'

'Oh, no,' says Yuri, as if it is the most ordinary thing in the world. 'My new, new papa's come home, so she's busy today.'

Soon, the city gutters away. On either side, the forest rushes past. The boy keeps his head down, at once both hungry to look and desperate not to see.

413

It is not the first time he has seen the forest. In the beginning, he forced them to make him come. If they did not – and, on occasion, they refused – they would find him gone in the morning, and have to pick him up on the side of the road. The truth is, every time he ran, he wanted them to come after. If he had wanted to disappear again, into the snow dark beneath the trees, he would have disappeared and never been found. Sometimes, he would reach the edge of the city, the first line of forest, and simply wait until they came. He would turn his back to the trees and listen to them whisper, and count himself strong that he did not go to them, not even when they begged. He would wonder: was this what it was like for my papa, through all those years of his life? The trees begged him to come back and live wild, but he was strong enough to resist them, all until he made that promise to mama. Then the wild had won, but it was long seasons before the boy or old man could fully understand.

The car banks left, to follow the old trail. They emerge onto the top of the glade just as the first snow is breaking from the sky, and weave slowly down to the front of the house.

Elenya is hanging from the front door before they have reached halfway. In her stocking feet she bounds across the snow to reach them. Her father barks some command at her, but she does not seem to listen. Instead, she grapples the boy out of the car and smothers him with kisses.

'Get off me!'

'I won't,' she declares, dragging him to the house. 'I think you could use a bath.'

She does not really mean it; it is an old joke now, because she finds it delightful to remind him of that time she dunked him in the bubbles and raised him up from dark brown soup. Together, they go inside. In the living room, a tree is bedecked

414

in gold and silver tassels. The star on top shines with silver light.

A puppy runs circles around them. Elenya bats it back, but it wants to go to the boy and releases a succession of shrill yaps whenever he stops teasing the scruff of its neck. At last, Yuri scampers off with it, to cavort in front of the wood-burner, or in the cubbyholes under the dining table.

Soon, there will be dinner – but, as Nikolai and Nastya ferry Ana into the house, to be cooed over by Elenya's mother, Elenya drags him upstairs. In her bedroom, the spoils of the morning are laid out. She has got dresses and scarves, embroidered gloves and new winter boots. A framed picture of Mishka sits at the side of her bed.

'Now we can get to it. What shall we play?'

It doesn't matter what he says; they always end up playing whatever game Elenya decides. She drags out board games and stuffed animals, the rancid end of the last bone Mishka ever chewed, but today none of them will do. At last, she produces a box wrapped in red paper, with a silver bow and a card he cannot read.

'Well, go on,' she says. 'It's for you.'

Inside lies a book. As is the girl's way, it is a book he has seen before – and not one she ought to be giving. He opens the first pages – and there, before the story of Baba Yaga, she has written him a note:

For the Wild Boy

Before he closes it, he remembers: 'I never said thank you.'

'Well, you can say it now.'

'Not for this. For . . . the eiderdown. For last year.'

'Oh, *that*,' grins Elenya. 'I got such a telling off for *that*, even after . . .' The rest of the story remains unsaid.

'I . . . gave it to my papa,' says the boy. 'To keep out the forest.'

'An eiderdown's not enough to keep out the forest, though, is it?'

The boy shakes his head; you need walls and roofs and roads and clothes.

'They never found your papa, did they?'

They did not. Woodsmen, police, roamed far and wide, but all they found were the trees. No campsites. No fires. No snares set and checked for squirrels, rabbits, the other lowly creatures of the forest. If there was a body, they said, the beasts of the wild had left nothing to be scavenged. The boy knows the truth more keenly than any: he crossed the marshes, into that older wild. There, the trees would drink him up, turn him into the new shoots of spring, the green leaves of summer, the forest mulch on the winter ground. That is why, when he looks through Elenya's window, he sees not only the tops of the trees bound up again in ice, but his family in the forest.

There was a tale told in the days after his papa came to pick him up from school. It lingers still, in the corners of classrooms, where children are forbidden to speak of it but find, neverthe-less, a story too delicious to ignore. Once upon a while, the wild man of the forests came to the city. On legs like roots and arms like briars, he circled the schoolhouse.

Let me in, let me in, he cried, with a voice made of wind.

Never, said the schoolhouse, whose voice was made of bricks.

Then I'll crow and I'll snow and I'll blow your house down . . .

All at once, the wild man called up a blizzard. Wind clawed down, and the schoolhouse doors came apart.

The wild man came into school on a carpet of thorns. When he reached the classroom door, he found it locked.

Let me in, let me in, he cried, with a voice made of wind.

If I let you in, you'll take my kin, said the door, whose voice was made of paint and varnish.

Then I'll crow and I'll snow and I'll blow this door down . . .

At once, the blizzard roared through the schoolhouse halls. The classroom door flew in, and the wild man stalked among the children, touching each with a finger cold as death.

I am a man of winter, I am a man of ice. Which of you is naughty, and which of you is nice?

But none of the children would answer. And when none of the children would tell which was good and which was bad, the wild man wept. He lifted one little boy, put him over his shoulder, and dragged him, sobbing, back to the forests. That little boy was never seen again. And from that day to this, whenever a mother should want to admonish her children, she would tell them: be good, be kind, or the wild man of the woods will come and take you away.

There comes a call from beyond the bedroom door: the familiar bark of Elenya's father. This time, he is not barracking her for her latest attempt at best behaviour. He is only announcing the serving of a New Year's goose.

Elenya is already opening the door by the time she realizes the boy has not followed. He appears stuck in the window frame. He inches his way to the pane and smears his face there, so that it looks as if the snowflakes are settling on him instead of the glass.

'Come on, Alek. Yuri will gobble it all if we don't . . .'

'I want to go out,' whispers the boy.

'Go out?'

'Not into the trees. Just into the garden.'

'Mr Navitski wouldn't allow it.'

The boy scowls, 'But Mr Navitski isn't my papa.'

They stand in silence. A great hand of snow slides down the window glass, revealing greater portions of the garden.

'Come on, then,' Elenya whispers. 'While they're busy in the kitchen . . .'

In the living room, the puppy gambols with Yuri, who seems as intent as the dog on gnawing on a great bone wrapped in ribbon. Ana is already at the table, bouncing in her high chair, but the adults are swilling drinks in the kitchen.

They cannot leave through there, so instead they go through the front door. He can feel the icy prick of each snowflake, but it is a comforting sensation.

They round the corner of the house, onto the untouched snows at the back. At the edge of the forest, the trees gather – but he has to think hard to remember which is mama's tree. Soon, he supposes, he'll forget altogether.

'Did you want to . . . go under?' asks Elenya, temptation in her voice. It is a remarkable thing to the boy, but even after what his papa did, she would still dare to go into the forest.

He shakes his head.

'Why not? You've never been to your gingerbread house . . .'

He has not. Sometimes he thinks: I've forgotten it. But even the act of forgetting is a kind of memory, and the harder he tries to keep it at bay, the more it flashes across the backs of his eyes or grows into a fairytale castle of ivy and thorns in his dreams. How could he possibly tell Elenya how much he wants to go back to it, yet still deny her the thrill of taking him under the trees? How could he tell her: if I go under the trees, I might turn wild like my papa; I'll fight against it all of my life, just like my papa, and only the seasons will tell if I win or fail. How could he say: my papa lived in the tenement all of his life, but he never stopped being wild. Not really. He pretended and

418

pretended, and then it burst out of him, and it was roots and shoots and gnarled branches and bared teeth. And how could he say: now, I have to pretend as well.

A sound, a hammering, fists on the glass. The boy whips his hand from Elenya's, turns around. In the frosted glass, there hangs Elenya's father. The door flies open, spilling light, spilling songs, spilling the smells of fat roast sausage.

Elenya's father is about to roar out, when Mr Navitski lays a hand on his shoulder.

'I'll sort them,' he says.

Once Elenya's father has trudged back inside, Navitski comes to the step. 'Come on you two. It's being served.'

Shrugging at the boy, Elenya squirms back past Mr Navitski. 'Alek?'

The boy nods, puts one foot on the step. That is enough to make Mr Navitski drift off.

Tempted by the heat, the boy crosses the threshold. Inside, he turns back to close the door. It is almost shut, but he cannot quite bear to close it altogether. Snow eddies towards him. He breathes it in, pitches forward to breathe in more.

Only then does he see the marks at the edge of the garden. A chasm opens in his chest. He opens the door again, tumbles from the step. Two steps, and then another, the snow climbing past his ankles and shins.

At the edge of the garden: a thin trench, wending its way out of the trees, wending its way back again.

Something takes flight inside him. He staggers forward, plunging into yet more snow. Smells come alive. Sounds, so distant and near. The sting of a nettle. The groaning of branches bearing too much ice. The soft pull of a cattail root as it is hauled out of the ground.

Click and soft thump. Click and soft thump.

He crawls through the snow to the edge of the forest. He sits, with his feet betraying the edge of the trench. Laces done up tight. Socks to keep out the cold. He takes them off, casts them aside. Too many buttons on his shirt, too many zips and buckles and pins.

'Alek, are you coming inside?'

Mr Navitski has himself stepped out of the house. Even now, he is striding across the garden.

The boy takes back his socks, puts them on his feet; takes back his shoes, slips them over socks sodden and cold.

'What is it, Alek?'

One last look into the snow dark, and then: 'Nothing, Mr Navitski.'

'I thought you called me Nikolai?'

The boy crosses the garden again, taking the teacher's hand. It is as if he is asking to be led inside – but the boy knows different; he is the one leading Navitski.

He hurtles down the length of the kitchen, finds Elenya at the table and takes her wrist. She comes with him, back to the frosted glass.

'What is it?'

The boy forces open the window. Outside, the snow is tumbling over the trees. It comes more fiercely now. He has to squint to see.

'There,' he says, his eyes seeking out the edge of the trench. 'There, and there . . .'

But Elenya cannot, will not see. She steps back, dusted in snowflakes. 'It's *dinner*, Alek. You haven't forgotten *dinner* again, have you?'

So he must stand alone – but now the snow is too thick, and now even his own footprints are disappearing, the ground a white so perfect that only the trees could tell he was ever there at all.

Click and soft thump. Click and soft thump.

Something wild inside him, and something wild, out there, in the night.

ACKNOWLEDGEMENTS

Many thanks to: Cassie Browne, Katie Espiner, Charlotte Cray and everyone at HarperCollins; Euan Thorneycroft, Jennifer Custer and Helene Ferey at AM Heath; my mother, for not leaving me to run too wild in the woodland when I was a boy, and especially Dad, for all of his woodland lore.

And, of course, to Kirstie and Esther, for everything else.

BALTIC SEA

THE
IRON
WALL

King in
the West